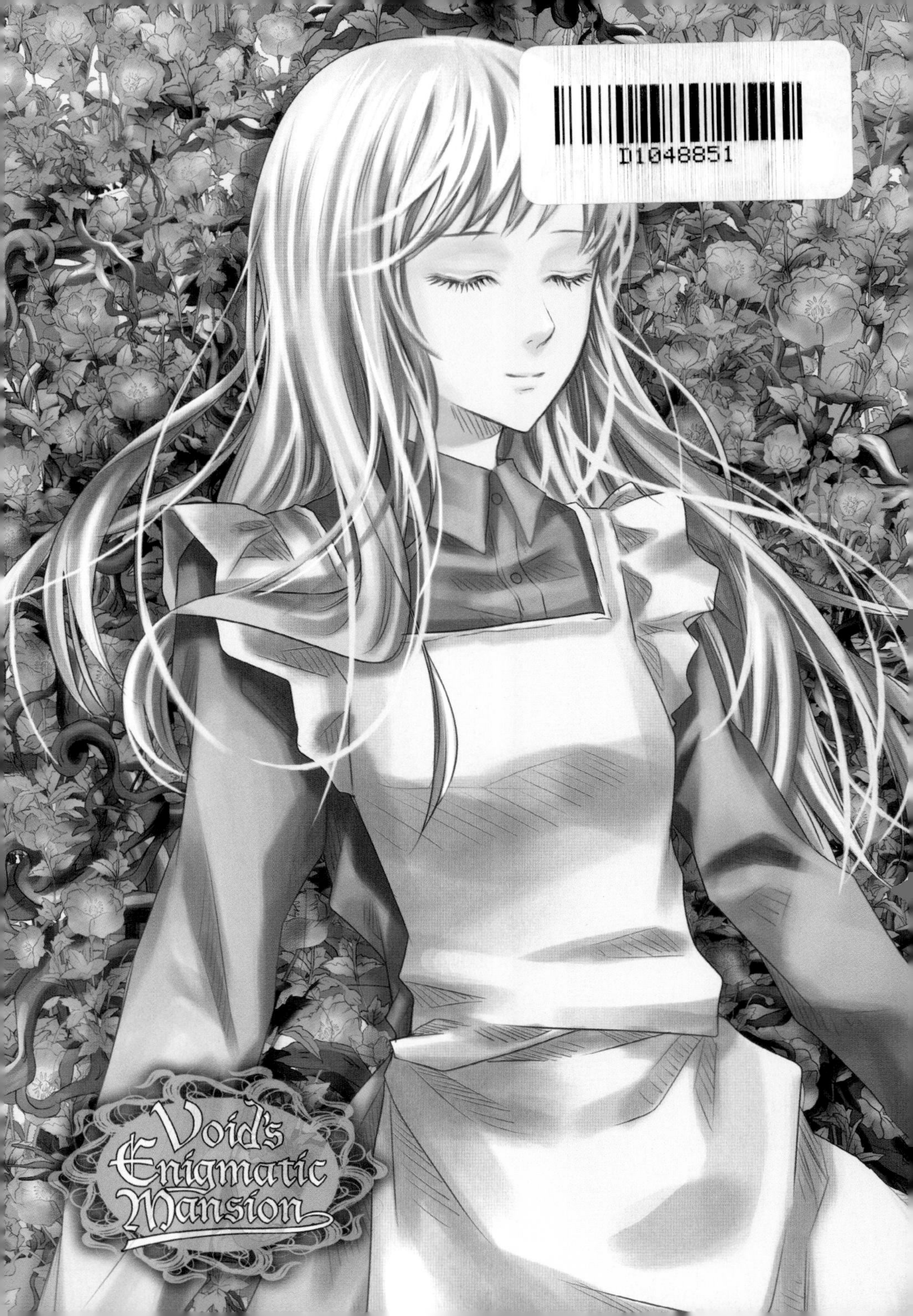
Void's
Enigmatic
Mansion

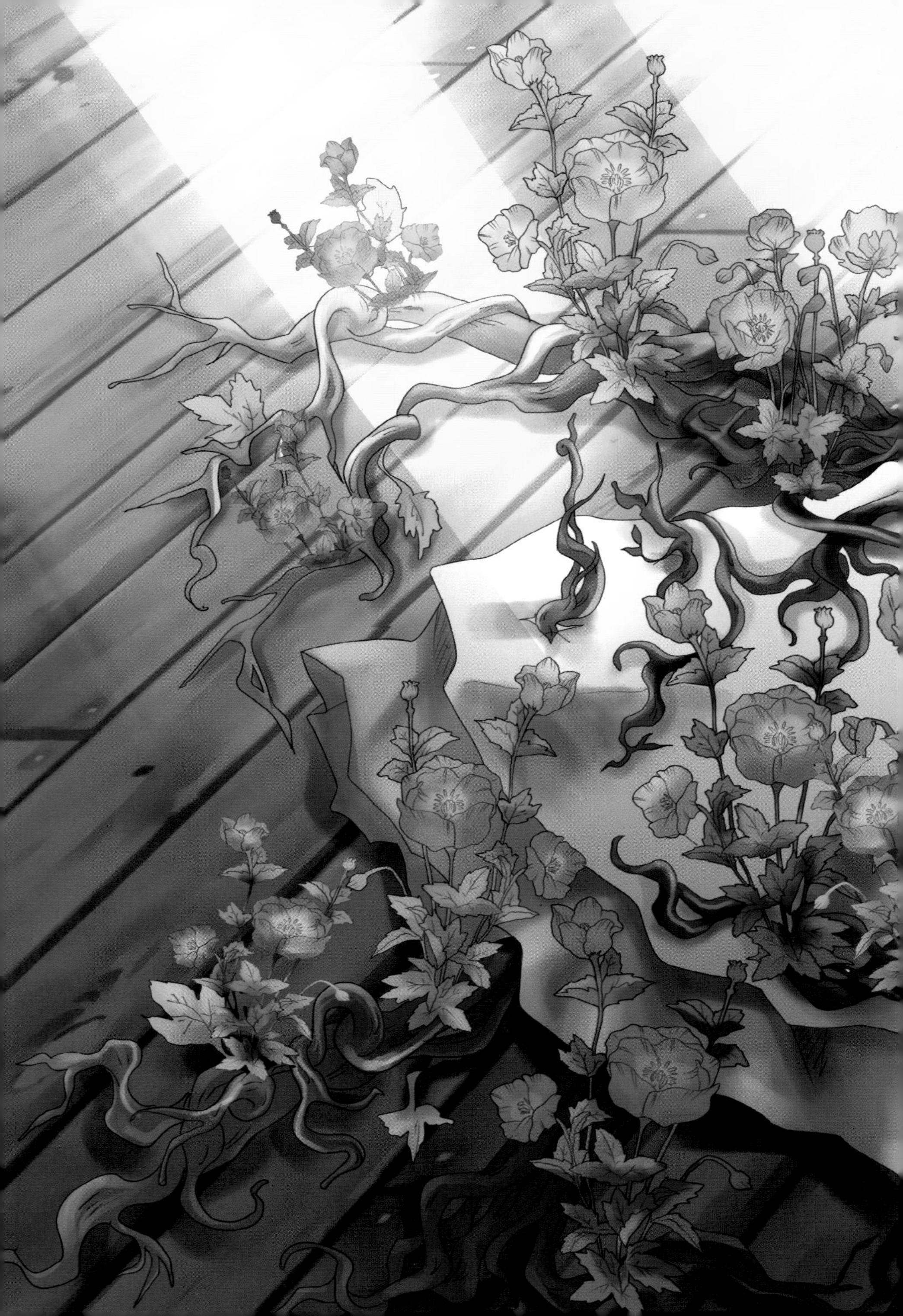

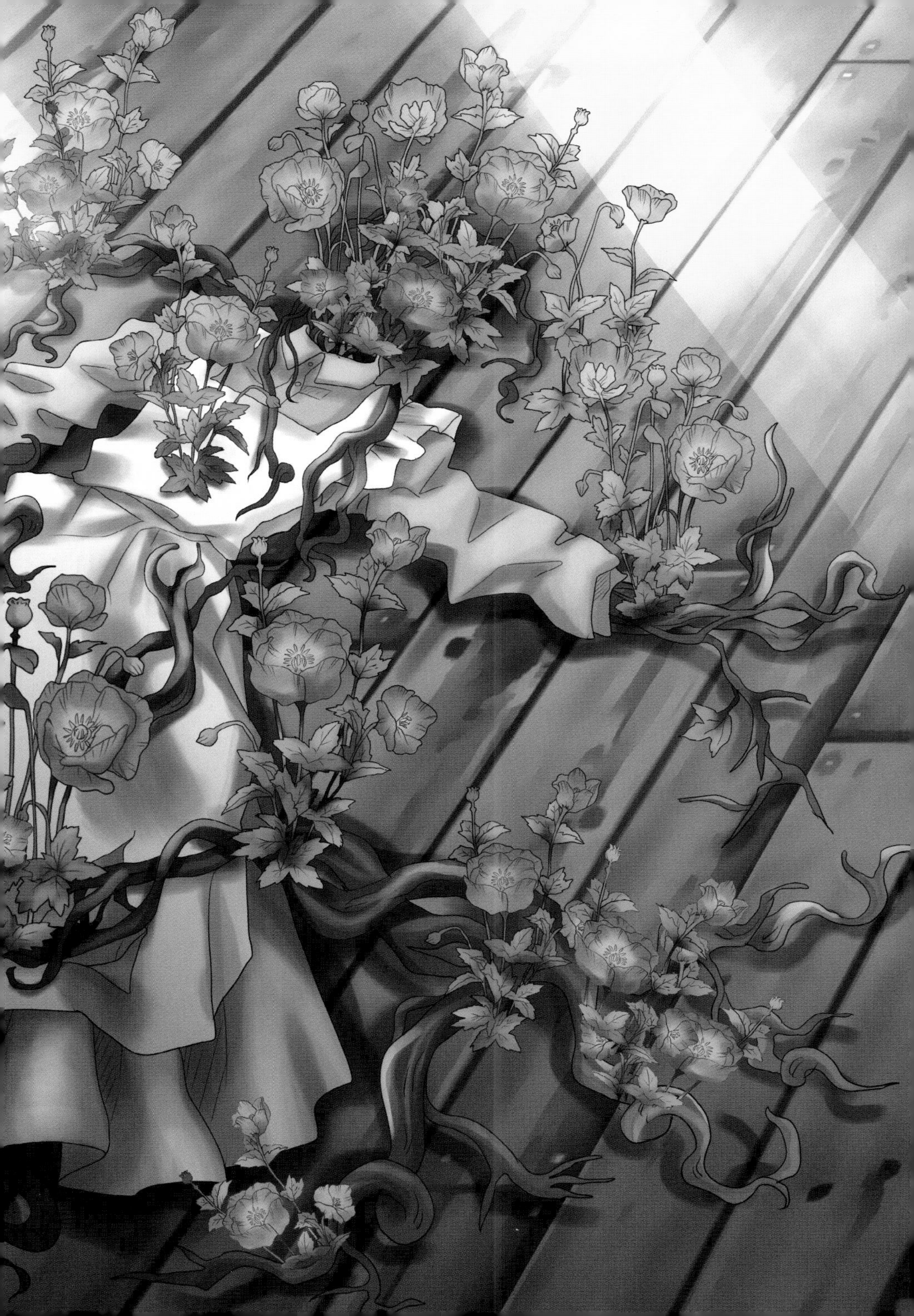

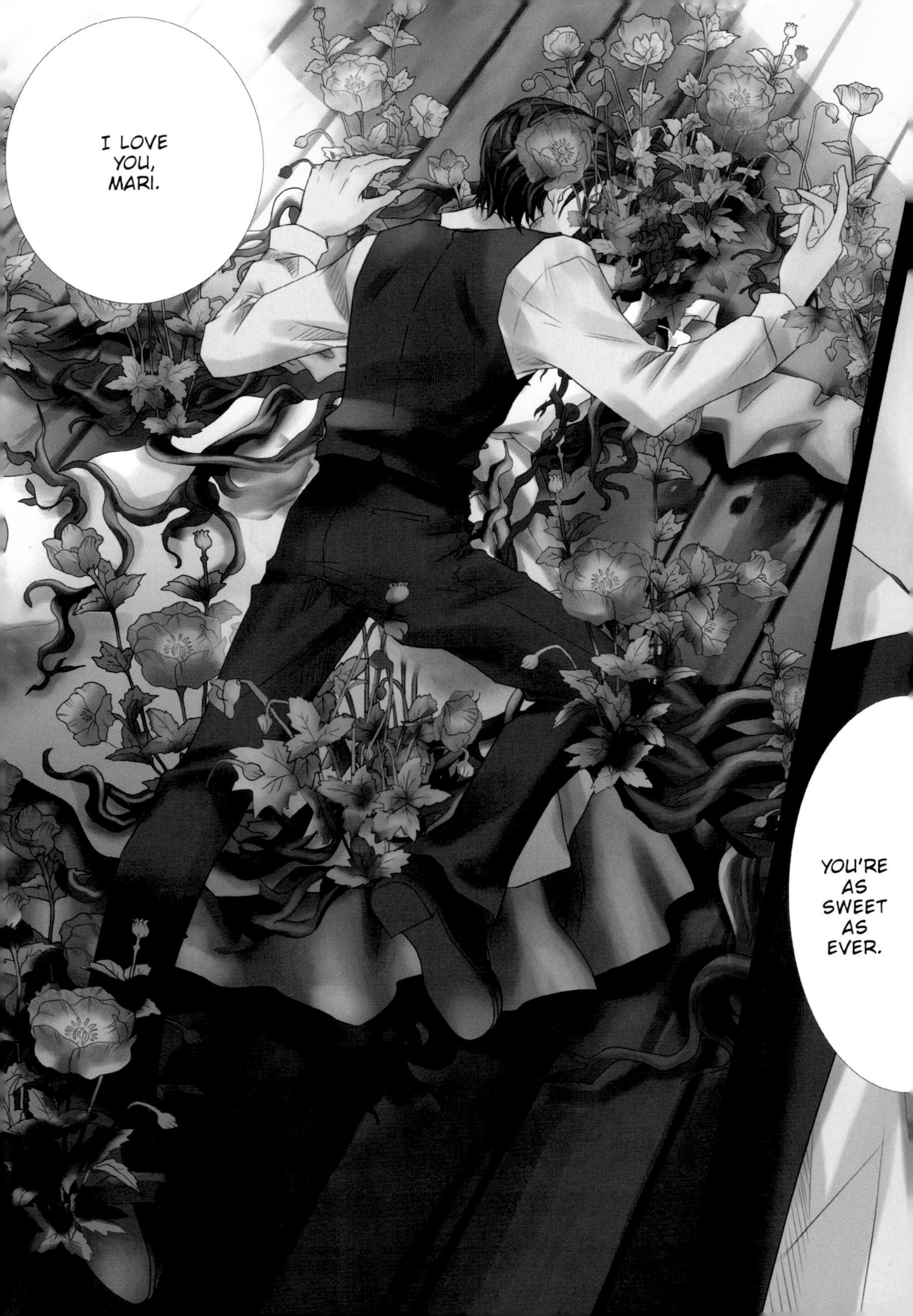
I LOVE YOU, MARI.
YOU'RE AS SWEET AS EVER.

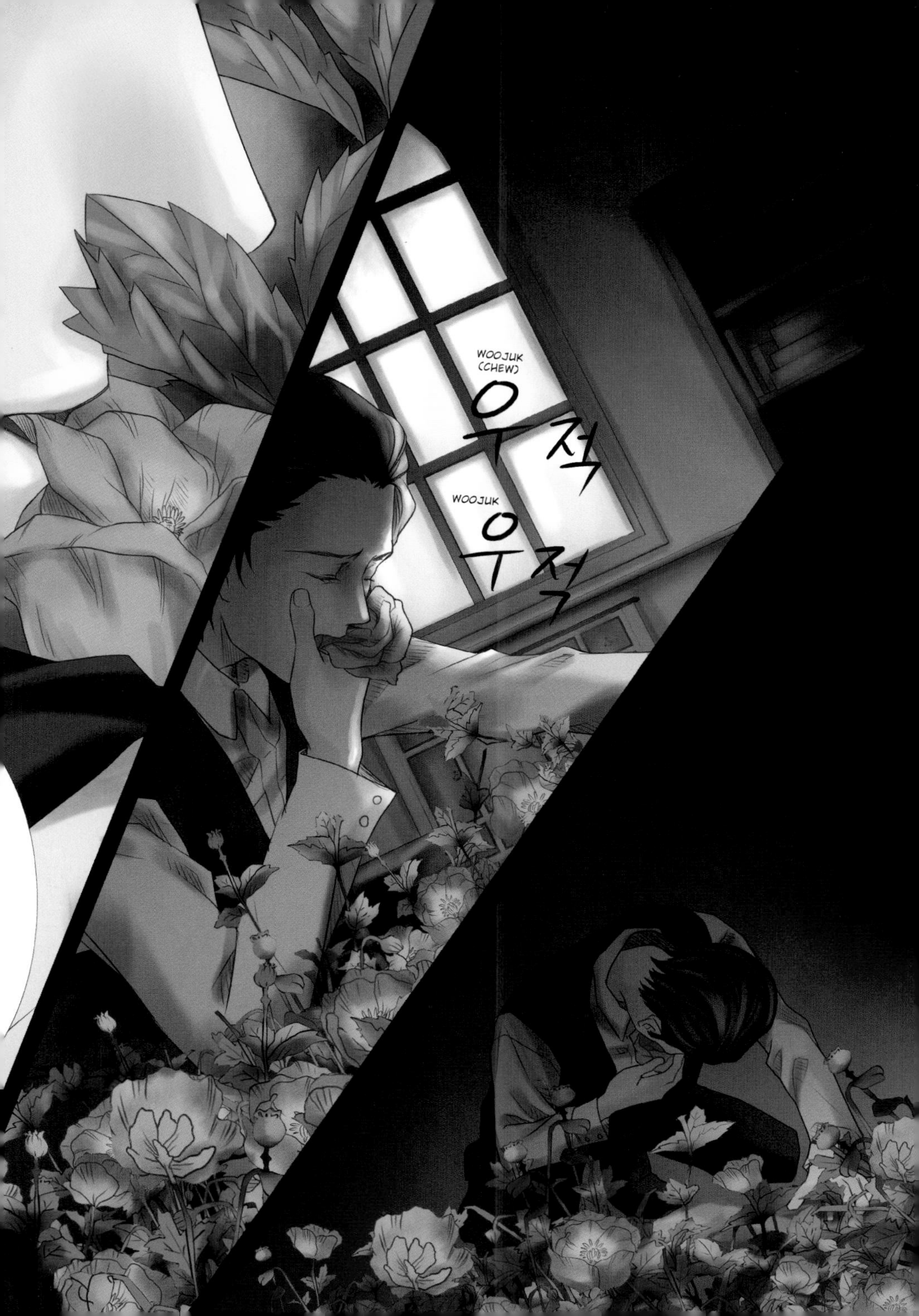

WOOJUK (CHEW)
우적
WOOJUK
우적

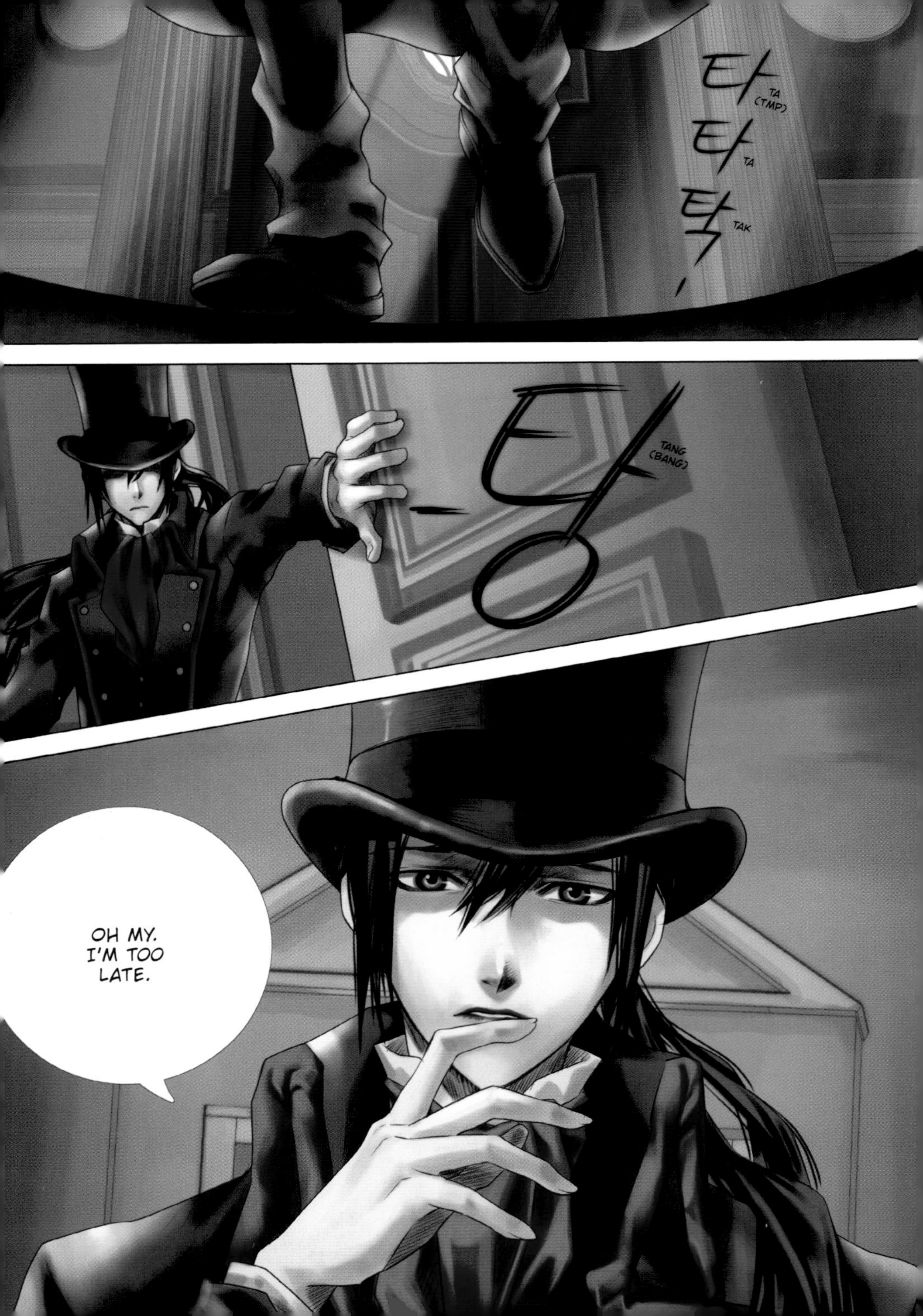

타
TA (TMP)
타
TA
탁
TAK
탕
TANG (BANG)
OH MY. I'M TOO LATE.

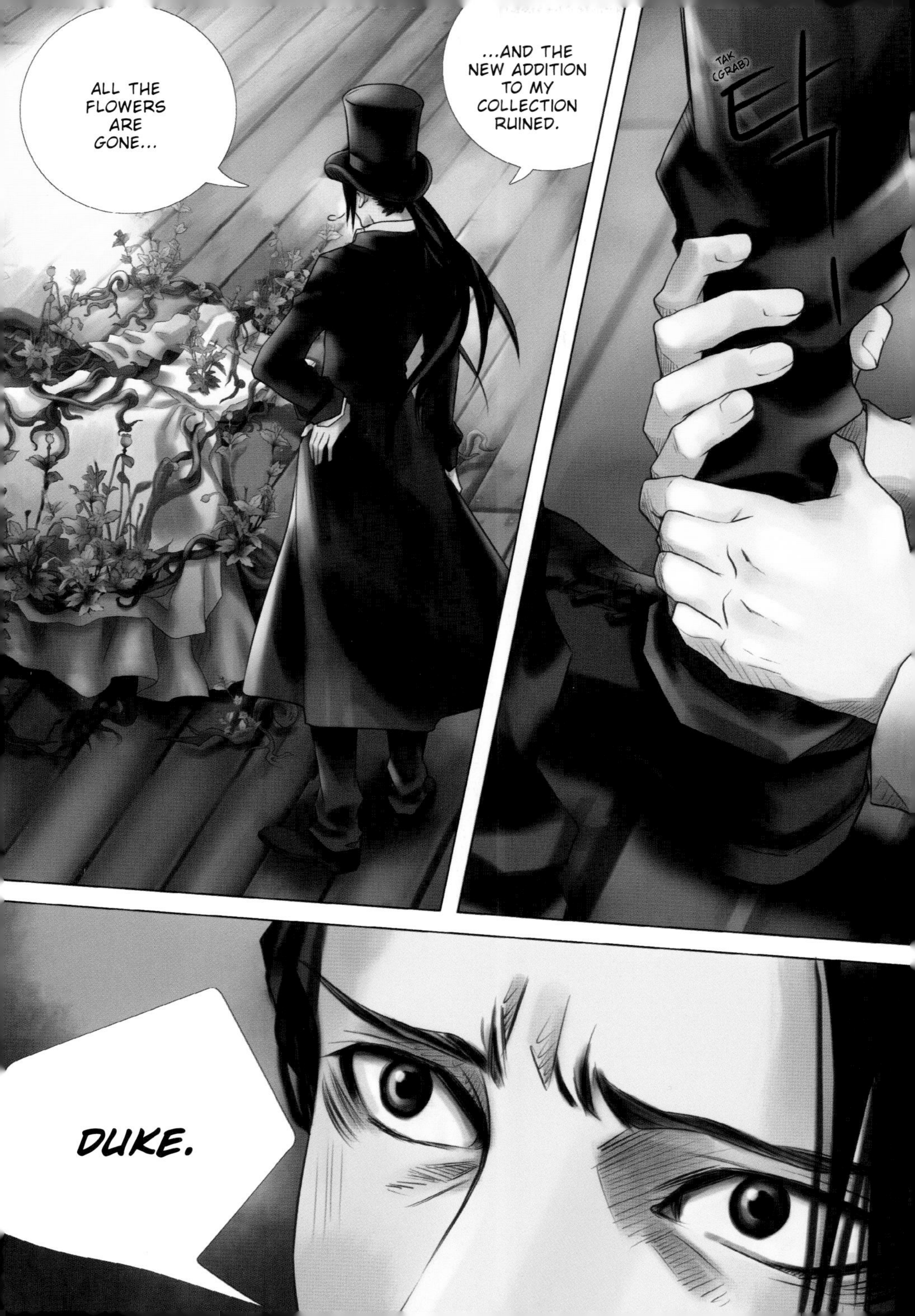
ALL THE FLOWERS ARE GONE...
...AND THE NEW ADDITION TO MY COLLECTION RUINED.
TAK (GRAB)
DUKE.

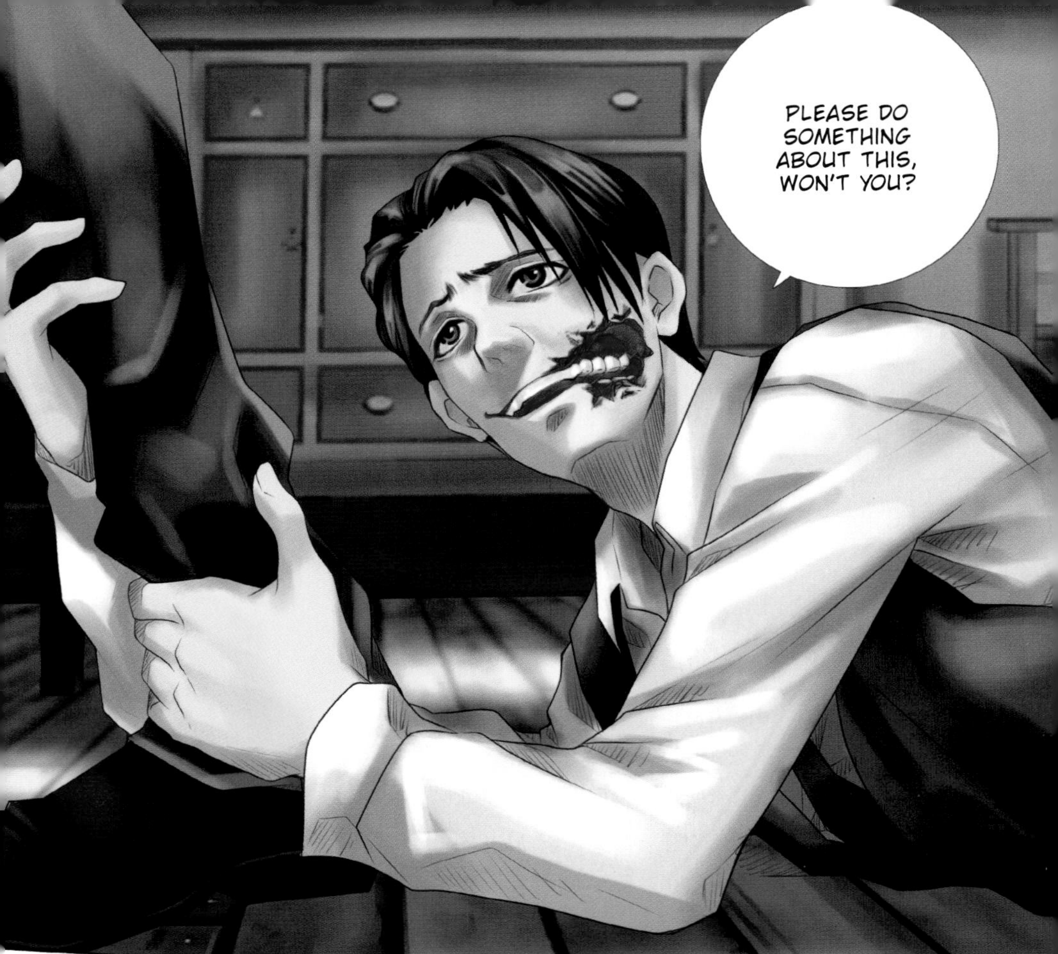
PLEASE DO SOMETHING ABOUT THIS, WON'T YOU?
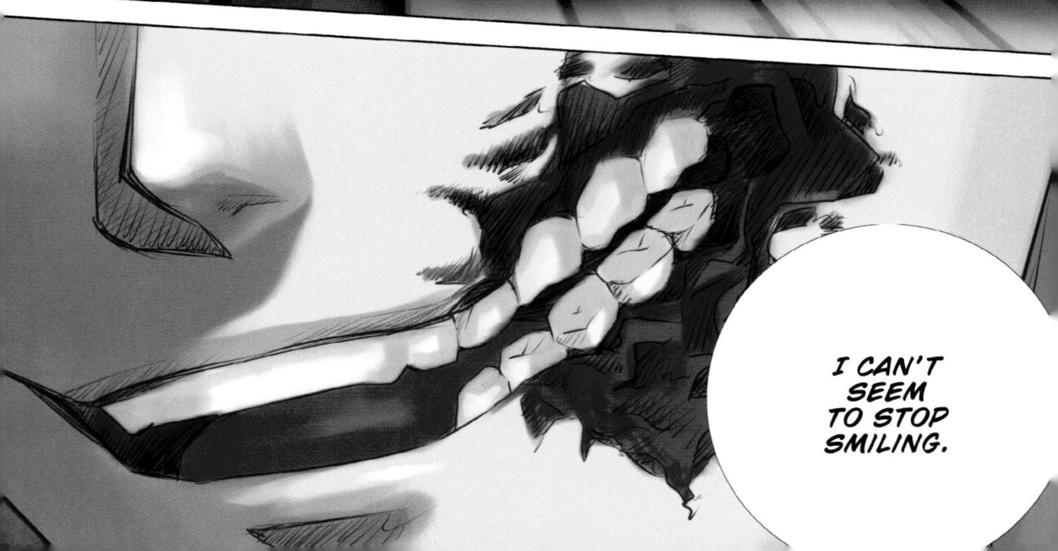
I CAN'T SEEM TO STOP SMILING.

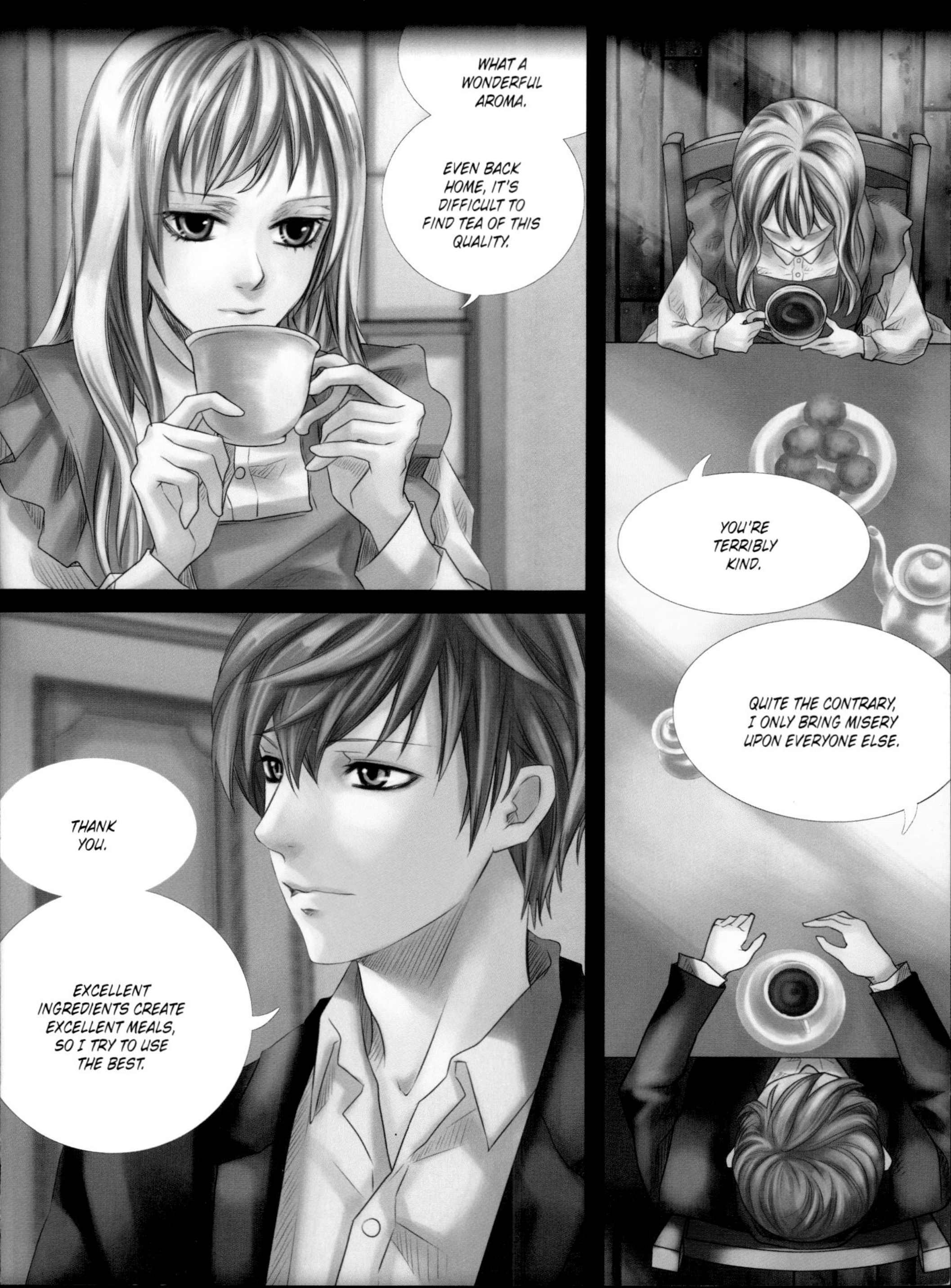
WHAT A WONDERFUL AROMA.
EVEN BACK HOME, IT'S DIFFICULT TO FIND TEA OF THIS QUALITY.
THANK YOU.
EXCELLENT INGREDIENTS CREATE EXCELLENT MEALS, SO I TRY TO USE THE BEST.
YOU'RE TERRIBLY KIND.
QUITE THE CONTRARY, I ONLY BRING MISERY UPON EVERYONE ELSE.

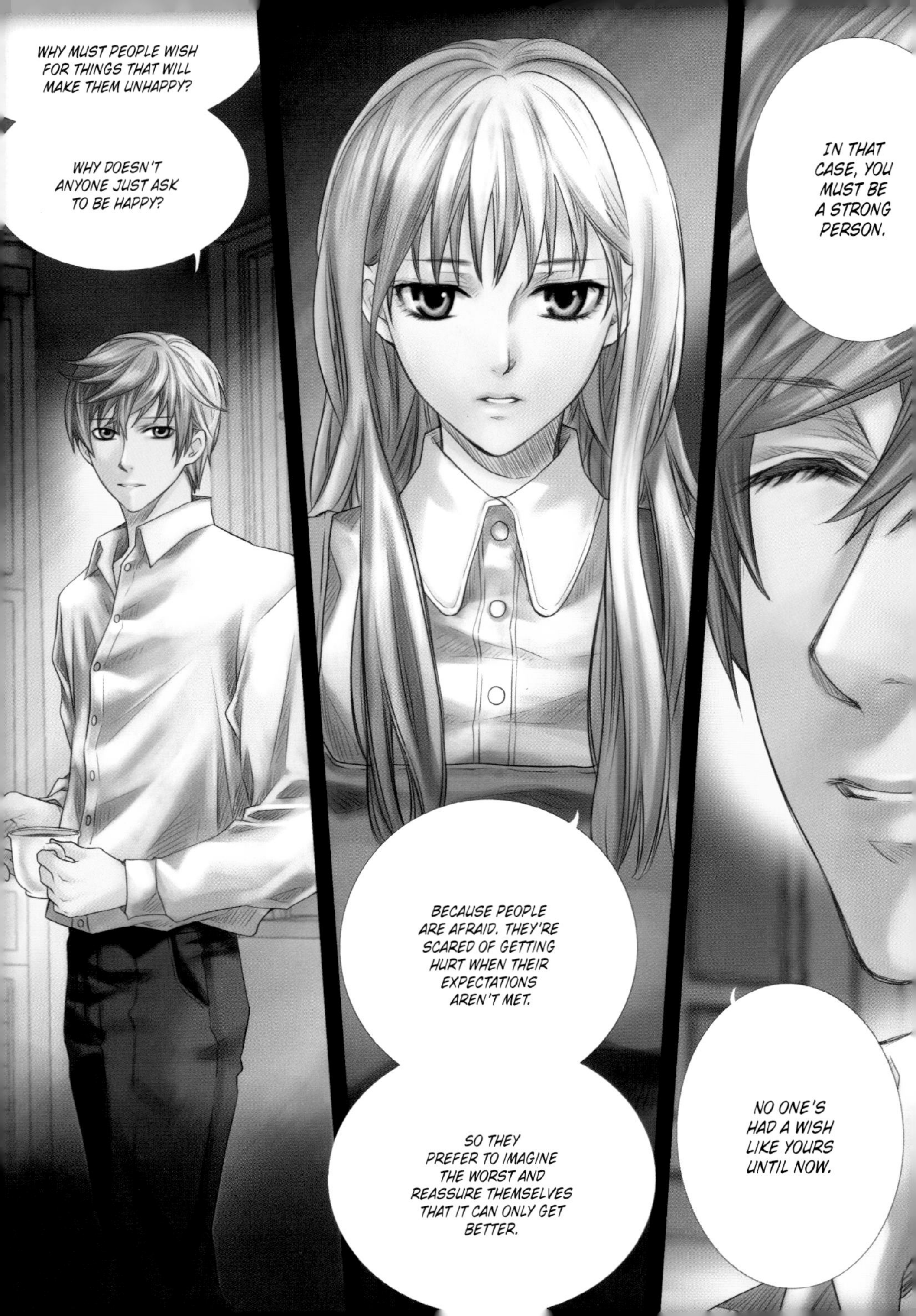
WHY MUST PEOPLE WISH FOR THINGS THAT WILL MAKE THEM UNHAPPY?
WHY DOESN'T ANYONE JUST ASK TO BE HAPPY?
BECAUSE PEOPLE ARE AFRAID. THEY'RE SCARED OF GETTING HURT WHEN THEIR EXPECTATIONS AREN'T MET.
SO THEY PREFER TO IMAGINE THE WORST AND REASSURE THEMSELVES THAT IT CAN ONLY GET BETTER.
IN THAT CASE, YOU MUST BE A STRONG PERSON.
NO ONE'S HAD A WISH LIKE YOURS UNTIL NOW.

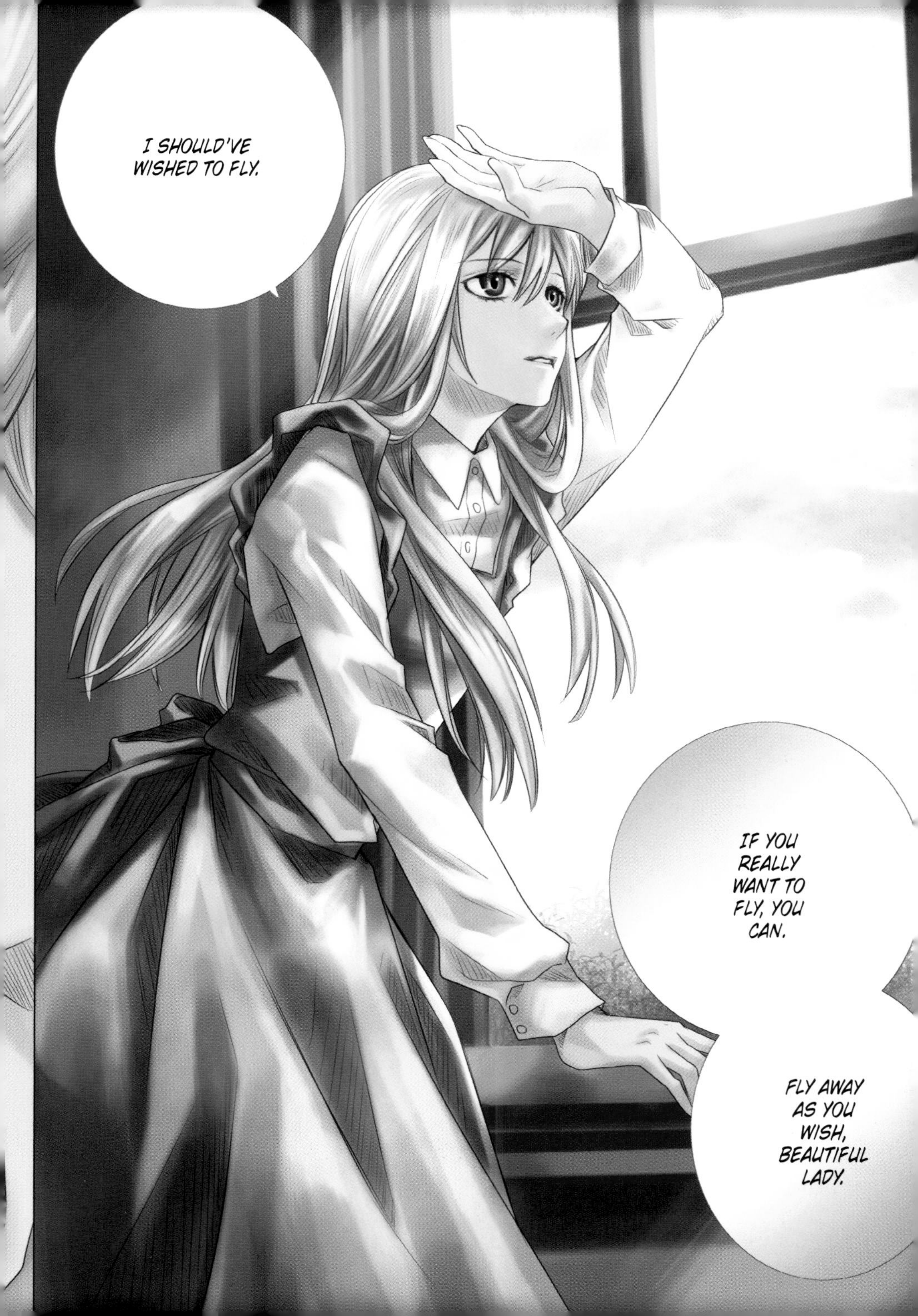
I SHOULD'VE WISHED TO FLY.
IF YOU REALLY WANT TO FLY, YOU CAN.
FLY AWAY AS YOU WISH, BEAUTIFUL LADY.

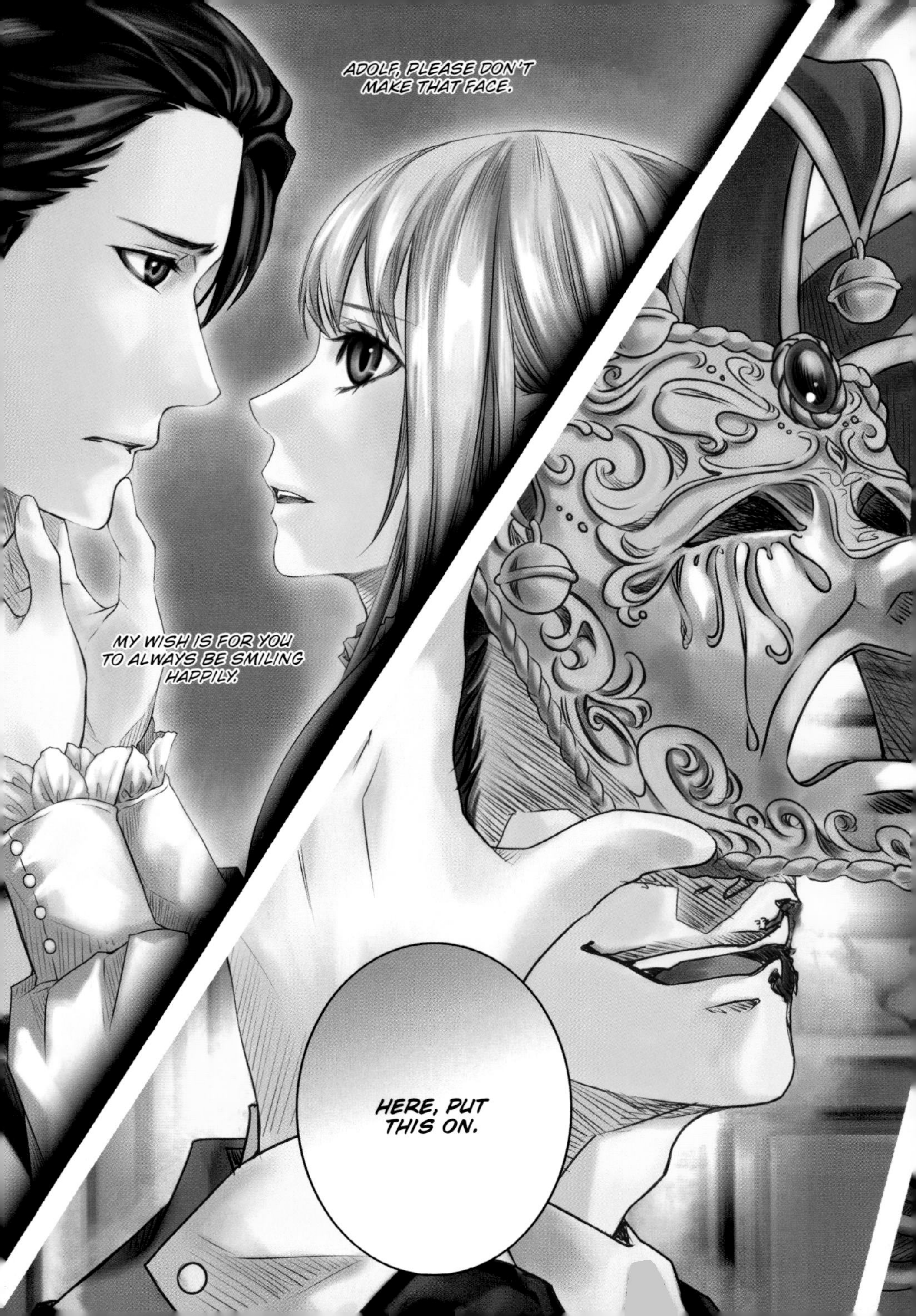
ADOLF, PLEASE DON'T MAKE THAT FACE.
MY WISH IS FOR YOU TO ALWAYS BE SMILING HAPPILY.
HERE, PUT THIS ON.

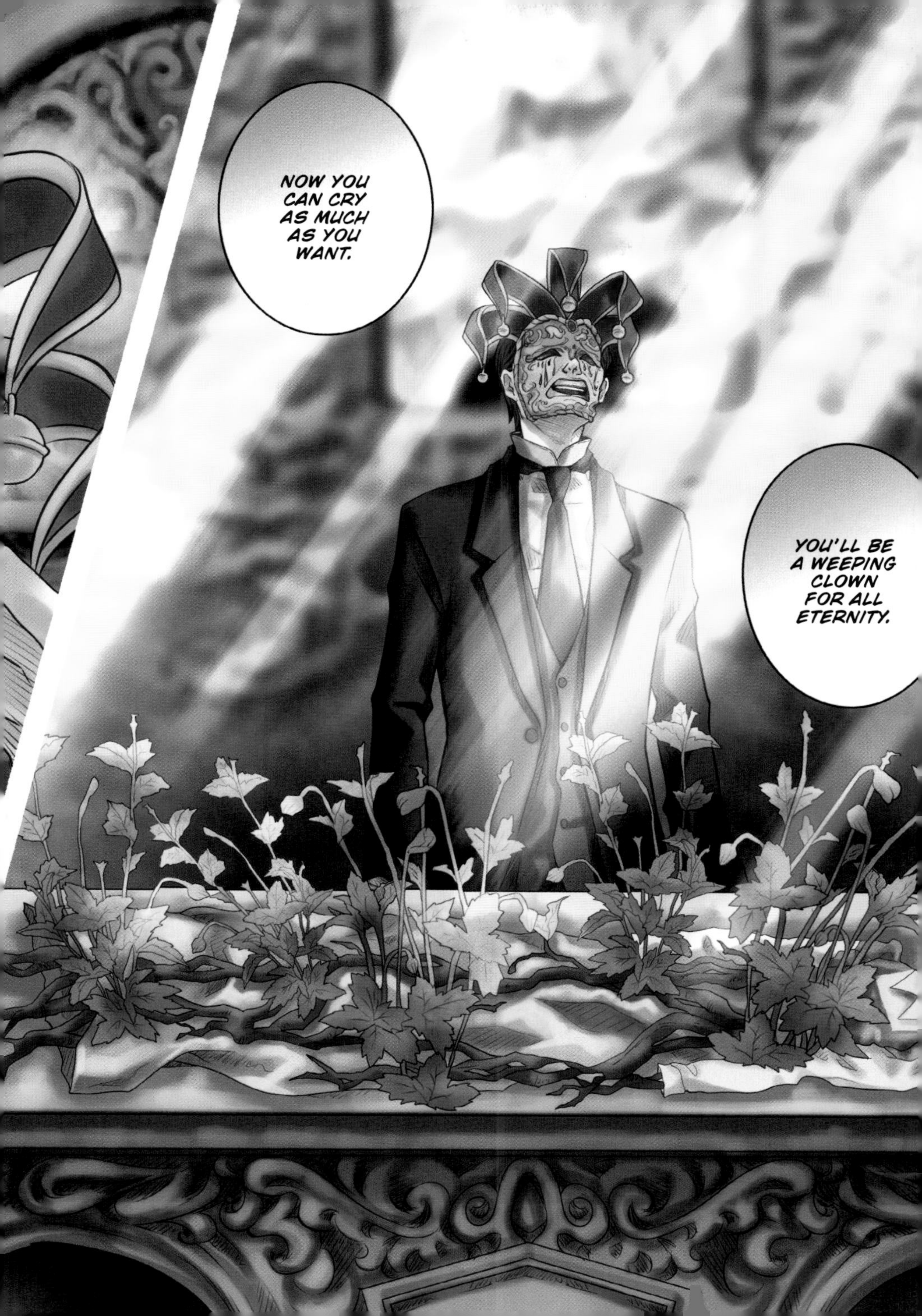
NOW YOU CAN CRY AS MUCH AS YOU WANT.
YOU'LL BE A WEEPING CLOWN FOR ALL ETERNITY.

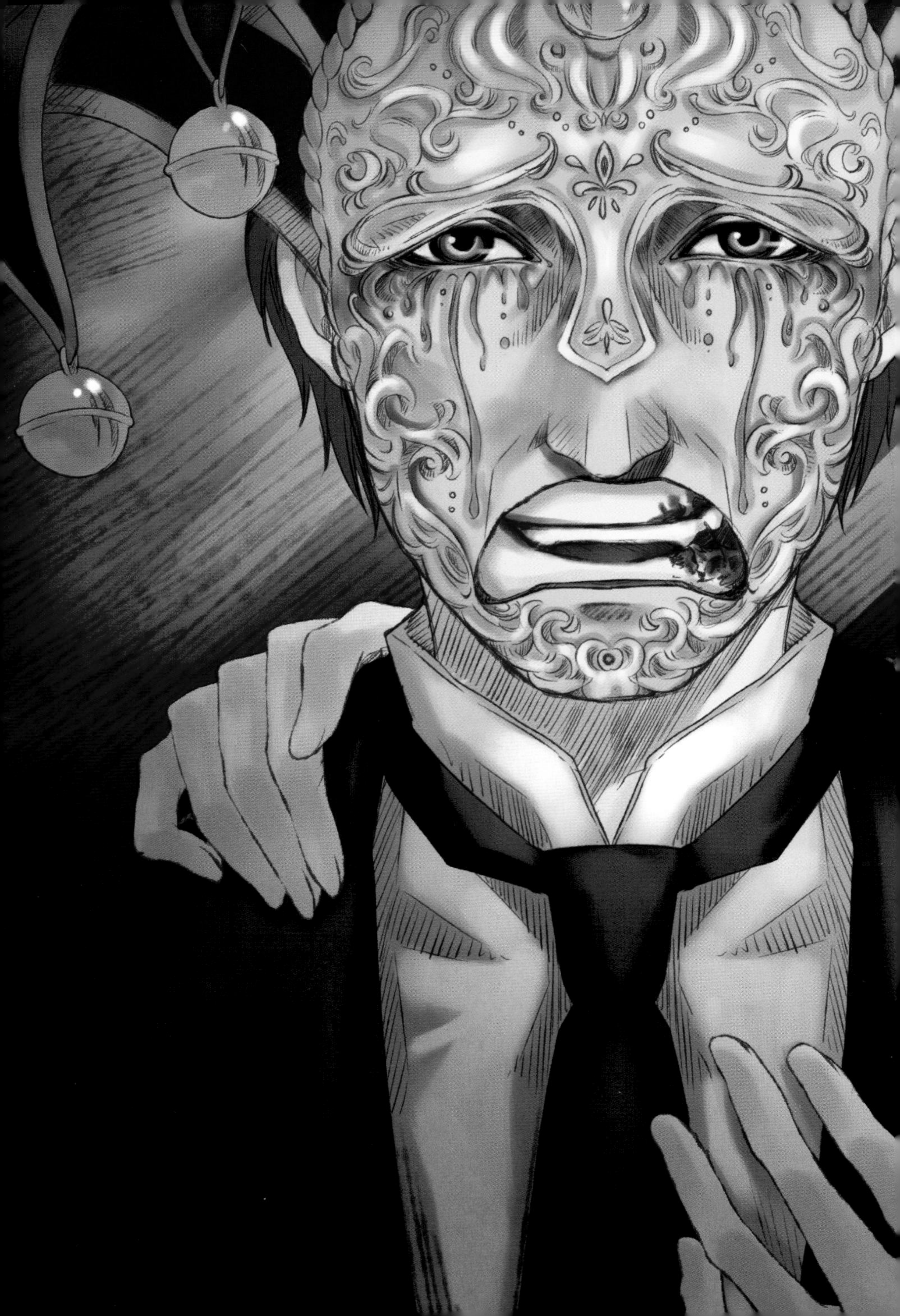

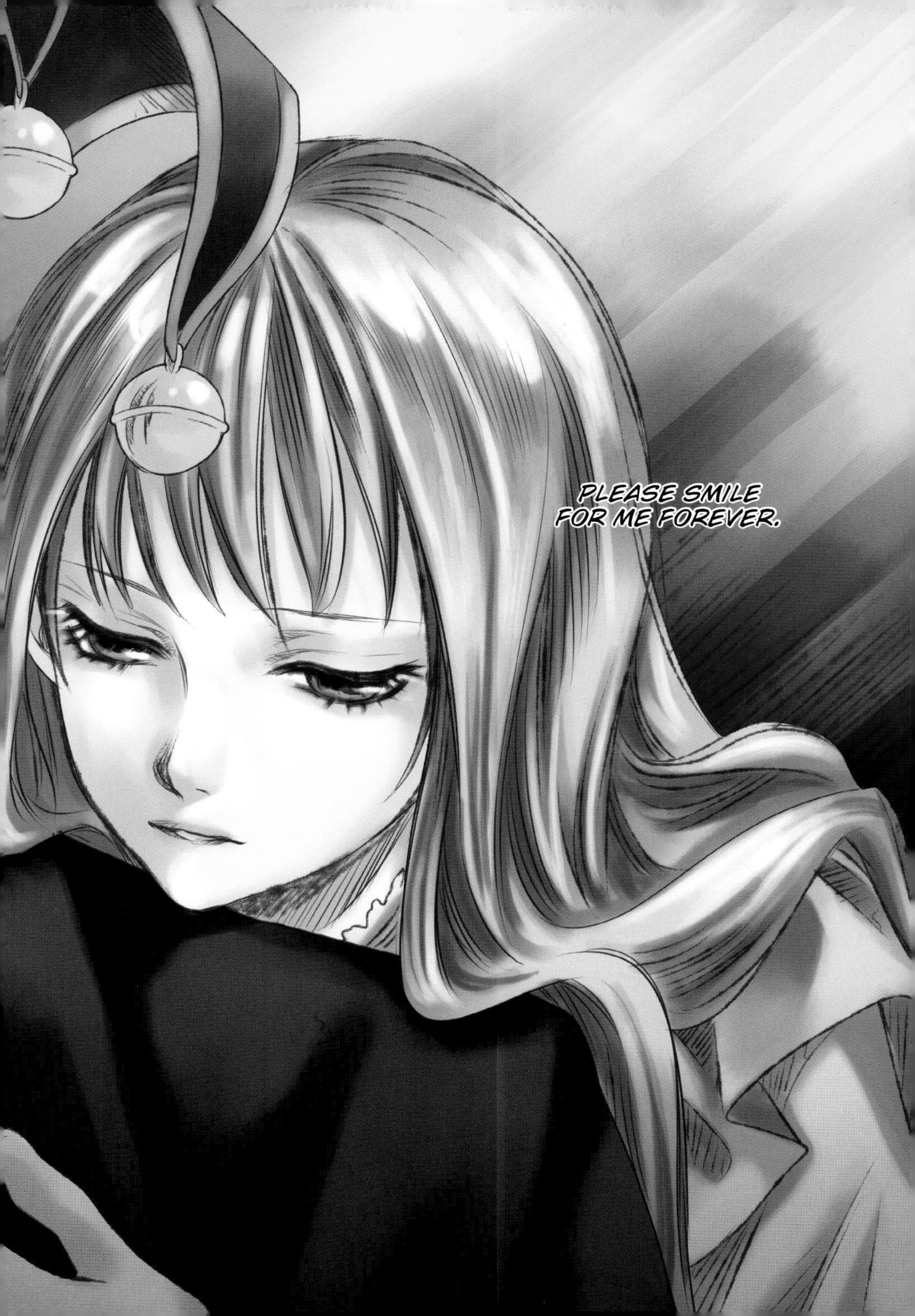
PLEASE SMILE FOR ME FOREVER.

Void's Enigmatic Mansion

"

Then why doesn't
someone make
a wish for him
instead?

"

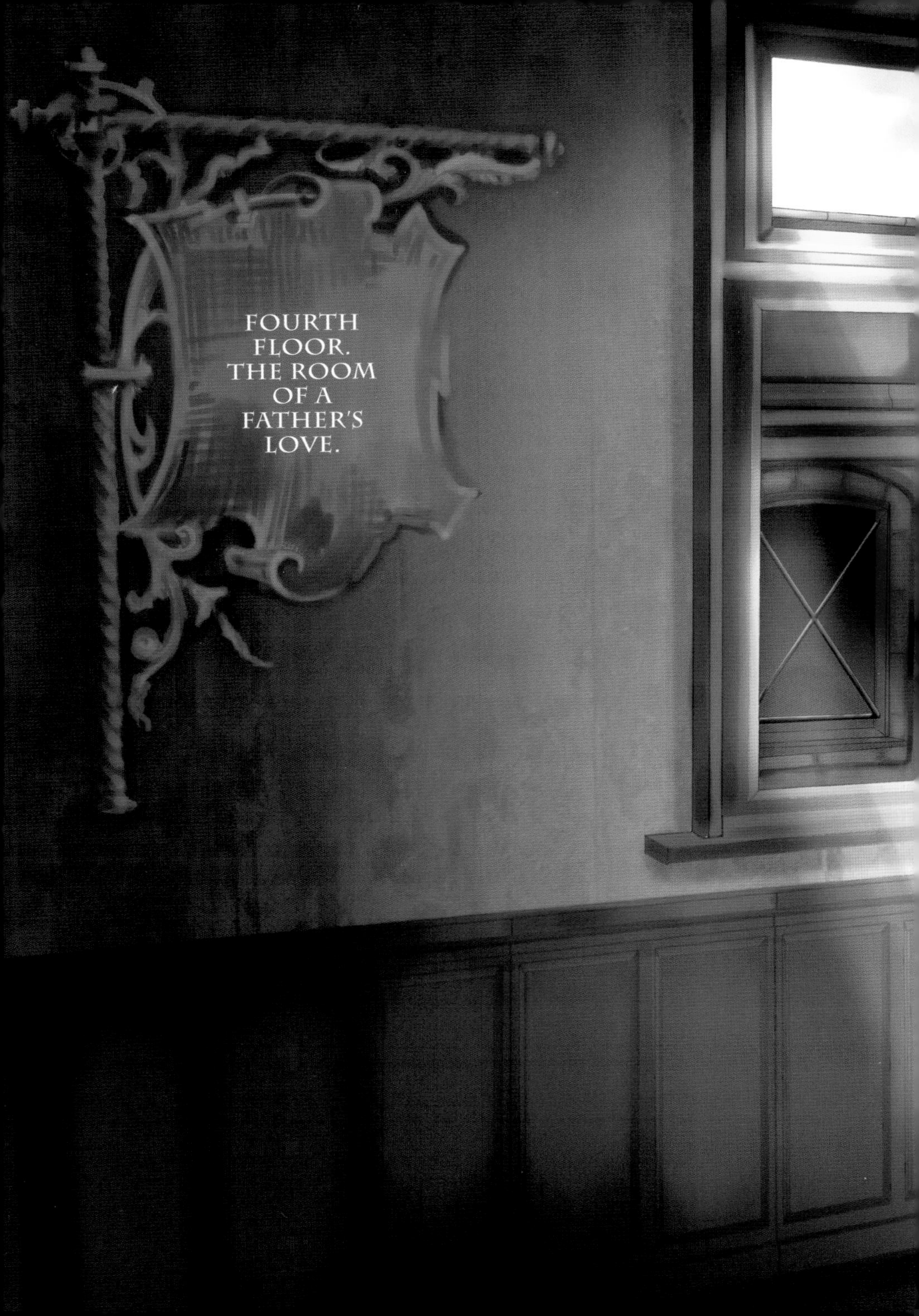
FOURTH FLOOR. THE ROOM OF A FATHER'S LOVE.

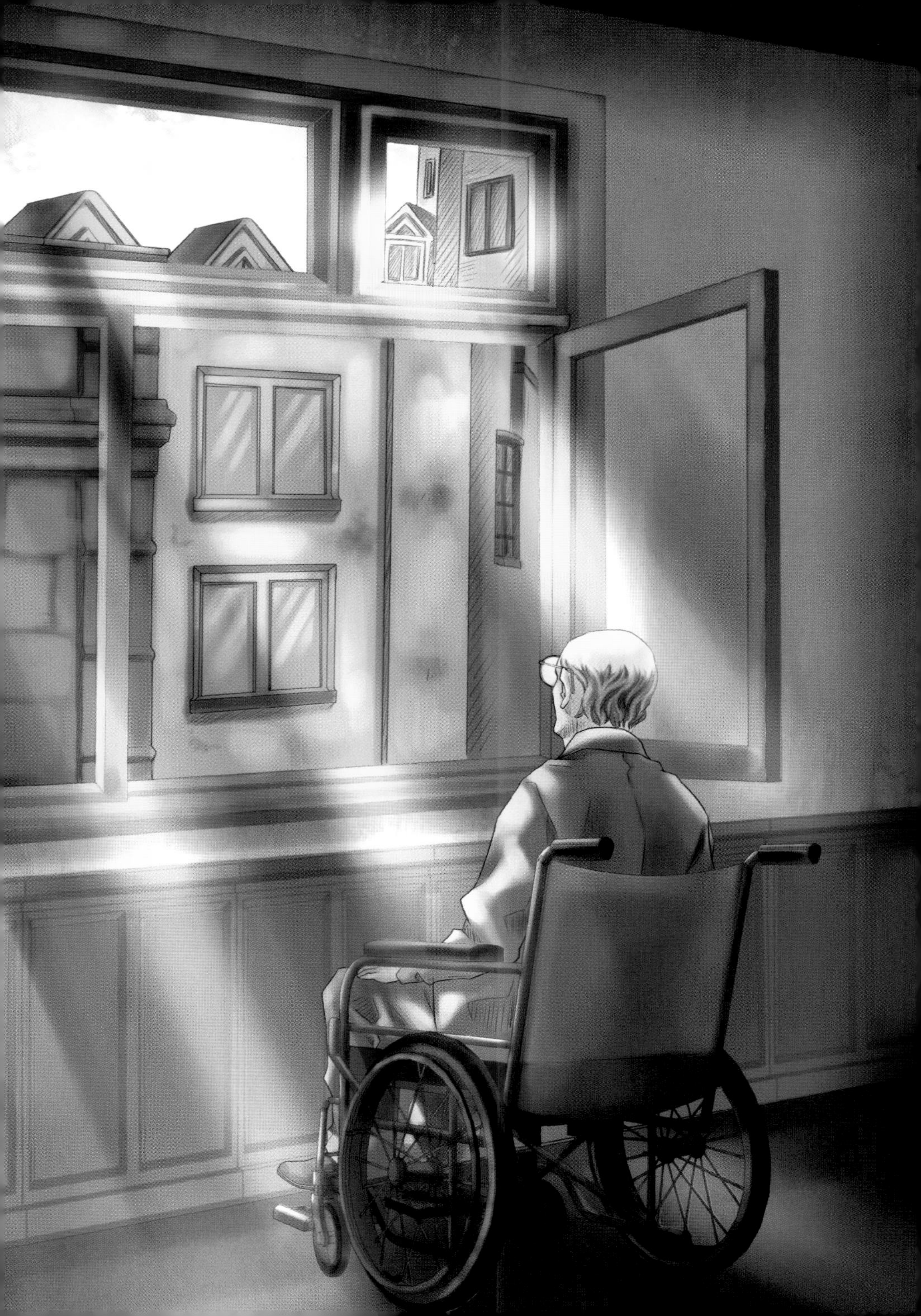

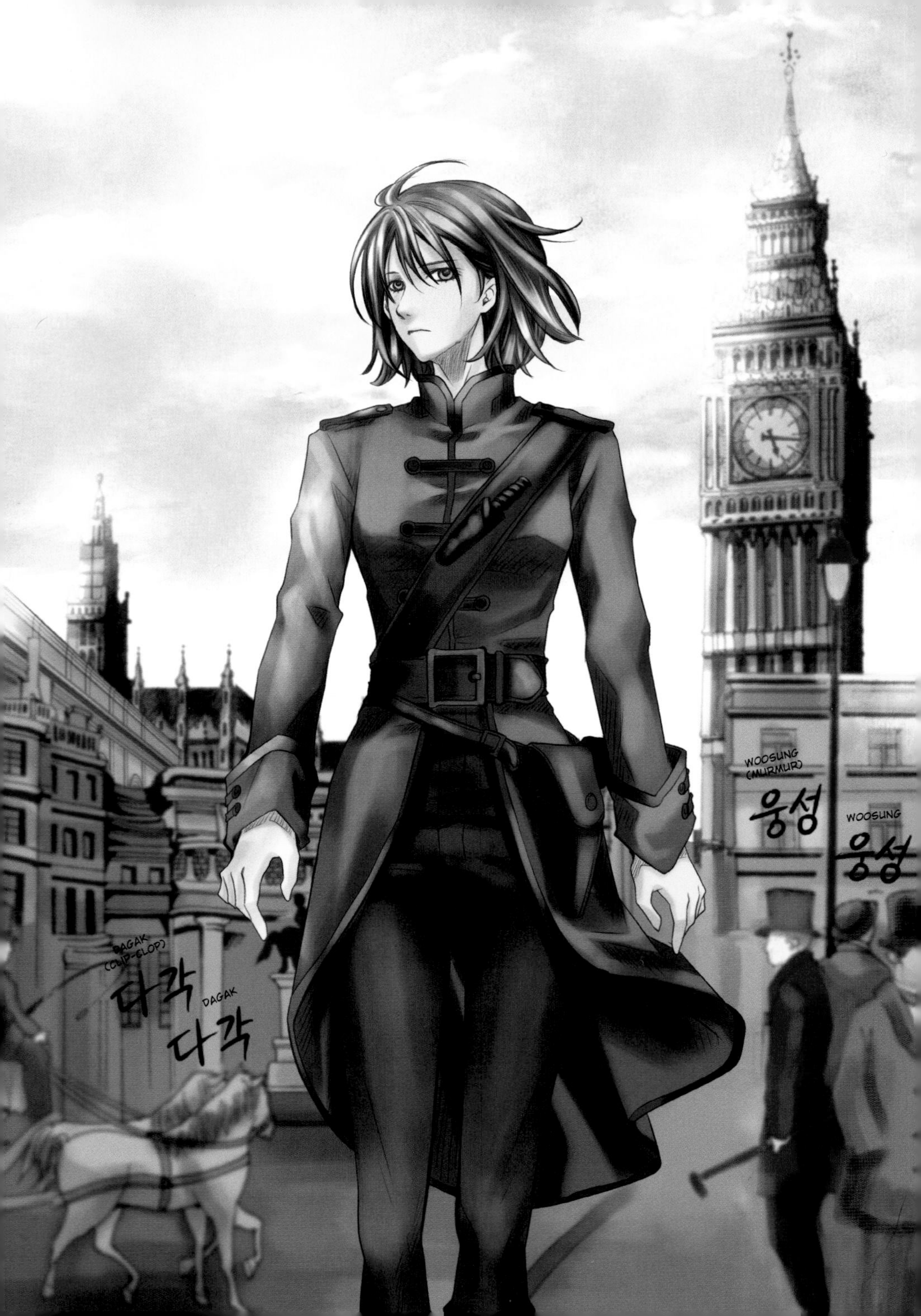
WOOSUNG (MURMUR)
웅성
WOOSUNG
웅성
DAGAK (CLIP-CLOP)
다각
DAGAK
다각

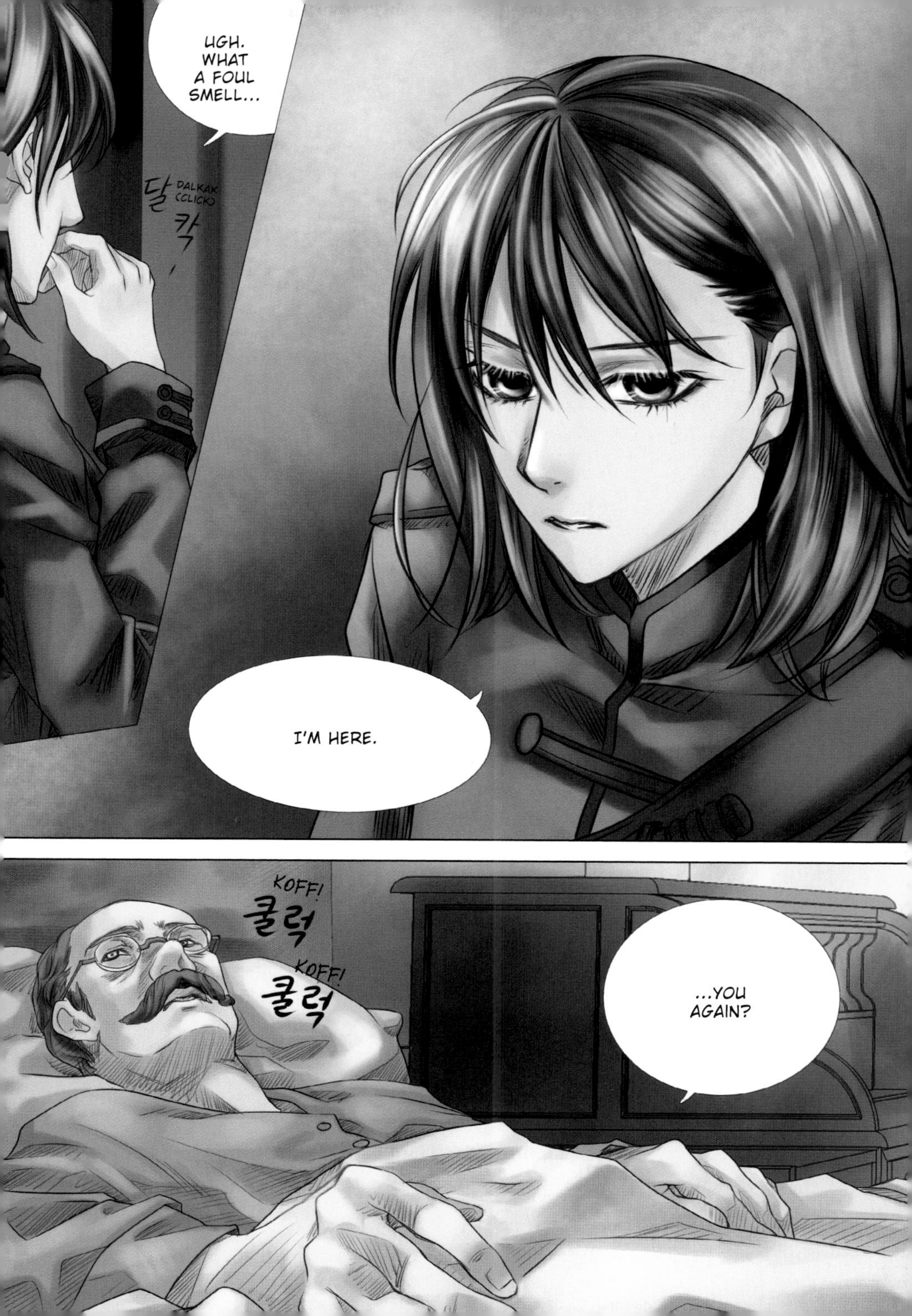
UGH. WHAT A FOUL SMELL...
달칵
DALKAK (CLICK)
I'M HERE.
KOFF!
쿨럭
KOFF!
쿨럭
...YOU AGAIN?

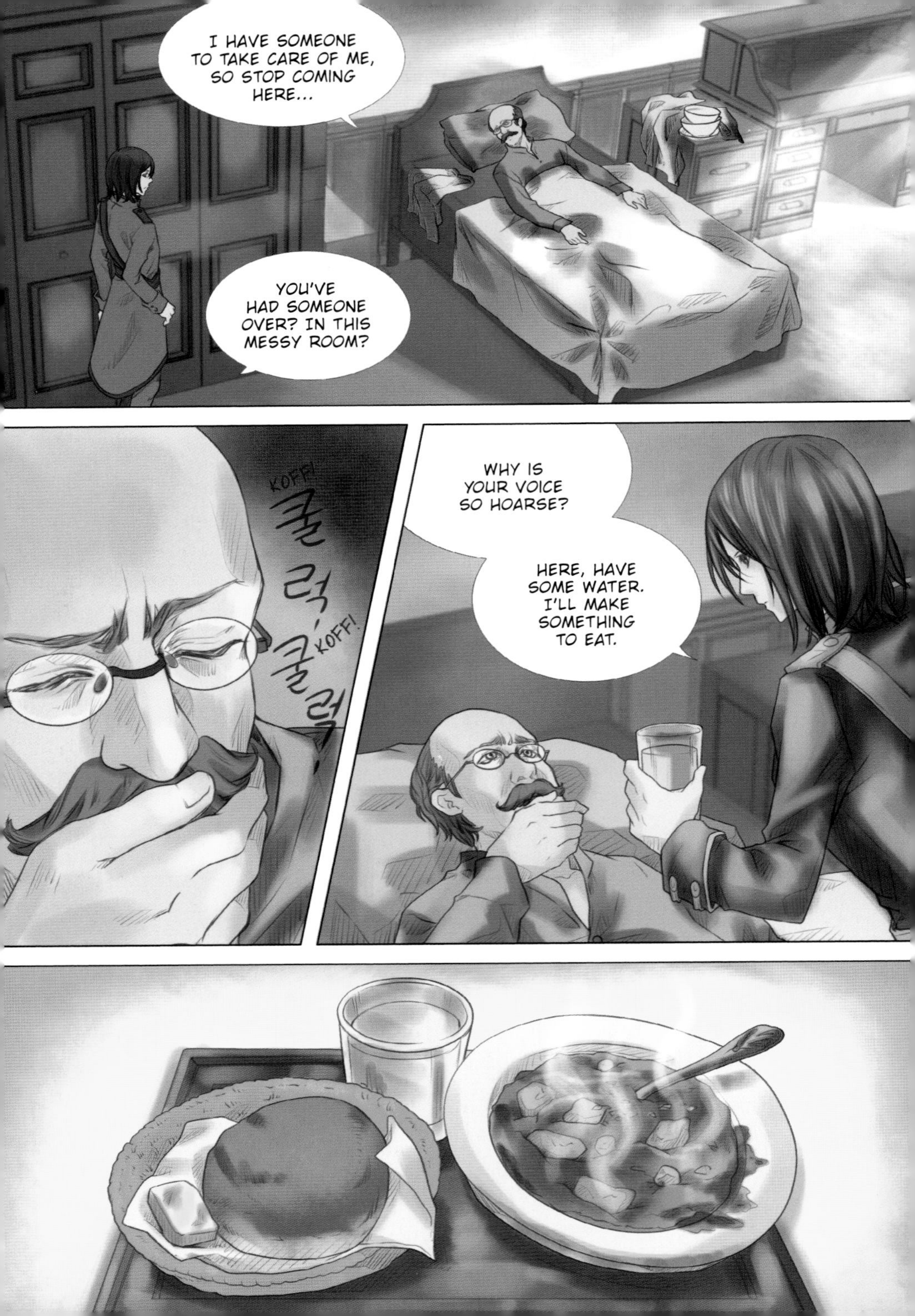
I HAVE SOMEONE TO TAKE CARE OF ME, SO STOP COMING HERE...
YOU'VE HAD SOMEONE OVER? IN THIS MESSY ROOM?
KOFF!
쿨럭,
KOFF!
쿨럭
WHY IS YOUR VOICE SO HOARSE?
HERE, HAVE SOME WATER. I'LL MAKE SOMETHING TO EAT.

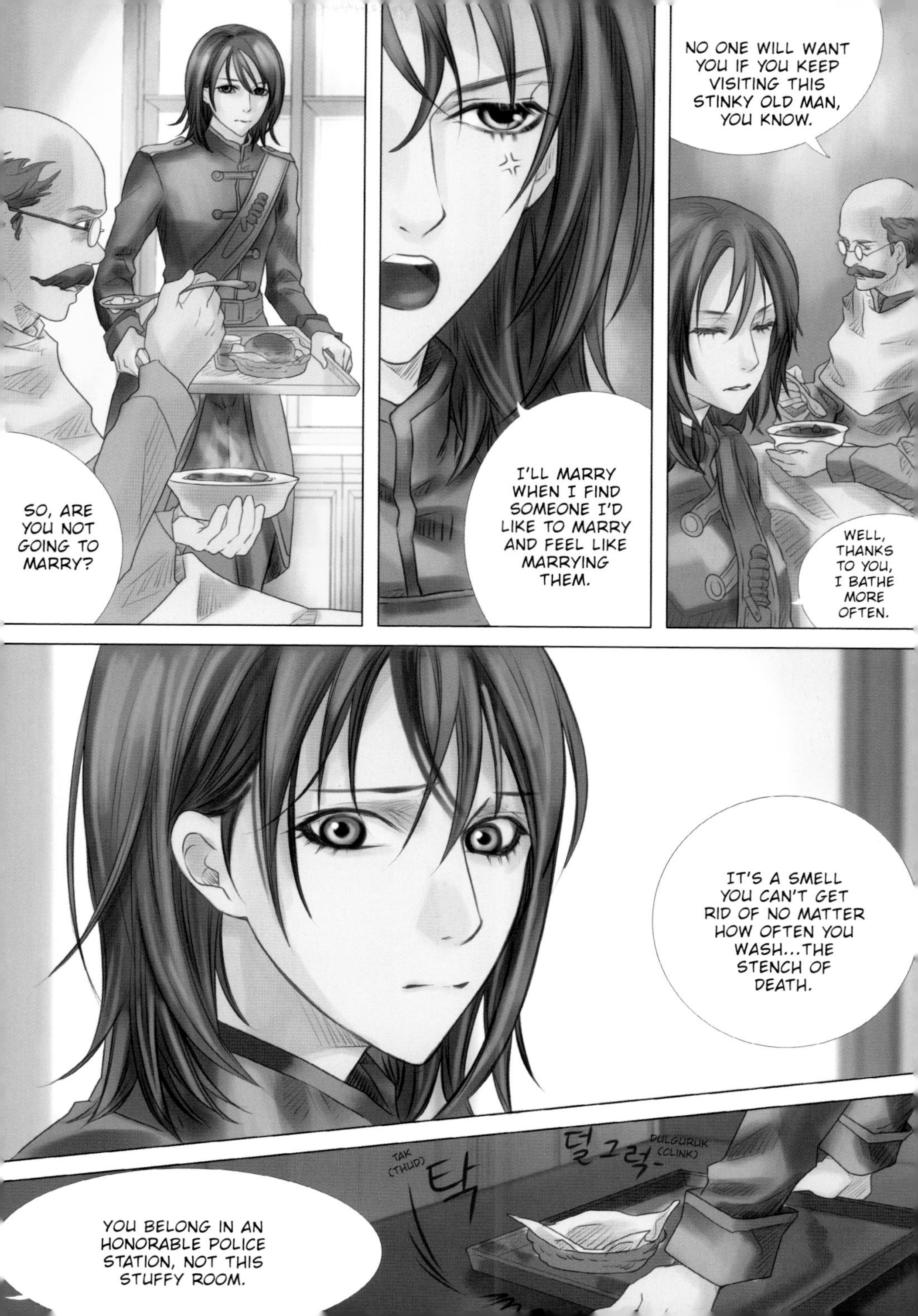
SO, ARE YOU NOT GOING TO MARRY?
I'LL MARRY WHEN I FIND SOMEONE I'D LIKE TO MARRY AND FEEL LIKE MARRYING THEM.
NO ONE WILL WANT YOU IF YOU KEEP VISITING THIS STINKY OLD MAN, YOU KNOW.
WELL, THANKS TO YOU, I BATHE MORE OFTEN.
IT'S A SMELL YOU CAN'T GET RID OF NO MATTER HOW OFTEN YOU WASH...THE STENCH OF DEATH.
TAK (THUD)
탁
덜그럭
DULGURUK (CLINK)
YOU BELONG IN AN HONORABLE POLICE STATION, NOT THIS STUFFY ROOM.

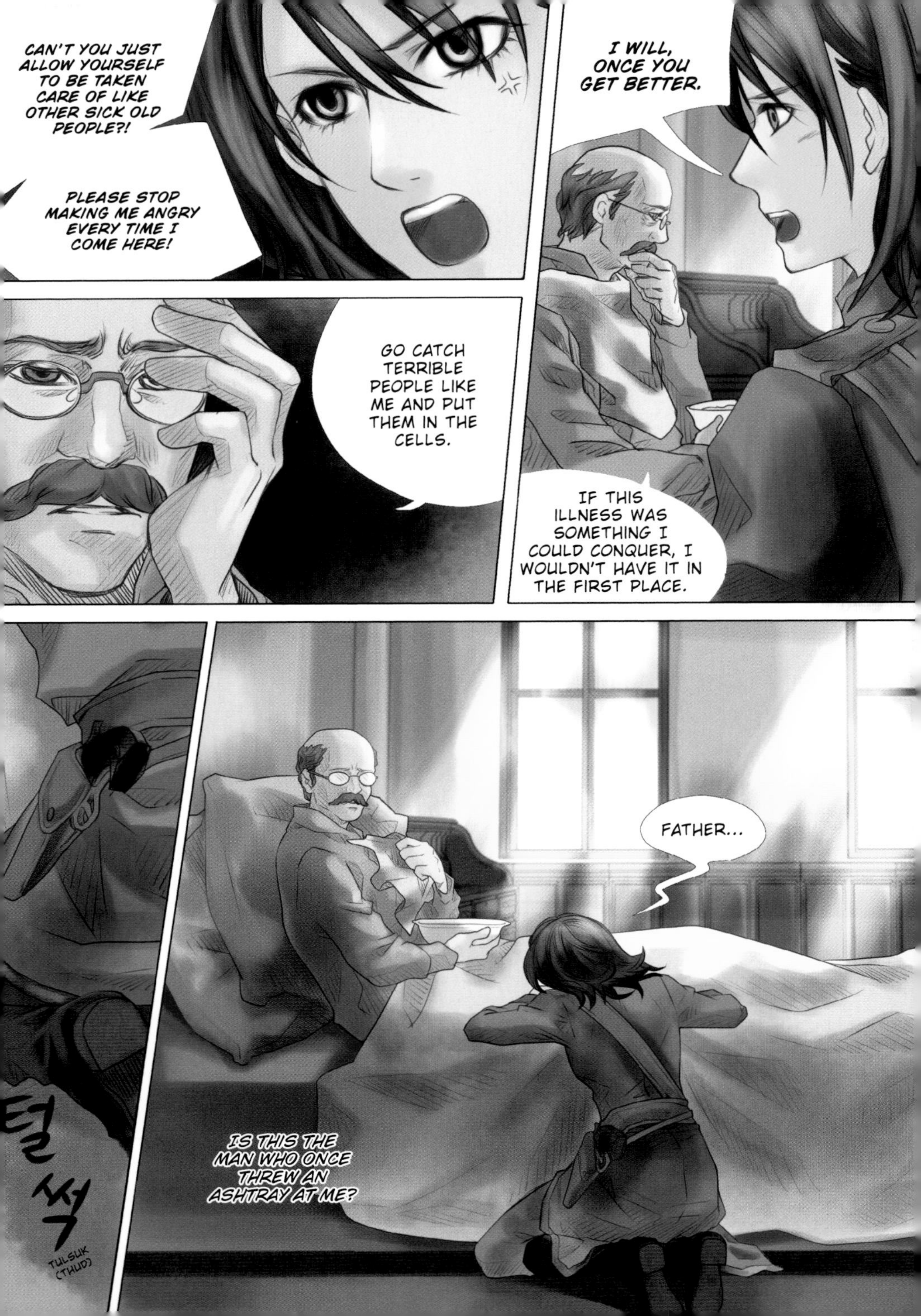
CAN'T YOU JUST ALLOW YOURSELF TO BE TAKEN CARE OF LIKE OTHER SICK OLD PEOPLE?!
PLEASE STOP MAKING ME ANGRY EVERY TIME I COME HERE!
I WILL, ONCE YOU GET BETTER.
GO CATCH TERRIBLE PEOPLE LIKE ME AND PUT THEM IN THE CELLS.
IF THIS ILLNESS WAS SOMETHING I COULD CONQUER, I WOULDN'T HAVE IT IN THE FIRST PLACE.
털썩
TULSUK (THUD)
IS THIS THE MAN WHO ONCE THREW AN ASHTRAY AT ME?
FATHER...

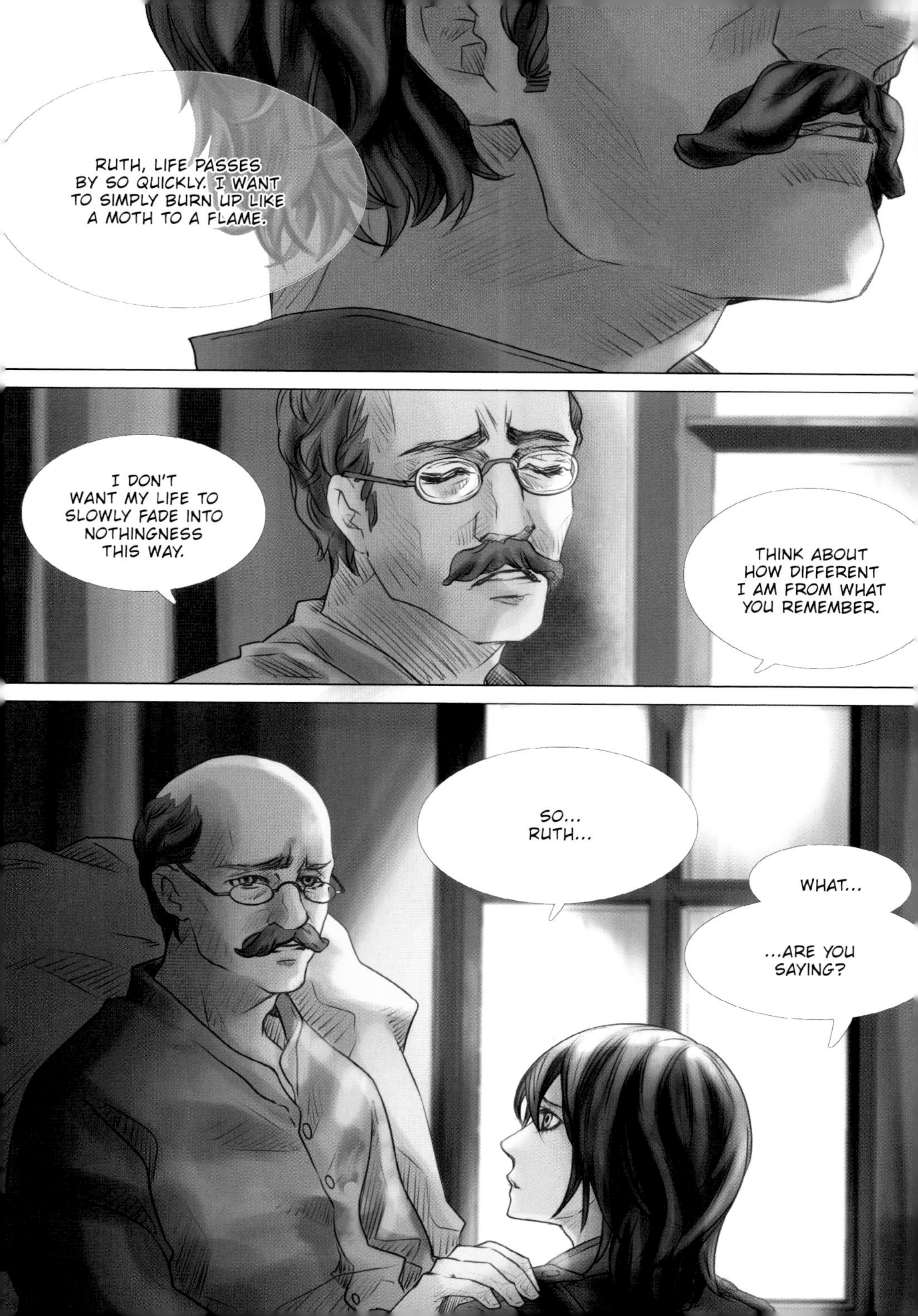
RUTH, LIFE PASSES BY SO QUICKLY. I WANT TO SIMPLY BURN UP LIKE A MOTH TO A FLAME.
I DON'T WANT MY LIFE TO SLOWLY FADE INTO NOTHINGNESS THIS WAY.
THINK ABOUT HOW DIFFERENT I AM FROM WHAT YOU REMEMBER.
SO... RUTH...
WHAT...
...ARE YOU SAYING?

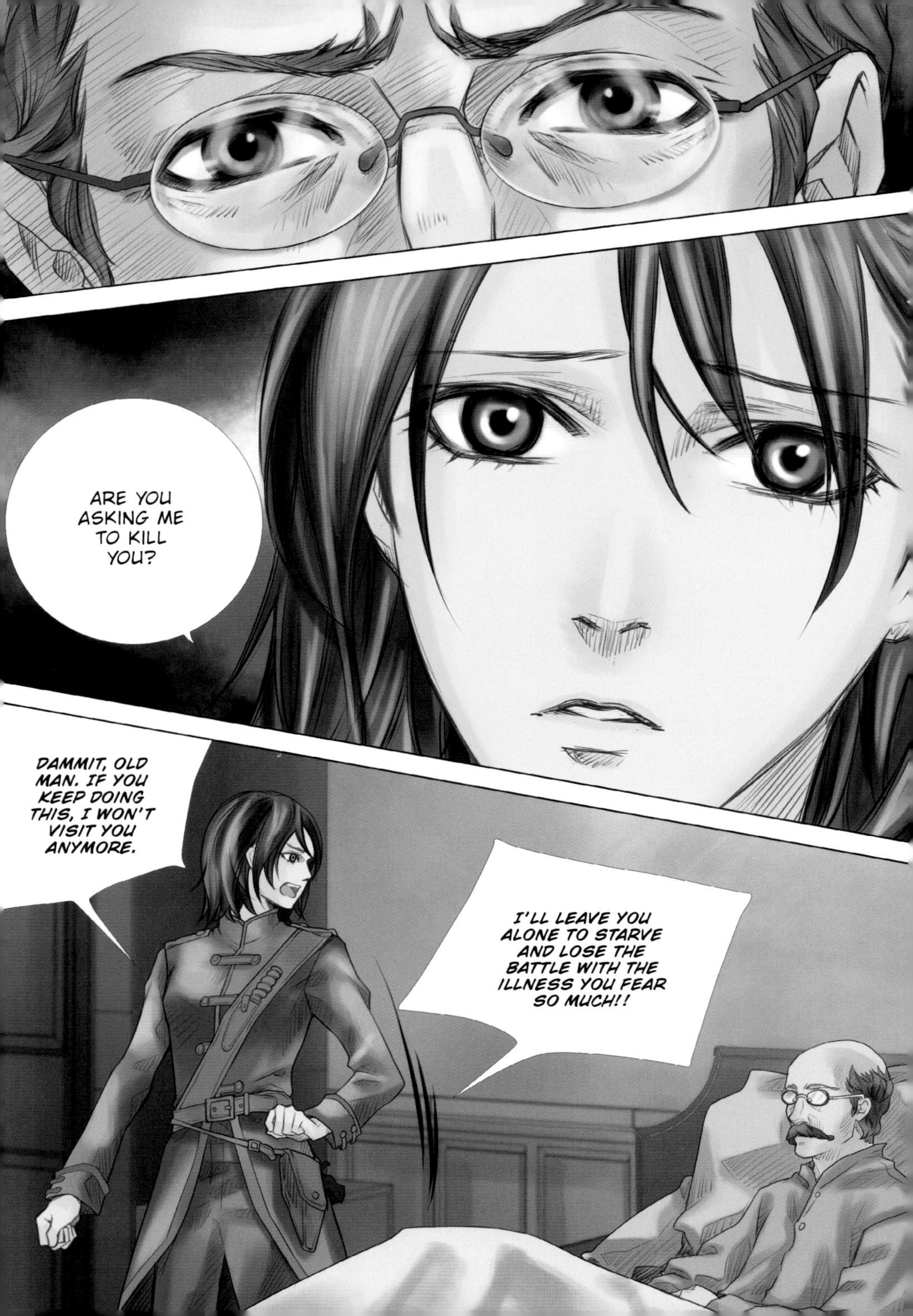
ARE YOU ASKING ME TO KILL YOU?
DAMMIT, OLD MAN. IF YOU KEEP DOING THIS, I WON'T VISIT YOU ANYMORE.
I'LL LEAVE YOU ALONE TO STARVE AND LOSE THE BATTLE WITH THE ILLNESS YOU FEAR SO MUCH!!

IF YOU AREN'T GOING TO FINISH ME NOW, THEN JUST GO.

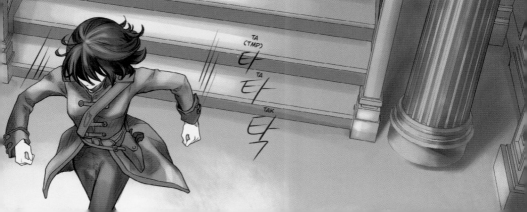

TA
(TMP)

TA

TAK

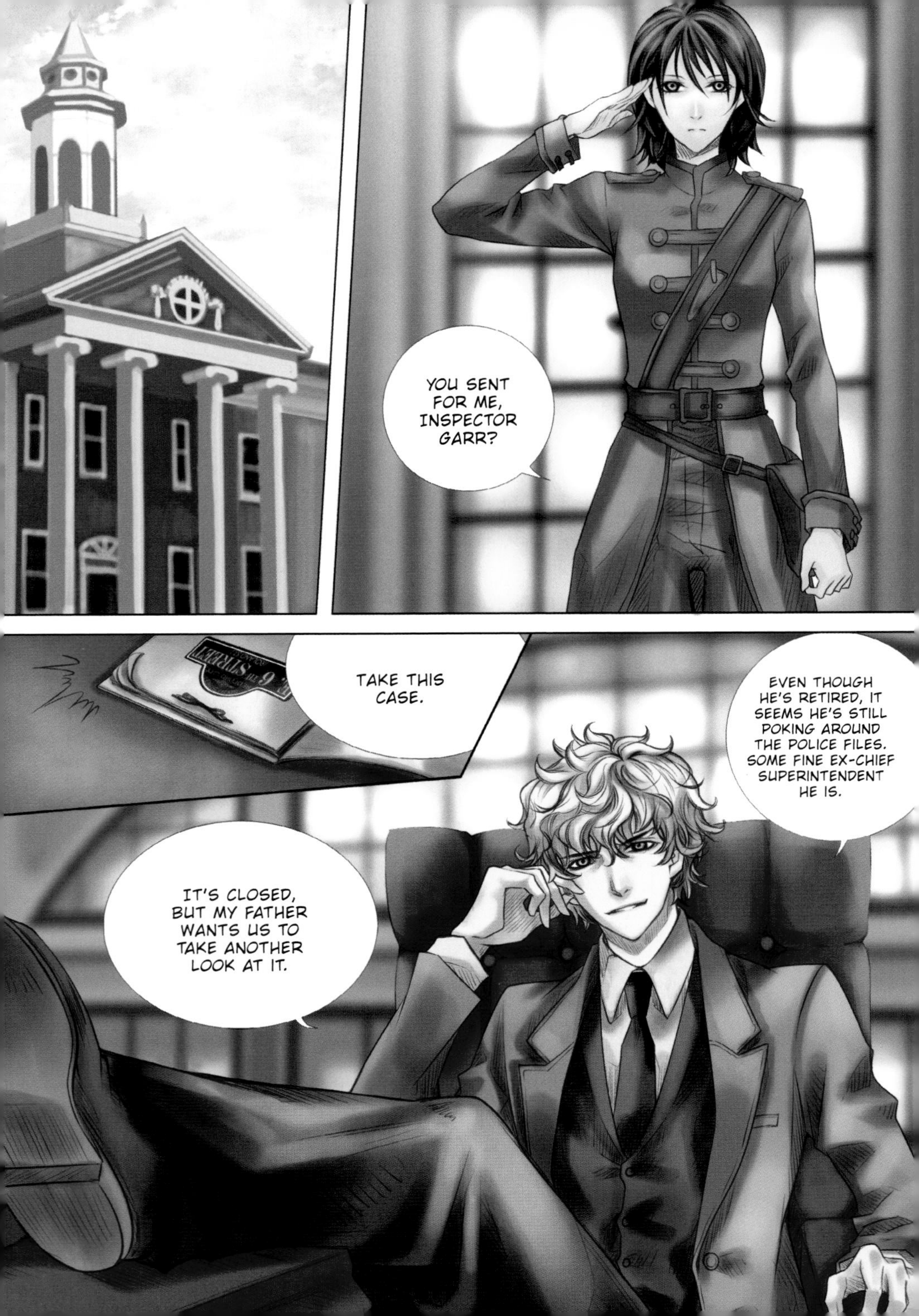
YOU SENT FOR ME, INSPECTOR GARR?
TAKE THIS CASE.
IT'S CLOSED, BUT MY FATHER WANTS US TO TAKE ANOTHER LOOK AT IT.
EVEN THOUGH HE'S RETIRED, IT SEEMS HE'S STILL POKING AROUND THE POLICE FILES. SOME FINE EX-CHIEF SUPERINTENDENT HE IS.

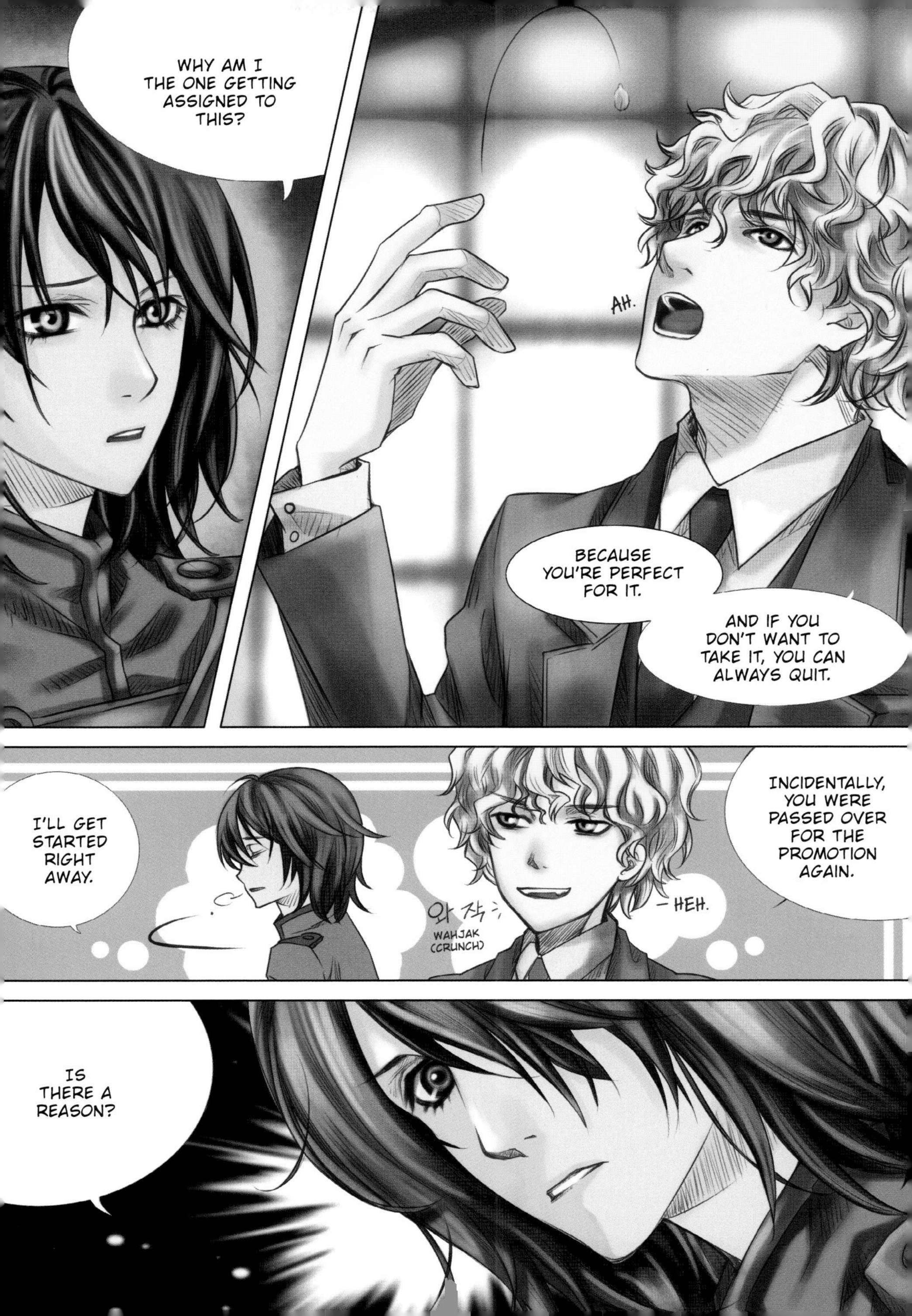
WHY AM I THE ONE GETTING ASSIGNED TO THIS?
AH.
BECAUSE YOU'RE PERFECT FOR IT.
AND IF YOU DON'T WANT TO TAKE IT, YOU CAN ALWAYS QUIT.
I'LL GET STARTED RIGHT AWAY.
와작
WAHJAK (CRUNCH)
—HEH.
INCIDENTALLY, YOU WERE PASSED OVER FOR THE PROMOTION AGAIN.
IS THERE A REASON?

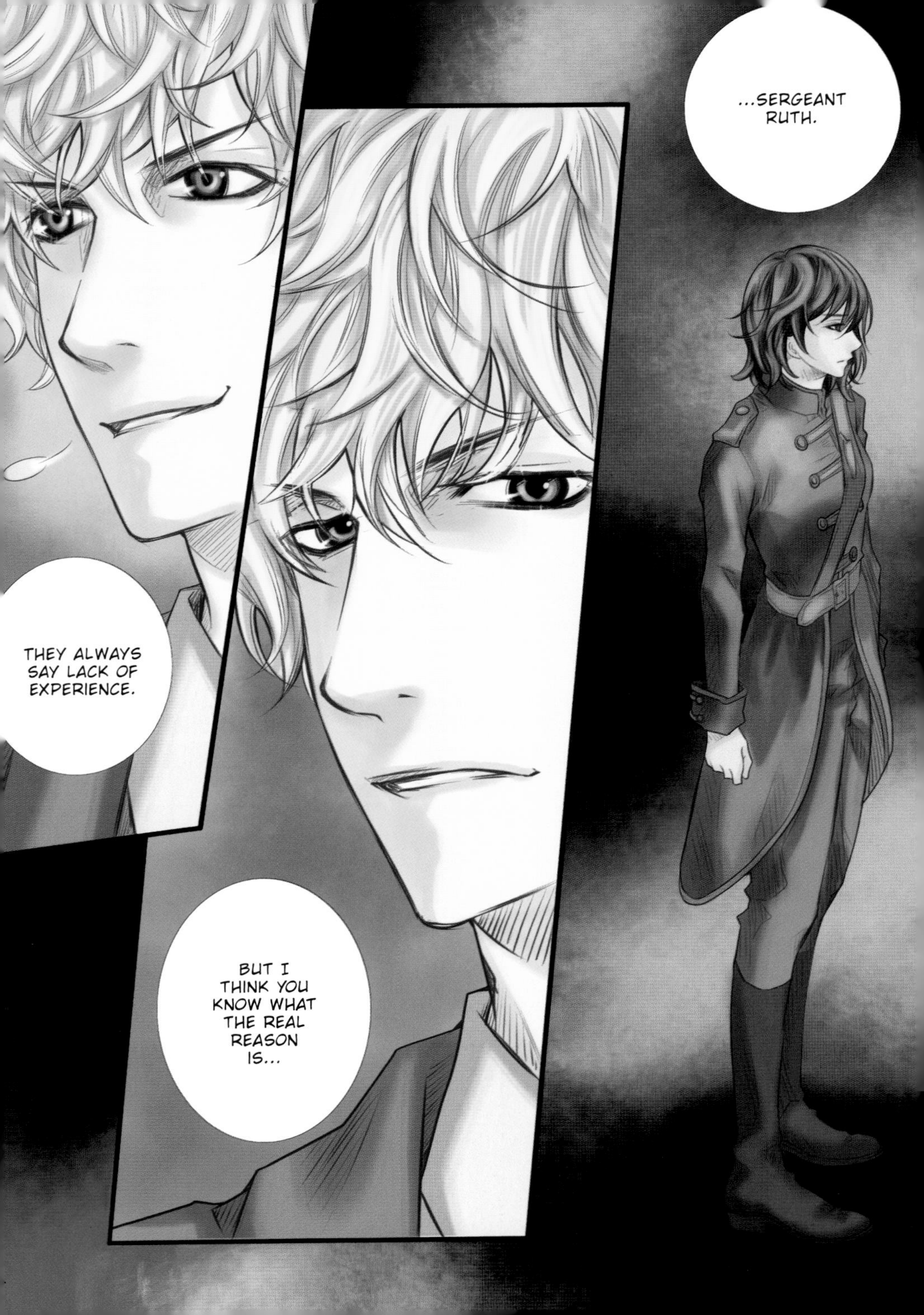
THEY ALWAYS SAY LACK OF EXPERIENCE.
BUT I THINK YOU KNOW WHAT THE REAL REASON IS...
...SERGEANT RUTH.

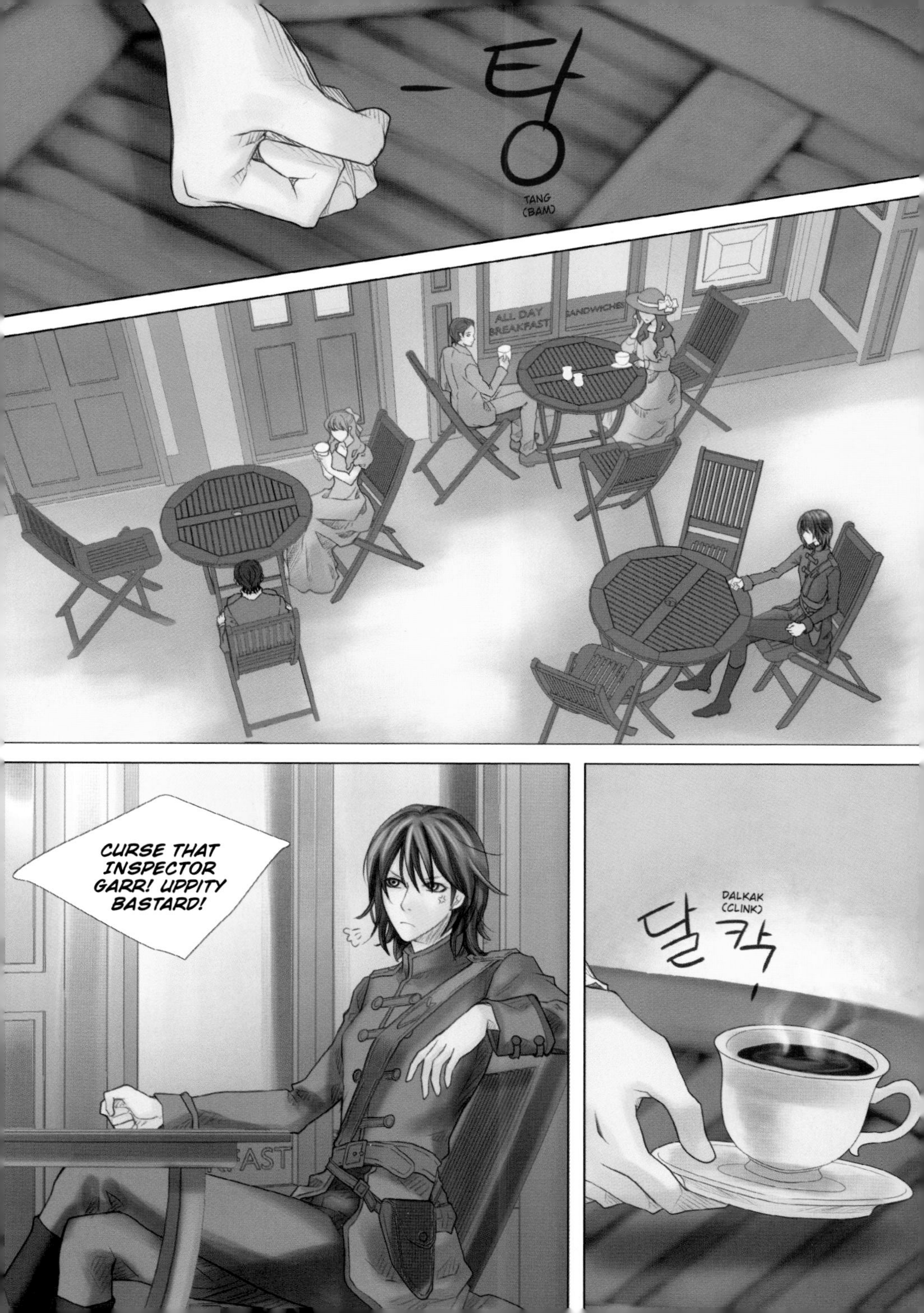
탕
TANG
(BAM)
ALL DAY
BREAKFAST
SANDWICHES
CURSE THAT INSPECTOR GARR! UPPITY BASTARD!
FAST
달칵
DALKAK
(CLINK)

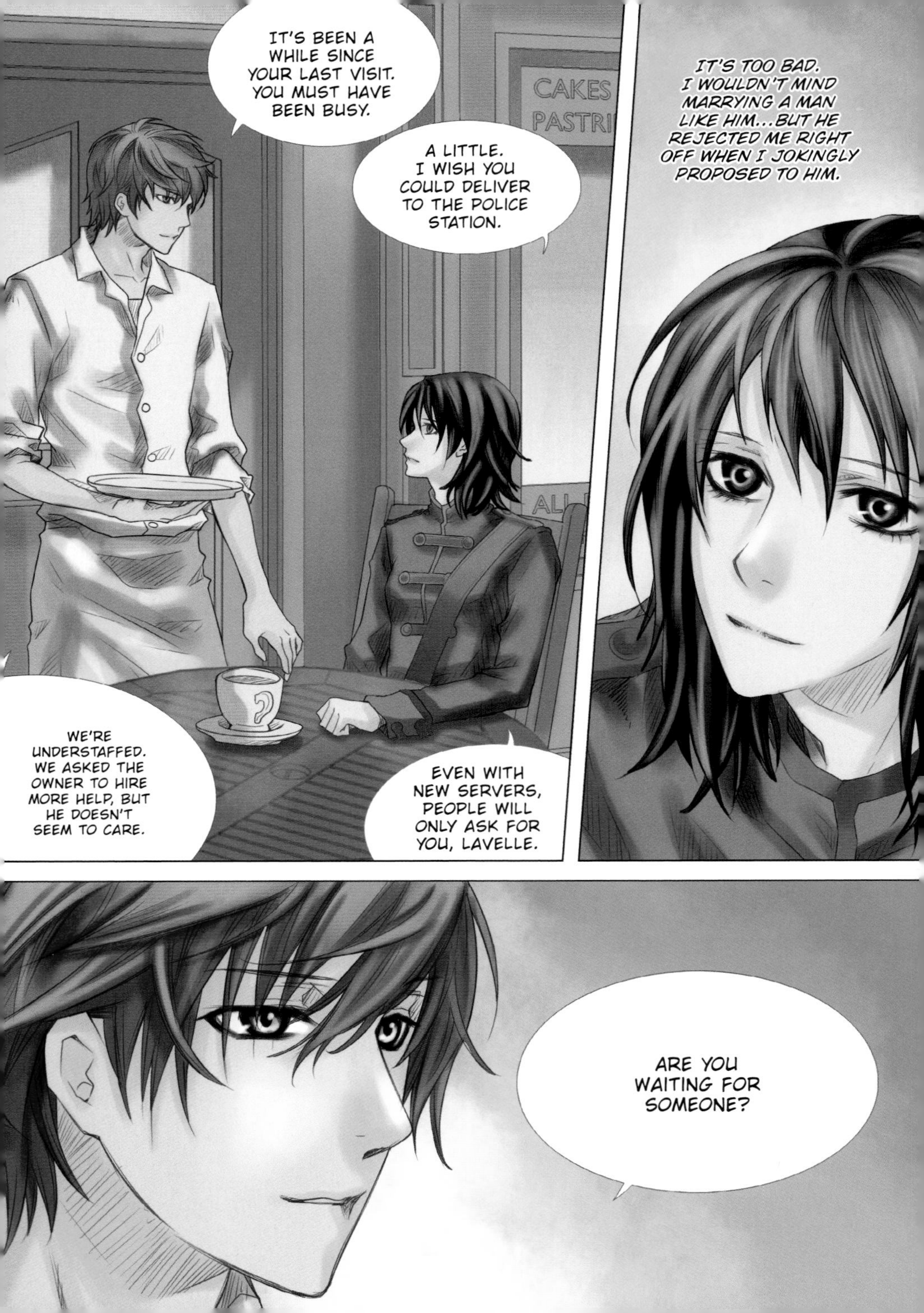
IT'S BEEN A WHILE SINCE YOUR LAST VISIT. YOU MUST HAVE BEEN BUSY.
CAKES PASTRI
A LITTLE. I WISH YOU COULD DELIVER TO THE POLICE STATION.
WE'RE UNDERSTAFFED. WE ASKED THE OWNER TO HIRE MORE HELP, BUT HE DOESN'T SEEM TO CARE.
EVEN WITH NEW SERVERS, PEOPLE WILL ONLY ASK FOR YOU, LAVELLE.
IT'S TOO BAD. I WOULDN'T MIND MARRYING A MAN LIKE HIM...BUT HE REJECTED ME RIGHT OFF WHEN I JOKINGLY PROPOSED TO HIM.
ARE YOU WAITING FOR SOMEONE?

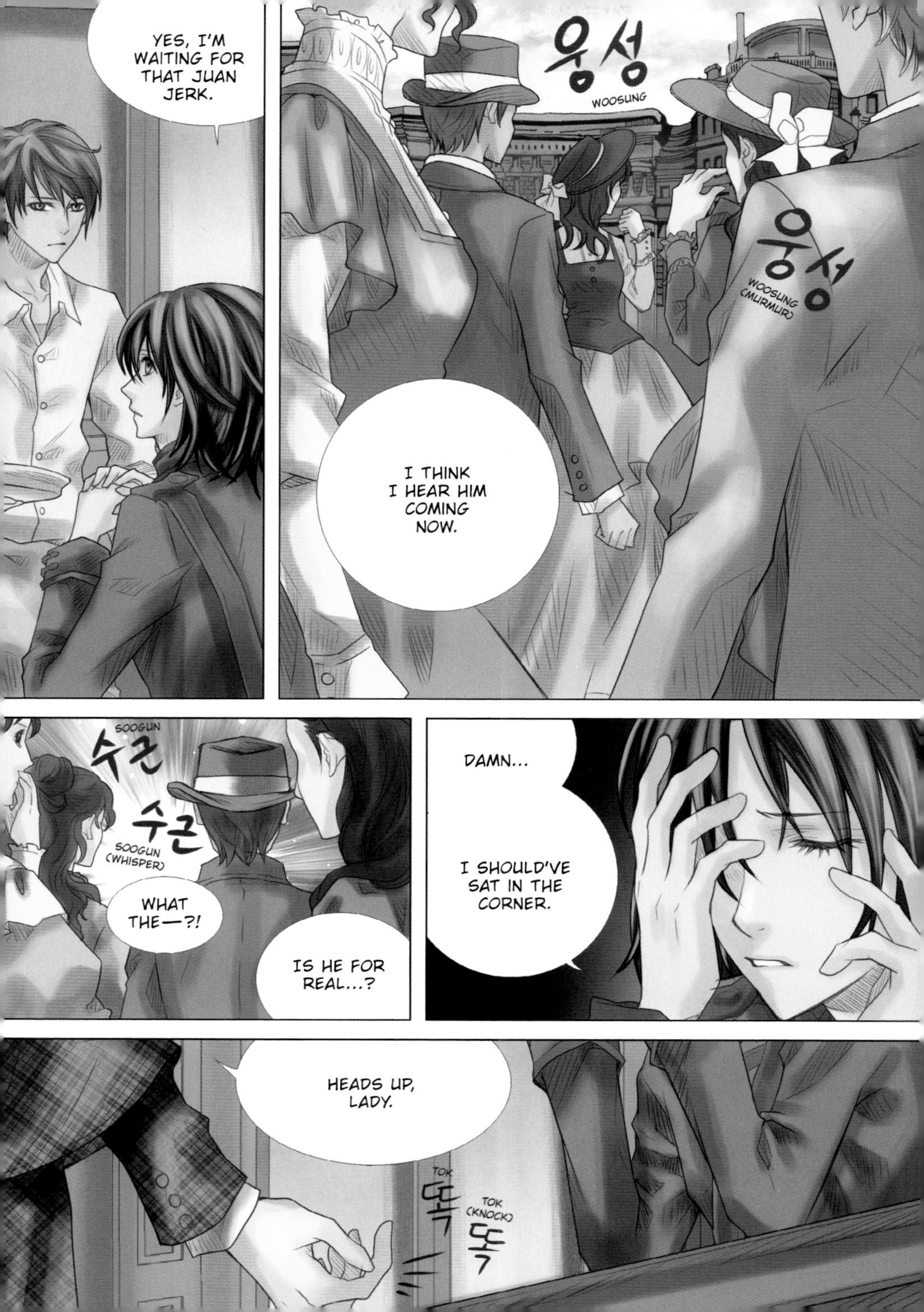
YES, I'M WAITING FOR THAT JUAN JERK.
웅성
WOOSUNG
웅성
WOOSUNG (MURMUR)
I THINK I HEAR HIM COMING NOW.
SOOGUN
수군
수군
SOOGUN (WHISPER)
WHAT THE—?!
IS HE FOR REAL...?
DAMN...
I SHOULD'VE SAT IN THE CORNER.
HEADS UP, LADY.
TOK
똑
TOK (KNOCK)
똑

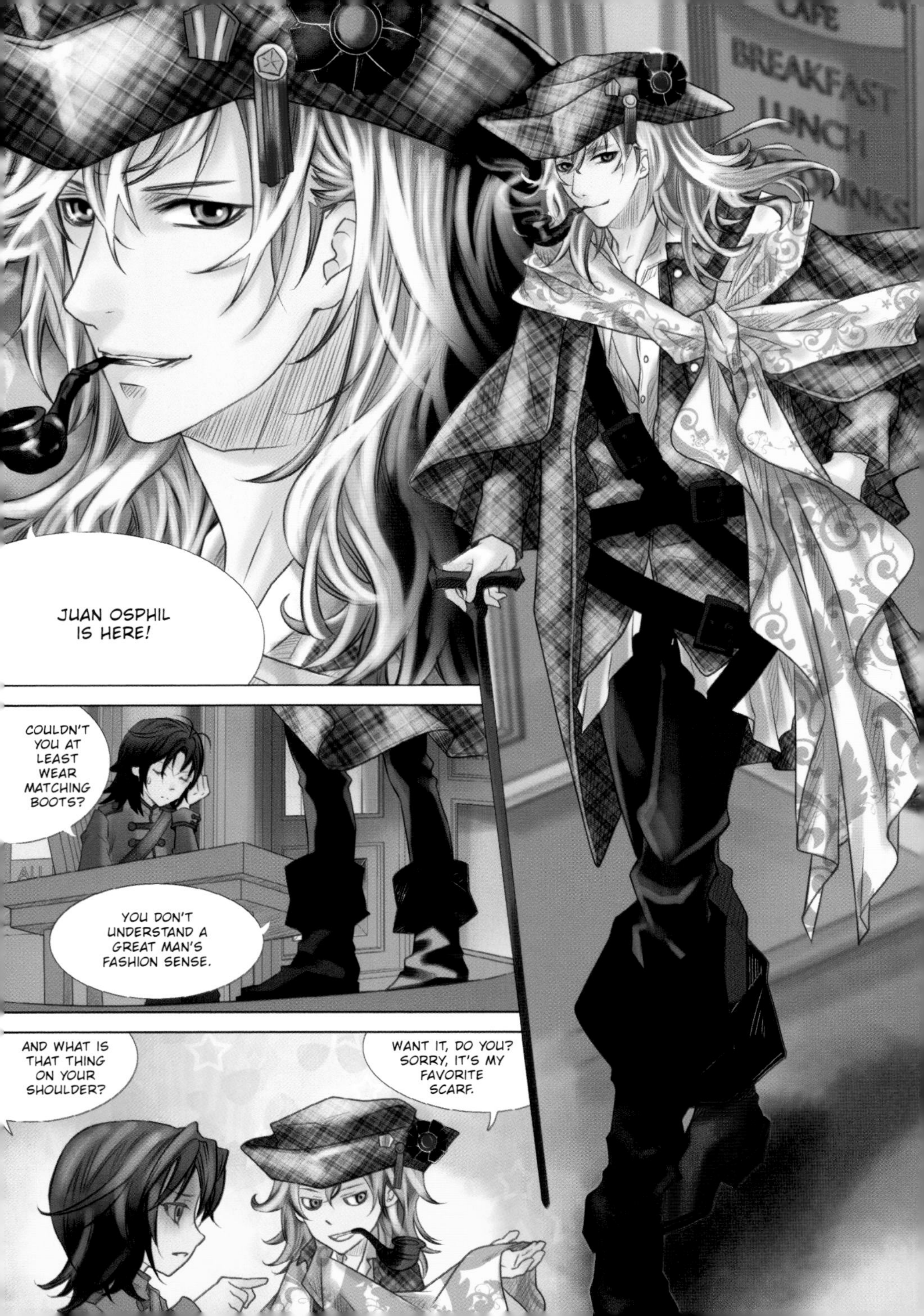
CAFE
BREAKFAST
LUNCH
DRINKS
JUAN OSPHIL IS HERE!
COULDN'T YOU AT LEAST WEAR MATCHING BOOTS?
YOU DON'T UNDERSTAND A GREAT MAN'S FASHION SENSE.
AND WHAT IS THAT THING ON YOUR SHOULDER?
WANT IT, DO YOU? SORRY, IT'S MY FAVORITE SCARF.

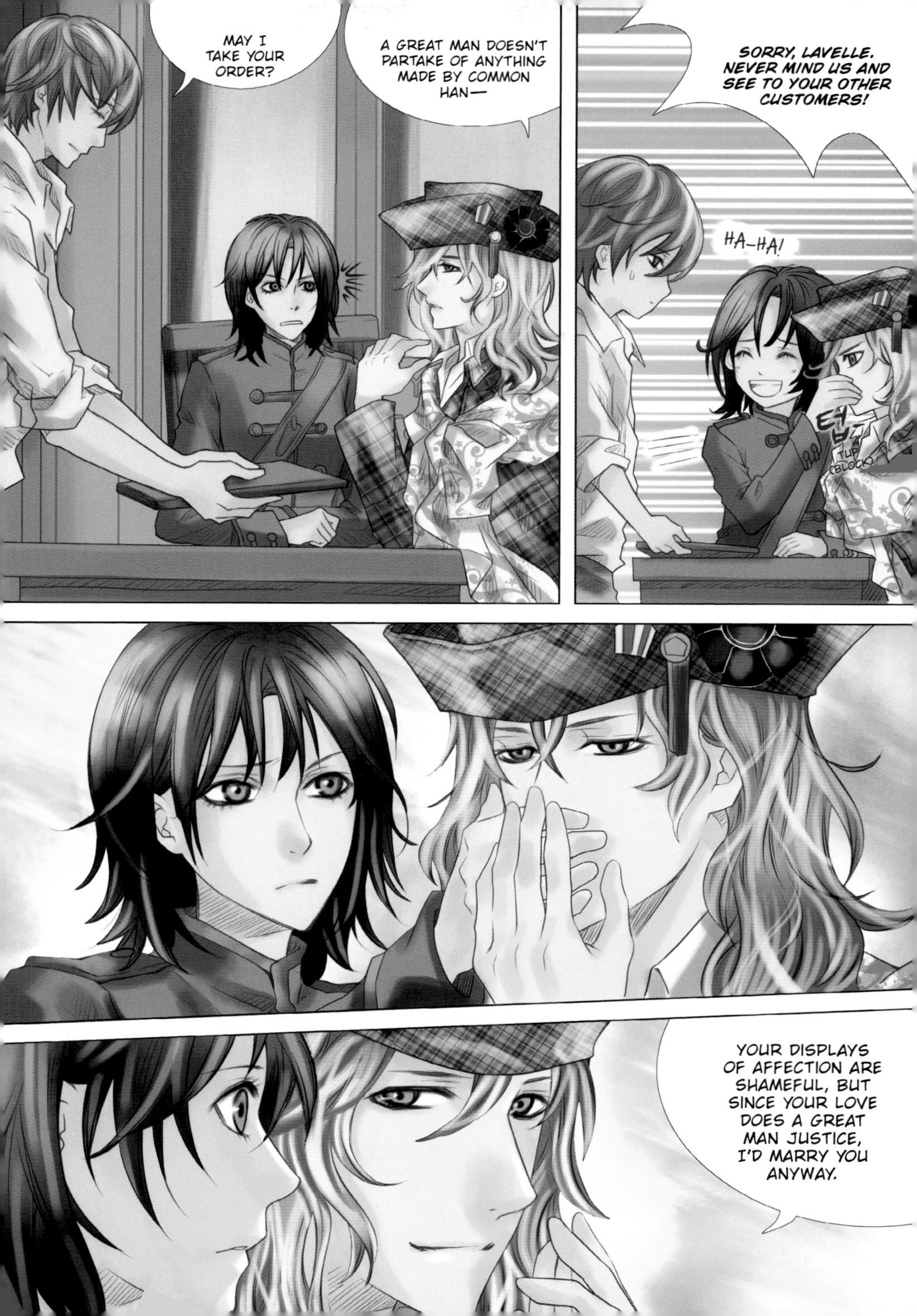
MAY I TAKE YOUR ORDER?
A GREAT MAN DOESN'T PARTAKE OF ANYTHING MADE BY COMMON HAN—
SORRY, LAVELLE. NEVER MIND US AND SEE TO YOUR OTHER CUSTOMERS!
HA-HA!
TUP (BLOCK)
YOUR DISPLAYS OF AFFECTION ARE SHAMEFUL, BUT SINCE YOUR LOVE DOES A GREAT MAN JUSTICE, I'D MARRY YOU ANYWAY.

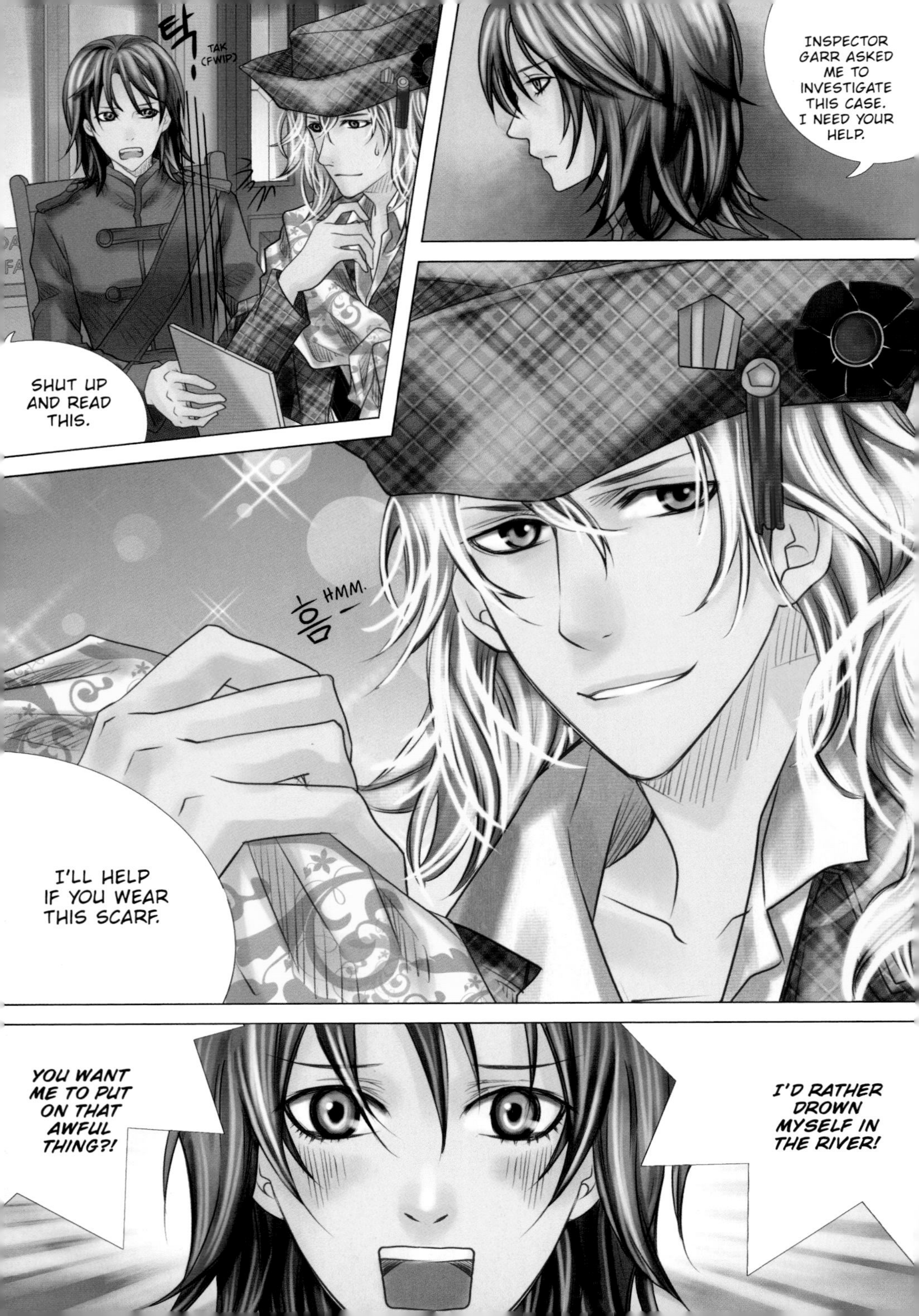
탁
TAK (FWIP)
SHUT UP AND READ THIS.
INSPECTOR GARR ASKED ME TO INVESTIGATE THIS CASE. I NEED YOUR HELP.
흠
HMM.
I'LL HELP IF YOU WEAR THIS SCARF.
YOU WANT ME TO PUT ON THAT AWFUL THING?!
I'D RATHER DROWN MYSELF IN THE RIVER!

THERE. HAPPY NOW?

HEH HEH

HEH.

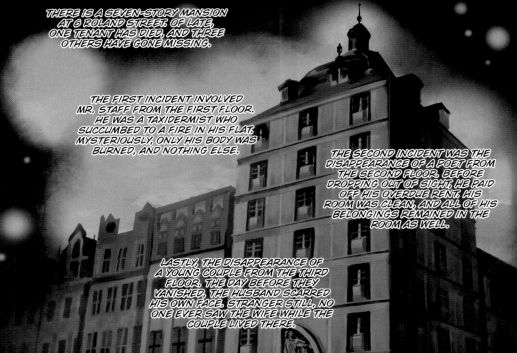

THERE IS A SEVEN-STORY MANSION AT 6 ROLAND STREET. OF LATE, ONE TENANT HAS DIED, AND THREE OTHERS HAVE GONE MISSING.

THE FIRST INCIDENT INVOLVED MR. STAFF FROM THE FIRST FLOOR. HE WAS A TAXIDERMIST WHO SUCCUMBED TO A FIRE IN HIS FLAT. MYSTERIOUSLY, ONLY HIS BODY WAS BURNED, AND NOTHING ELSE.

THE SECOND INCIDENT WAS THE DISAPPEARANCE OF A POET FROM THE SECOND FLOOR. BEFORE DROPPING OUT OF SIGHT, HE PAID OFF HIS OVERDUE RENT. HIS ROOM WAS CLEAN, AND ALL OF HIS BELONGINGS REMAINED IN THE ROOM AS WELL.

LASTLY, THE DISAPPEARANCE OF A YOUNG COUPLE FROM THE THIRD FLOOR. THE DAY BEFORE THEY VANISHED, THE HUSBAND SCARRED HIS OWN FACE. STRANGER STILL, NO ONE EVER SAW THE WIFE WHILE THE COUPLE LIVED THERE.

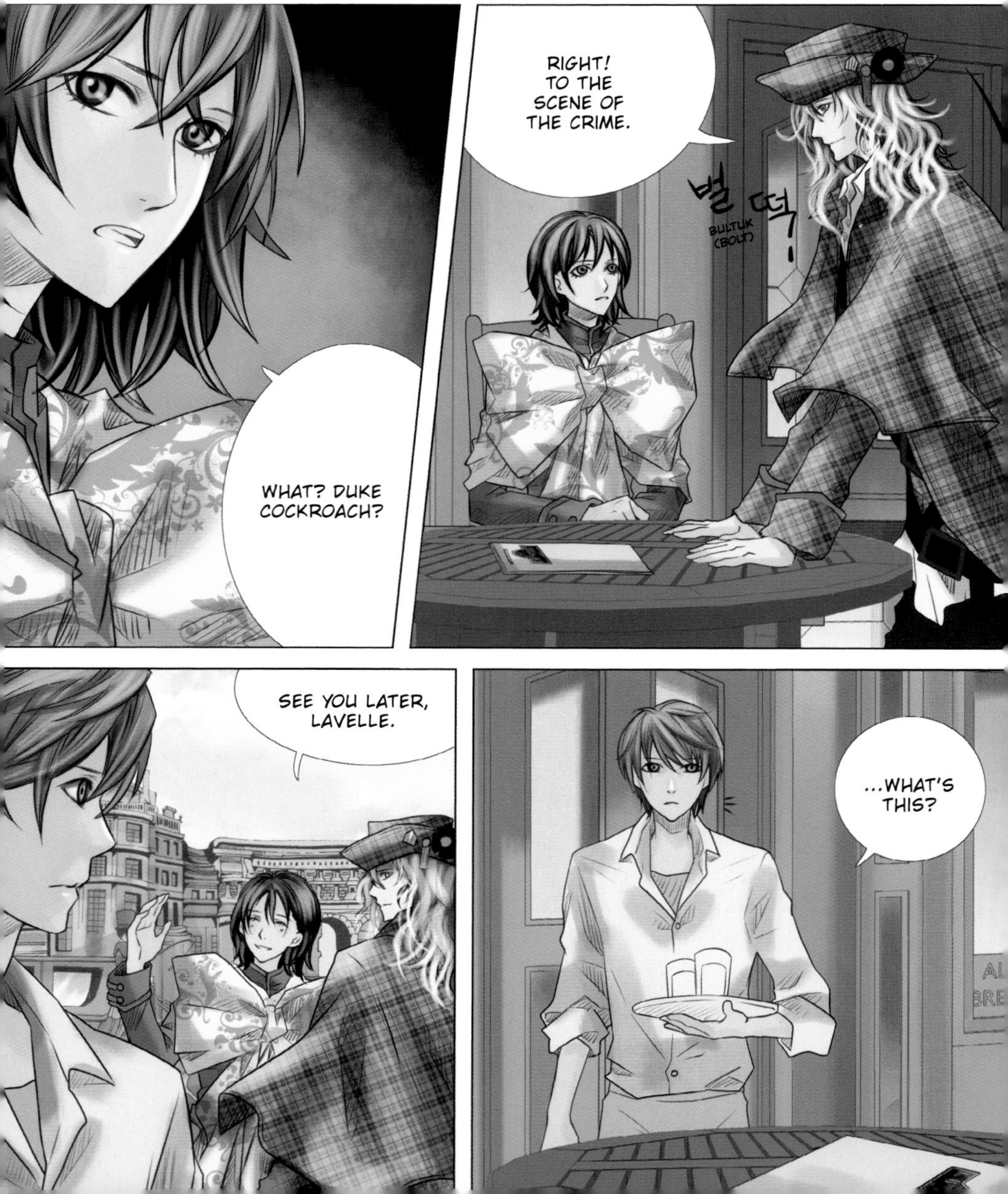
WHAT? DUKE COCKROACH?
RIGHT! TO THE SCENE OF THE CRIME.
벌떡
BULTUK (BOLT)
SEE YOU LATER, LAVELLE.
...WHAT'S THIS?

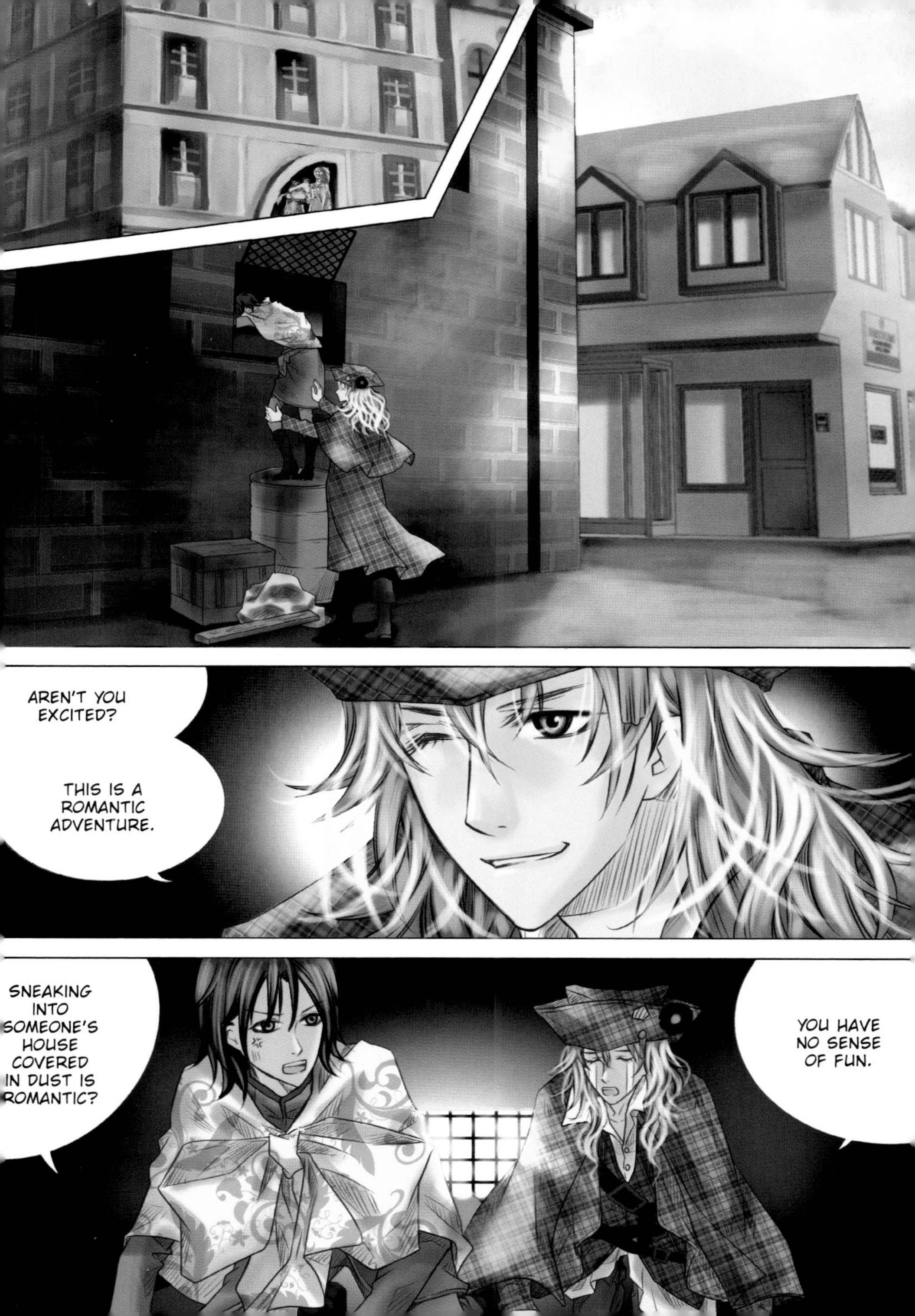
AREN'T YOU EXCITED?
THIS IS A ROMANTIC ADVENTURE.
SNEAKING INTO SOMEONE'S HOUSE COVERED IN DUST IS ROMANTIC?
YOU HAVE NO SENSE OF FUN.

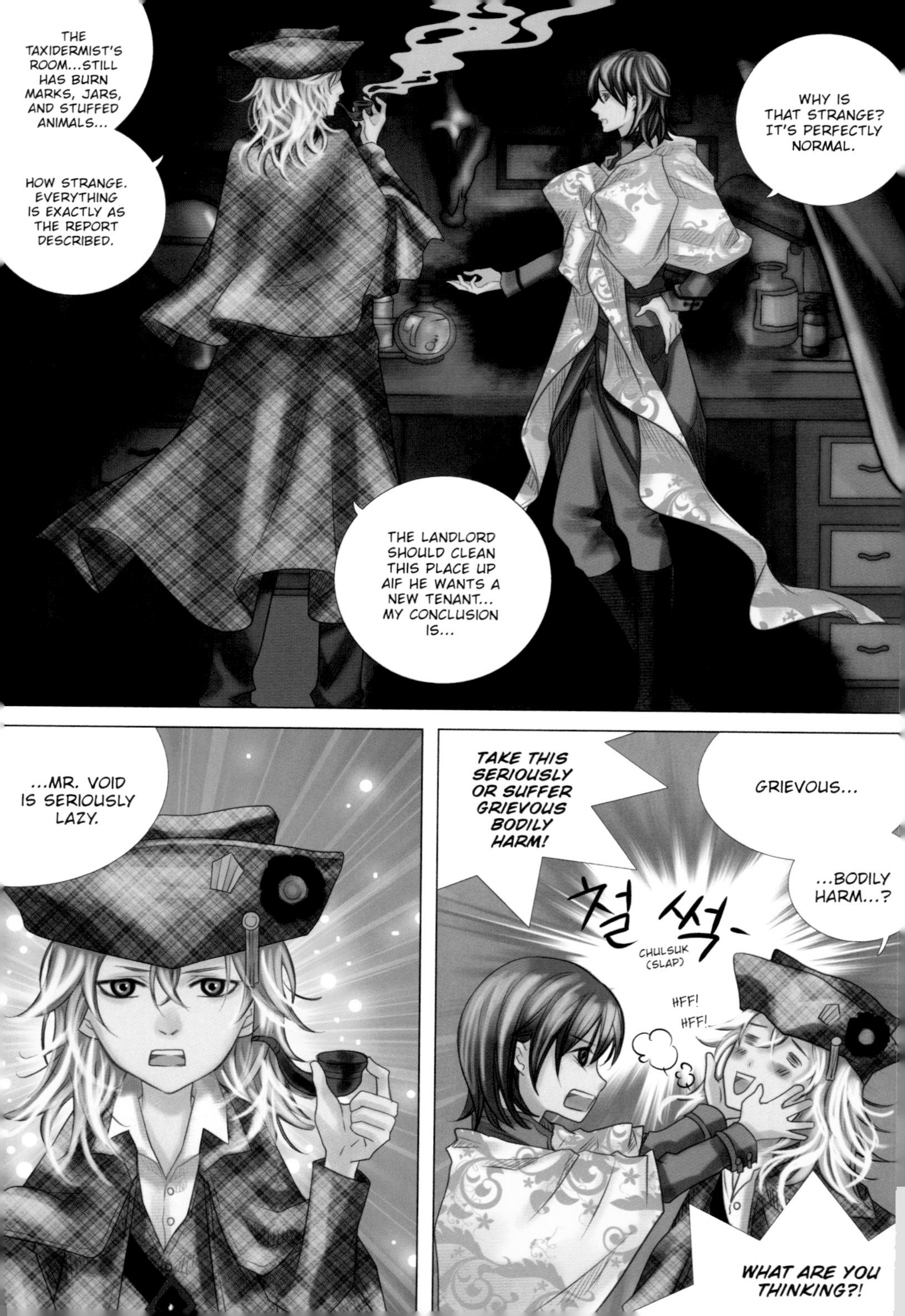
THE TAXIDERMIST'S ROOM...STILL HAS BURN MARKS, JARS, AND STUFFED ANIMALS...
HOW STRANGE. EVERYTHING IS EXACTLY AS THE REPORT DESCRIBED.
WHY IS THAT STRANGE? IT'S PERFECTLY NORMAL.
THE LANDLORD SHOULD CLEAN THIS PLACE UP AIF HE WANTS A NEW TENANT... MY CONCLUSION IS...
...MR. VOID IS SERIOUSLY LAZY.
TAKE THIS SERIOUSLY OR SUFFER GRIEVOUS BODILY HARM!
GRIEVOUS...
...BODILY HARM...?
철썩-
CHULSUK (SLAP)
HFF! HFF!
WHAT ARE YOU THINKING?!

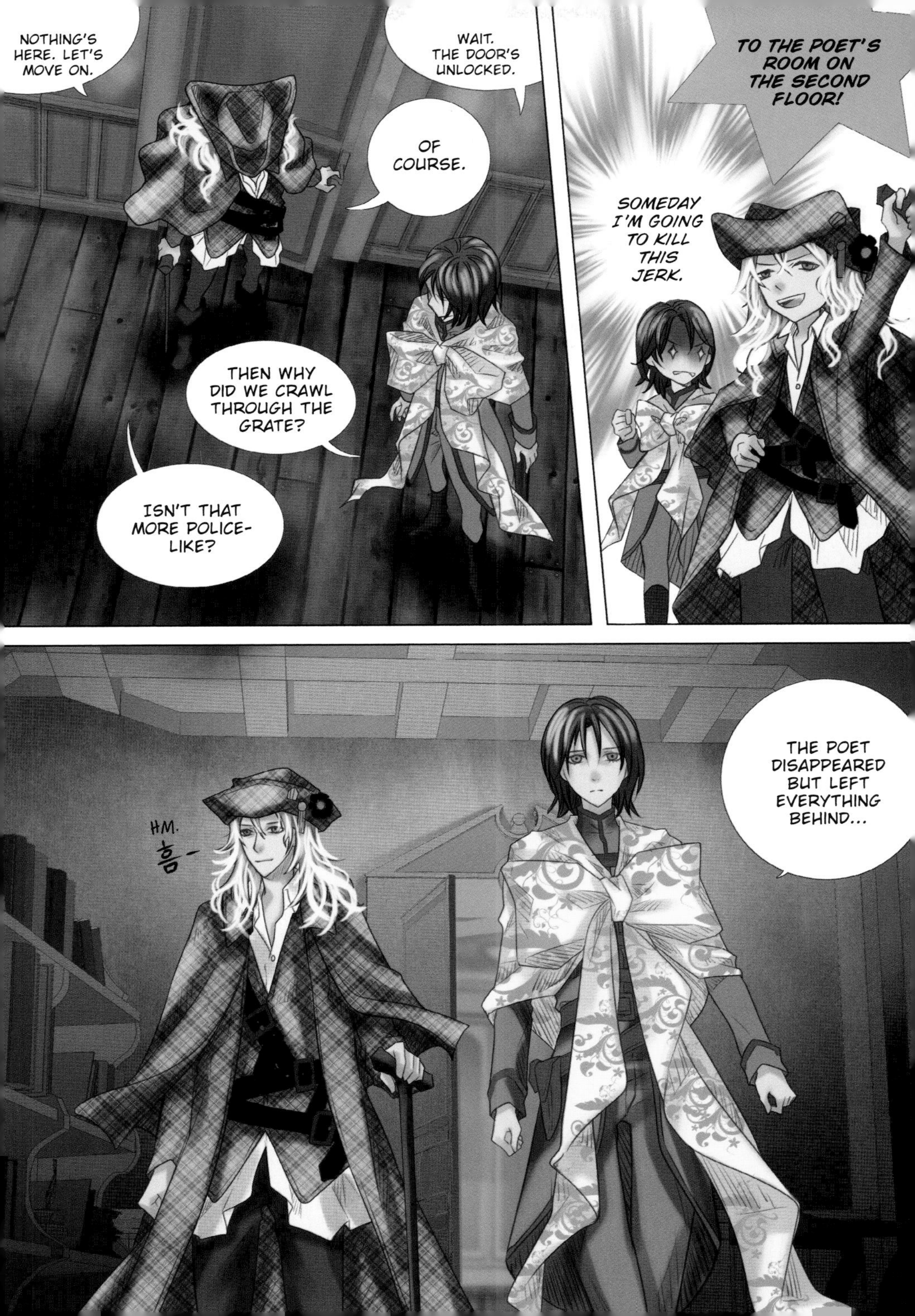
NOTHING'S HERE. LET'S MOVE ON.
WAIT. THE DOOR'S UNLOCKED.
OF COURSE.
THEN WHY DID WE CRAWL THROUGH THE GRATE?
ISN'T THAT MORE POLICE-LIKE?
TO THE POET'S ROOM ON THE SECOND FLOOR!
SOMEDAY I'M GOING TO KILL THIS JERK.
HM.
흠-
THE POET DISAPPEARED BUT LEFT EVERYTHING BEHIND...

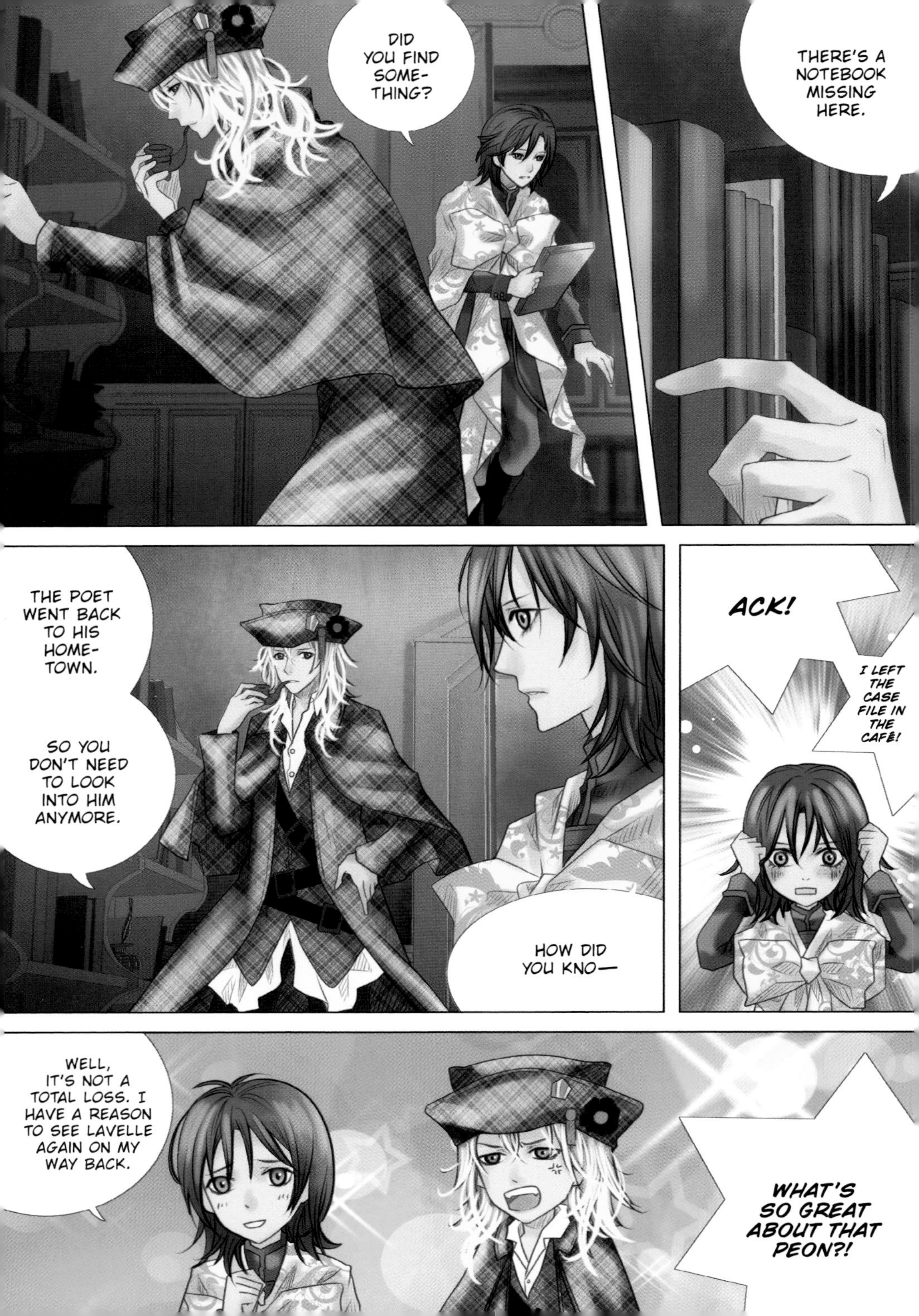
DID YOU FIND SOME-THING?
THERE'S A NOTEBOOK MISSING HERE.
THE POET WENT BACK TO HIS HOME-TOWN.
SO YOU DON'T NEED TO LOOK INTO HIM ANYMORE.
HOW DID YOU KNO—
ACK!
I LEFT THE CASE FILE IN THE CAFÉ!
WELL, IT'S NOT A TOTAL LOSS. I HAVE A REASON TO SEE LAVELLE AGAIN ON MY WAY BACK.
WHAT'S SO GREAT ABOUT THAT PEON?!

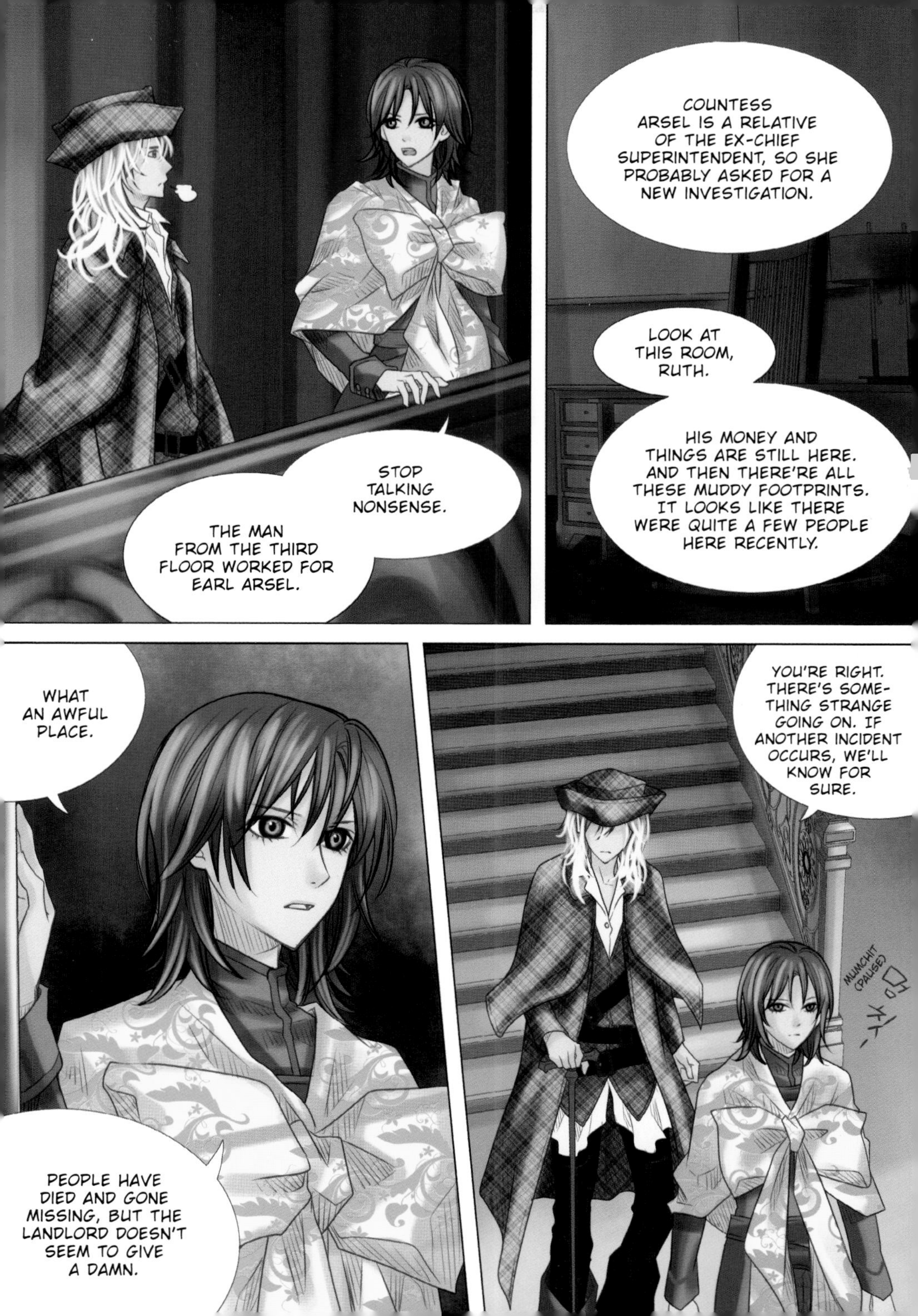
STOP TALKING NONSENSE.
THE MAN FROM THE THIRD FLOOR WORKED FOR EARL ARSEL.
COUNTESS ARSEL IS A RELATIVE OF THE EX-CHIEF SUPERINTENDENT, SO SHE PROBABLY ASKED FOR A NEW INVESTIGATION.
LOOK AT THIS ROOM, RUTH.
HIS MONEY AND THINGS ARE STILL HERE. AND THEN THERE'RE ALL THESE MUDDY FOOTPRINTS. IT LOOKS LIKE THERE WERE QUITE A FEW PEOPLE HERE RECENTLY.
WHAT AN AWFUL PLACE.
PEOPLE HAVE DIED AND GONE MISSING, BUT THE LANDLORD DOESN'T SEEM TO GIVE A DAMN.
YOU'RE RIGHT. THERE'S SOME-THING STRANGE GOING ON. IF ANOTHER INCIDENT OCCURS, WE'LL KNOW FOR SURE.
MUMCHIT (PAUSE)

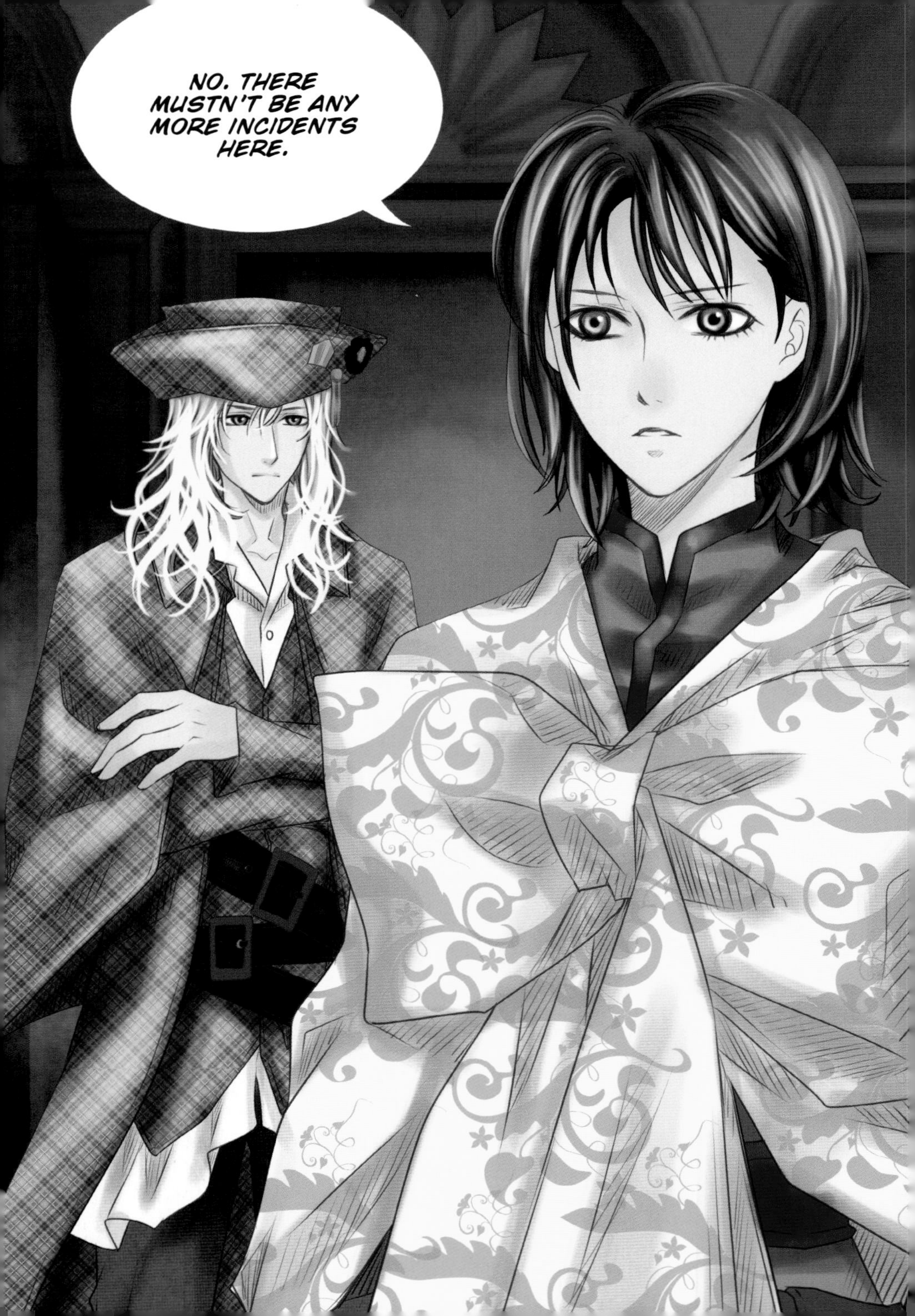
NO. THERE MUSTN'T BE ANY MORE INCIDENTS HERE.

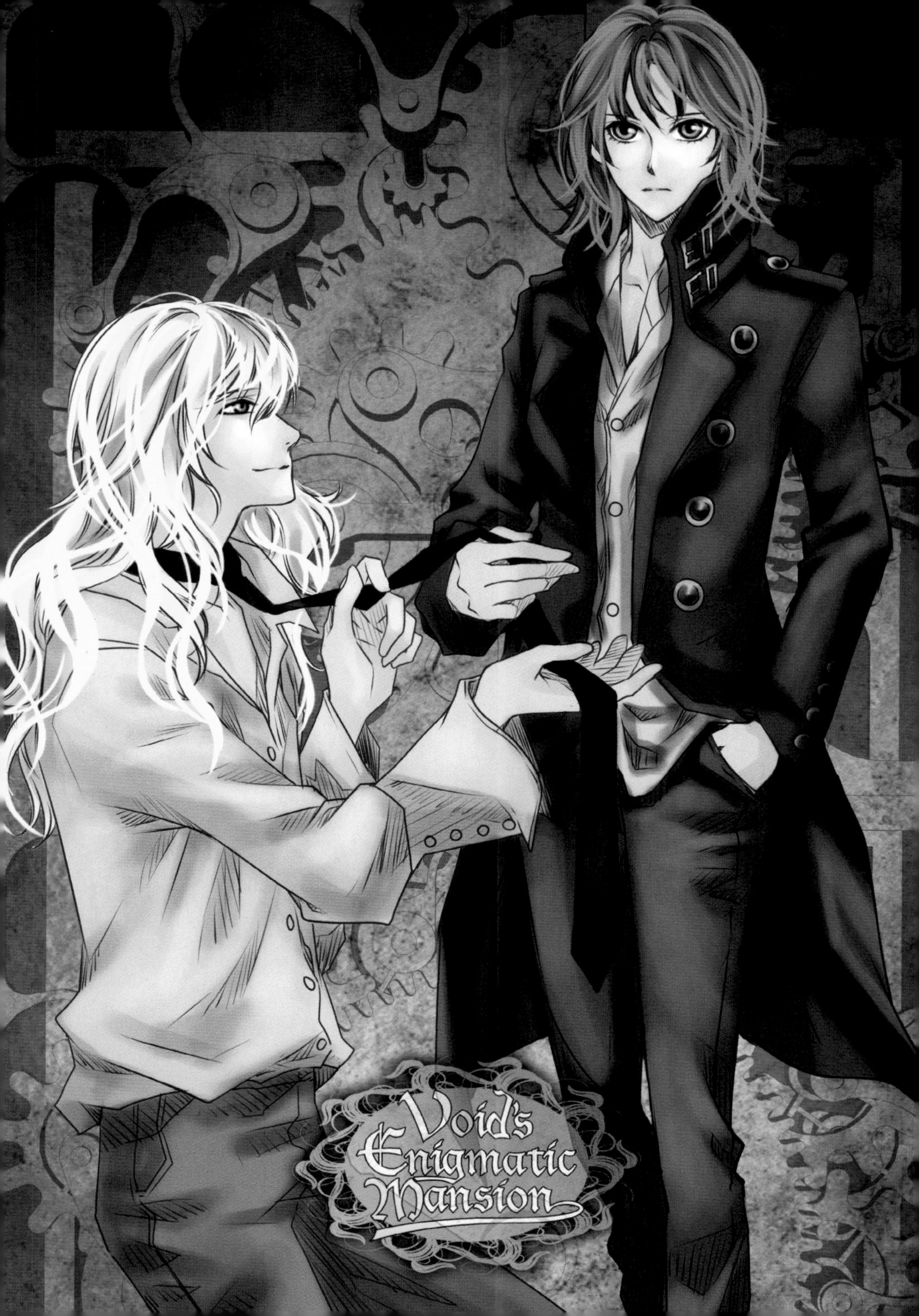
Void's
Enigmatic
Mansion

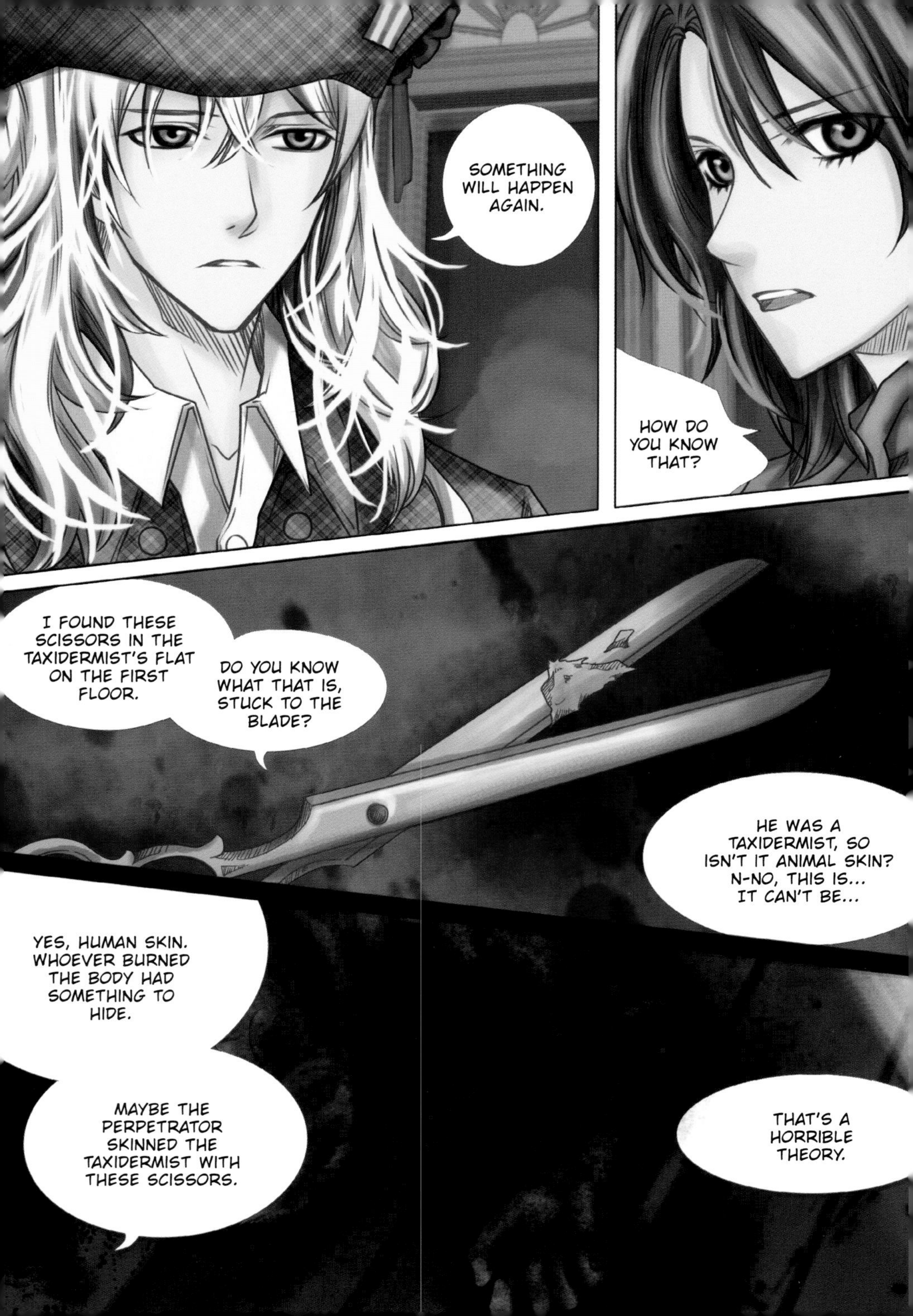
SOMETHING WILL HAPPEN AGAIN.
HOW DO YOU KNOW THAT?
I FOUND THESE SCISSORS IN THE TAXIDERMIST'S FLAT ON THE FIRST FLOOR.
DO YOU KNOW WHAT THAT IS, STUCK TO THE BLADE?
HE WAS A TAXIDERMIST, SO ISN'T IT ANIMAL SKIN? N-NO, THIS IS... IT CAN'T BE...
YES, HUMAN SKIN. WHOEVER BURNED THE BODY HAD SOMETHING TO HIDE.
MAYBE THE PERPETRATOR SKINNED THE TAXIDERMIST WITH THESE SCISSORS.
THAT'S A HORRIBLE THEORY.

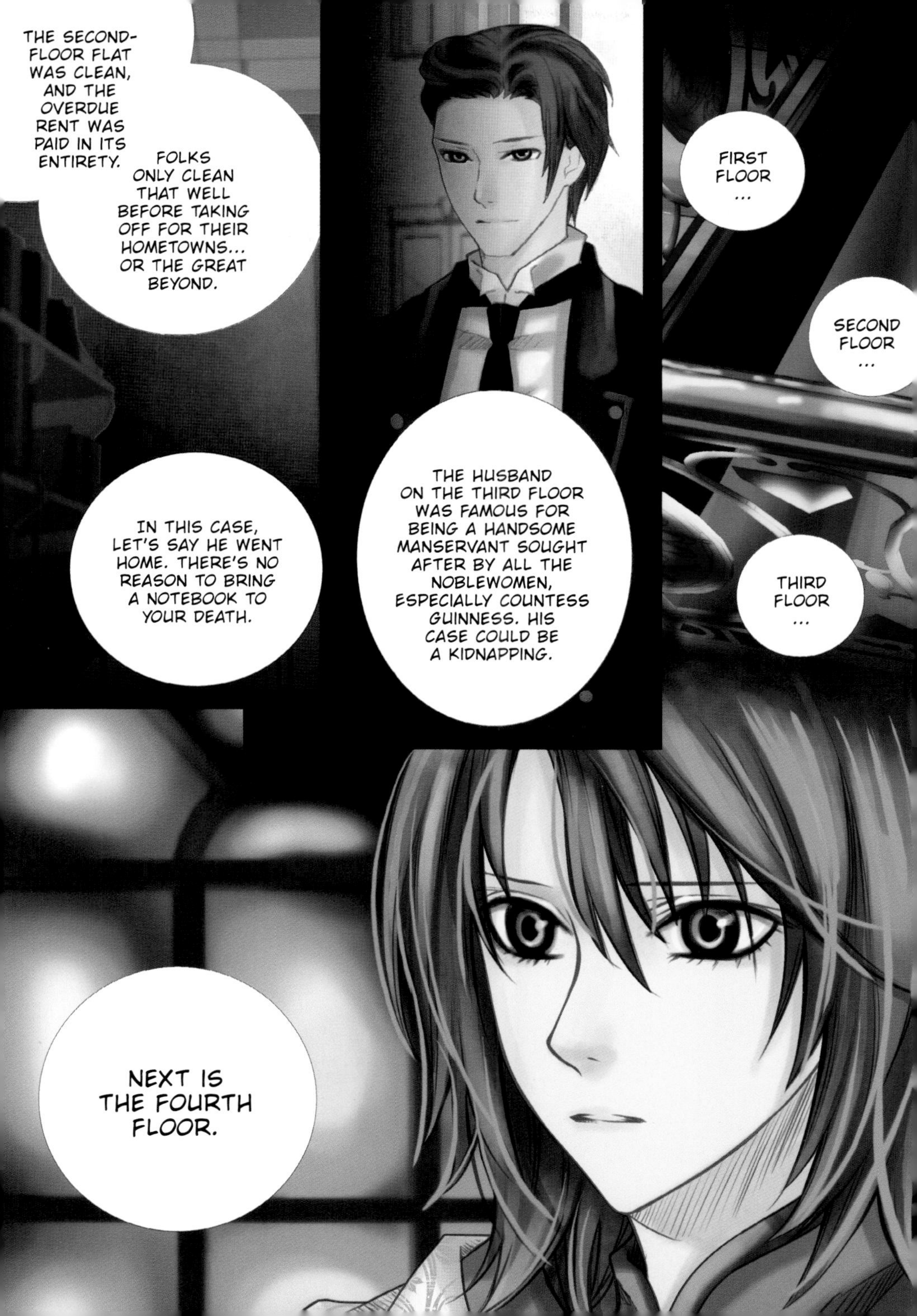

THE SECOND-FLOOR FLAT WAS CLEAN, AND THE OVERDUE RENT WAS PAID IN ITS ENTIRETY.
FOLKS ONLY CLEAN THAT WELL BEFORE TAKING OFF FOR THEIR HOMETOWNS... OR THE GREAT BEYOND.
IN THIS CASE, LET'S SAY HE WENT HOME. THERE'S NO REASON TO BRING A NOTEBOOK TO YOUR DEATH.
THE HUSBAND ON THE THIRD FLOOR WAS FAMOUS FOR BEING A HANDSOME MANSERVANT SOUGHT AFTER BY ALL THE NOBLEWOMEN, ESPECIALLY COUNTESS GUINNESS. HIS CASE COULD BE A KIDNAPPING.
FIRST FLOOR...
SECOND FLOOR...
THIRD FLOOR...
NEXT IS THE FOURTH FLOOR.

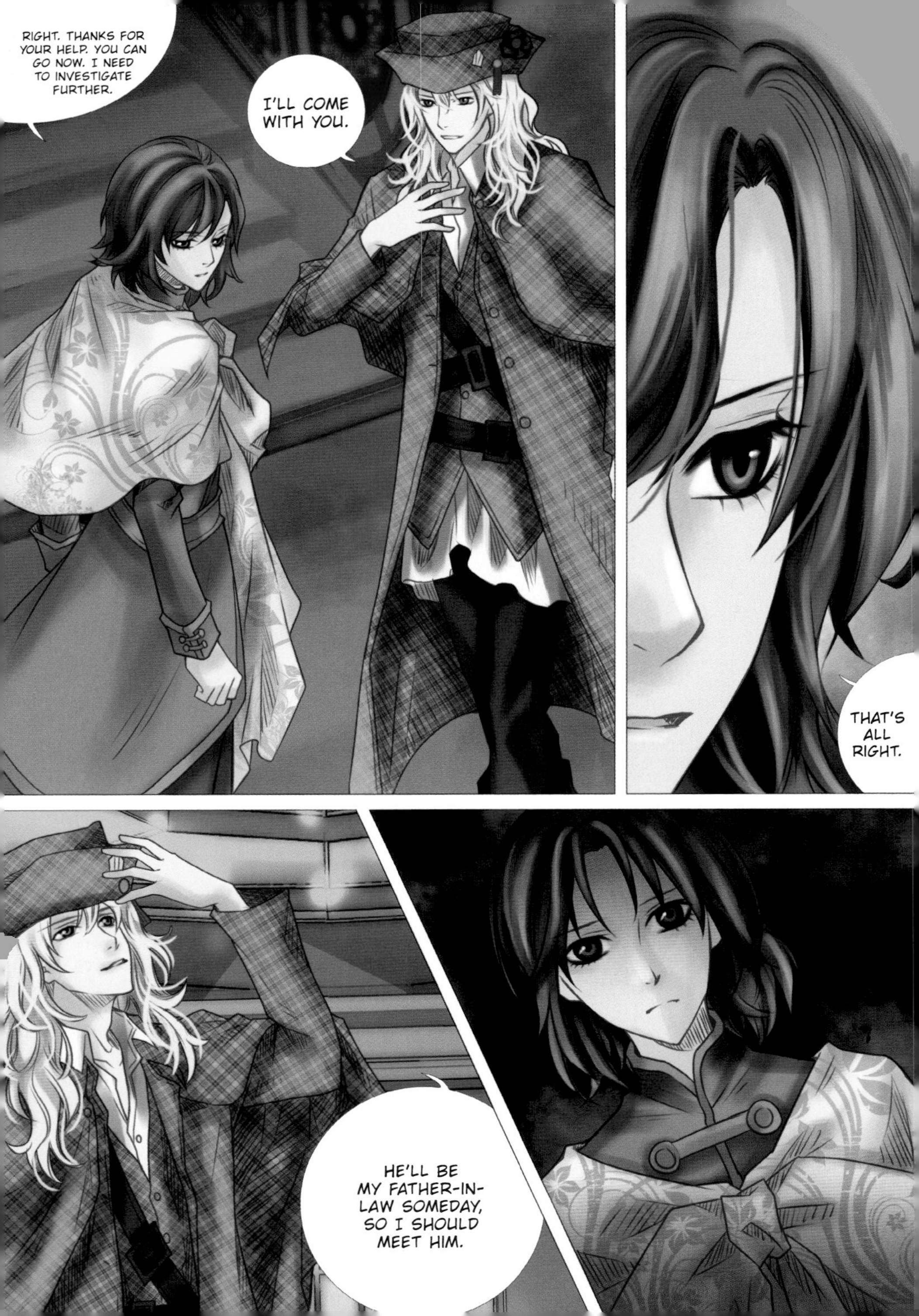
RIGHT. THANKS FOR YOUR HELP. YOU CAN GO NOW. I NEED TO INVESTIGATE FURTHER.
I'LL COME WITH YOU.
THAT'S ALL RIGHT.
HE'LL BE MY FATHER-IN-LAW SOMEDAY, SO I SHOULD MEET HIM.

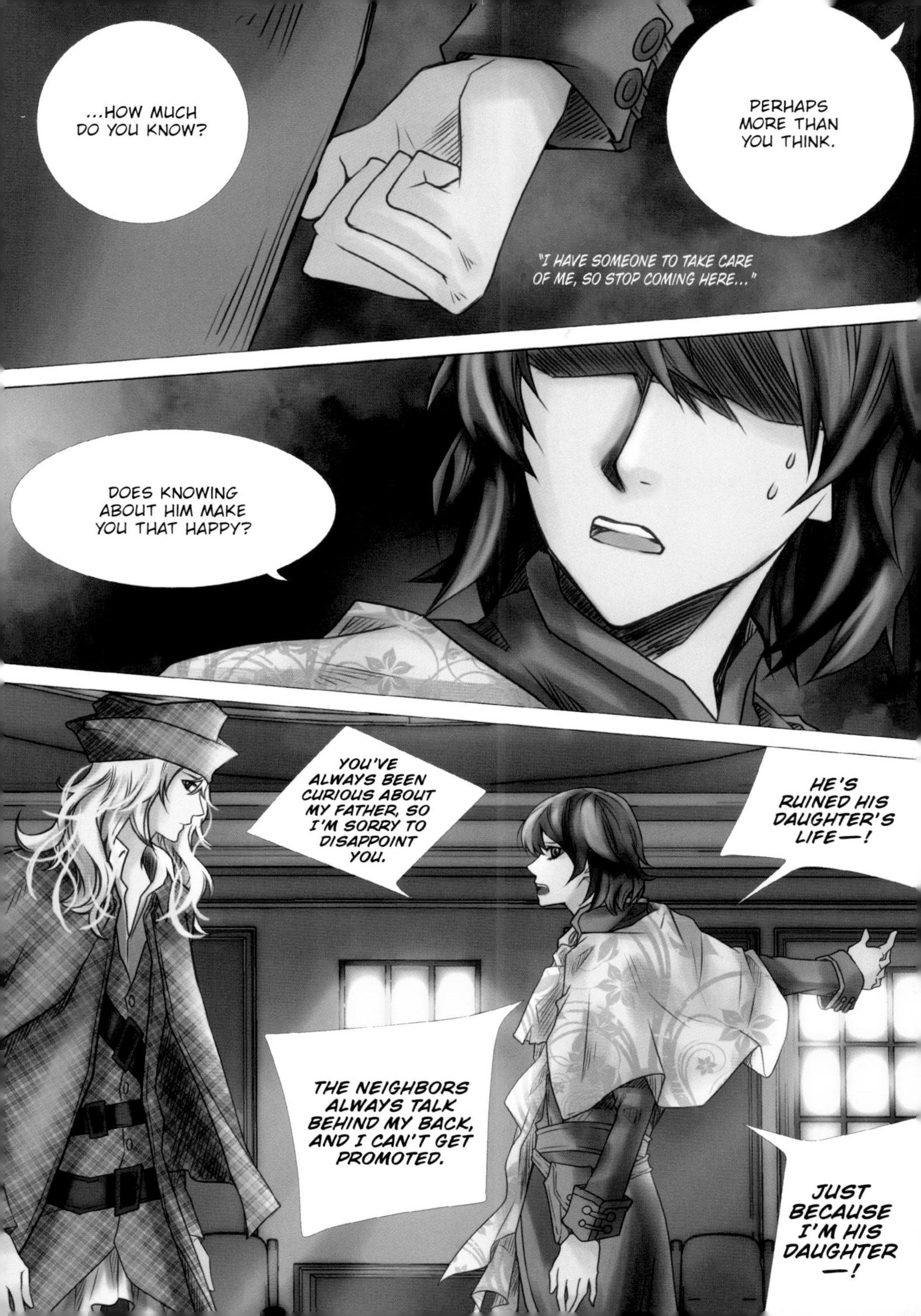
...HOW MUCH DO YOU KNOW?
PERHAPS MORE THAN YOU THINK.
"I HAVE SOMEONE TO TAKE CARE OF ME, SO STOP COMING HERE..."
DOES KNOWING ABOUT HIM MAKE YOU THAT HAPPY?
YOU'VE ALWAYS BEEN CURIOUS ABOUT MY FATHER, SO I'M SORRY TO DISAPPOINT YOU.
HE'S RUINED HIS DAUGHTER'S LIFE—!
THE NEIGHBORS ALWAYS TALK BEHIND MY BACK, AND I CAN'T GET PROMOTED.
JUST BECAUSE I'M HIS DAUGHTER—!

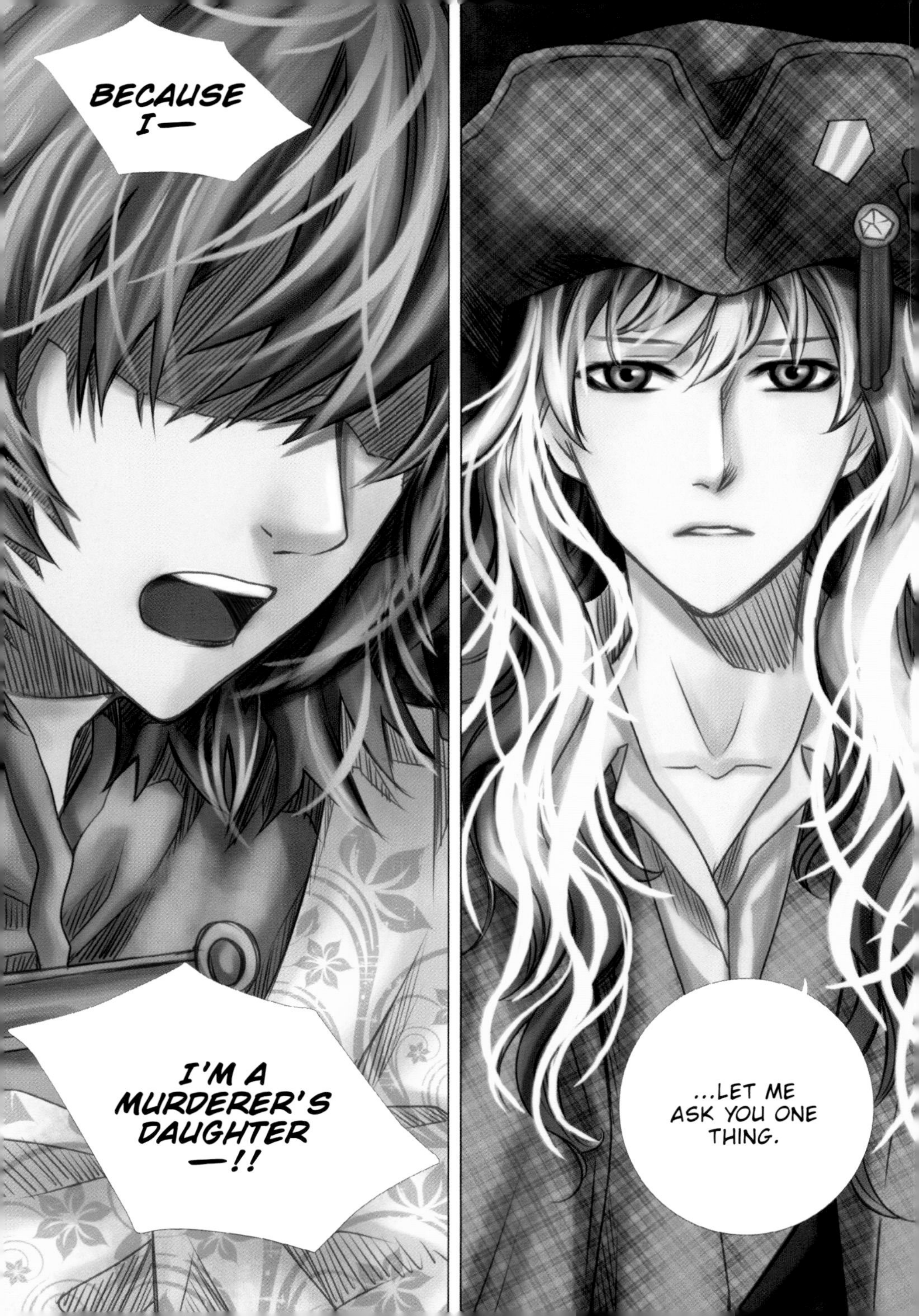
BECAUSE I—
I'M A MURDERER'S DAUGHTER—!!
...LET ME ASK YOU ONE THING.

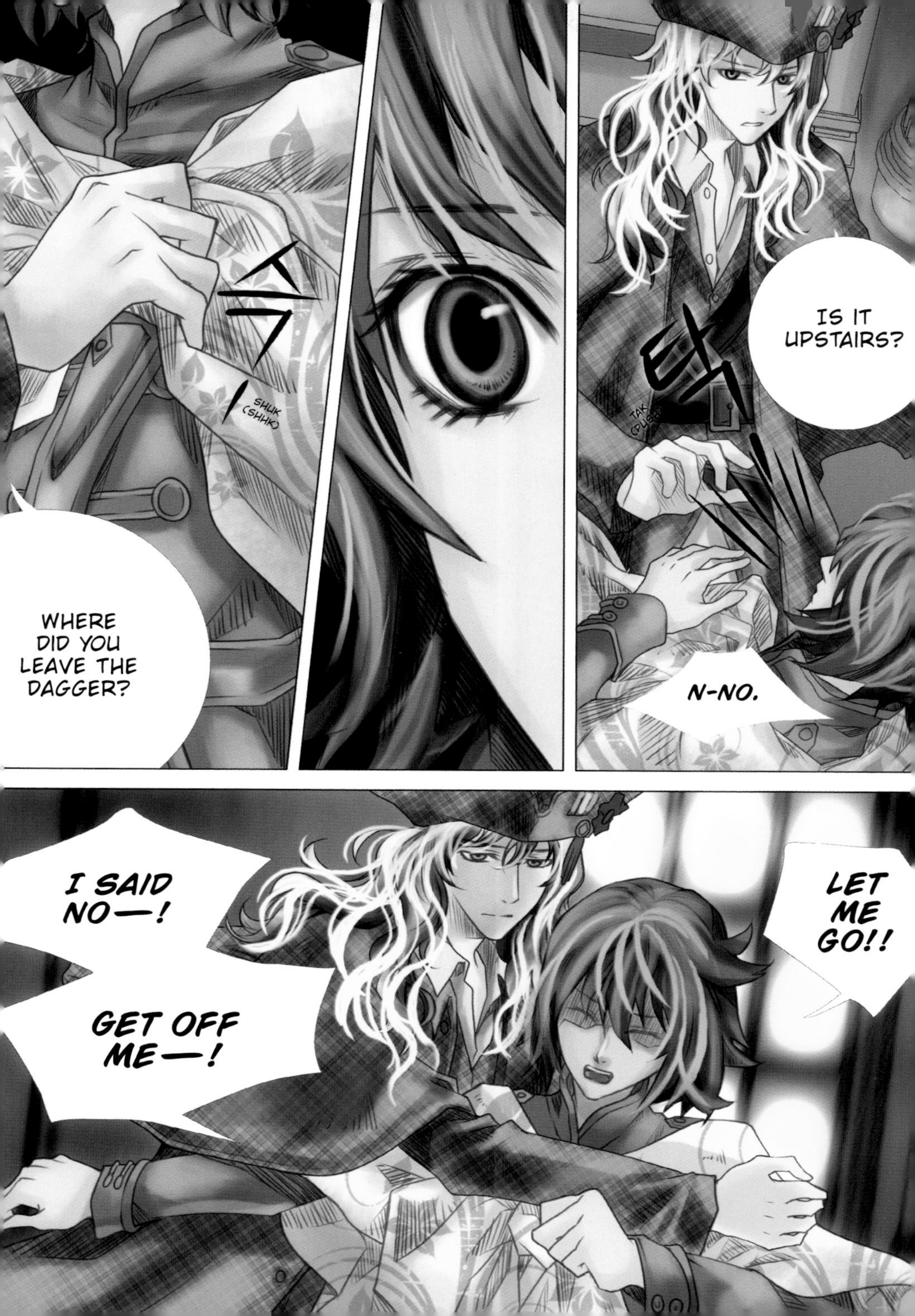
SHUK (SHHK)
WHERE DID YOU LEAVE THE DAGGER?
IS IT UPSTAIRS?
TAK
N-NO.
I SAID NO—!
GET OFF ME—!
LET ME GO!!

CALM DOWN AND LOOK AT ME.

I DIDN'T PUT THAT SCARF ON YOU FOR NO REASON.

WHATEVER YOU'VE DONE, I'M ON YOUR SIDE. I'LL DO MY BEST TO PROTECT YOU.

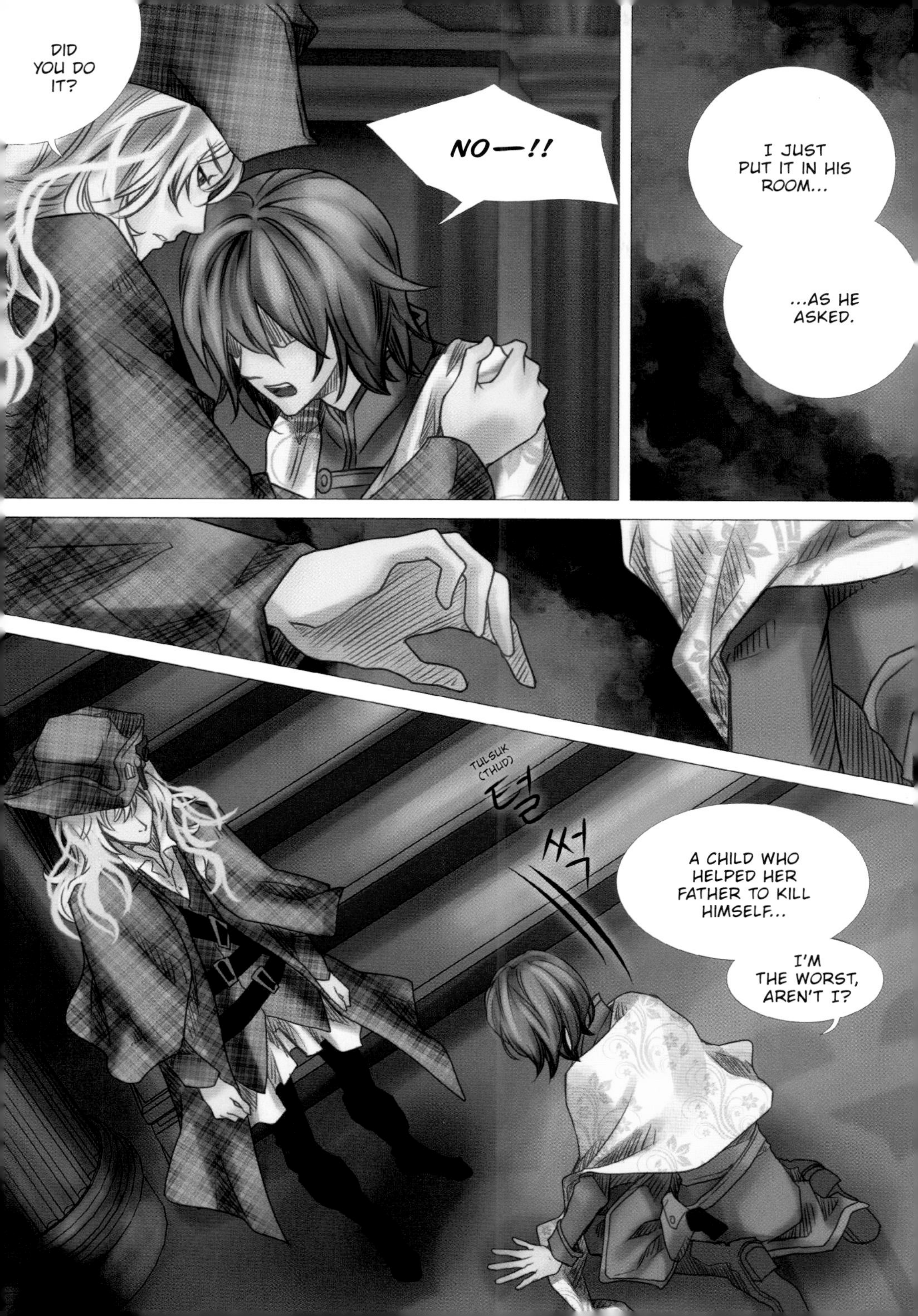
DID YOU DO IT?
NO—!!
I JUST PUT IT IN HIS ROOM...
...AS HE ASKED.
TULSUK (THUD)
털썩
A CHILD WHO HELPED HER FATHER TO KILL HIMSELF...
I'M THE WORST, AREN'T I?

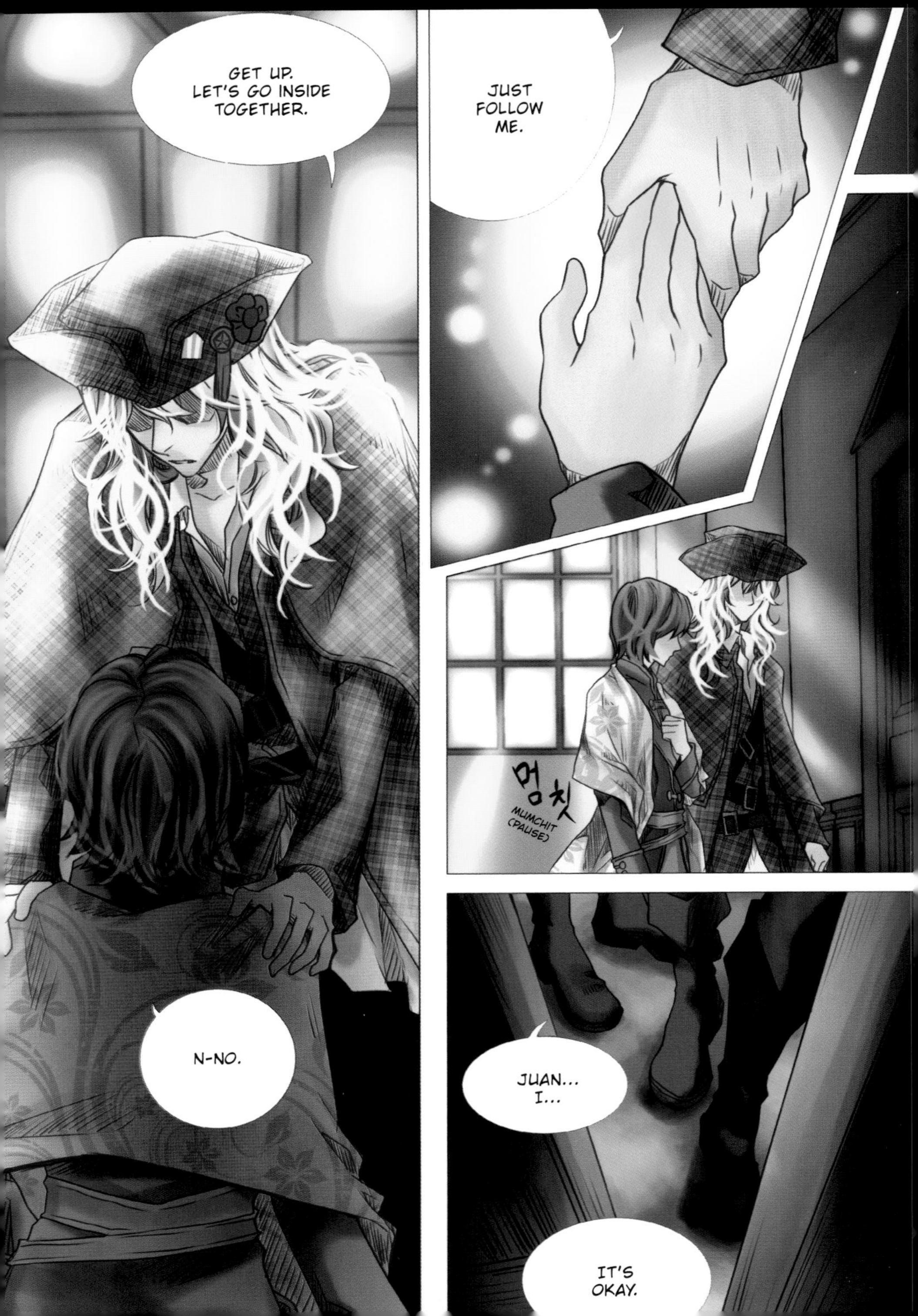
GET UP. LET'S GO INSIDE TOGETHER.
N-NO.
JUST FOLLOW ME.
멈칫
MUMCHIT (PAUSE)
JUAN... I...
IT'S OKAY.

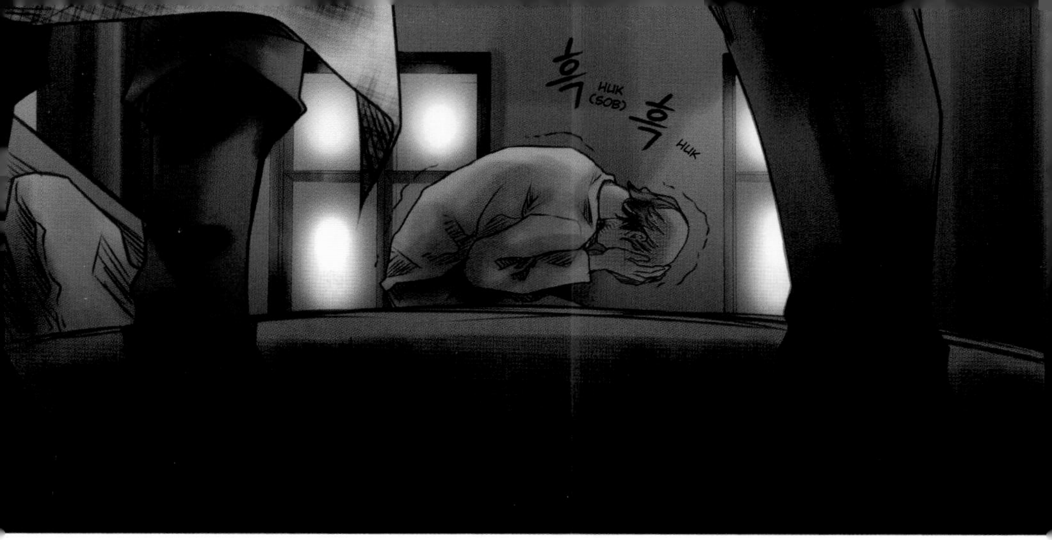
흑
HUK (SOB)
흑
HUK
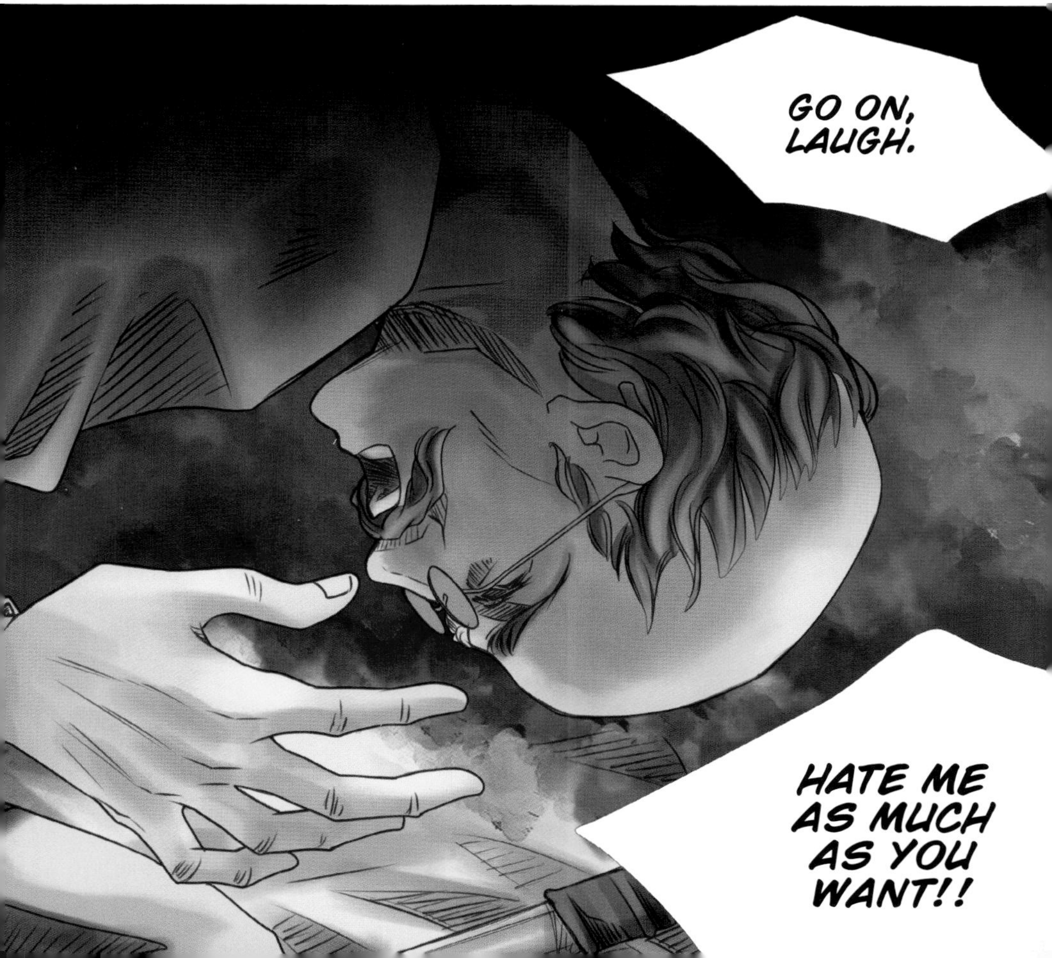
GO ON, LAUGH.
HATE ME AS MUCH AS YOU WANT!!

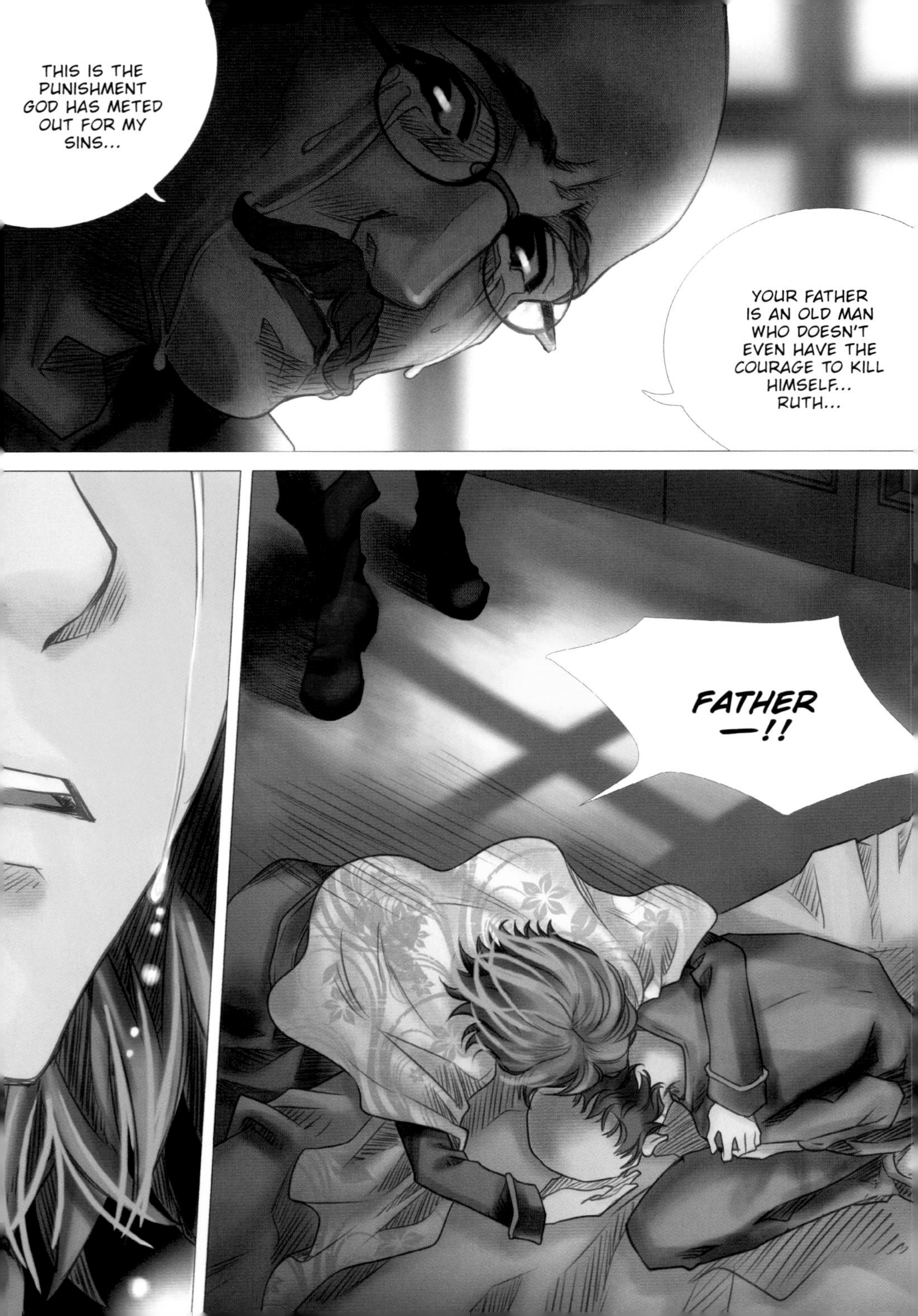
THIS IS THE PUNISHMENT GOD HAS METED OUT FOR MY SINS...
YOUR FATHER IS AN OLD MAN WHO DOESN'T EVEN HAVE THE COURAGE TO KILL HIMSELF... RUTH...
FATHER—!!

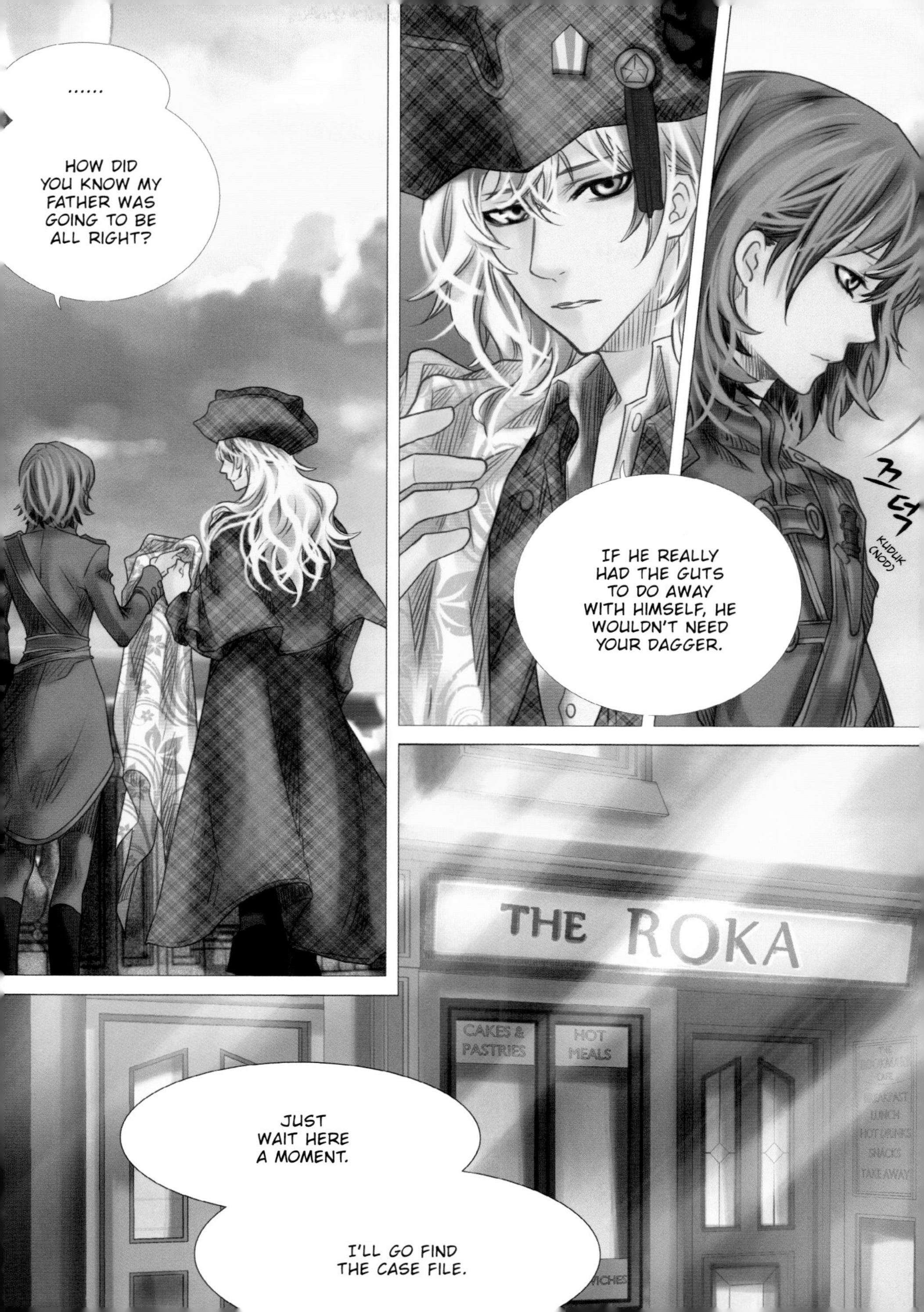

......
HOW DID YOU KNOW MY FATHER WAS GOING TO BE ALL RIGHT?
끄덕
KIDUK (NOD)
IF HE REALLY HAD THE GUTS TO DO AWAY WITH HIMSELF, HE WOULDN'T NEED YOUR DAGGER.
THE ROKA
CAKES & PASTRIES
HOT MEALS
JUST WAIT HERE A MOMENT.
I'LL GO FIND THE CASE FILE.

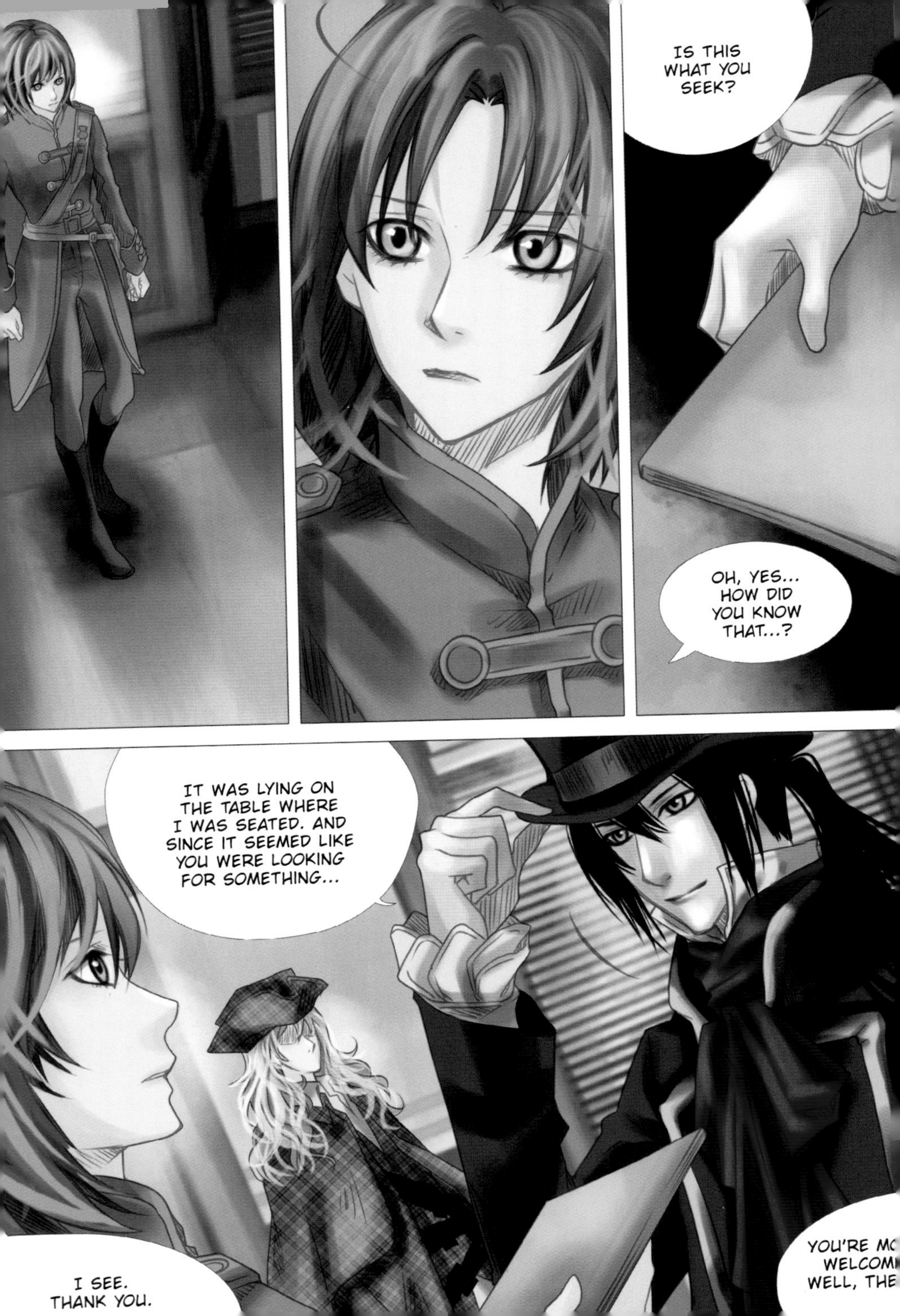
IS THIS WHAT YOU SEEK?
OH, YES... HOW DID YOU KNOW THAT...?
IT WAS LYING ON THE TABLE WHERE I WAS SEATED. AND SINCE IT SEEMED LIKE YOU WERE LOOKING FOR SOMETHING...
I SEE. THANK YOU.
YOU'RE MO WELCOM WELL, THE

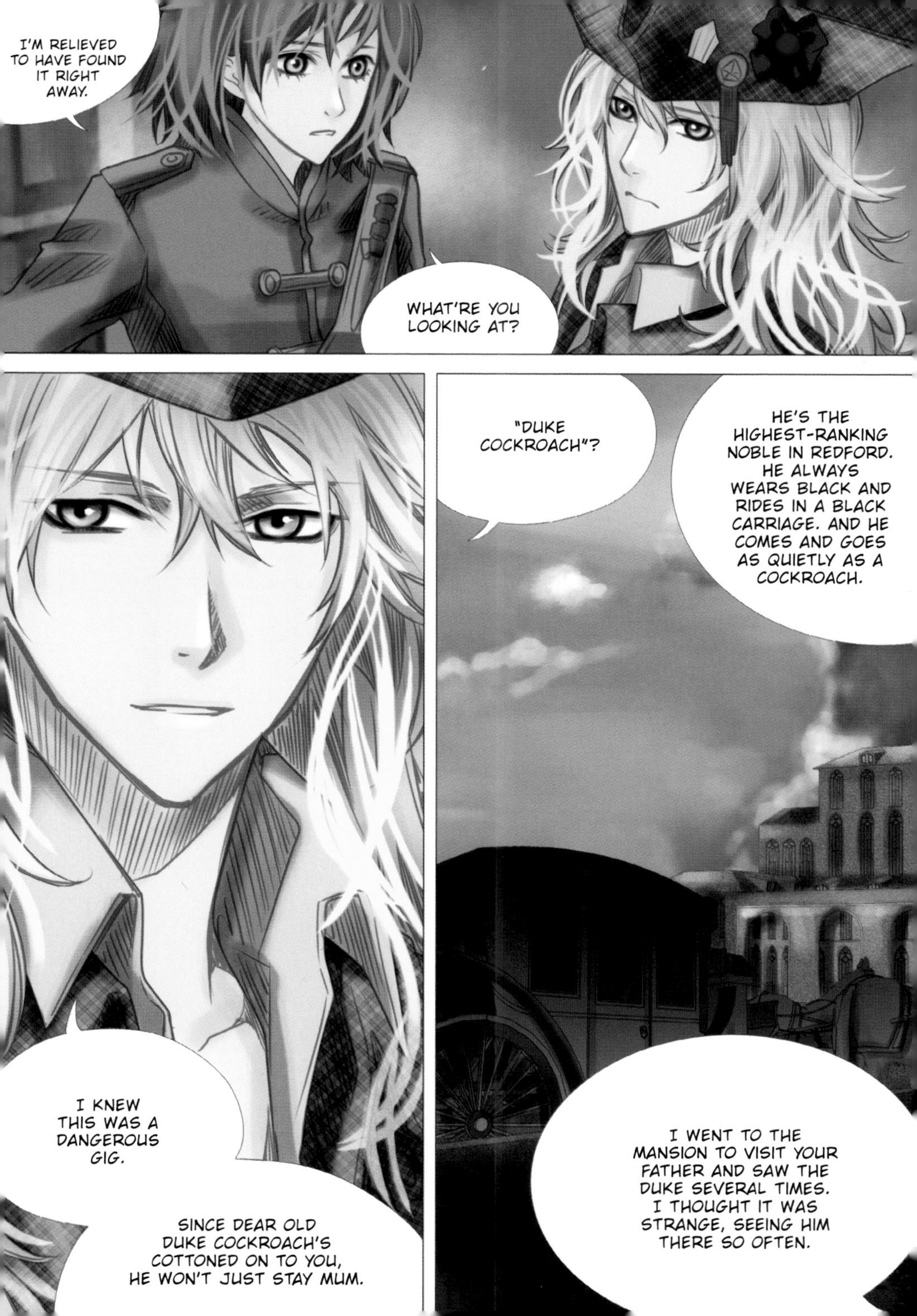
I'M RELIEVED TO HAVE FOUND IT RIGHT AWAY.
WHAT'RE YOU LOOKING AT?
I KNEW THIS WAS A DANGEROUS GIG.
SINCE DEAR OLD DUKE COCKROACH'S COTTONED ON TO YOU, HE WON'T JUST STAY MUM.
"DUKE COCKROACH"?
HE'S THE HIGHEST-RANKING NOBLE IN REDFORD. HE ALWAYS WEARS BLACK AND RIDES IN A BLACK CARRIAGE. AND HE COMES AND GOES AS QUIETLY AS A COCKROACH.
I WENT TO THE MANSION TO VISIT YOUR FATHER AND SAW THE DUKE SEVERAL TIMES. I THOUGHT IT WAS STRANGE, SEEING HIM THERE SO OFTEN.

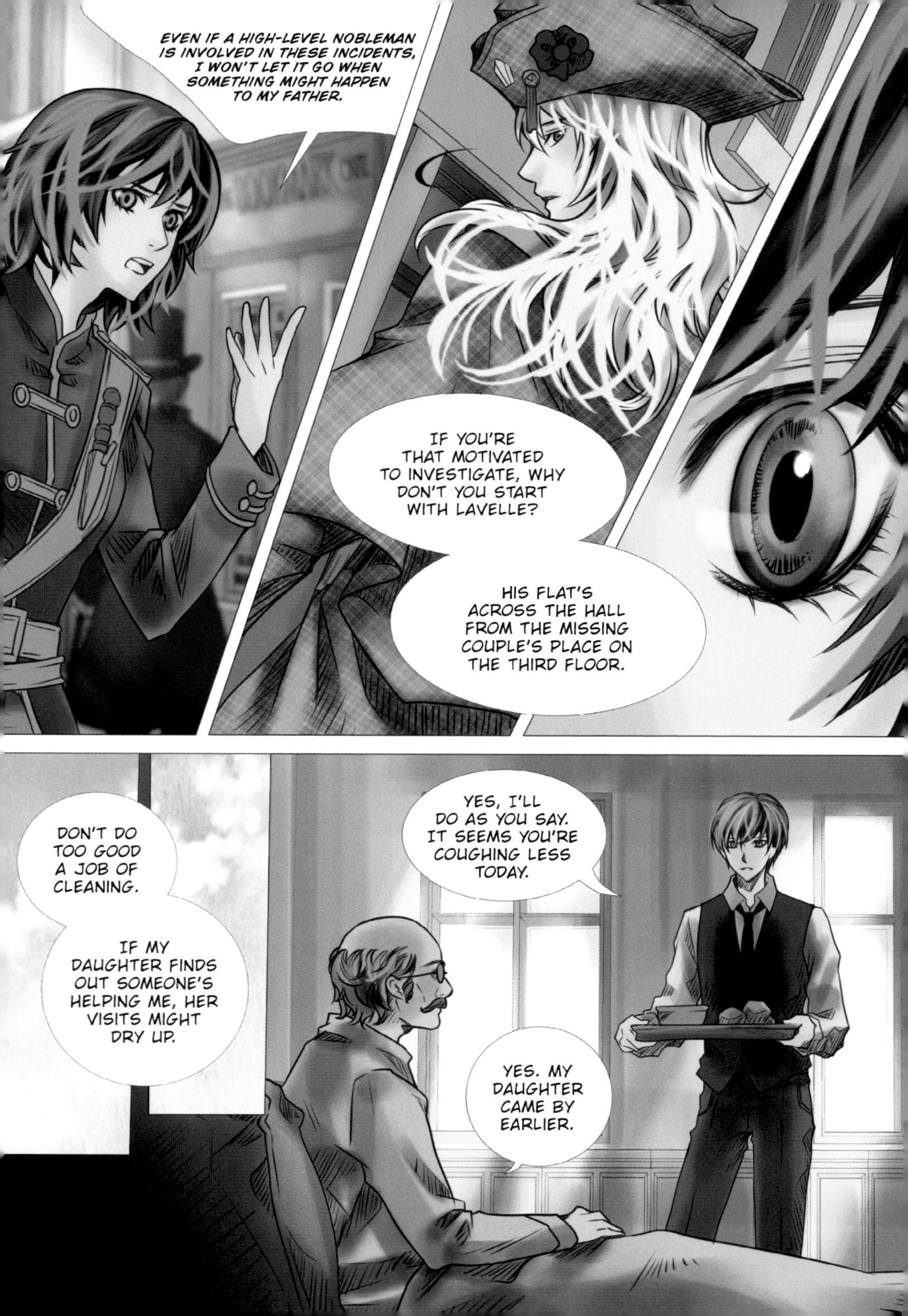
EVEN IF A HIGH-LEVEL NOBLEMAN IS INVOLVED IN THESE INCIDENTS, I WON'T LET IT GO WHEN SOMETHING MIGHT HAPPEN TO MY FATHER.
IF YOU'RE THAT MOTIVATED TO INVESTIGATE, WHY DON'T YOU START WITH LAVELLE?
HIS FLAT'S ACROSS THE HALL FROM THE MISSING COUPLE'S PLACE ON THE THIRD FLOOR.
DON'T DO TOO GOOD A JOB OF CLEANING.
IF MY DAUGHTER FINDS OUT SOMEONE'S HELPING ME, HER VISITS MIGHT DRY UP.
YES, I'LL DO AS YOU SAY. IT SEEMS YOU'RE COUGHING LESS TODAY.
YES. MY DAUGHTER CAME BY EARLIER.

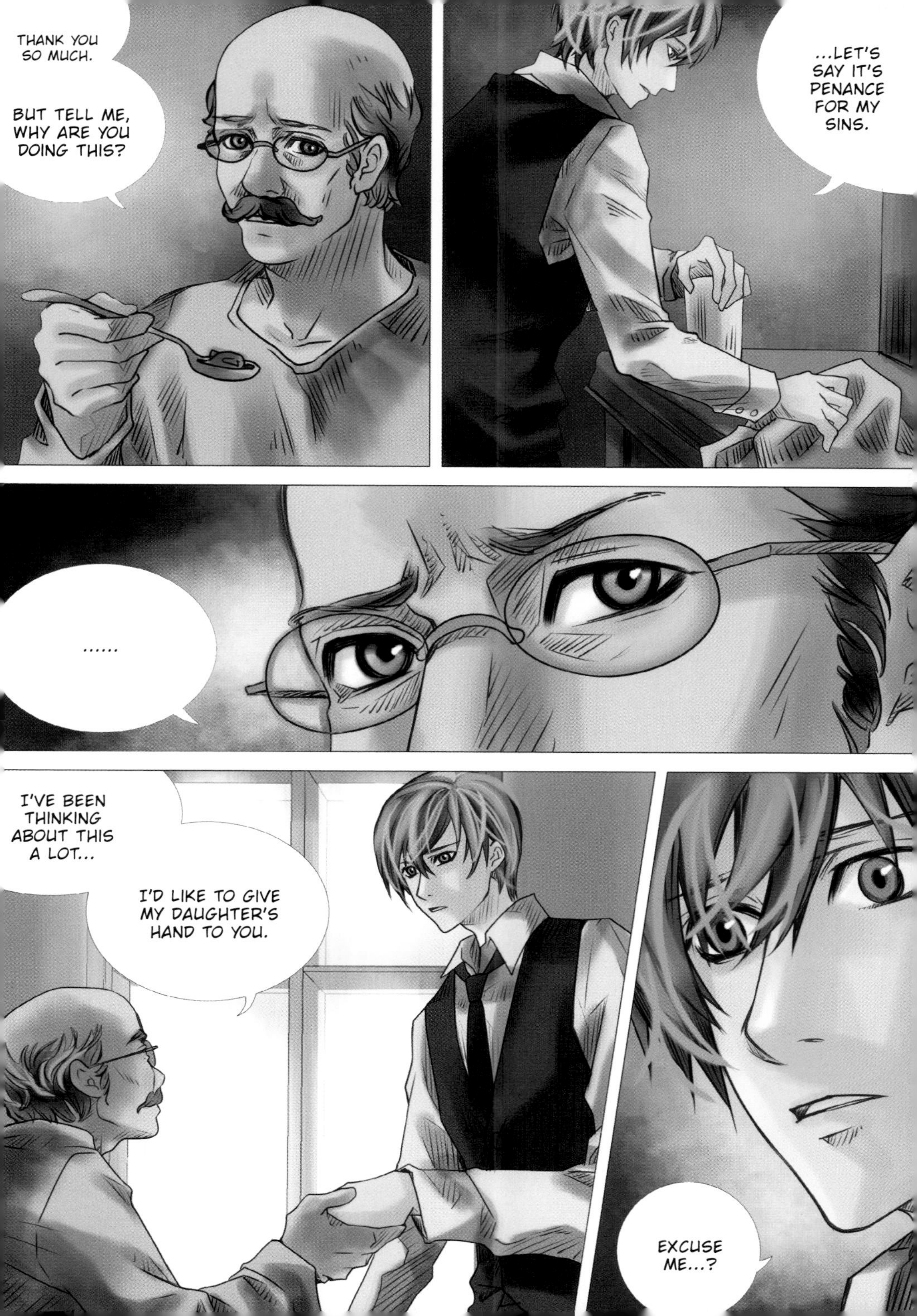
THANK YOU SO MUCH.
BUT TELL ME, WHY ARE YOU DOING THIS?
...LET'S SAY IT'S PENANCE FOR MY SINS.
......
I'VE BEEN THINKING ABOUT THIS A LOT...
I'D LIKE TO GIVE MY DAUGHTER'S HAND TO YOU.
EXCUSE ME...?

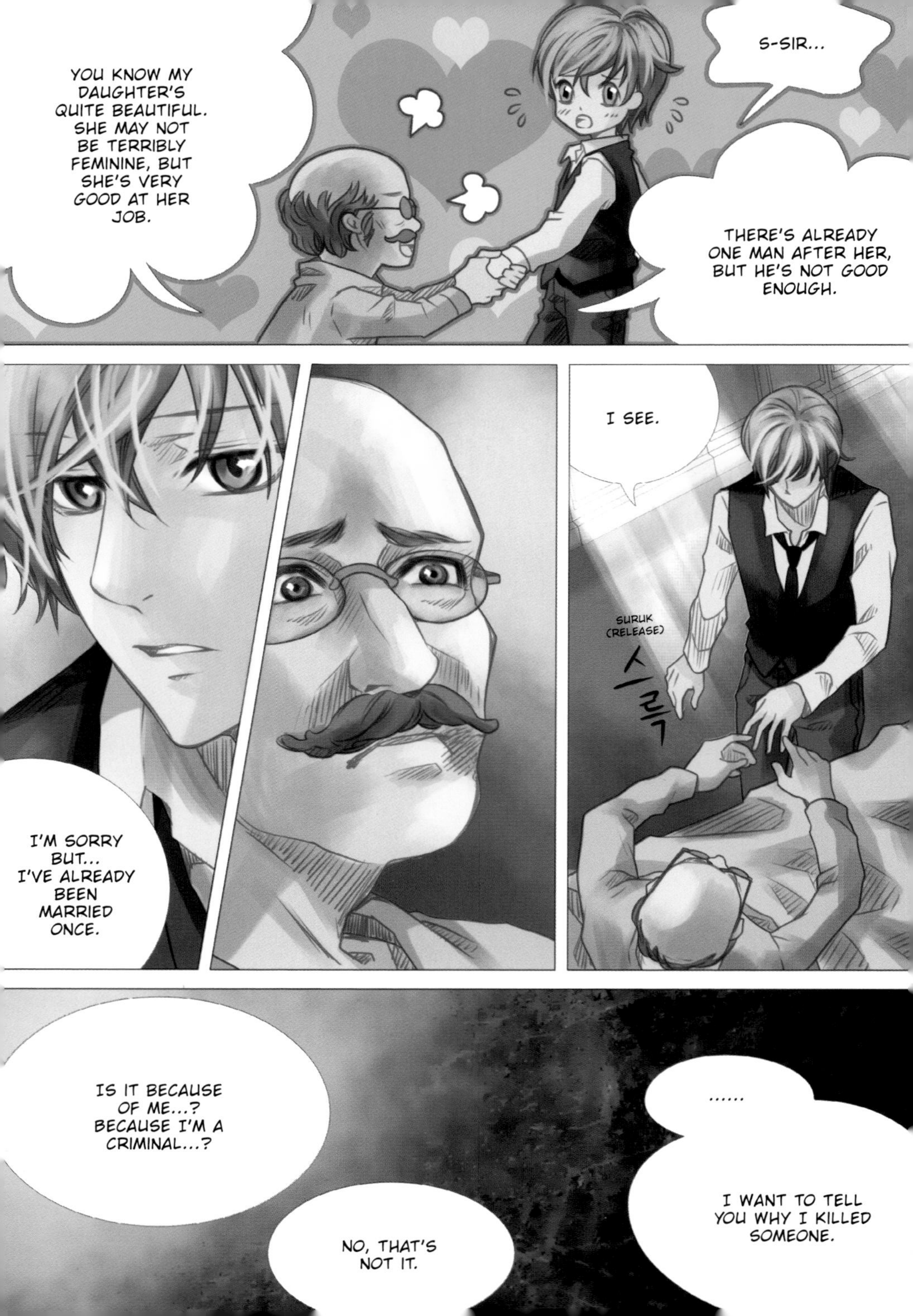
YOU KNOW MY DAUGHTER'S QUITE BEAUTIFUL. SHE MAY NOT BE TERRIBLY FEMININE, BUT SHE'S VERY GOOD AT HER JOB.
S-SIR...
THERE'S ALREADY ONE MAN AFTER HER, BUT HE'S NOT GOOD ENOUGH.
I'M SORRY BUT... I'VE ALREADY BEEN MARRIED ONCE.
I SEE.
SURUK (RELEASE)
스르륵
IS IT BECAUSE OF ME...? BECAUSE I'M A CRIMINAL...?
NO, THAT'S NOT IT.
......
I WANT TO TELL YOU WHY I KILLED SOMEONE.

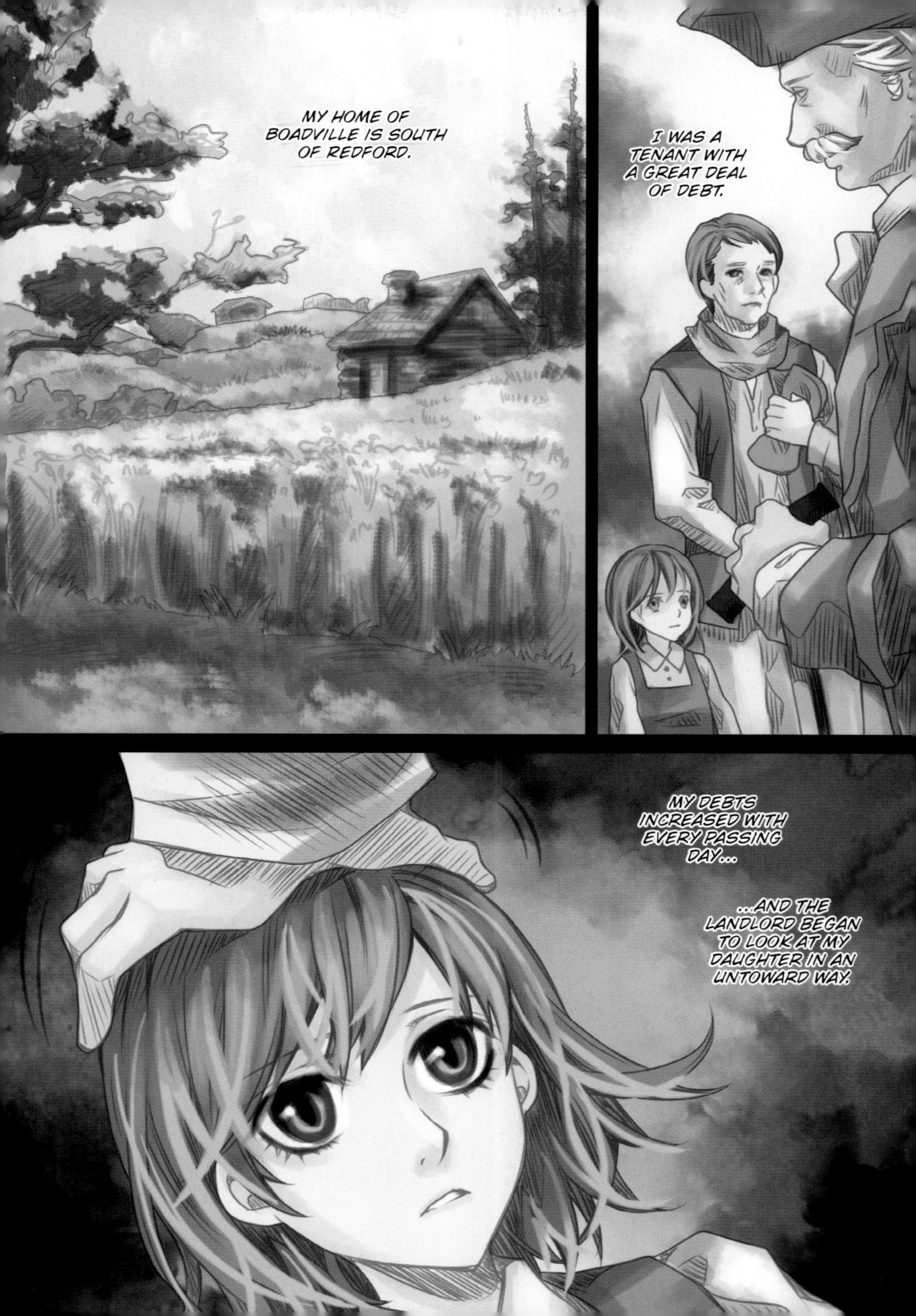
MY HOME OF BOADVILLE IS SOUTH OF REDFORD.
I WAS A TENANT WITH A GREAT DEAL OF DEBT.
MY DEBTS INCREASED WITH EVERY PASSING DAY...
...AND THE LANDLORD BEGAN TO LOOK AT MY DAUGHTER IN AN UNTOWARD WAY.

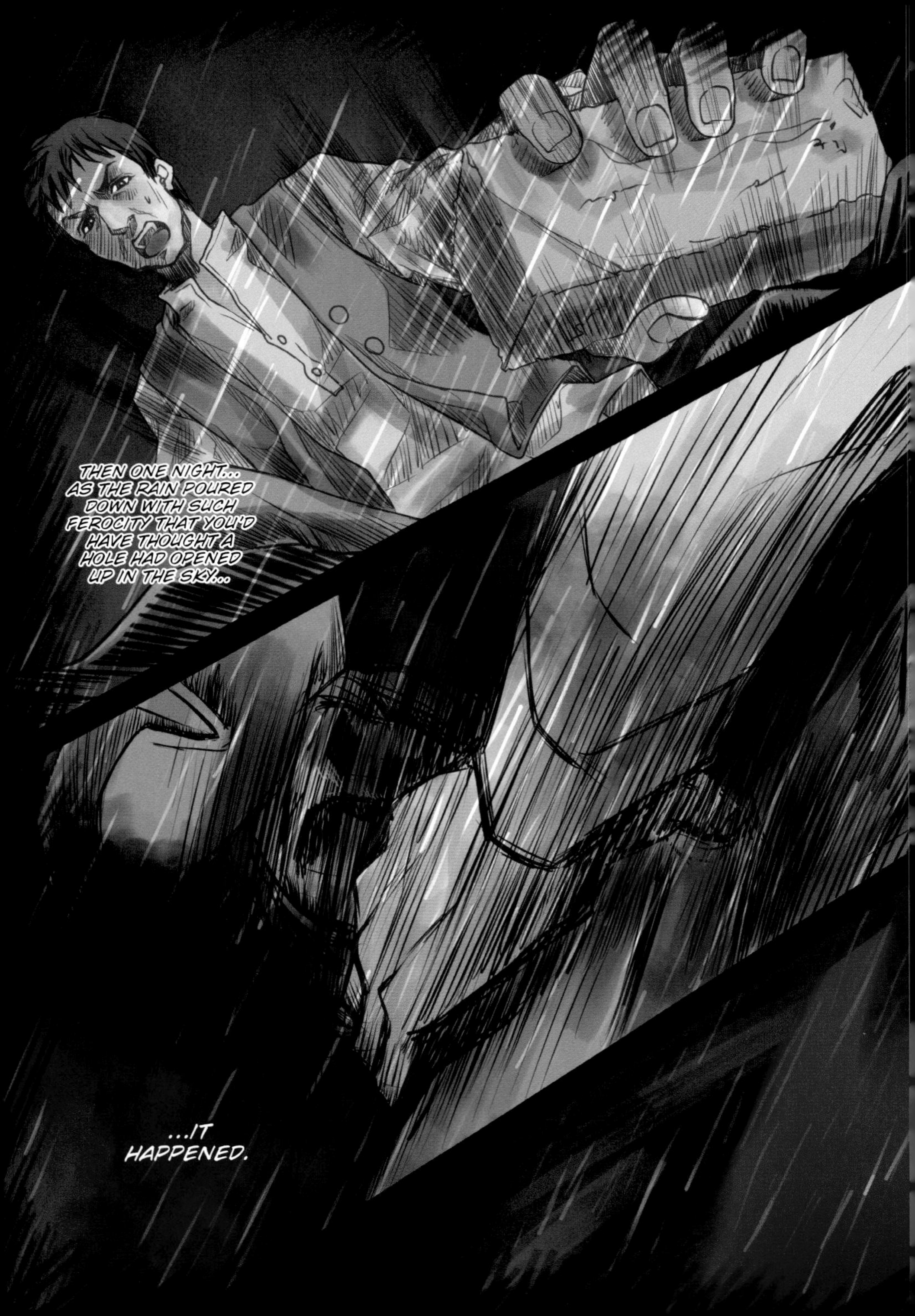
THEN ONE NIGHT... AS THE RAIN POURED DOWN WITH SUCH FEROCITY THAT YOU'D HAVE THOUGHT A HOLE HAD OPENED UP IN THE SKY...
...IT HAPPENED.

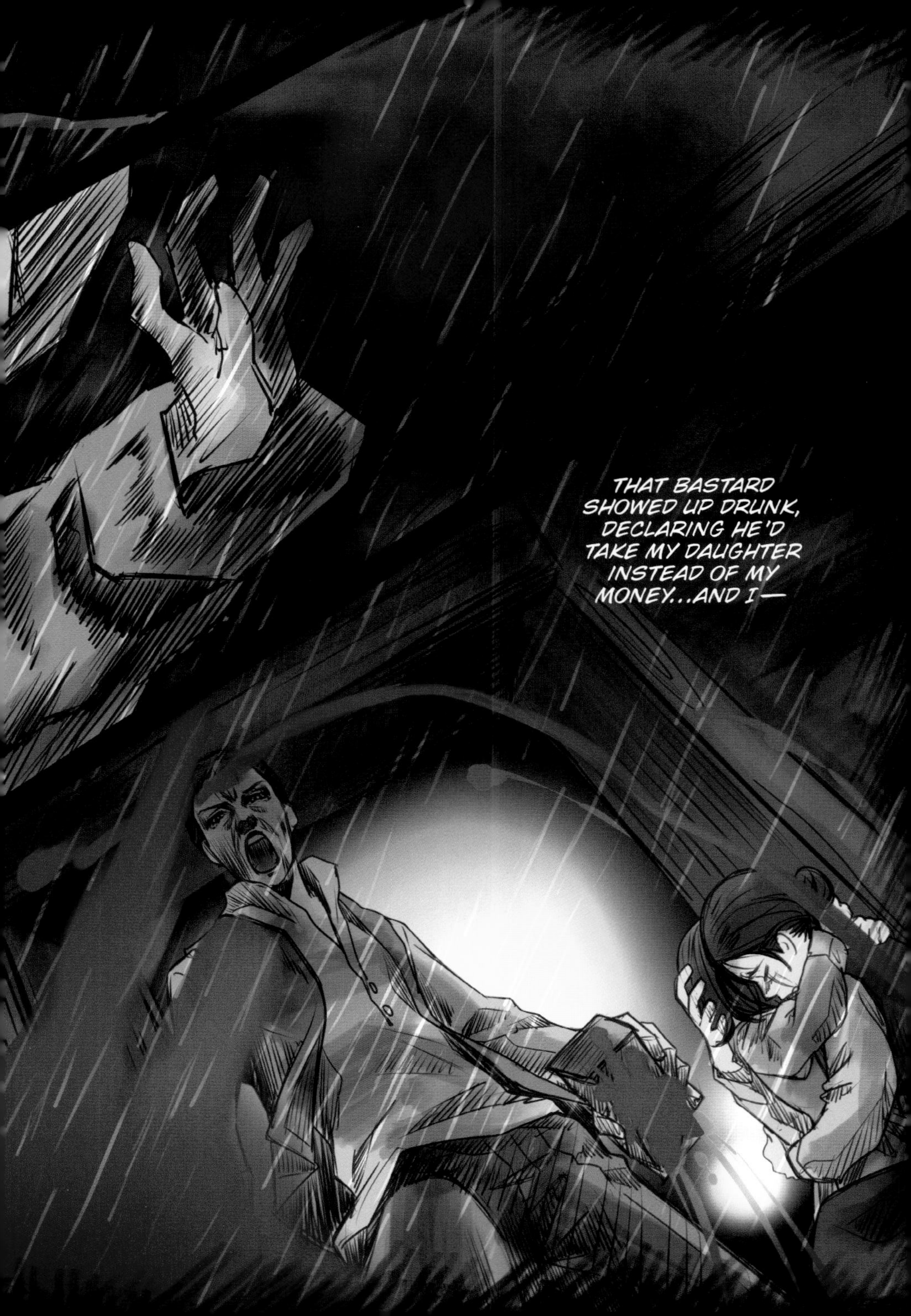
THAT BASTARD SHOWED UP DRUNK, DECLARING HE'D TAKE MY DAUGHTER INSTEAD OF MY MONEY...AND I—

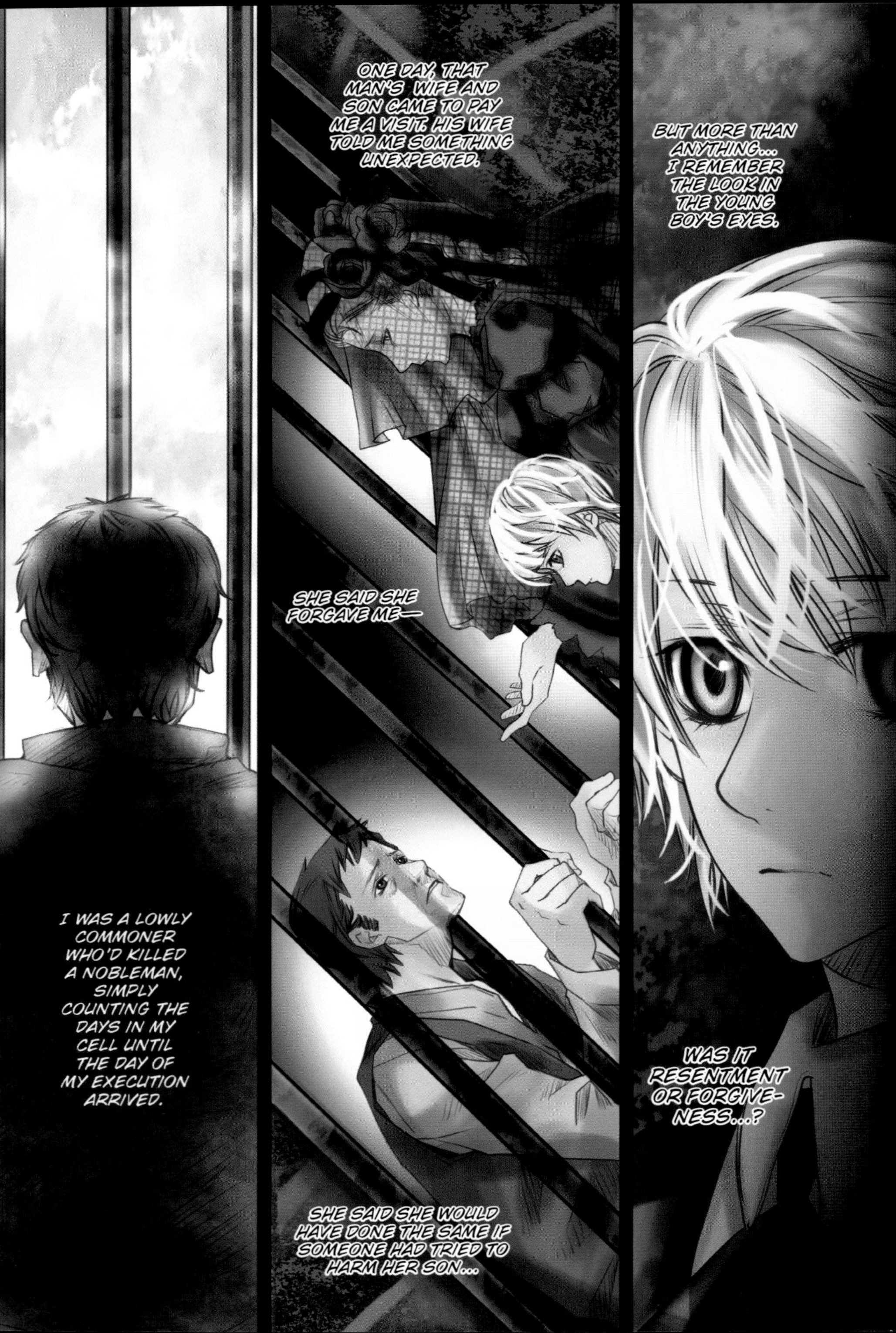
I WAS A LOWLY COMMONER WHO'D KILLED A NOBLEMAN, SIMPLY COUNTING THE DAYS IN MY CELL UNTIL THE DAY OF MY EXECUTION ARRIVED.
ONE DAY, THAT MAN'S WIFE AND SON CAME TO PAY ME A VISIT. HIS WIFE TOLD ME SOMETHING UNEXPECTED.
SHE SAID SHE FORGAVE ME—
SHE SAID SHE WOULD HAVE DONE THE SAME IF SOMEONE HAD TRIED TO HARM HER SON...
BUT MORE THAN ANYTHING... I REMEMBER THE LOOK IN THE YOUNG BOY'S EYES.
WAS IT RESENTMENT OR FORGIVE-NESS...?

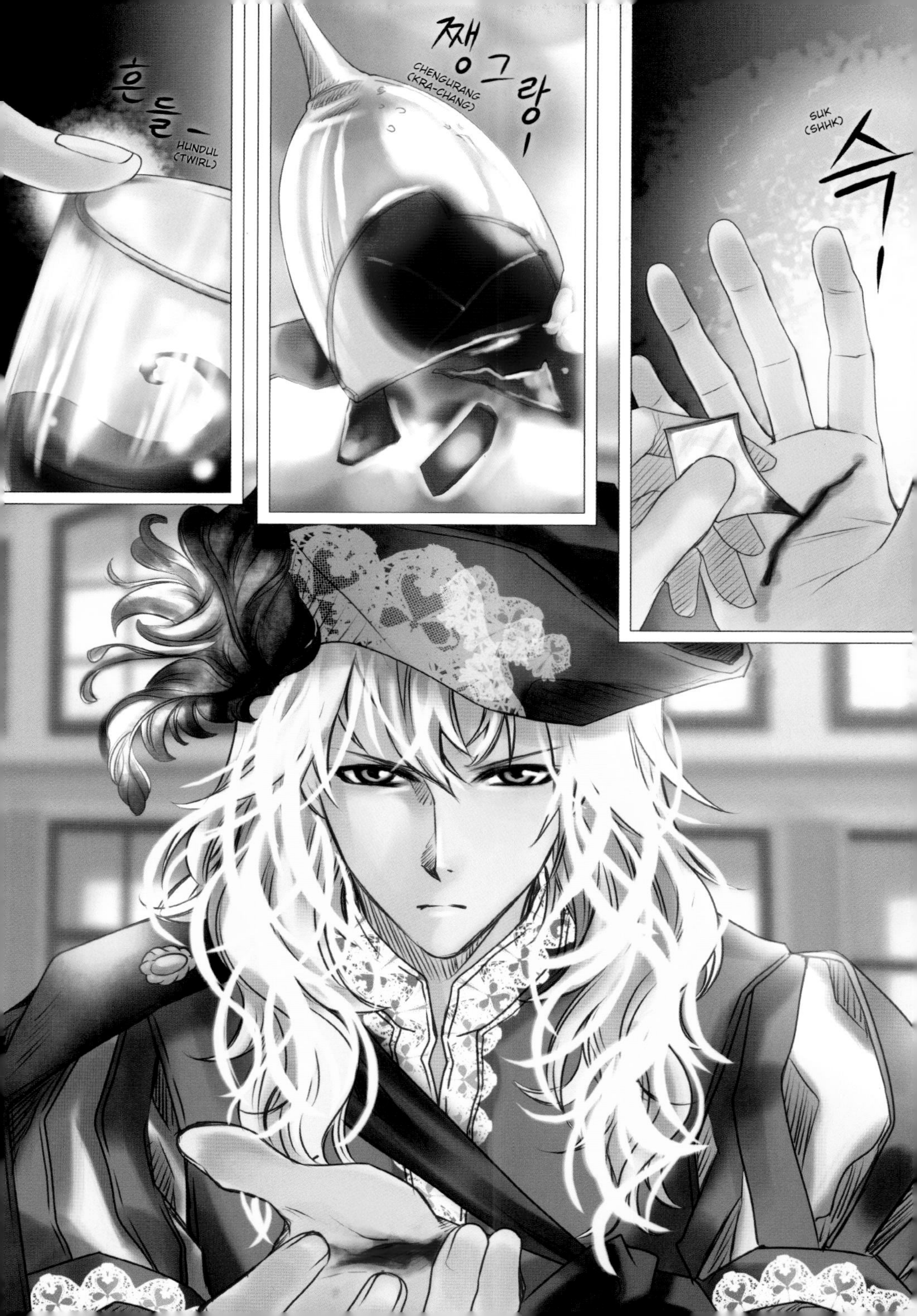
흔들-
HUNDUL
(TWIRL)
쨍그랑-
CHENGURANG
(KRA-CHANG)
SUK
(SHHK)
슥-!

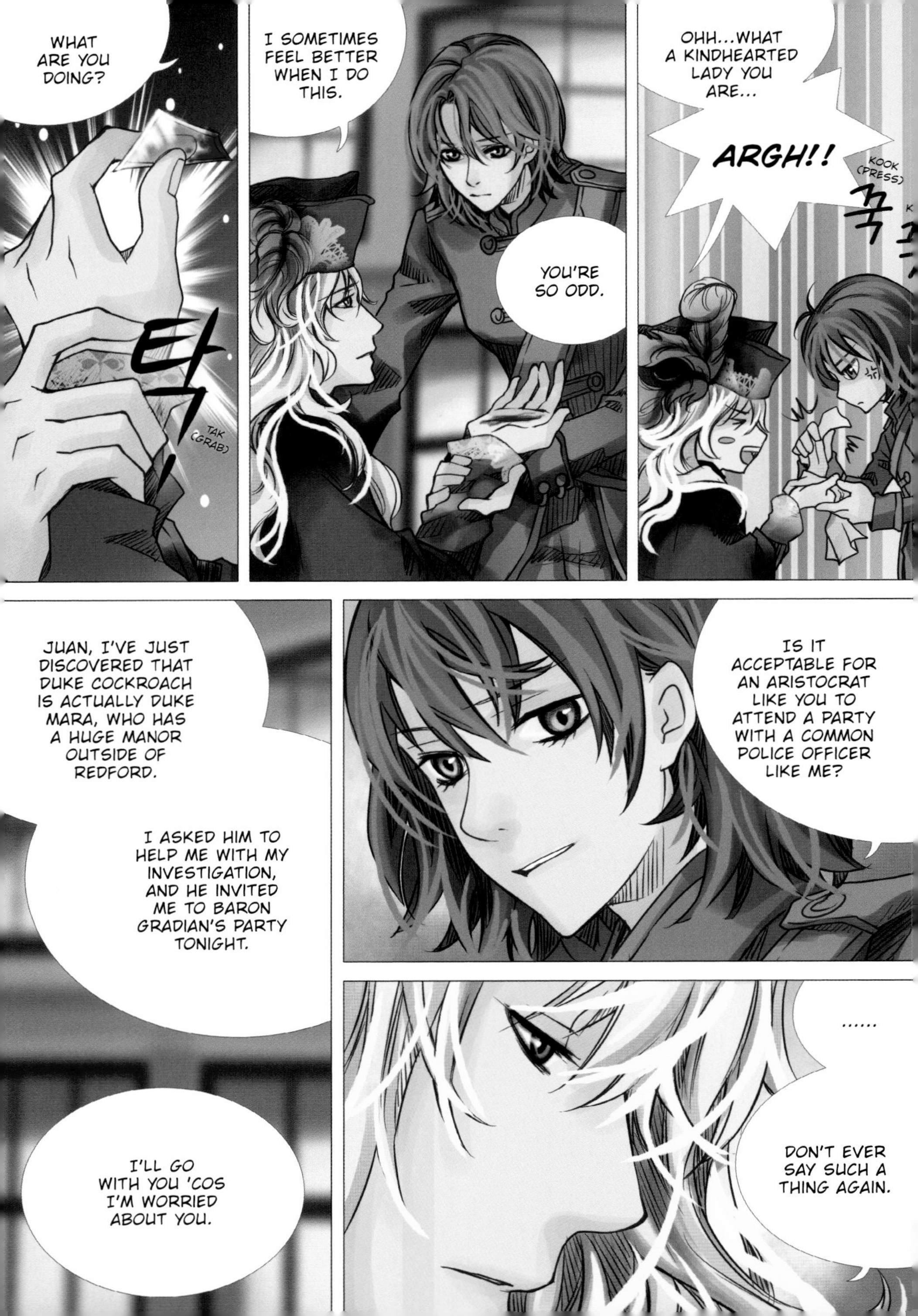
WHAT ARE YOU DOING?
탁
TAK (GRAB)
I SOMETIMES FEEL BETTER WHEN I DO THIS.
YOU'RE SO ODD.
OHH...WHAT A KINDHEARTED LADY YOU ARE...
ARGH!!
꾹
KOOK (PRESS)
JUAN, I'VE JUST DISCOVERED THAT DUKE COCKROACH IS ACTUALLY DUKE MARA, WHO HAS A HUGE MANOR OUTSIDE OF REDFORD.
I ASKED HIM TO HELP ME WITH MY INVESTIGATION, AND HE INVITED ME TO BARON GRADIAN'S PARTY TONIGHT.
I'LL GO WITH YOU 'COS I'M WORRIED ABOUT YOU.
IS IT ACCEPTABLE FOR AN ARISTOCRAT LIKE YOU TO ATTEND A PARTY WITH A COMMON POLICE OFFICER LIKE ME?
......
DON'T EVER SAY SUCH A THING AGAIN.

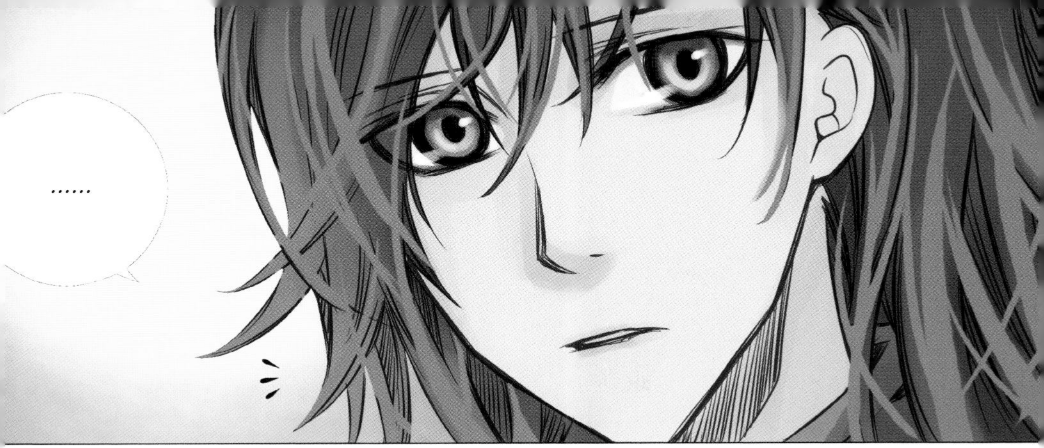
……
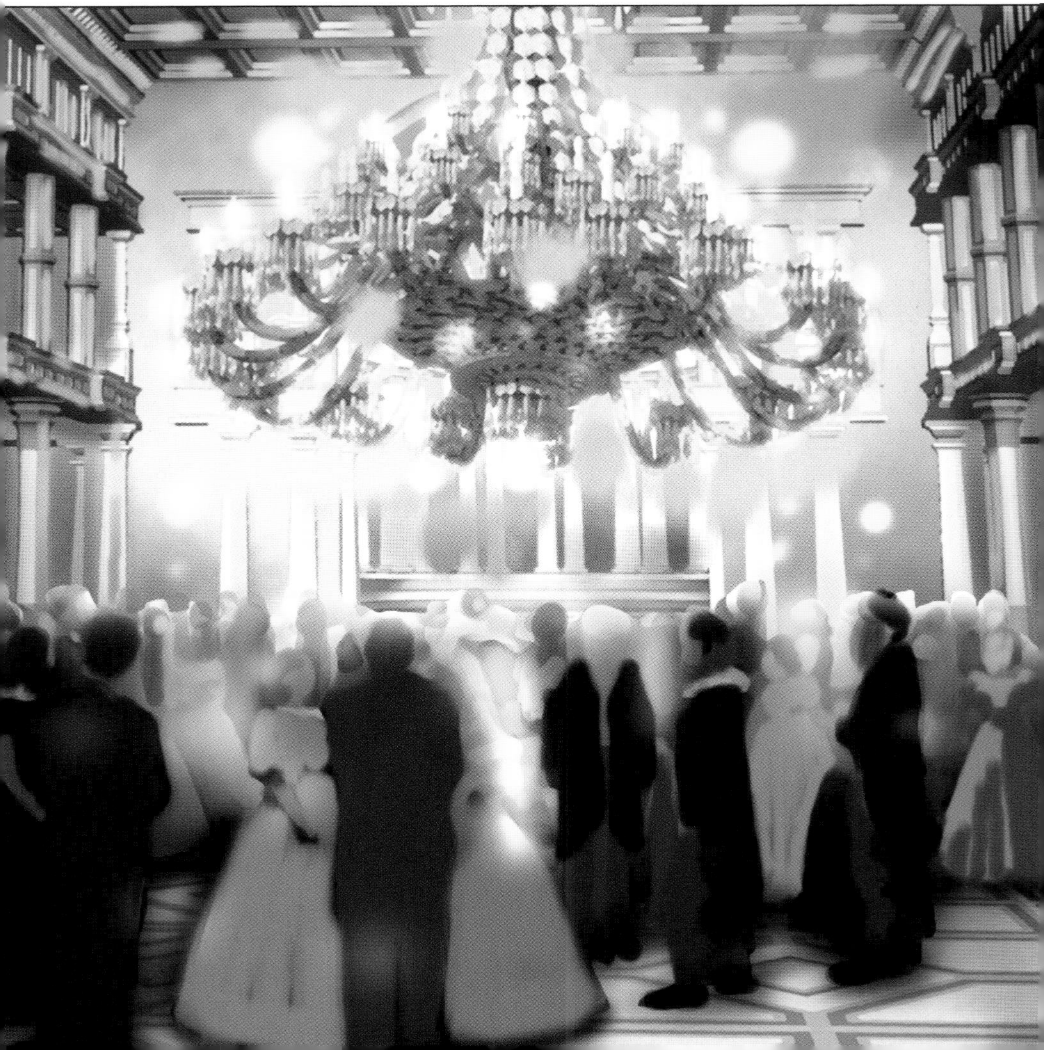

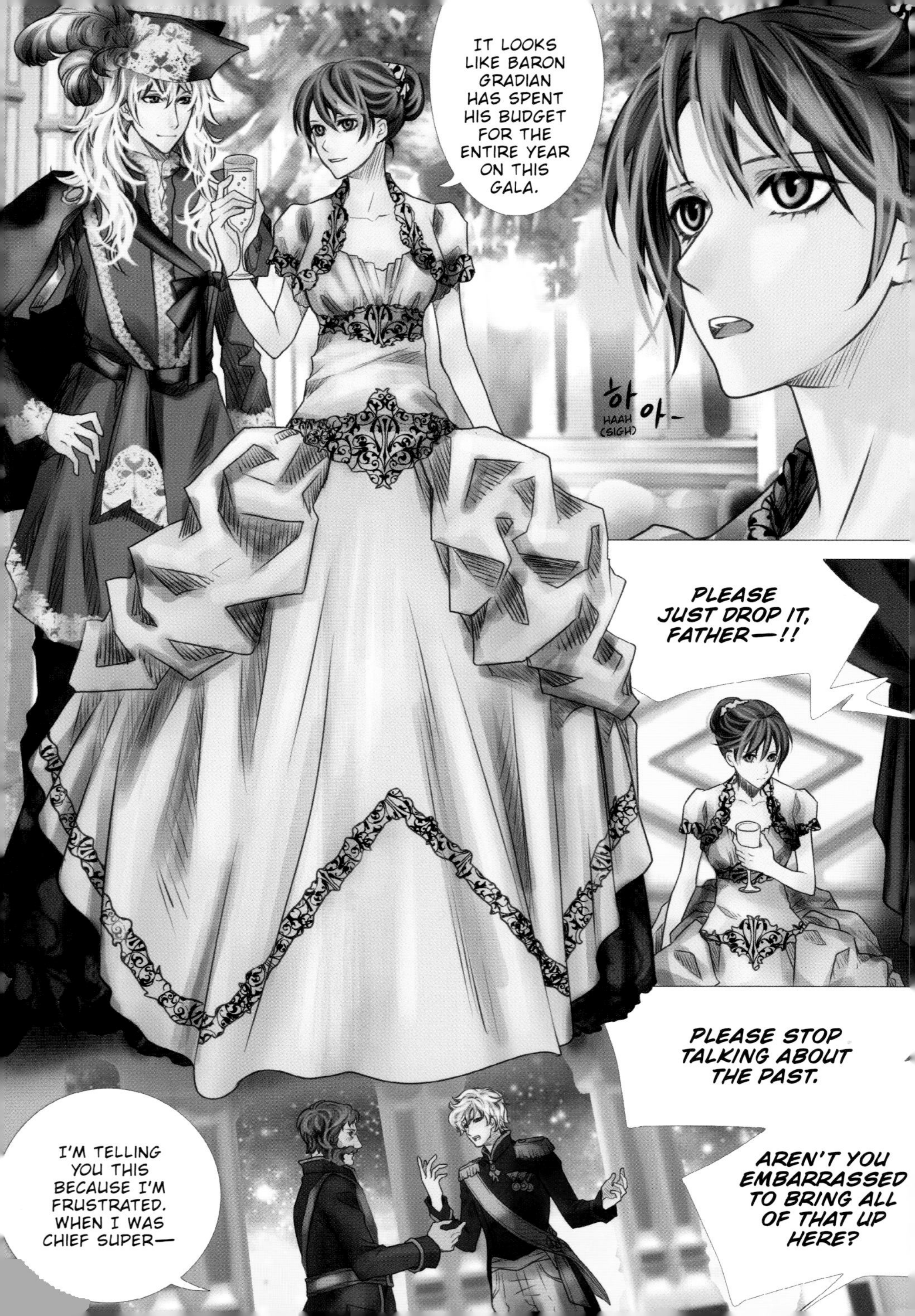
IT LOOKS LIKE BARON GRADIAN HAS SPENT HIS BUDGET FOR THE ENTIRE YEAR ON THIS GALA.
하아-
HAAH (SIGH)
PLEASE JUST DROP IT, FATHER—!!
I'M TELLING YOU THIS BECAUSE I'M FRUSTRATED. WHEN I WAS CHIEF SUPER—
PLEASE STOP TALKING ABOUT THE PAST.
AREN'T YOU EMBARRASSED TO BRING ALL OF THAT UP HERE?

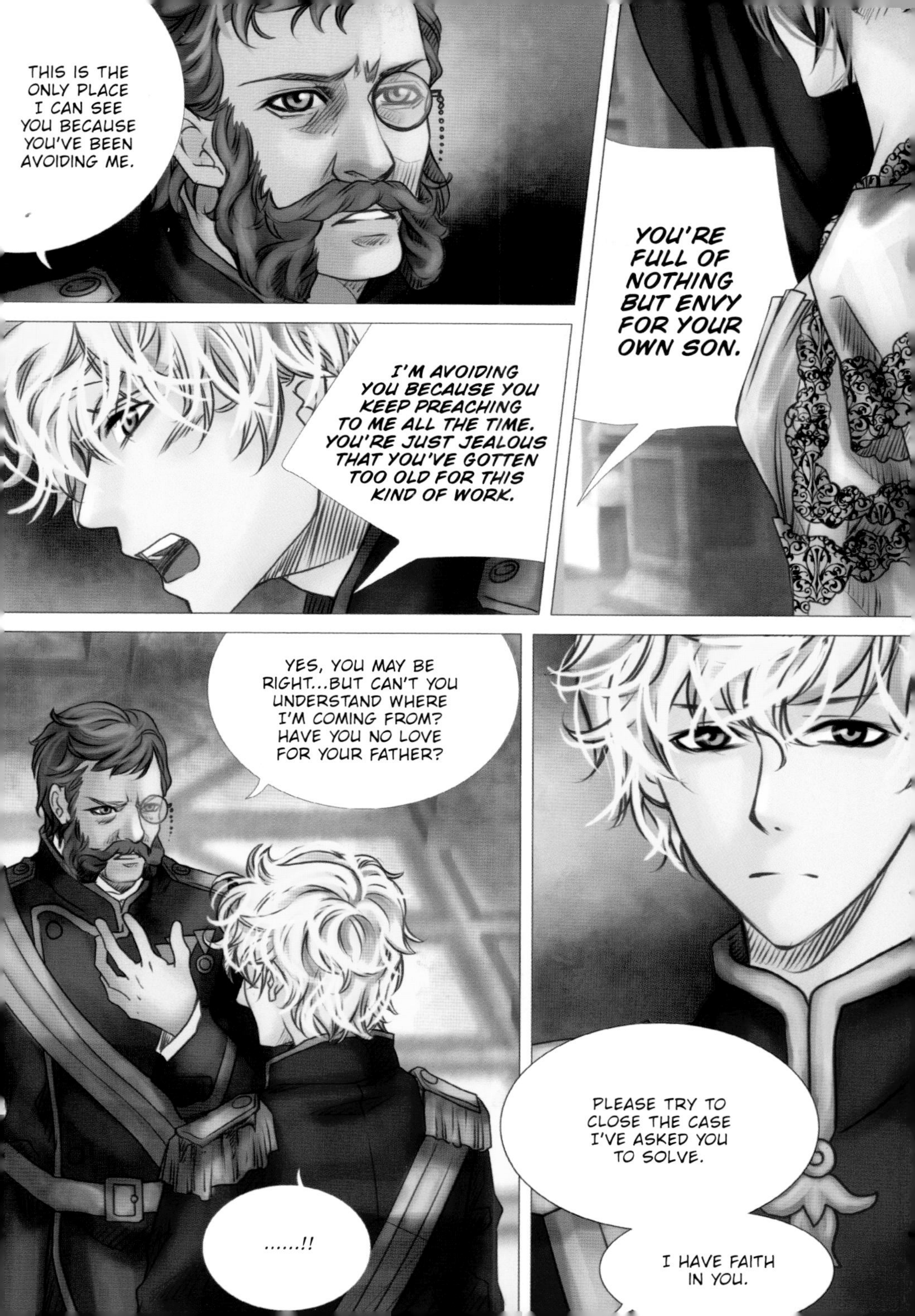
THIS IS THE ONLY PLACE I CAN SEE YOU BECAUSE YOU'VE BEEN AVOIDING ME.
I'M AVOIDING YOU BECAUSE YOU KEEP PREACHING TO ME ALL THE TIME. YOU'RE JUST JEALOUS THAT YOU'VE GOTTEN TOO OLD FOR THIS KIND OF WORK.
YOU'RE FULL OF NOTHING BUT ENVY FOR YOUR OWN SON.
YES, YOU MAY BE RIGHT...BUT CAN'T YOU UNDERSTAND WHERE I'M COMING FROM? HAVE YOU NO LOVE FOR YOUR FATHER?
......!!
PLEASE TRY TO CLOSE THE CASE I'VE ASKED YOU TO SOLVE.
I HAVE FAITH IN YOU.

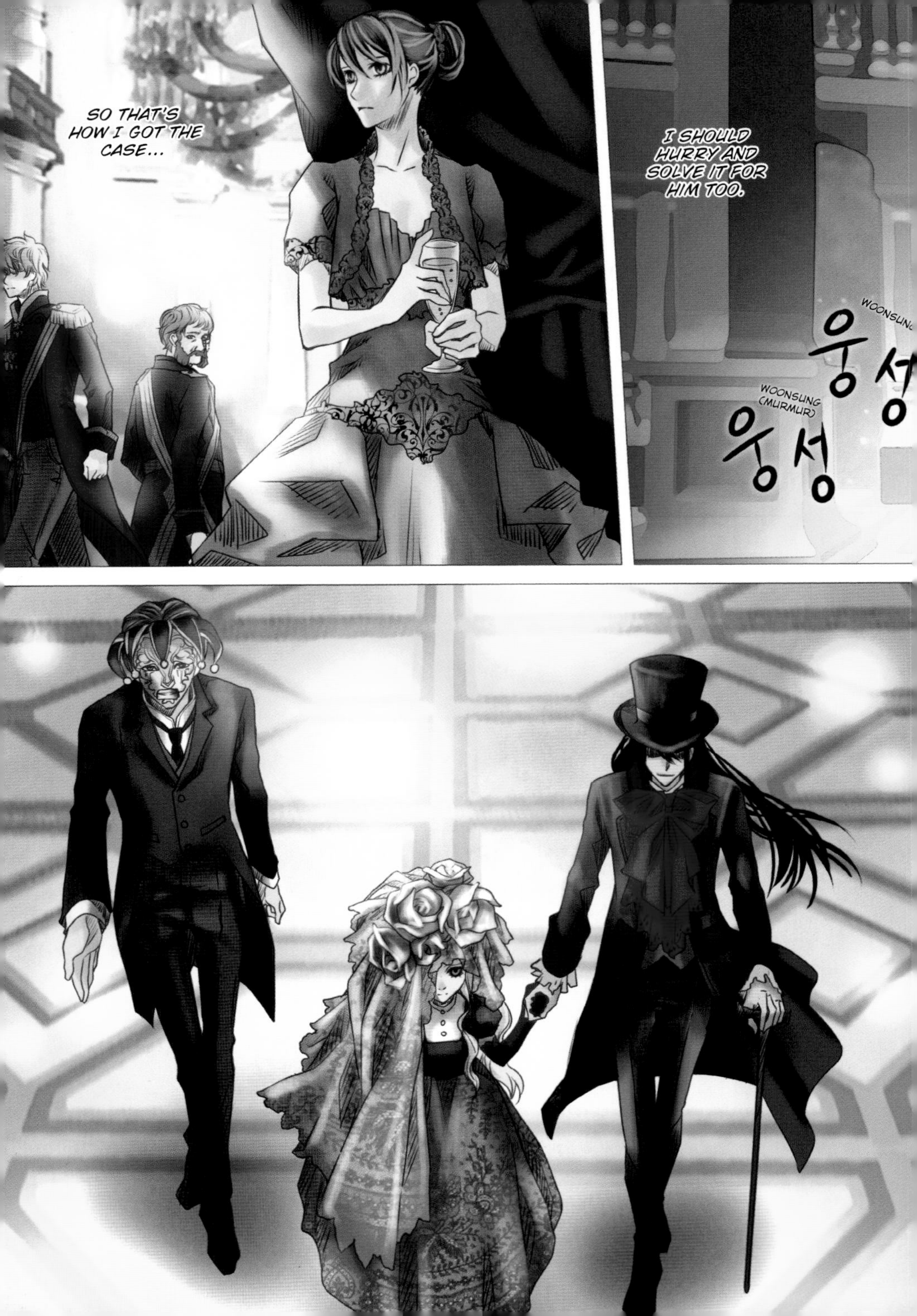
SO THAT'S HOW I GOT THE CASE...
I SHOULD HURRY AND SOLVE IT FOR HIM TOO.
WOONSUNG
웅성
WOONSUNG (MURMUR)
웅성

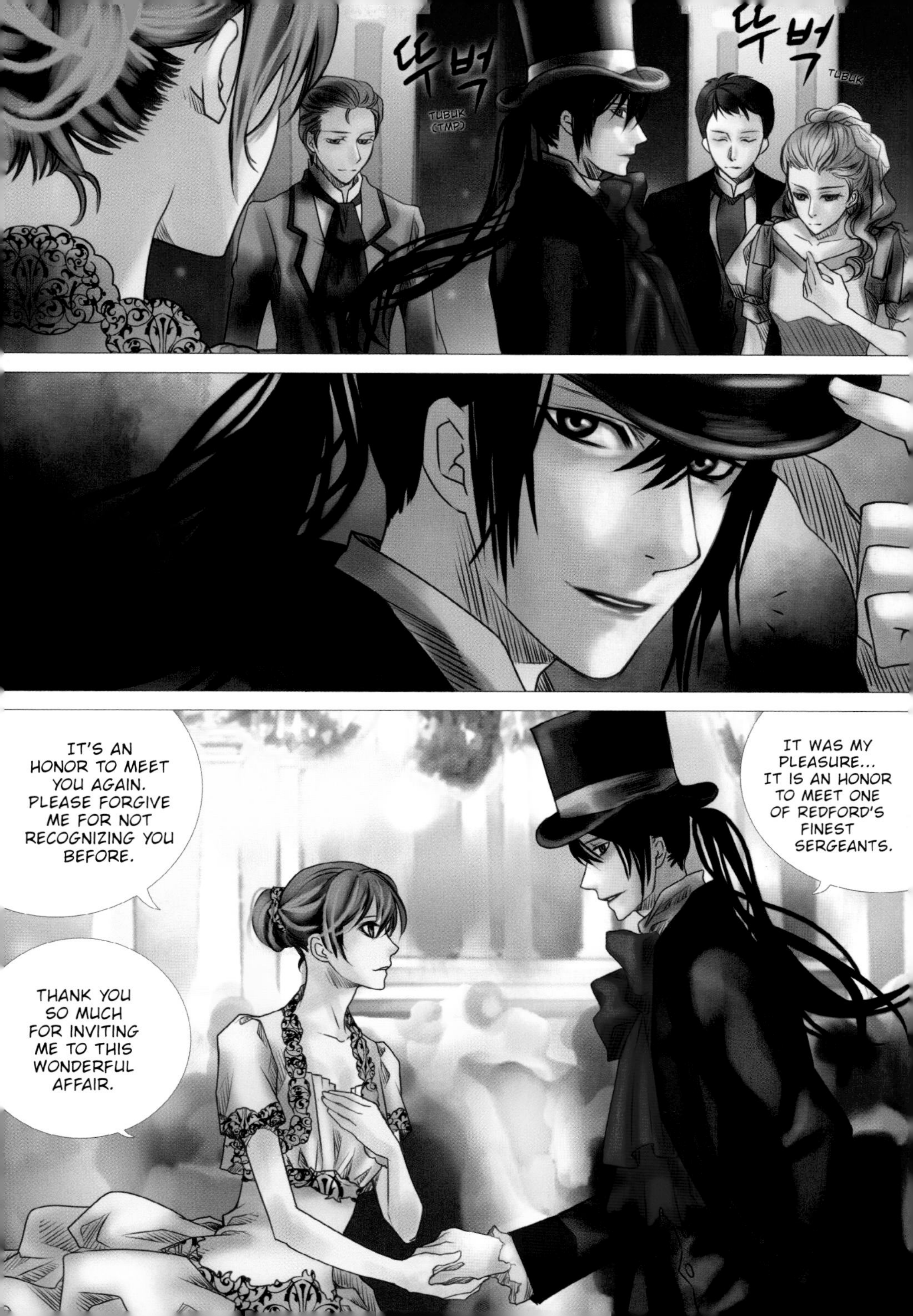
뚜벅
TUBUK (TMP)
뚜벅
TUBUK
IT'S AN HONOR TO MEET YOU AGAIN. PLEASE FORGIVE ME FOR NOT RECOGNIZING YOU BEFORE.
THANK YOU SO MUCH FOR INVITING ME TO THIS WONDERFUL AFFAIR.
IT WAS MY PLEASURE... IT IS AN HONOR TO MEET ONE OF REDFORD'S FINEST SERGEANTS.

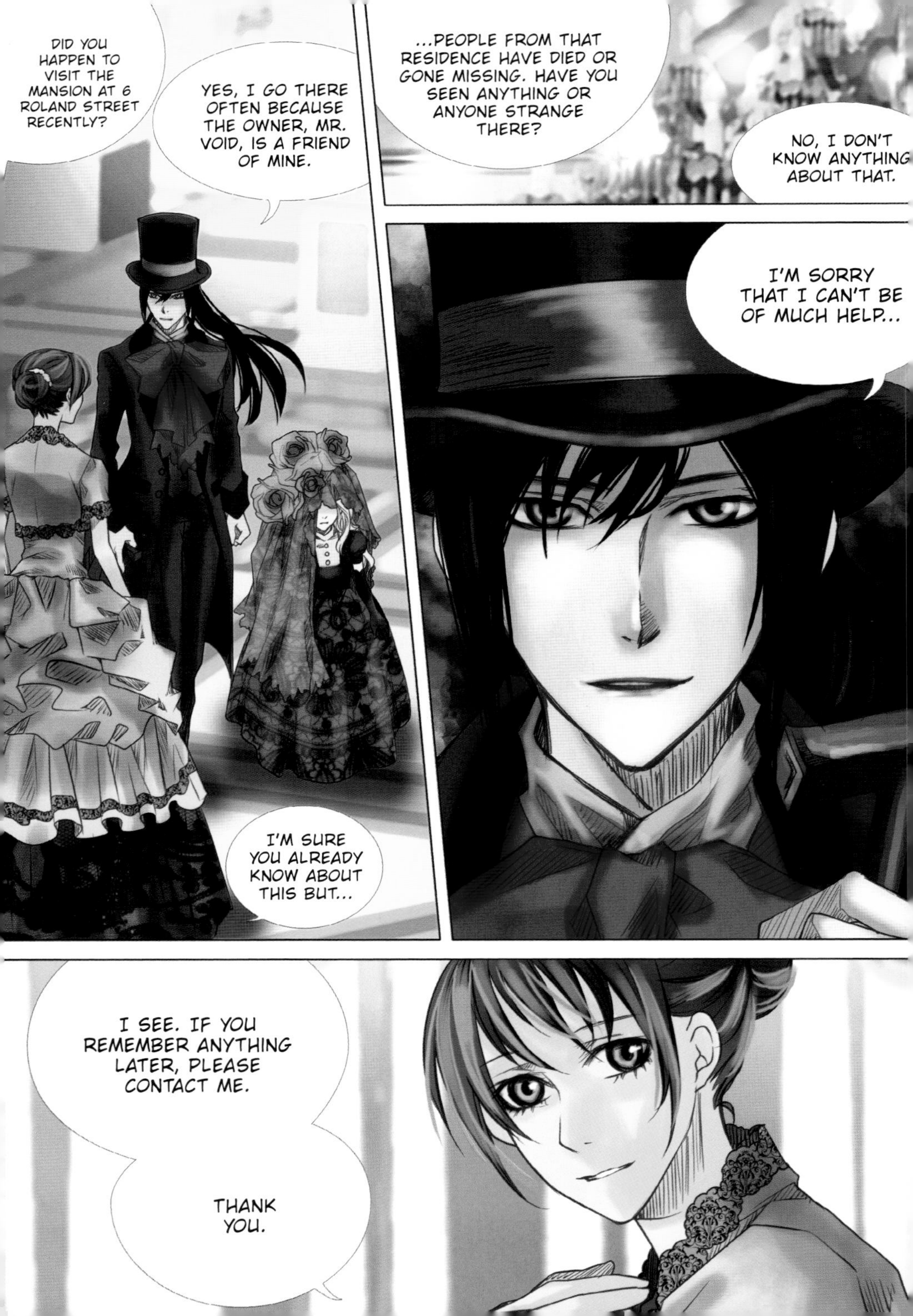
DID YOU HAPPEN TO VISIT THE MANSION AT 6 ROLAND STREET RECENTLY?
YES, I GO THERE OFTEN BECAUSE THE OWNER, MR. VOID, IS A FRIEND OF MINE.
I'M SURE YOU ALREADY KNOW ABOUT THIS BUT...
...PEOPLE FROM THAT RESIDENCE HAVE DIED OR GONE MISSING. HAVE YOU SEEN ANYTHING OR ANYONE STRANGE THERE?
NO, I DON'T KNOW ANYTHING ABOUT THAT.
I'M SORRY THAT I CAN'T BE OF MUCH HELP...
I SEE. IF YOU REMEMBER ANYTHING LATER, PLEASE CONTACT ME.
THANK YOU.

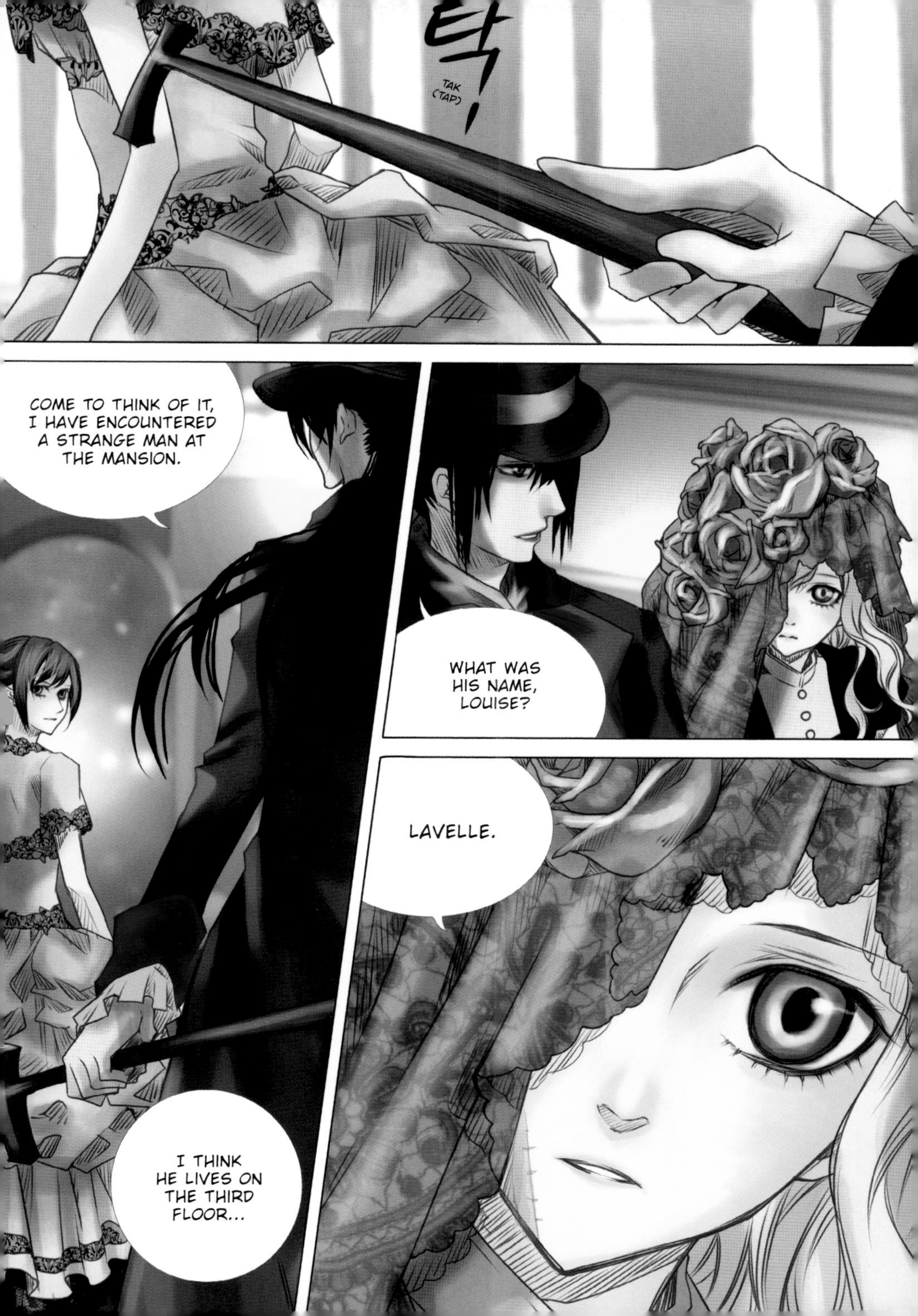
탁
TAK (TAP)
COME TO THINK OF IT, I HAVE ENCOUNTERED A STRANGE MAN AT THE MANSION.
I THINK HE LIVES ON THE THIRD FLOOR...
WHAT WAS HIS NAME, LOUISE?
LAVELLE.

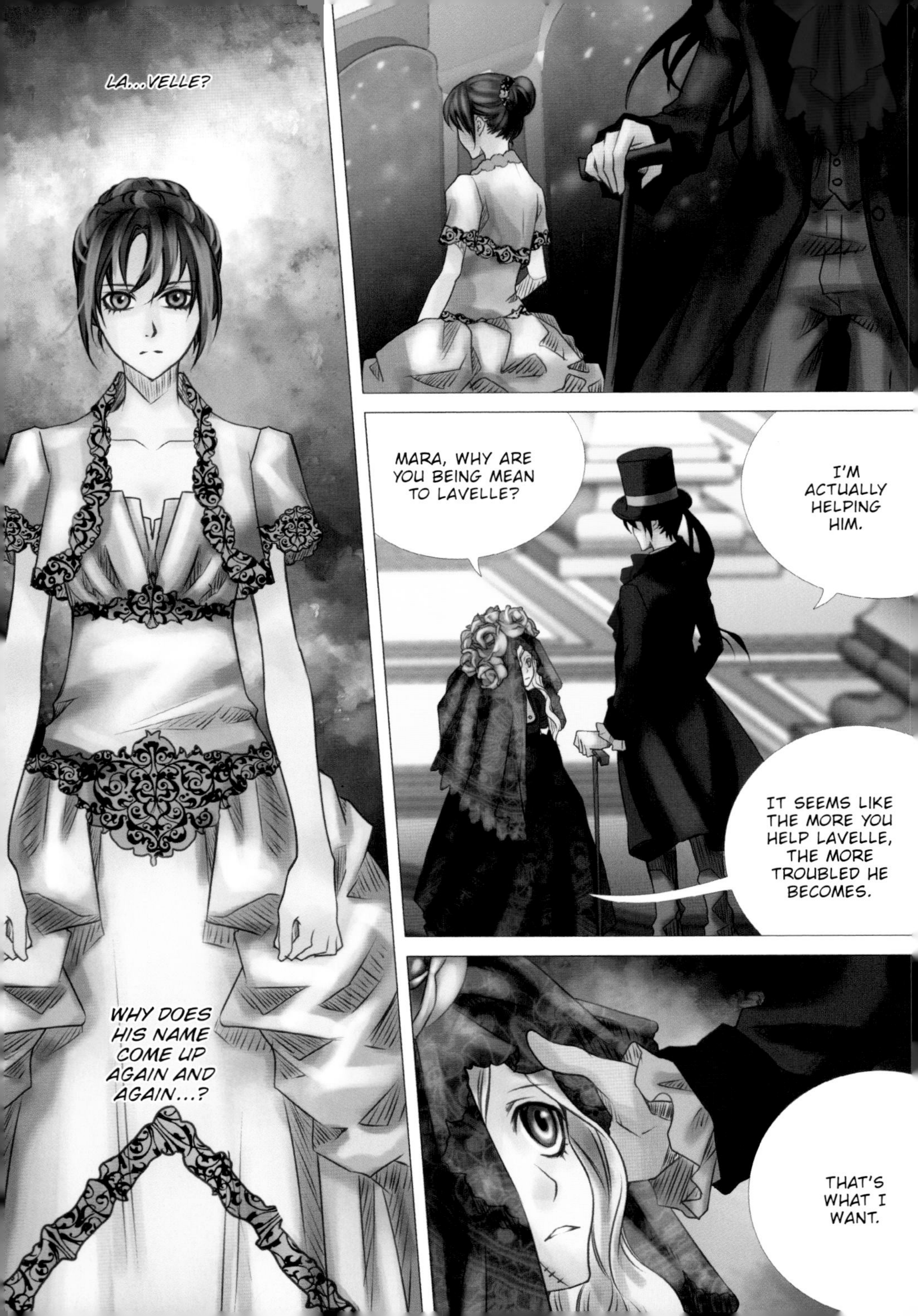
LA...VELLE?
WHY DOES HIS NAME COME UP AGAIN AND AGAIN...?
MARA, WHY ARE YOU BEING MEAN TO LAVELLE?
I'M ACTUALLY HELPING HIM.
IT SEEMS LIKE THE MORE YOU HELP LAVELLE, THE MORE TROUBLED HE BECOMES.
THAT'S WHAT I WANT.

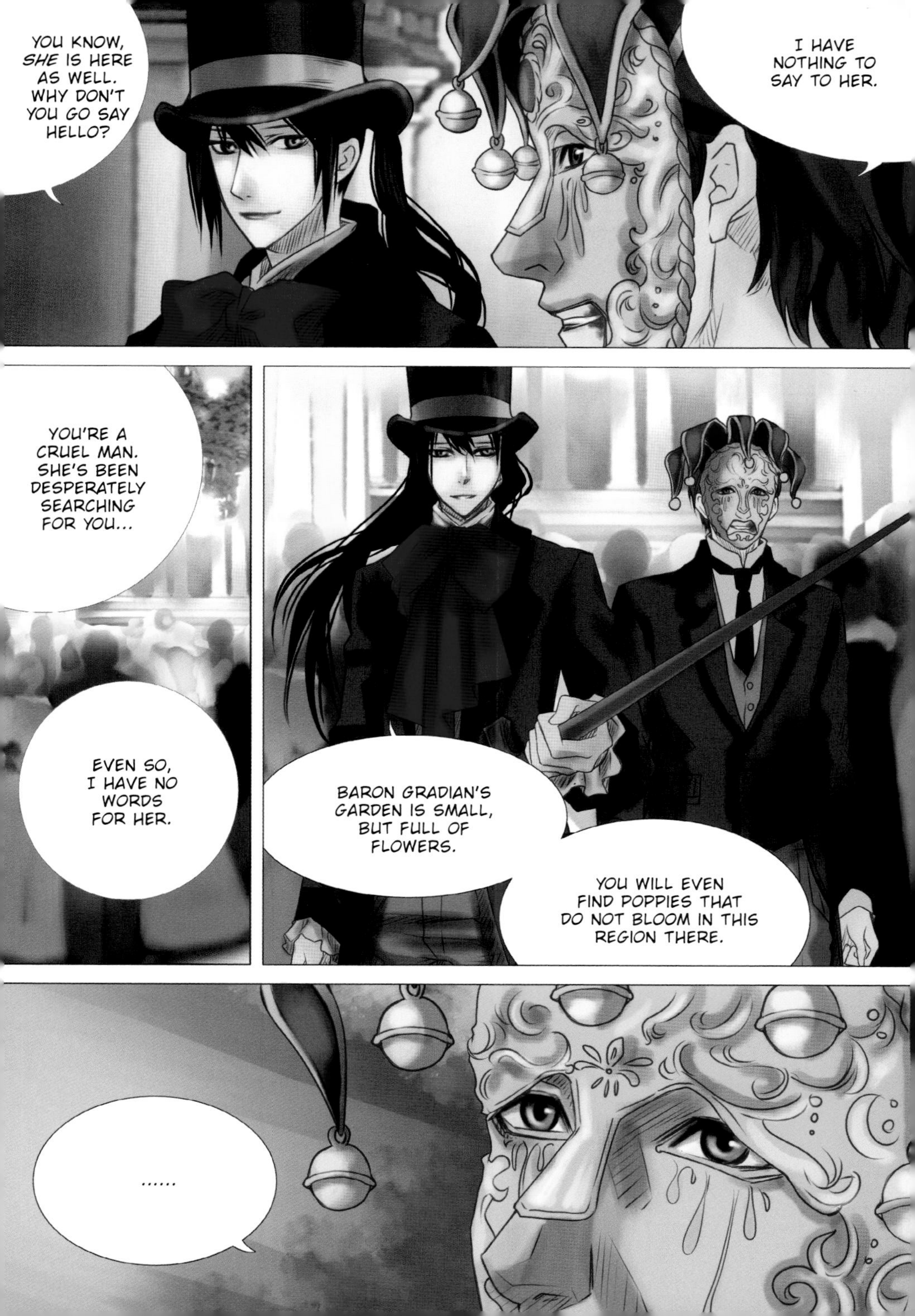
YOU KNOW, SHE IS HERE AS WELL. WHY DON'T YOU GO SAY HELLO?
I HAVE NOTHING TO SAY TO HER.
YOU'RE A CRUEL MAN. SHE'S BEEN DESPERATELY SEARCHING FOR YOU...
EVEN SO, I HAVE NO WORDS FOR HER.
BARON GRADIAN'S GARDEN IS SMALL, BUT FULL OF FLOWERS.
YOU WILL EVEN FIND POPPIES THAT DO NOT BLOOM IN THIS REGION THERE.
......

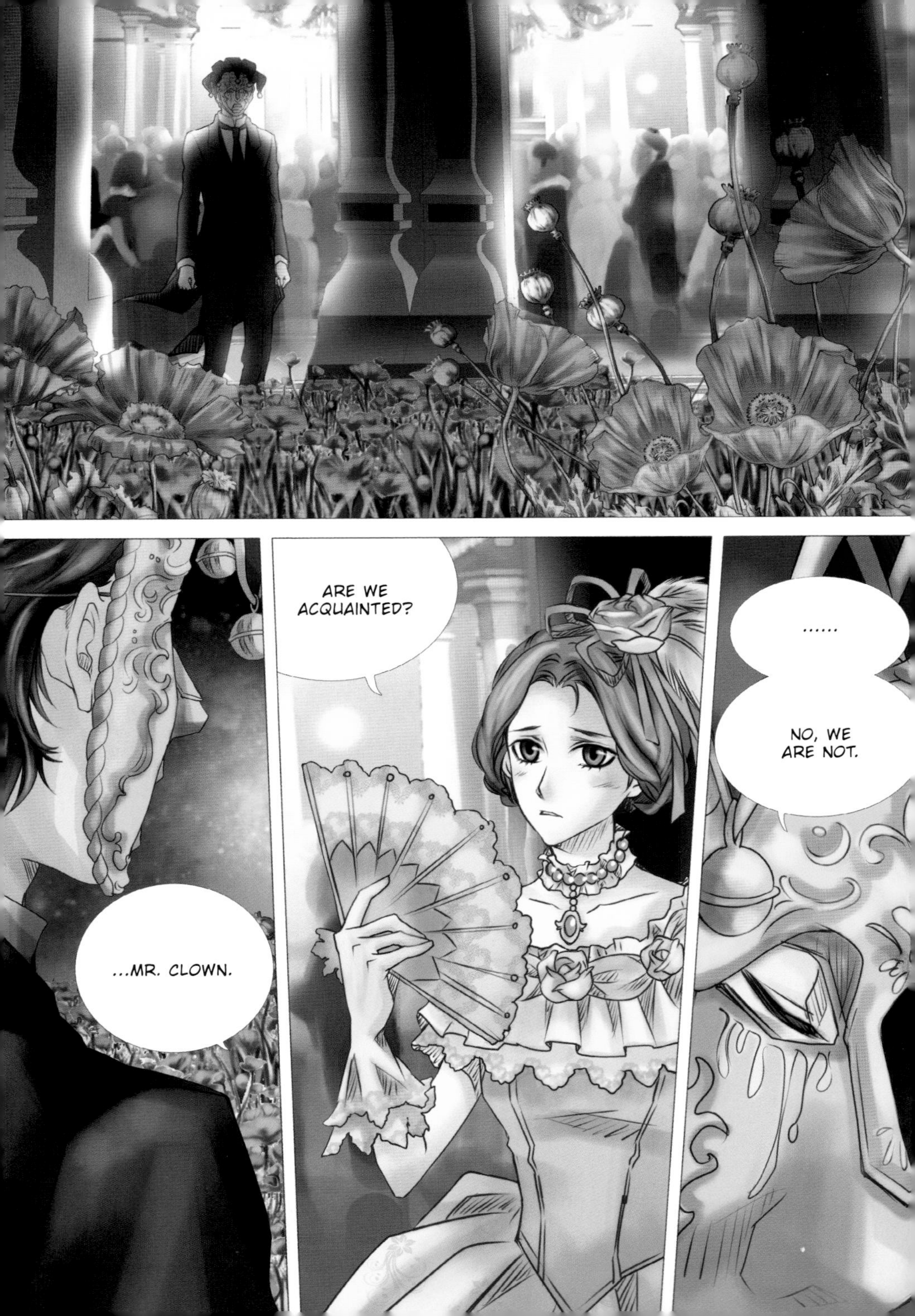
...MR. CLOWN.
ARE WE ACQUAINTED?
......
NO, WE ARE NOT.

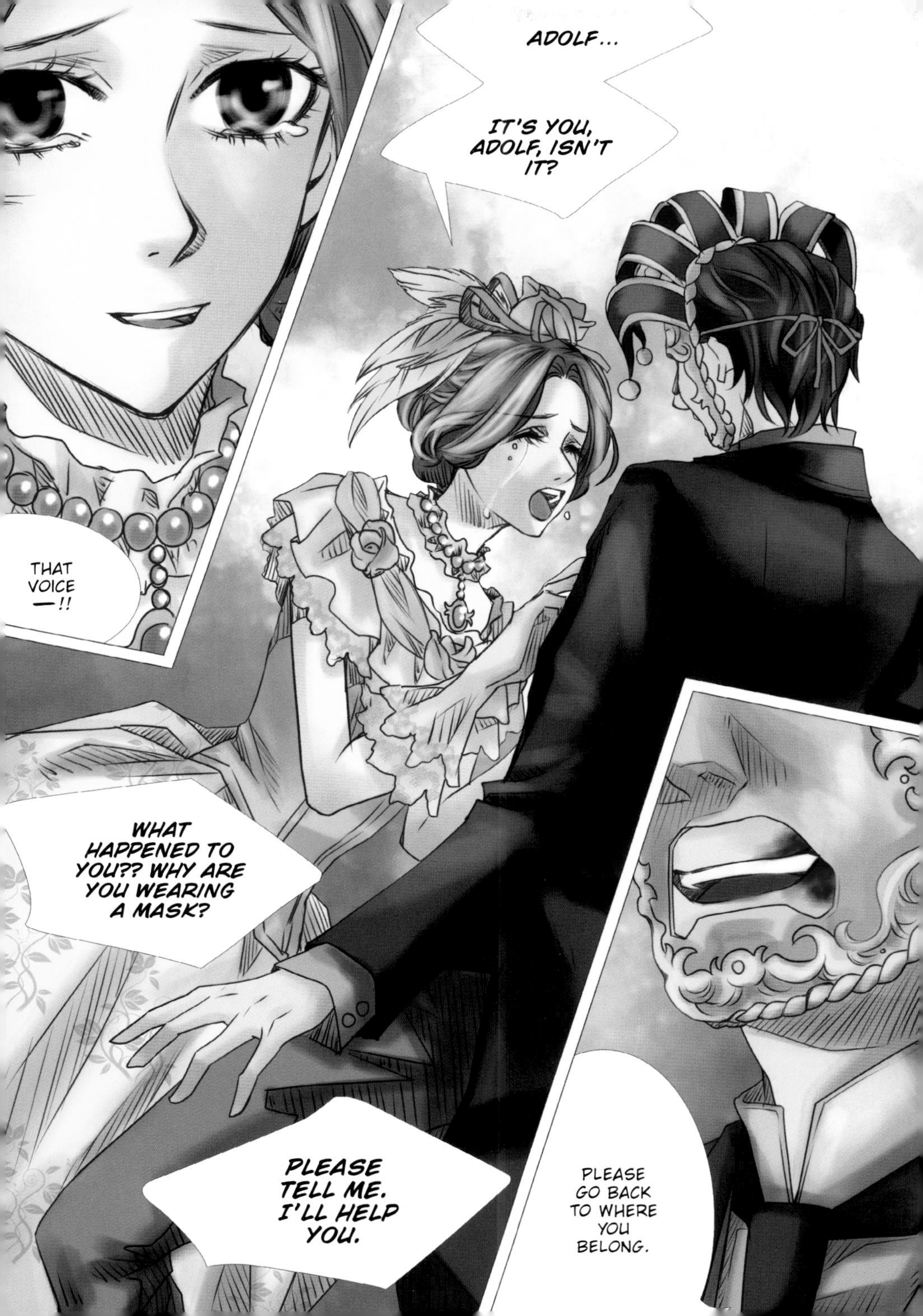
ADOLF...
IT'S YOU, ADOLF, ISN'T IT?
THAT VOICE —!!
WHAT HAPPENED TO YOU?? WHY ARE YOU WEARING A MASK?
PLEASE TELL ME. I'LL HELP YOU.
PLEASE GO BACK TO WHERE YOU BELONG.

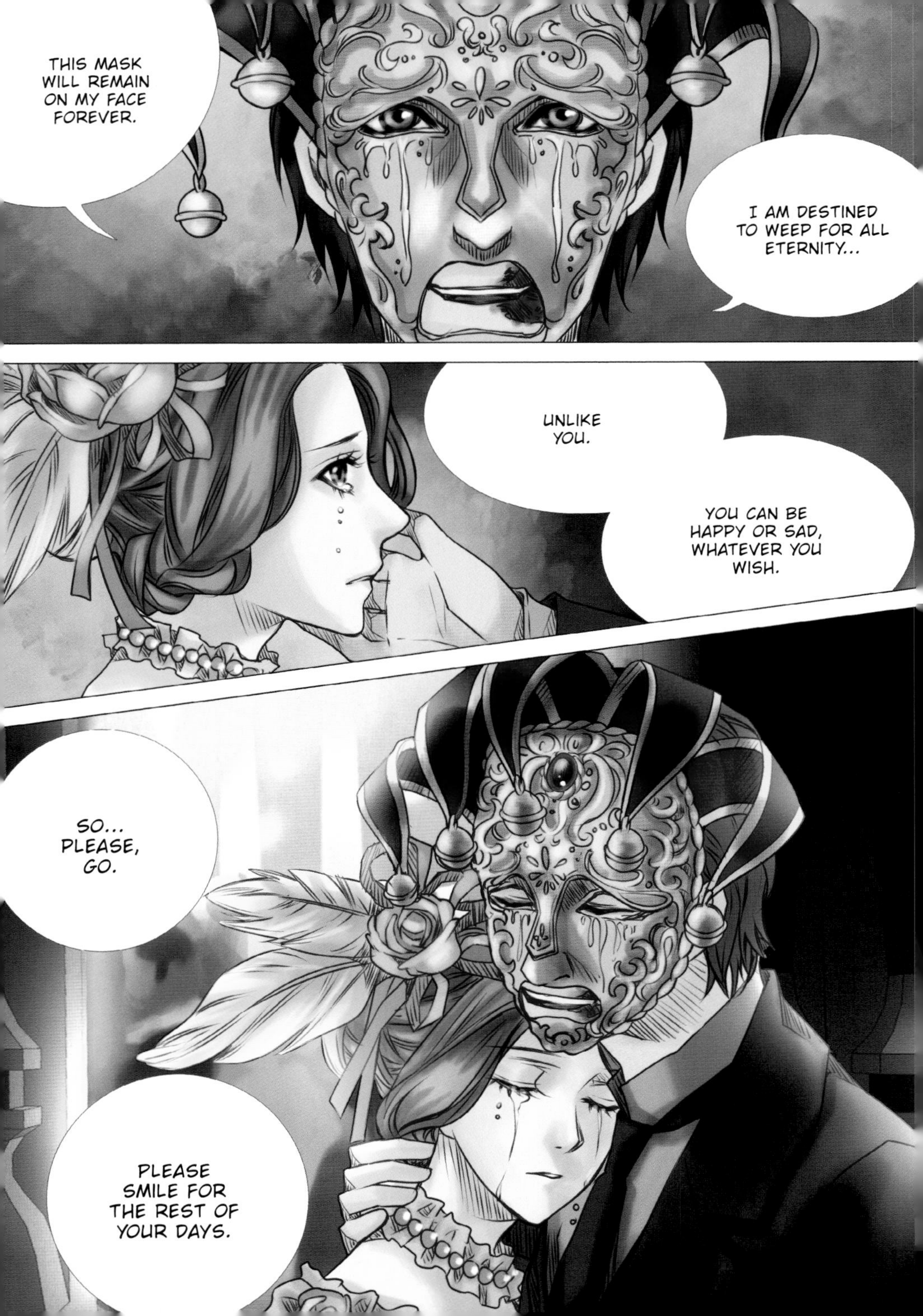
THIS MASK WILL REMAIN ON MY FACE FOREVER.
I AM DESTINED TO WEEP FOR ALL ETERNITY...
UNLIKE YOU.
YOU CAN BE HAPPY OR SAD, WHATEVER YOU WISH.
SO... PLEASE, GO.
PLEASE SMILE FOR THE REST OF YOUR DAYS.

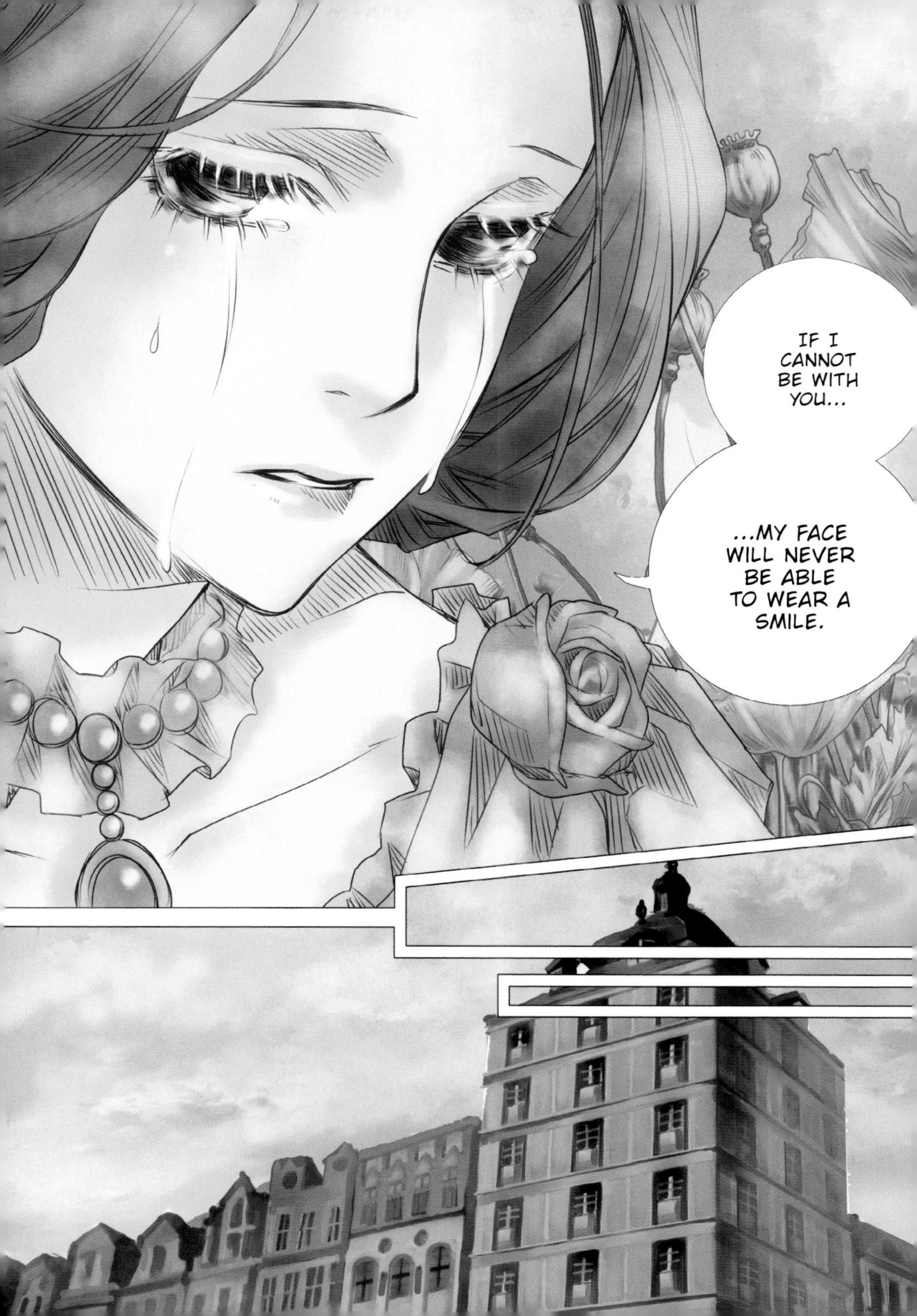
IF I CANNOT BE WITH YOU...
...MY FACE WILL NEVER BE ABLE TO WEAR A SMILE.

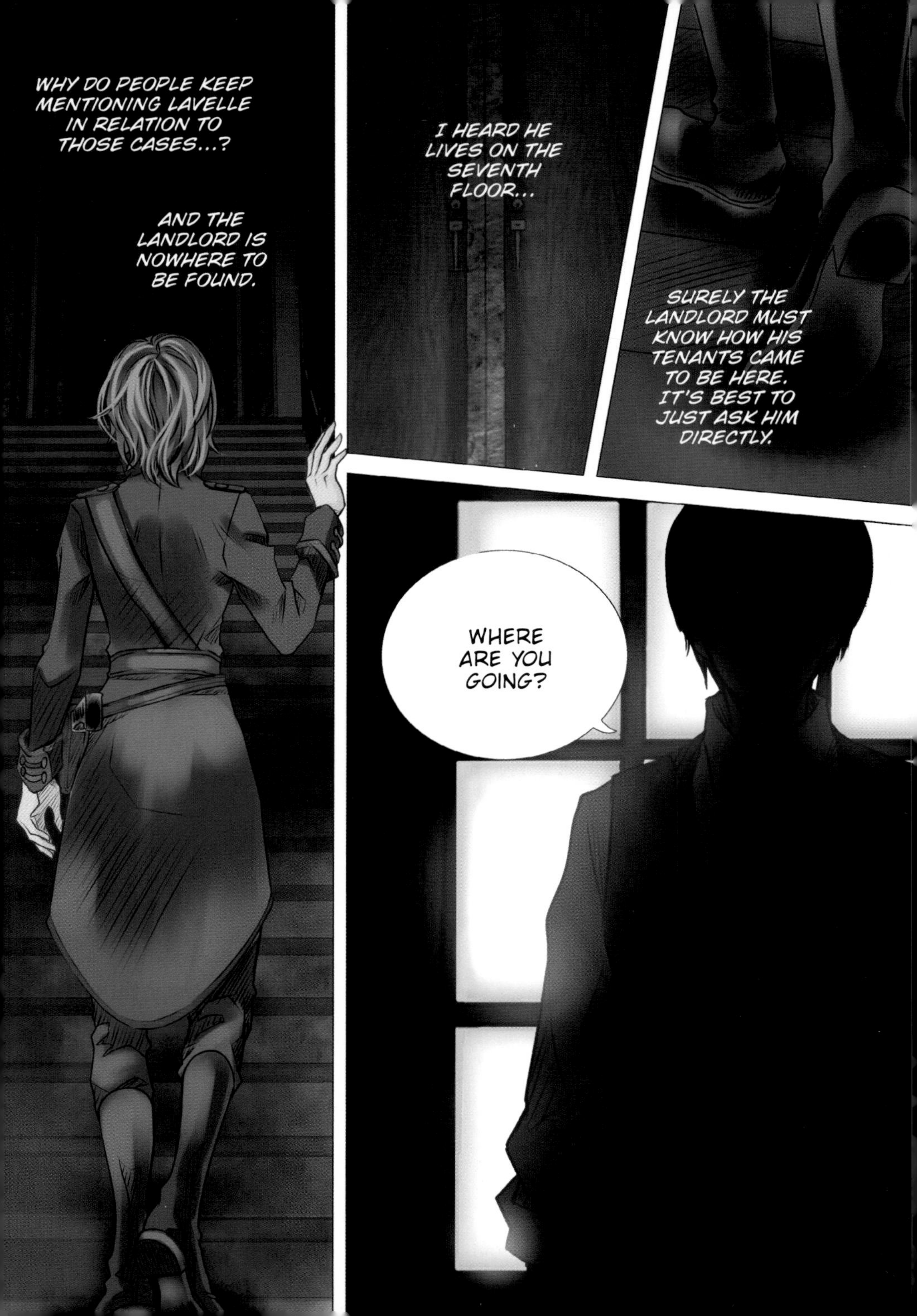
WHY DO PEOPLE KEEP MENTIONING LAVELLE IN RELATION TO THOSE CASES...?
AND THE LANDLORD IS NOWHERE TO BE FOUND.
I HEARD HE LIVES ON THE SEVENTH FLOOR...
SURELY THE LANDLORD MUST KNOW HOW HIS TENANTS CAME TO BE HERE. IT'S BEST TO JUST ASK HIM DIRECTLY.
WHERE ARE YOU GOING?

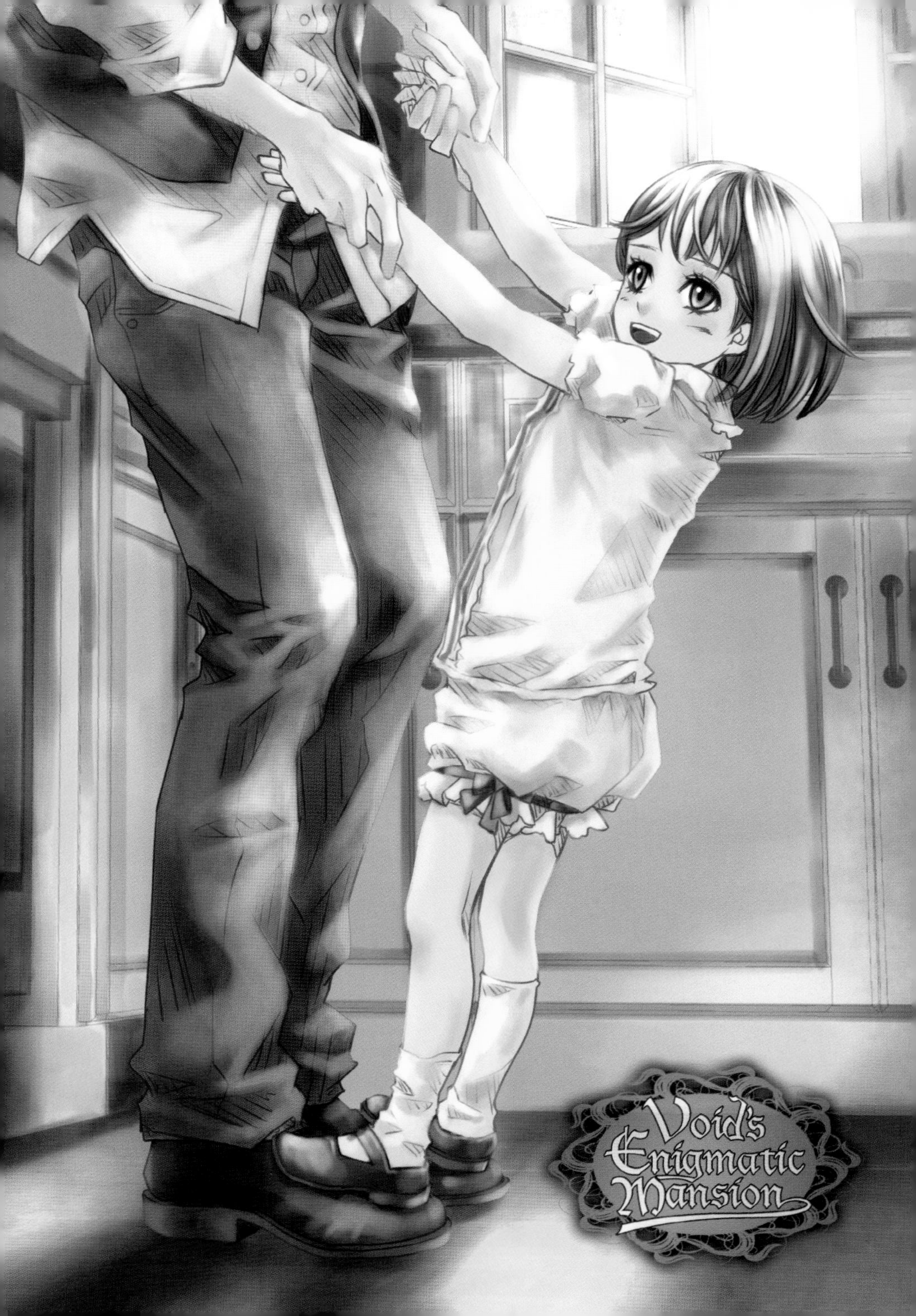
Void's
Enigmatic
Mansion

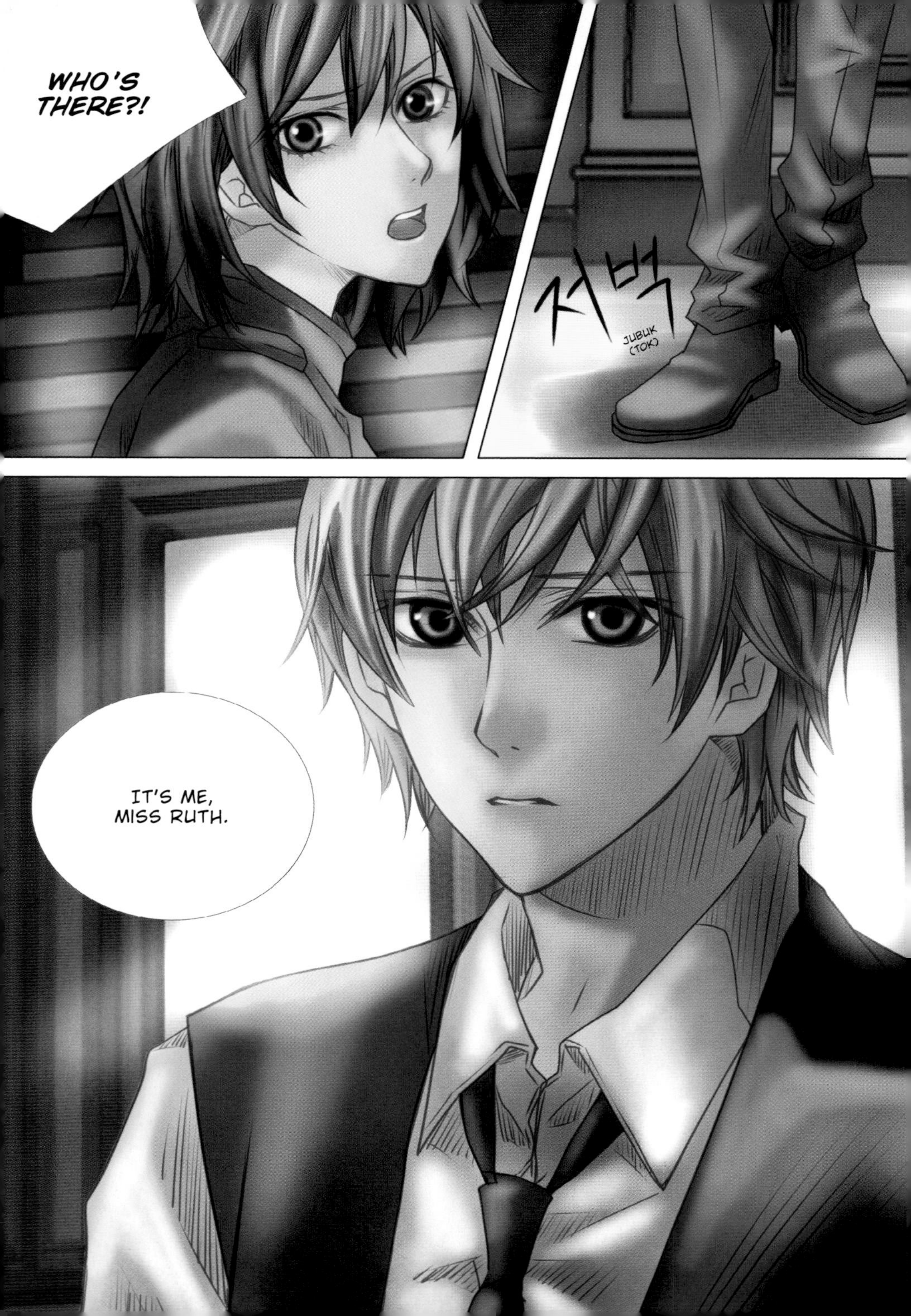
WHO'S THERE?!
저벅
JUBUK (TOK)
IT'S ME, MISS RUTH.

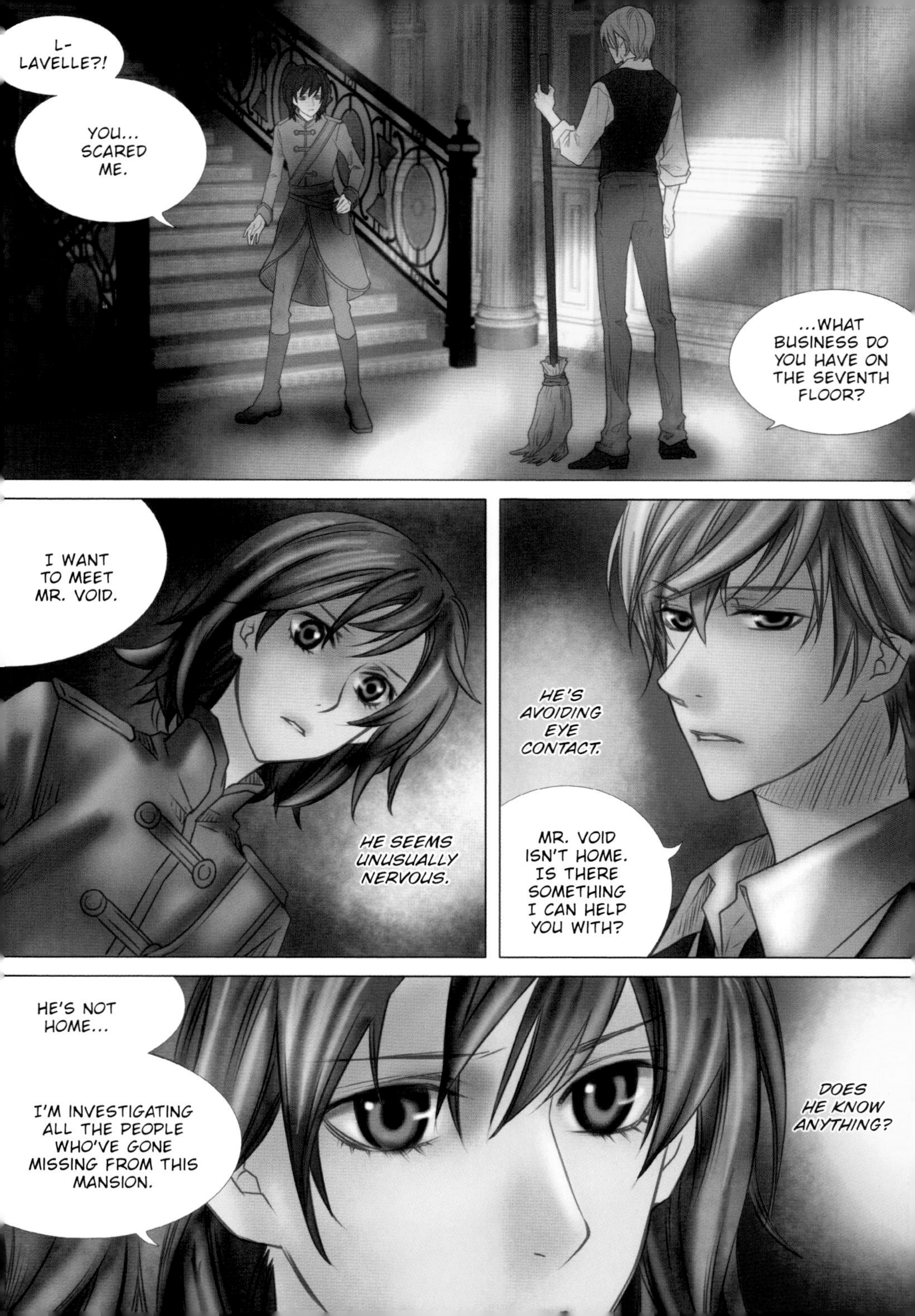
L-LAVELLE?!
YOU... SCARED ME.
...WHAT BUSINESS DO YOU HAVE ON THE SEVENTH FLOOR?
I WANT TO MEET MR. VOID.
HE SEEMS UNUSUALLY NERVOUS.
HE'S AVOIDING EYE CONTACT.
MR. VOID ISN'T HOME. IS THERE SOMETHING I CAN HELP YOU WITH?
HE'S NOT HOME...
I'M INVESTIGATING ALL THE PEOPLE WHO'VE GONE MISSING FROM THIS MANSION.
DOES HE KNOW ANYTHING?

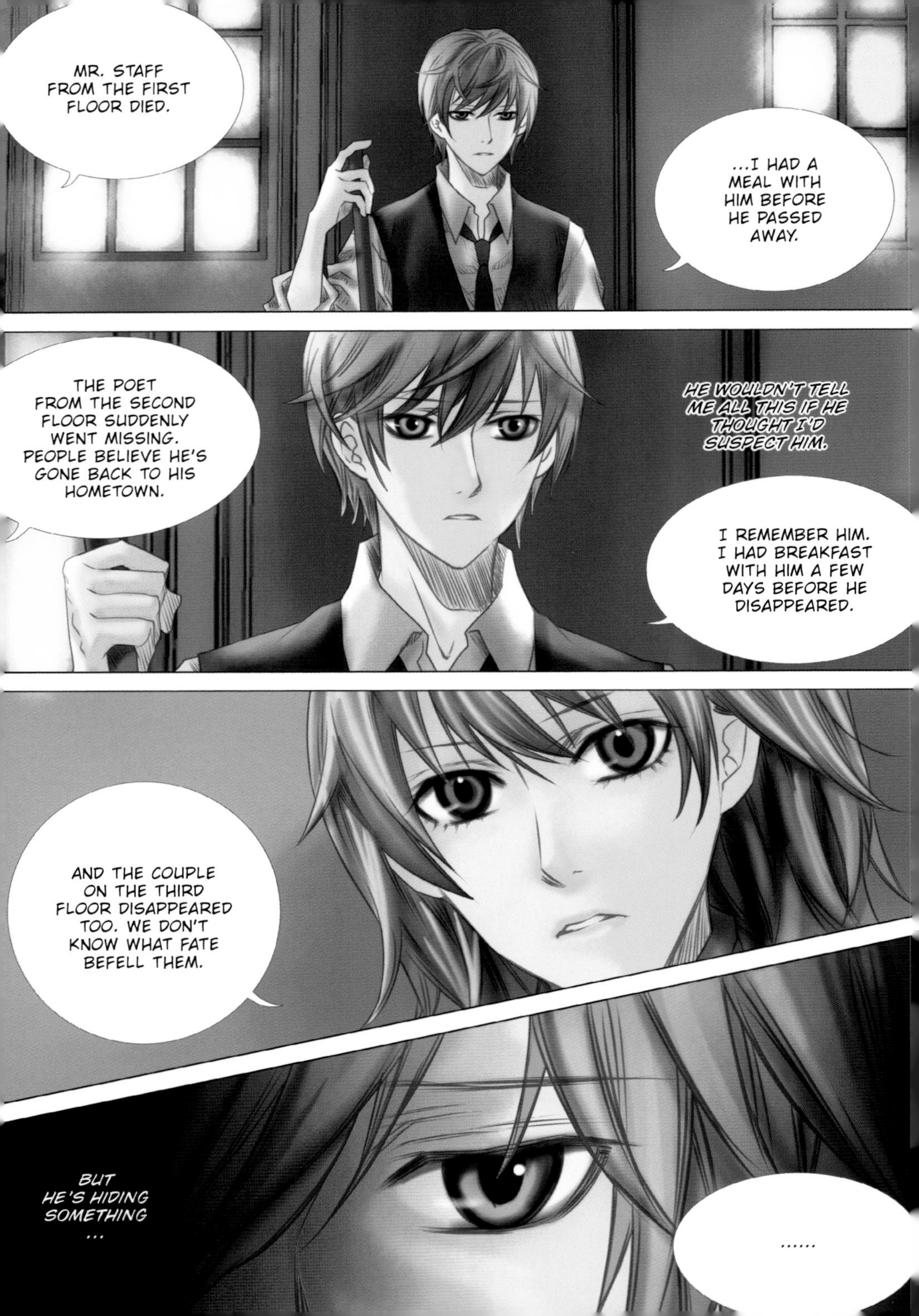
MR. STAFF FROM THE FIRST FLOOR DIED.
...I HAD A MEAL WITH HIM BEFORE HE PASSED AWAY.
THE POET FROM THE SECOND FLOOR SUDDENLY WENT MISSING. PEOPLE BELIEVE HE'S GONE BACK TO HIS HOMETOWN.
HE WOULDN'T TELL ME ALL THIS IF HE THOUGHT I'D SUSPECT HIM.
I REMEMBER HIM. I HAD BREAKFAST WITH HIM A FEW DAYS BEFORE HE DISAPPEARED.
AND THE COUPLE ON THE THIRD FLOOR DISAPPEARED TOO. WE DON'T KNOW WHAT FATE BEFELL THEM.
BUT HE'S HIDING SOMETHING ...
......

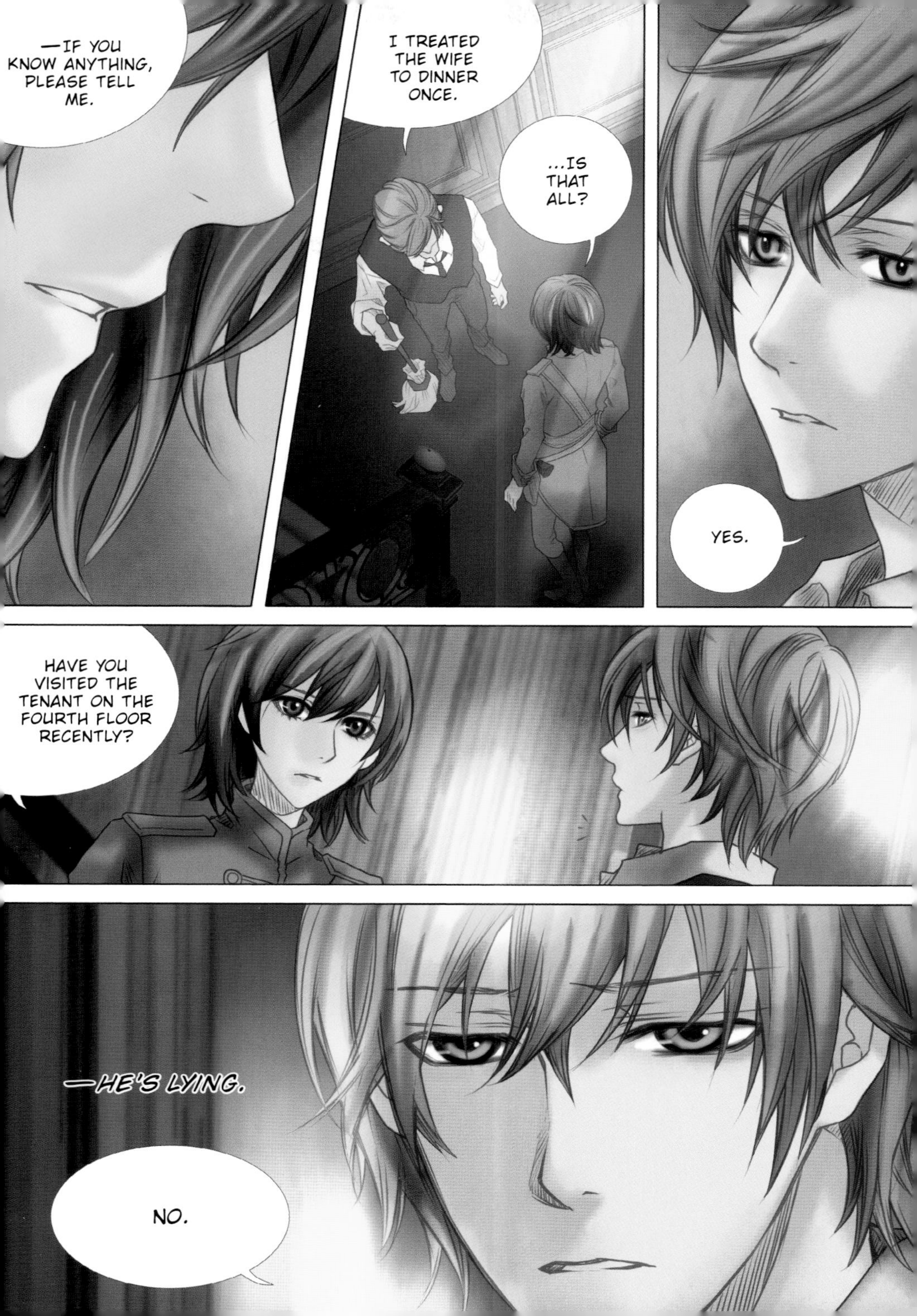
—IF YOU KNOW ANYTHING, PLEASE TELL ME.
I TREATED THE WIFE TO DINNER ONCE.
...IS THAT ALL?
YES.
HAVE YOU VISITED THE TENANT ON THE FOURTH FLOOR RECENTLY?
—HE'S LYING.
NO.

ALL RIGHT. IF I HAVE ANY MORE QUESTIONS, I'LL ASK YOU TO COME TO THE POLICE STATION.

YES, OF COURSE.

I'LL DO MY BEST TO COOPERATE.

HE'S HESITATING, AND HIS EYES LOOK SHIFTY...

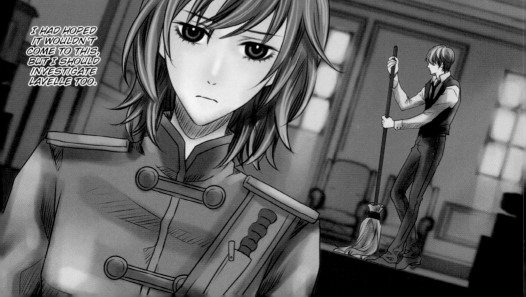

I HAD HOPED IT WOULDN'T COME TO THIS, BUT I SHOULD INVESTIGATE LAVELLE TOO.

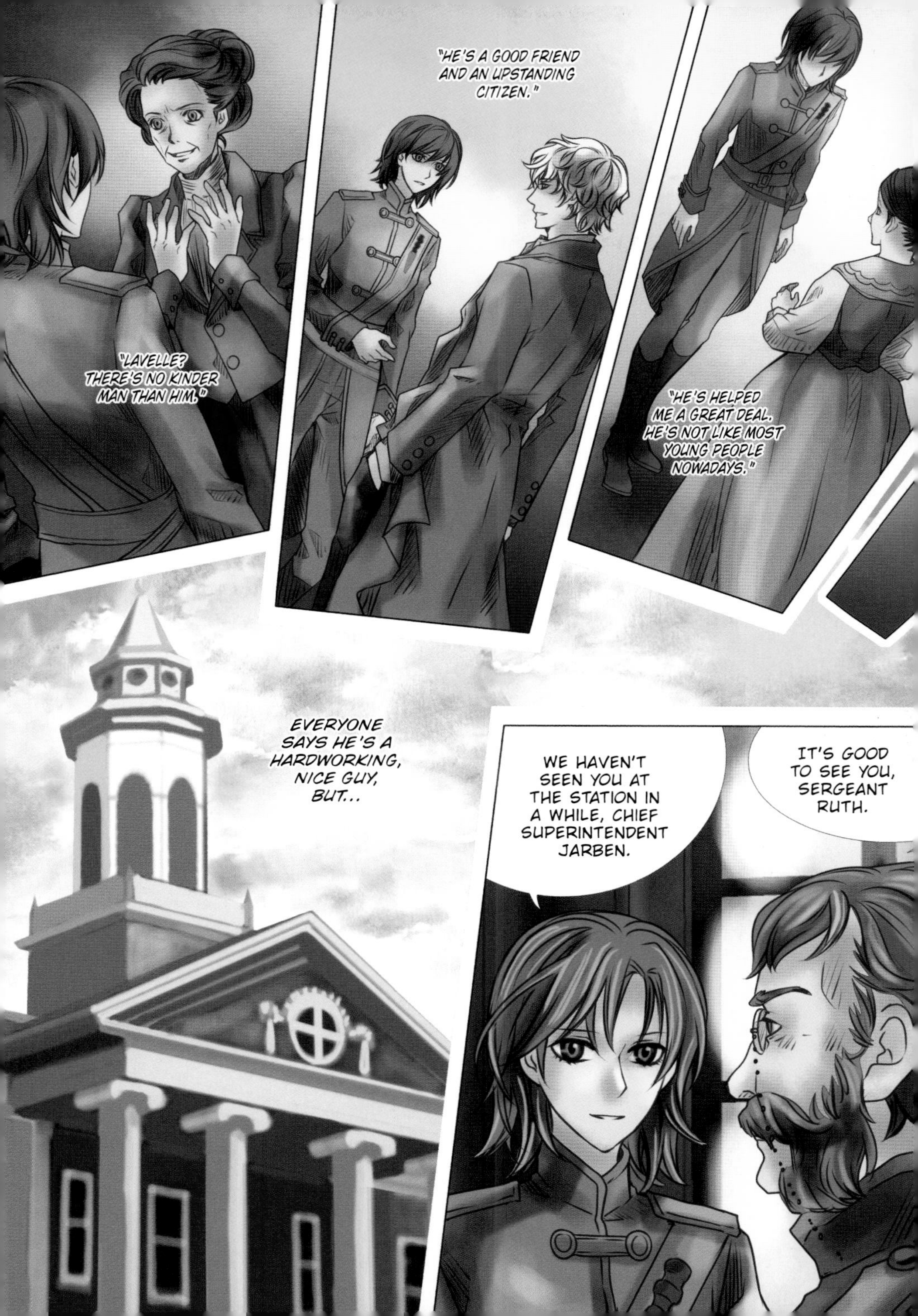
"LAVELLE? THERE'S NO KINDER MAN THAN HIM."
"HE'S A GOOD FRIEND AND AN UPSTANDING CITIZEN."
"HE'S HELPED ME A GREAT DEAL. HE'S NOT LIKE MOST YOUNG PEOPLE NOWADAYS."
EVERYONE SAYS HE'S A HARDWORKING, NICE GUY, BUT...
WE HAVEN'T SEEN YOU AT THE STATION IN A WHILE, CHIEF SUPERINTENDENT JARBEN.
IT'S GOOD TO SEE YOU, SERGEANT RUTH.

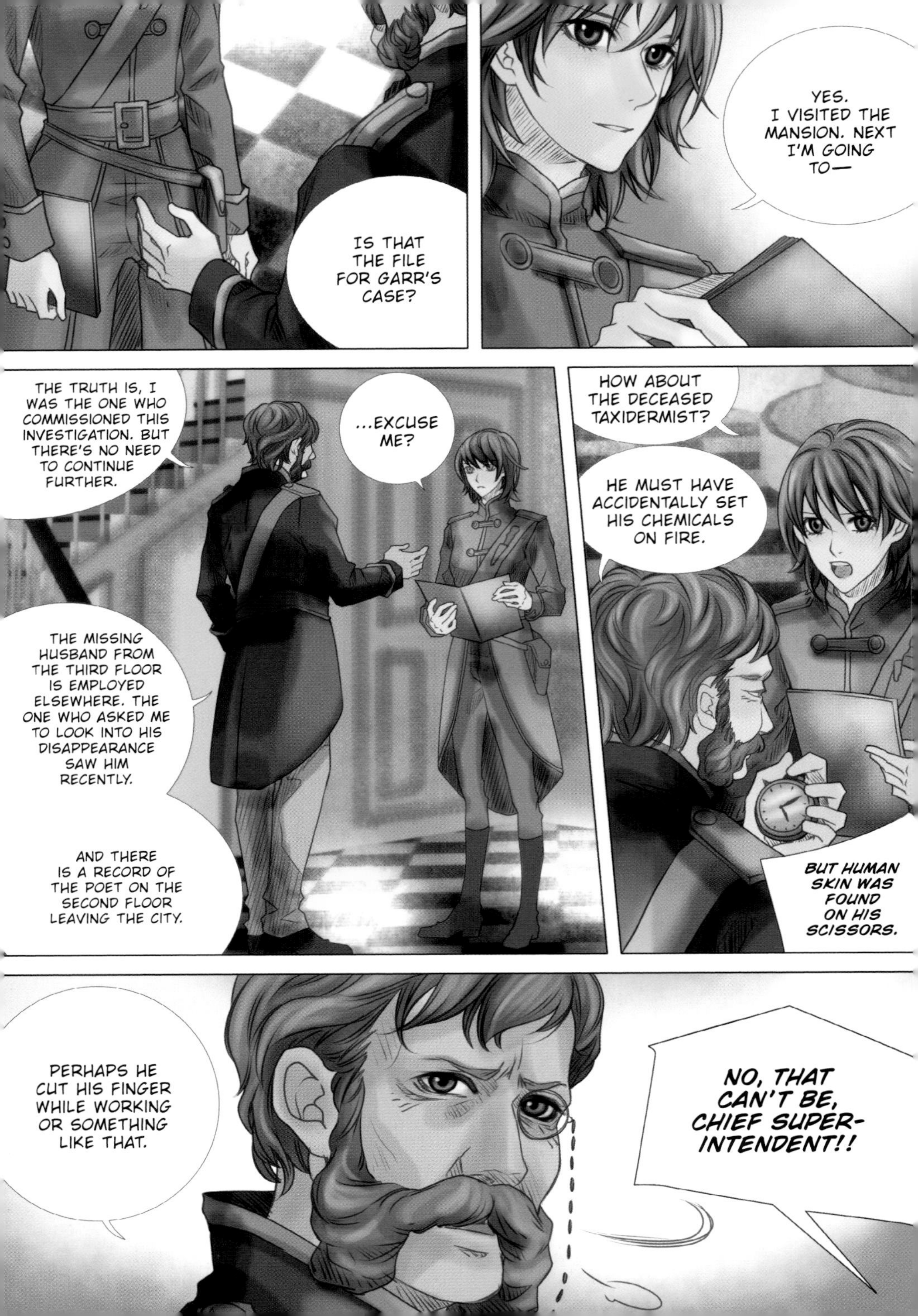
IS THAT THE FILE FOR GARR'S CASE?
YES. I VISITED THE MANSION. NEXT I'M GOING TO—
THE TRUTH IS, I WAS THE ONE WHO COMMISSIONED THIS INVESTIGATION. BUT THERE'S NO NEED TO CONTINUE FURTHER.
...EXCUSE ME?
THE MISSING HUSBAND FROM THE THIRD FLOOR IS EMPLOYED ELSEWHERE. THE ONE WHO ASKED ME TO LOOK INTO HIS DISAPPEARANCE SAW HIM RECENTLY.
AND THERE IS A RECORD OF THE POET ON THE SECOND FLOOR LEAVING THE CITY.
HOW ABOUT THE DECEASED TAXIDERMIST?
HE MUST HAVE ACCIDENTALLY SET HIS CHEMICALS ON FIRE.
BUT HUMAN SKIN WAS FOUND ON HIS SCISSORS.
PERHAPS HE CUT HIS FINGER WHILE WORKING OR SOMETHING LIKE THAT.
NO, THAT CAN'T BE, CHIEF SUPER-INTENDENT!!

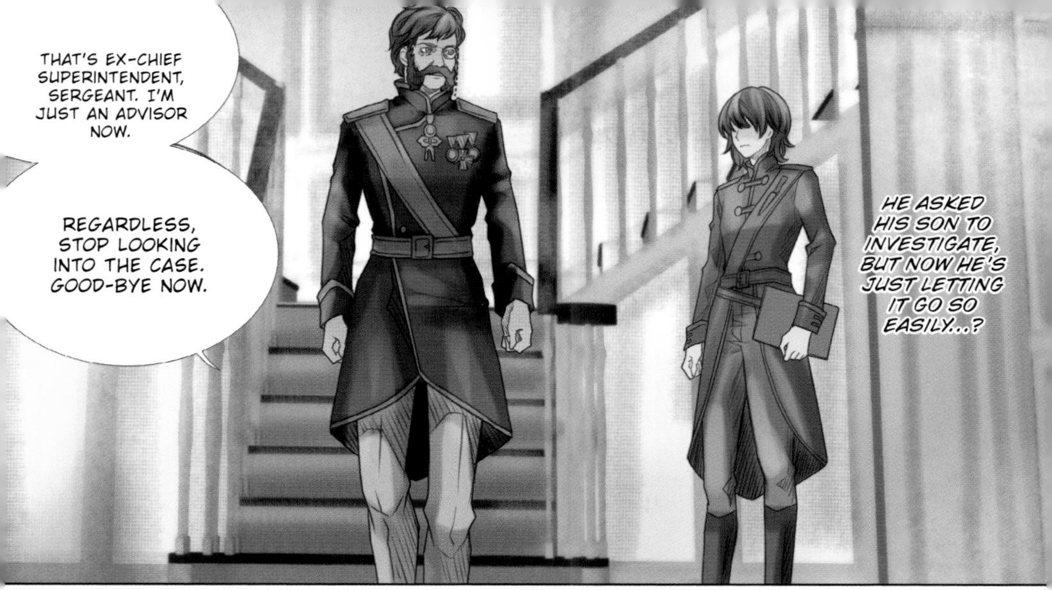
THAT'S EX-CHIEF SUPERINTENDENT, SERGEANT. I'M JUST AN ADVISOR NOW.
REGARDLESS, STOP LOOKING INTO THE CASE. GOOD-BYE NOW.
HE ASKED HIS SON TO INVESTIGATE, BUT NOW HE'S JUST LETTING IT GO SO EASILY...?
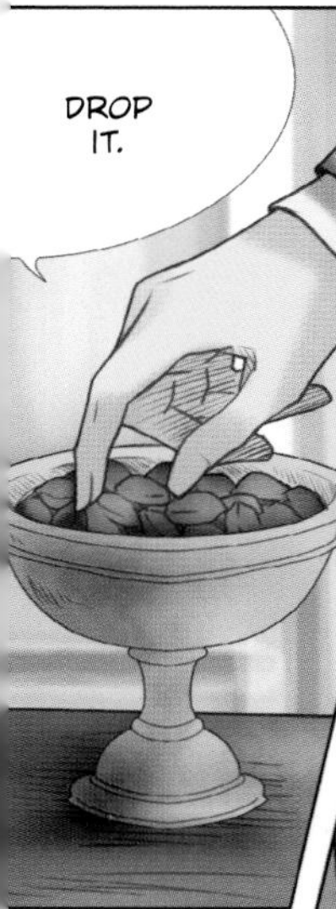
DROP IT.
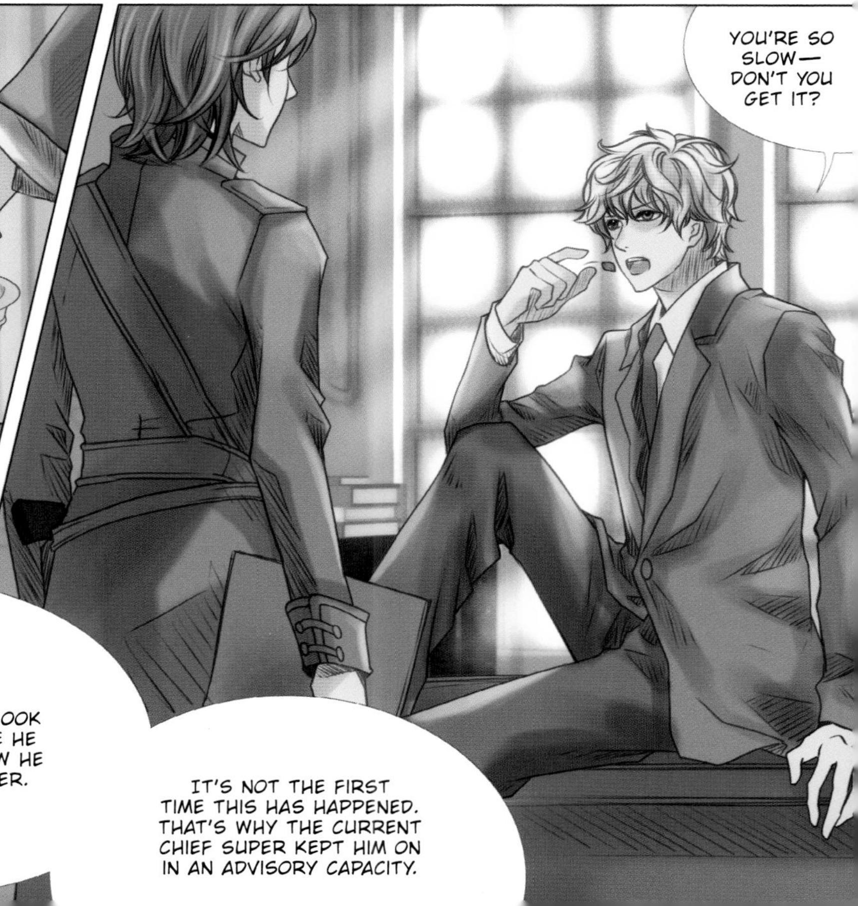
YOU'RE SO SLOW— DON'T YOU GET IT?
MY FATHER WANTED ME TO LOOK INTO IT BECAUSE HE WANTED TO SHOW HE STILL HAD POWER.
IT'S NOT THE FIRST TIME THIS HAS HAPPENED. THAT'S WHY THE CURRENT CHIEF SUPER KEPT HIM ON IN AN ADVISORY CAPACITY.

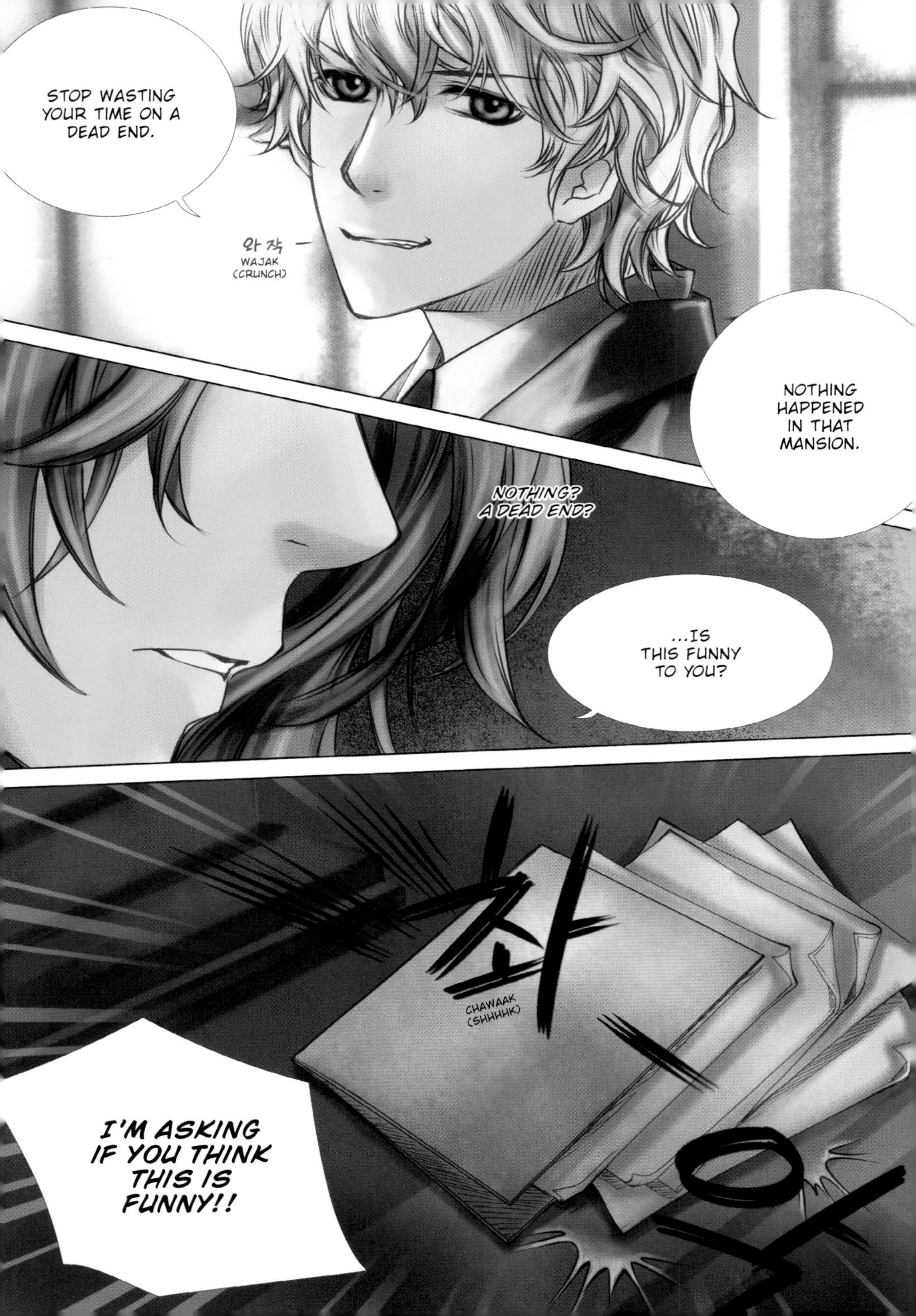
STOP WASTING YOUR TIME ON A DEAD END.
와 작 —
WAJAK (CRUNCH)
NOTHING HAPPENED IN THAT MANSION.
NOTHING? A DEAD END?
...IS THIS FUNNY TO YOU?
좌
CHAWAAK (SHHHHK)
I'M ASKING IF YOU THINK THIS IS FUNNY!!

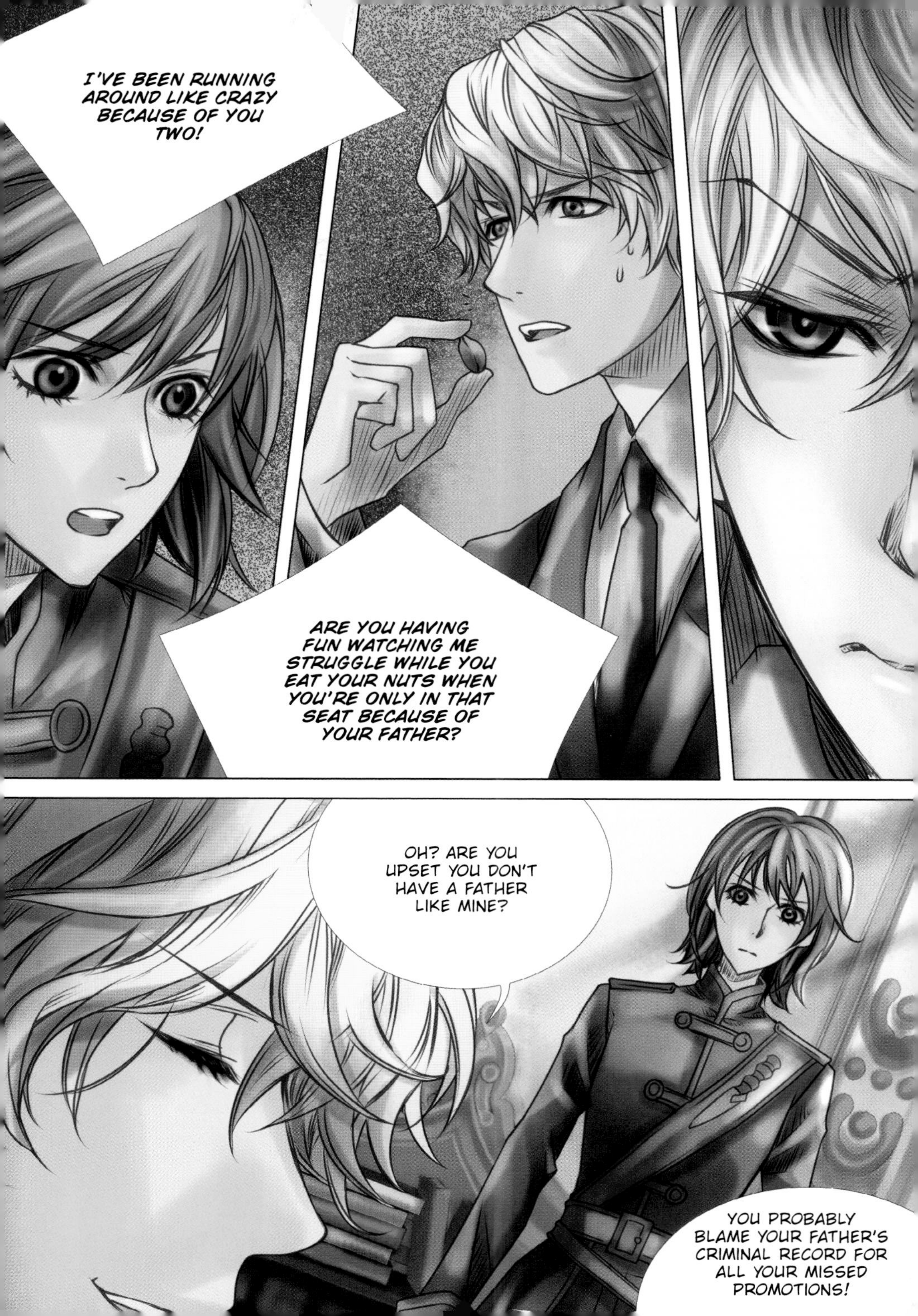
I'VE BEEN RUNNING AROUND LIKE CRAZY BECAUSE OF YOU TWO!
ARE YOU HAVING FUN WATCHING ME STRUGGLE WHILE YOU EAT YOUR NUTS WHEN YOU'RE ONLY IN THAT SEAT BECAUSE OF YOUR FATHER?
OH? ARE YOU UPSET YOU DON'T HAVE A FATHER LIKE MINE?
YOU PROBABLY BLAME YOUR FATHER'S CRIMINAL RECORD FOR ALL YOUR MISSED PROMOTIONS!

ISN'T THAT THE REASON?

YOU RELY ON GOOD LUCK AND THE HELP OF OTHERS INSTEAD OF YOUR OWN THOUGHTS AND JUDGMENTS.

!!

ALL YOU DID IN THE PAST SIX MONTHS WAS SOLVE A FEW CASES WITH THE HELP OF BARON JUAN.

THAT'S WHAT I CALL "LACK OF ABILITY," NOT "LACK OF EXPERIENCE."

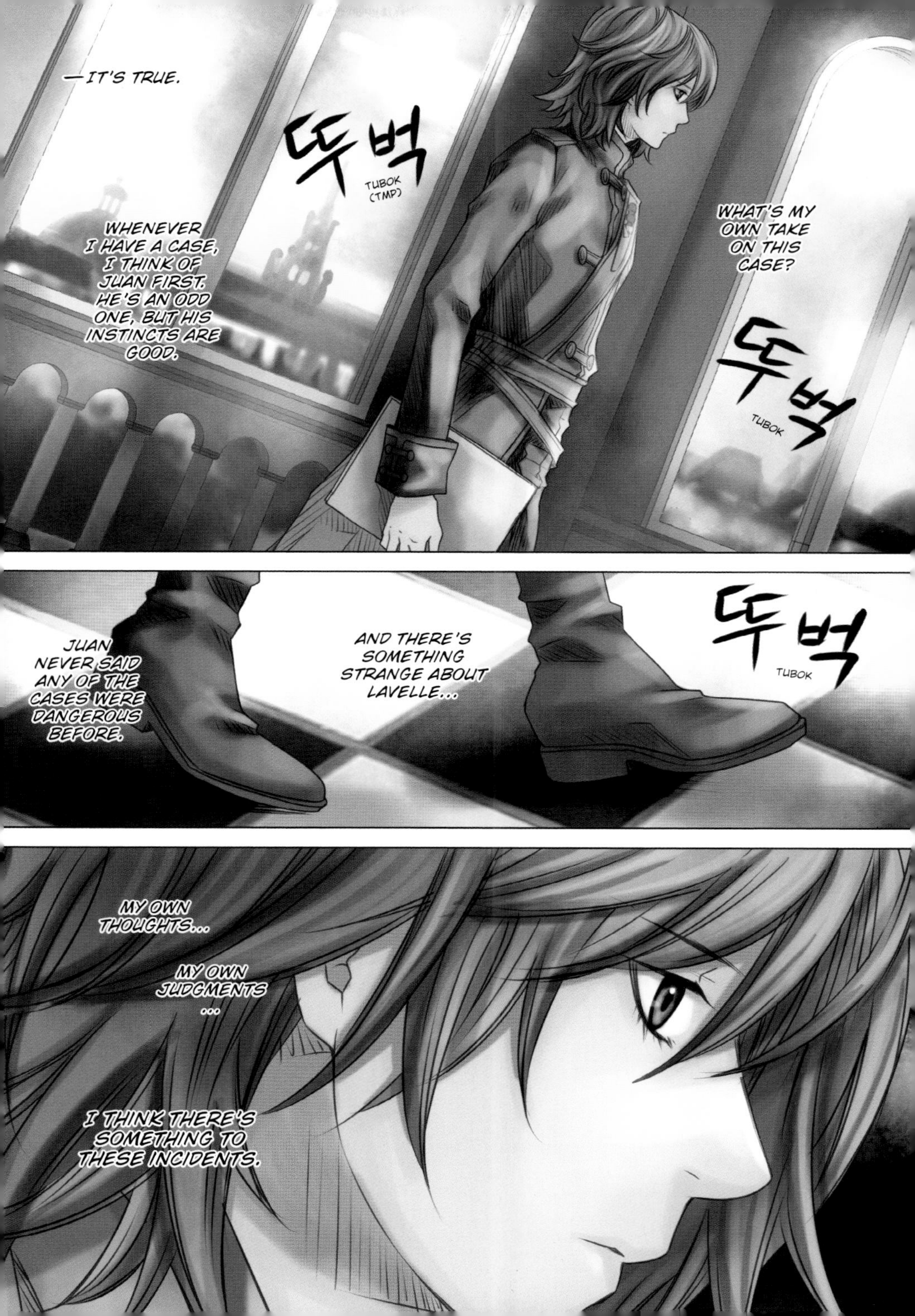
—IT'S TRUE.
뚜벅
TUBOK (TMP)
WHENEVER I HAVE A CASE, I THINK OF JUAN FIRST. HE'S AN ODD ONE, BUT HIS INSTINCTS ARE GOOD.
WHAT'S MY OWN TAKE ON THIS CASE?
뚜벅
TUBOK
JUAN NEVER SAID ANY OF THE CASES WERE DANGEROUS BEFORE.
AND THERE'S SOMETHING STRANGE ABOUT LAVELLE...
뚜벅
TUBOK
MY OWN THOUGHTS...
MY OWN JUDGMENTS...
I THINK THERE'S SOMETHING TO THESE INCIDENTS.

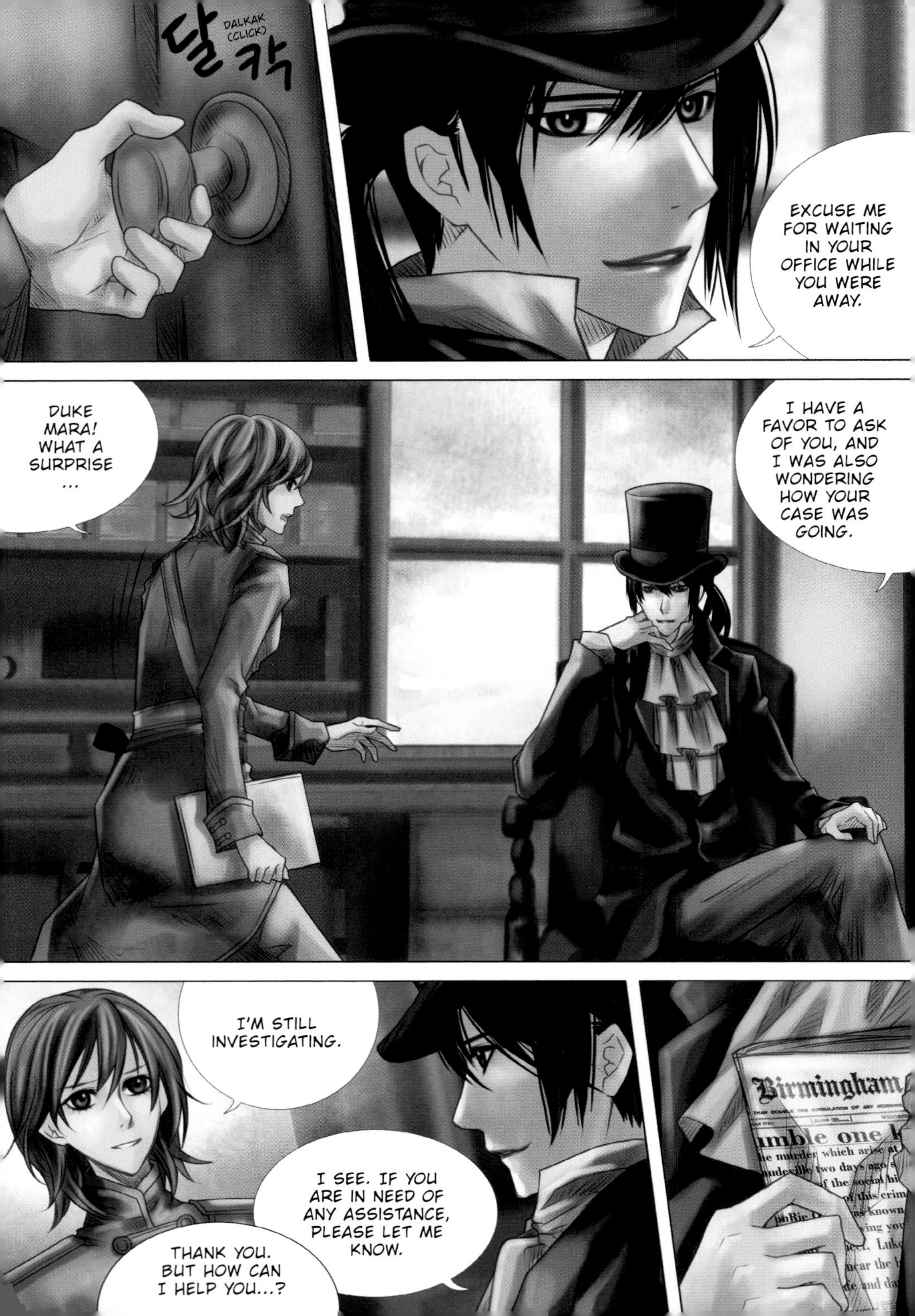

달칵
DALKAK (CLICK)
EXCUSE ME FOR WAITING IN YOUR OFFICE WHILE YOU WERE AWAY.
DUKE MARA! WHAT A SURPRISE ...
I HAVE A FAVOR TO ASK OF YOU, AND I WAS ALSO WONDERING HOW YOUR CASE WAS GOING.
I'M STILL INVESTIGATING.
I SEE. IF YOU ARE IN NEED OF ANY ASSISTANCE, PLEASE LET ME KNOW.
THANK YOU. BUT HOW CAN I HELP YOU...?
Birmingham

A LONG TIME AGO, AN ACQUAINTANCE PASSED AWAY UNDER UNFORTUNATE CIRCUMSTANCES. I'D BEEN TRYING TO FIND HIS REMAINING FAMILY MEMBERS.

I WANTED TO HELP HIS WIFE AND SON AFTER THE INCIDENT, BUT THEY'D DISAPPEARED.

HOWEVER, I'VE HEARD THAT THEY ARE HERE IN REDFORD RECENTLY.

gham Gazette

MORE THAN DOUBLE THE CIRCULATION OF ANY MORNING PAPER PRINTED IN THE MIDLANDS.

WEDNESDAY, 5 AUGUST, 1914.

"Gazette"
£1,000 Free
Insurance.

Humble one killed a noble

The murder which arise at the Vaudeville two days ago shows the collapse of the social hierarchy. The victim of this crime. Rie Ospil was know

I'LL LET YOU KNOW AS SOON AS I UNCOVER ANYTHING.

THANK YOU. SEE YOU, THEN.

I CAN'T BELIEVE SUCH A HIGH-RANKING ARISTOCRAT CAME TO PERSONALLY OFFER ME A NEW CASE?!

IT'S A GOOD OPPORTUNITY TO DISPLAY MY TALENTS TO THAT DAMNABLE GARR...

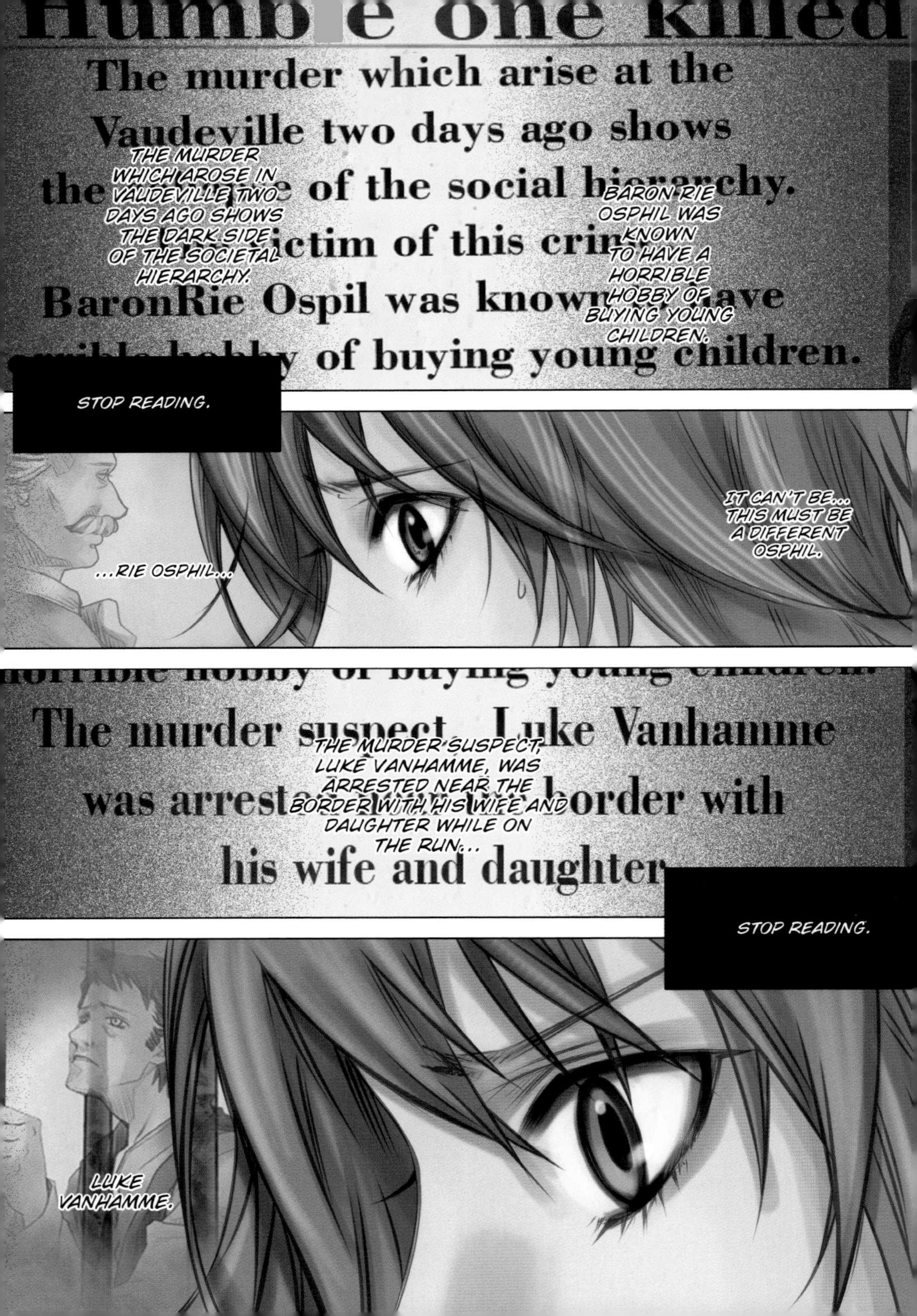
The murder which arise at the
Vaudeville two days ago shows
THE MURDER WHICH AROSE IN VAUDEVILLE TWO DAYS AGO SHOWS THE DARK SIDE OF THE SOCIETAL HIERARCHY.
BARON RIE OSPHIL WAS KNOWN TO HAVE A HORRIBLE HOBBY OF BUYING YOUNG CHILDREN.
STOP READING.
...RIE OSPHIL...
IT CAN'T BE... THIS MUST BE A DIFFERENT OSPHIL.
THE MURDER SUSPECT, LUKE VANHAMME, WAS ARRESTED NEAR THE BORDER WITH HIS WIFE AND DAUGHTER WHILE ON THE RUN...
STOP READING.
LUKE VANHAMME.

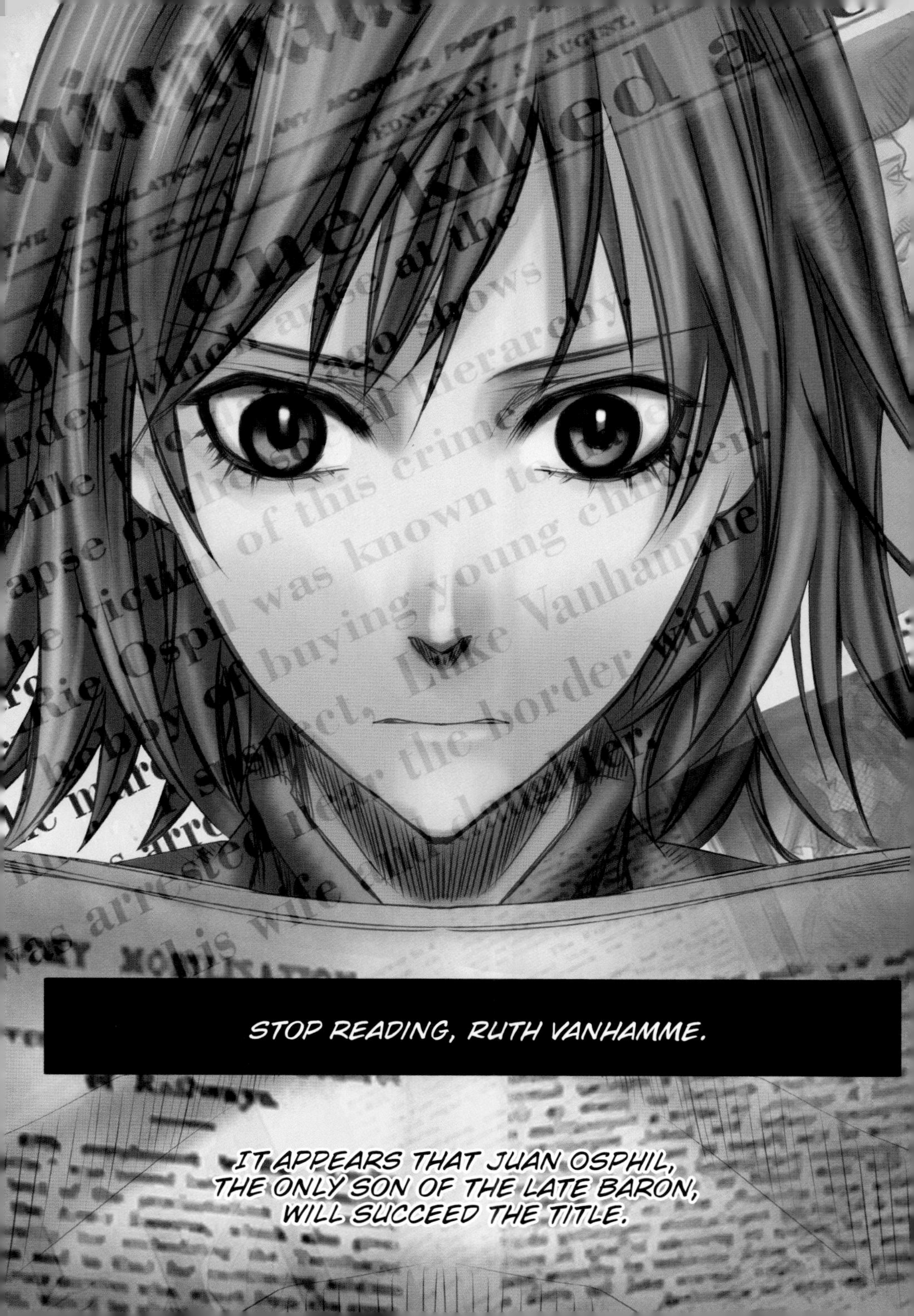
STOP READING, RUTH VANHAMME.
IT APPEARS THAT JUAN OSPHIL, THE ONLY SON OF THE LATE BARON, WILL SUCCEED THE TITLE.

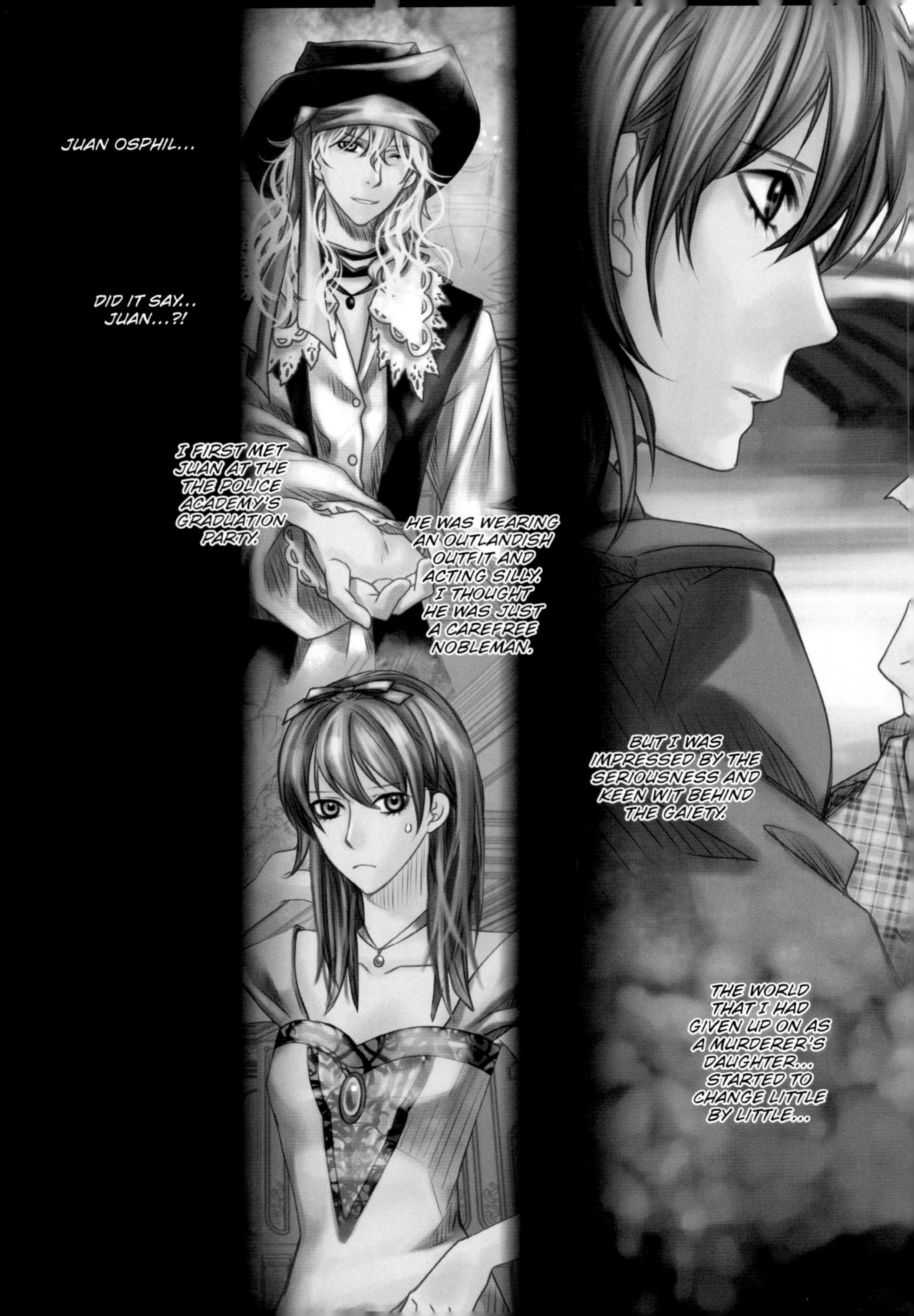
JUAN OSPHIL...
DID IT SAY... JUAN...?!
I FIRST MET JUAN AT THE THE POLICE ACADEMY'S GRADUATION PARTY.
HE WAS WEARING AN OUTLANDISH OUTFIT AND ACTING SILLY. I THOUGHT HE WAS JUST A CAREFREE NOBLEMAN.
BUT I WAS IMPRESSED BY THE SERIOUSNESS AND KEEN WIT BEHIND THE GAIETY.
THE WORLD THAT I HAD GIVEN UP ON AS A MURDERER'S DAUGHTER... STARTED TO CHANGE LITTLE BY LITTLE...

BUT...

BUT...

...I'M THE DAUGHTER OF HIS FATHER'S KILLER—?!

THAT CAN'T BE TRUE.

...ALL BECAUSE HE TRUSTED ME AND LOOKED OUT FOR ME.

NO!!

IF THIS IS TRUE—

TAK
(GRAB)

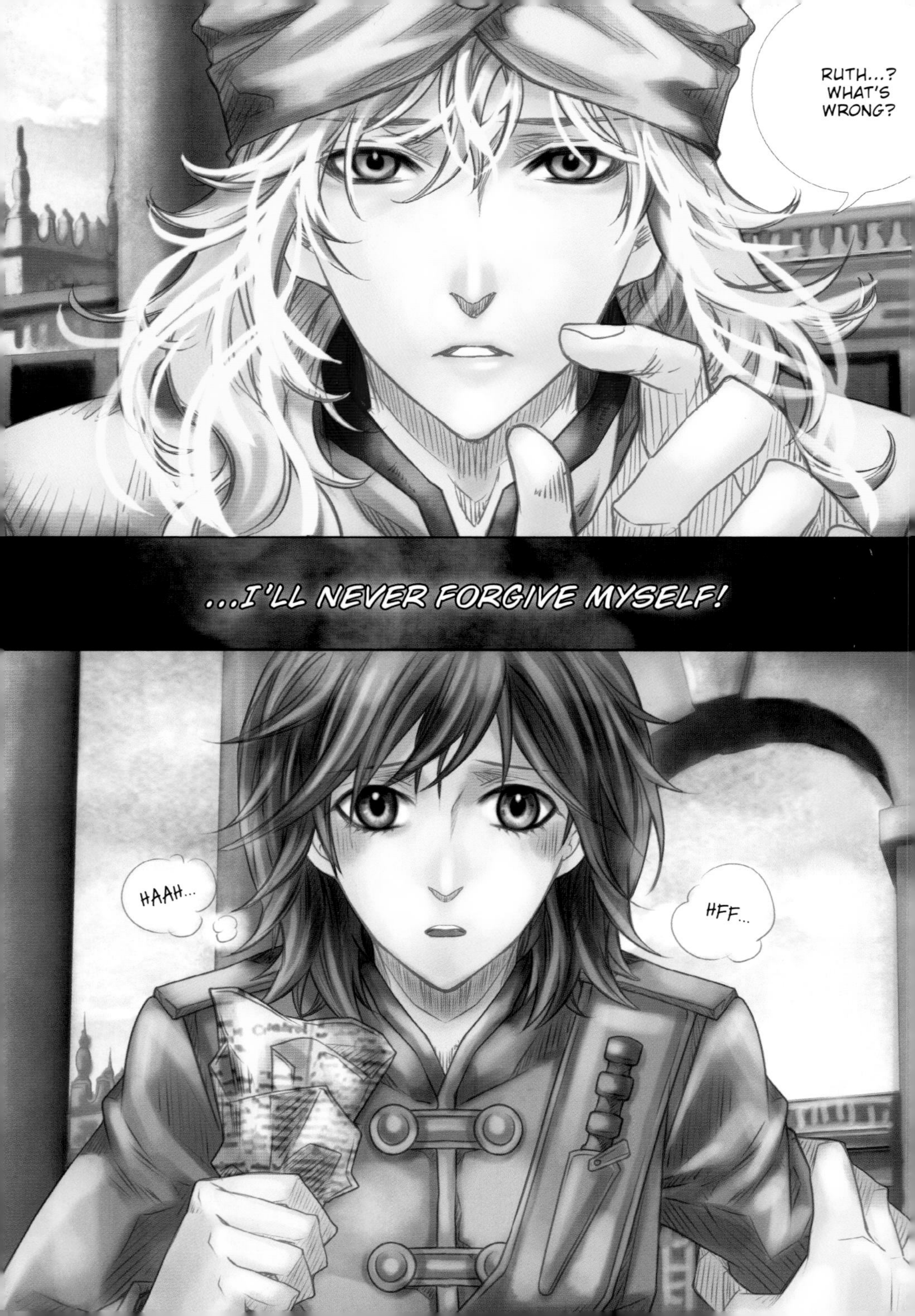
RUTH...? WHAT'S WRONG?
...I'LL NEVER FORGIVE MYSELF!
HAAH...
HFF...

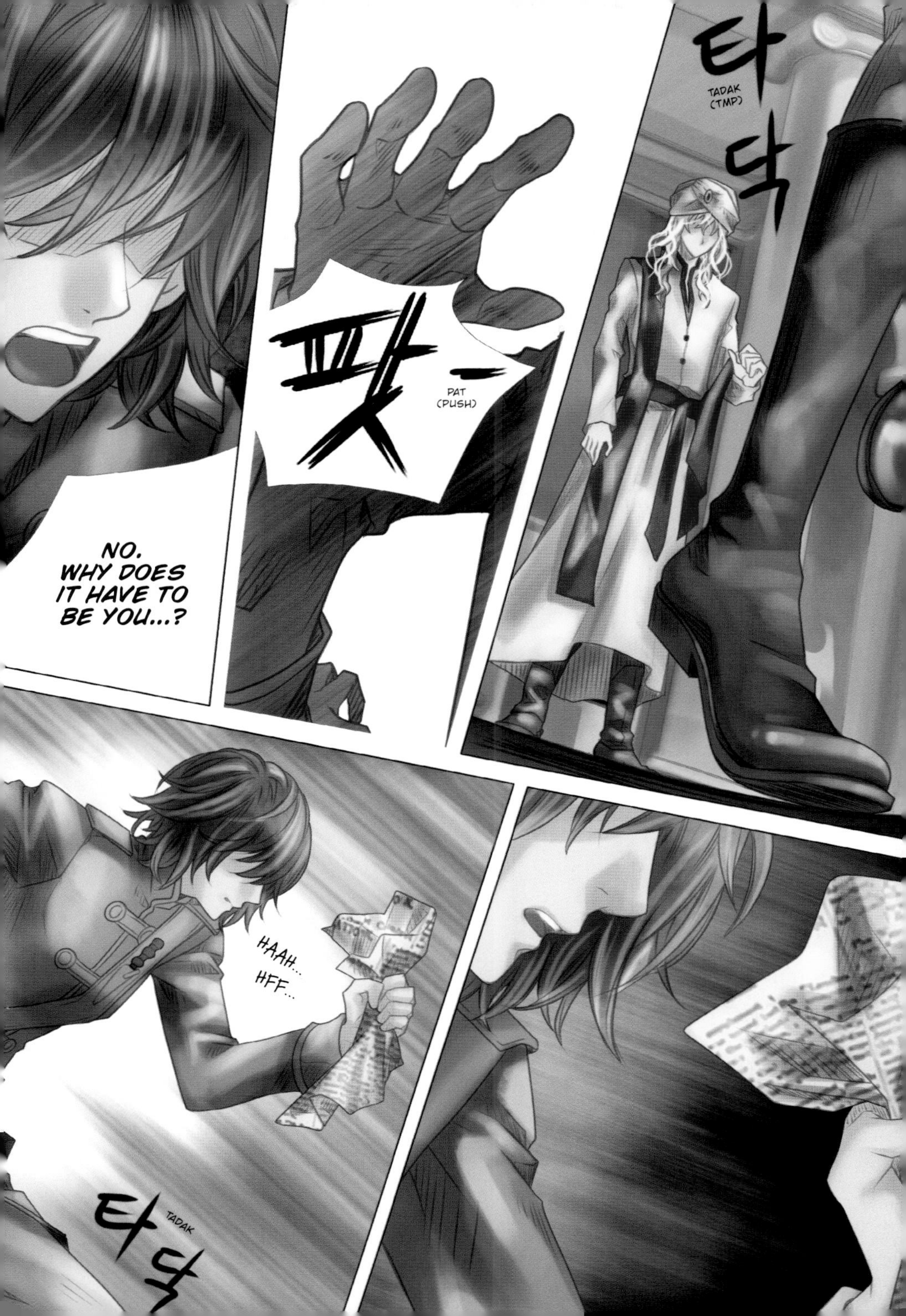
NO. WHY DOES IT HAVE TO BE YOU...?
팟
PAT (PUSH)
타닥
TADAK (TMP)
HAAH... HFF...
타닥
TADAK

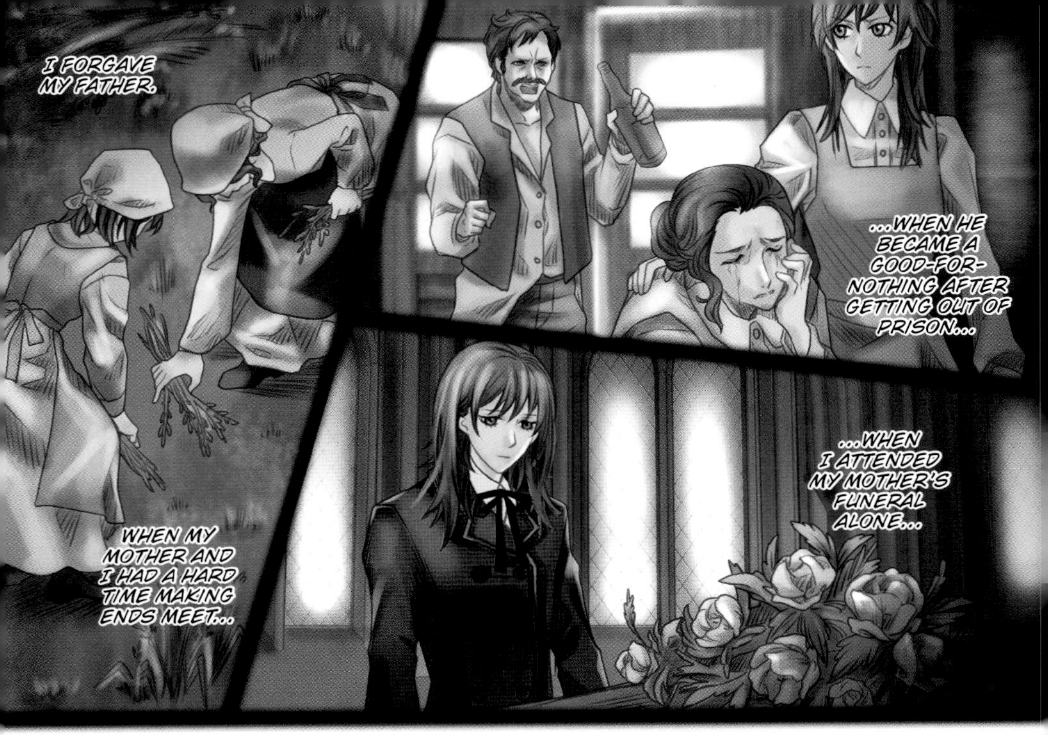
I FORGAVE MY FATHER.
WHEN MY MOTHER AND I HAD A HARD TIME MAKING ENDS MEET...
...WHEN HE BECAME A GOOD-FOR-NOTHING AFTER GETTING OUT OF PRISON...
...WHEN I ATTENDED MY MOTHER'S FUNERAL ALONE...
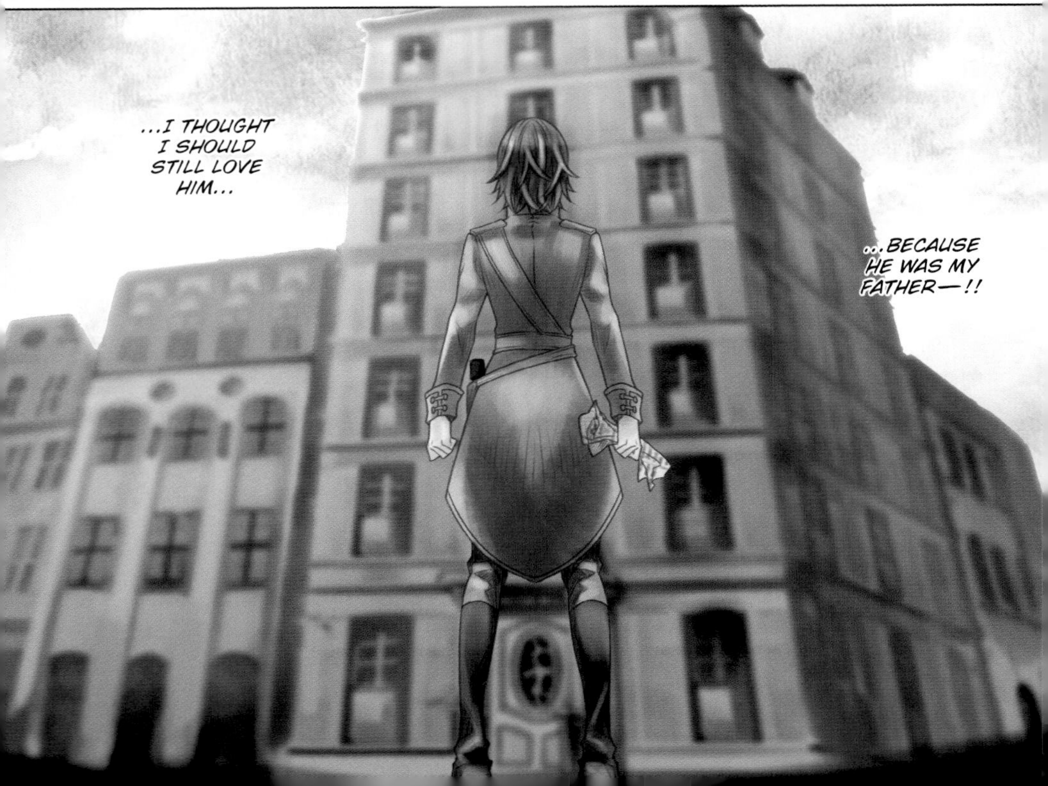
...I THOUGHT I SHOULD STILL LOVE HIM...
...BECAUSE HE WAS MY FATHER—!!

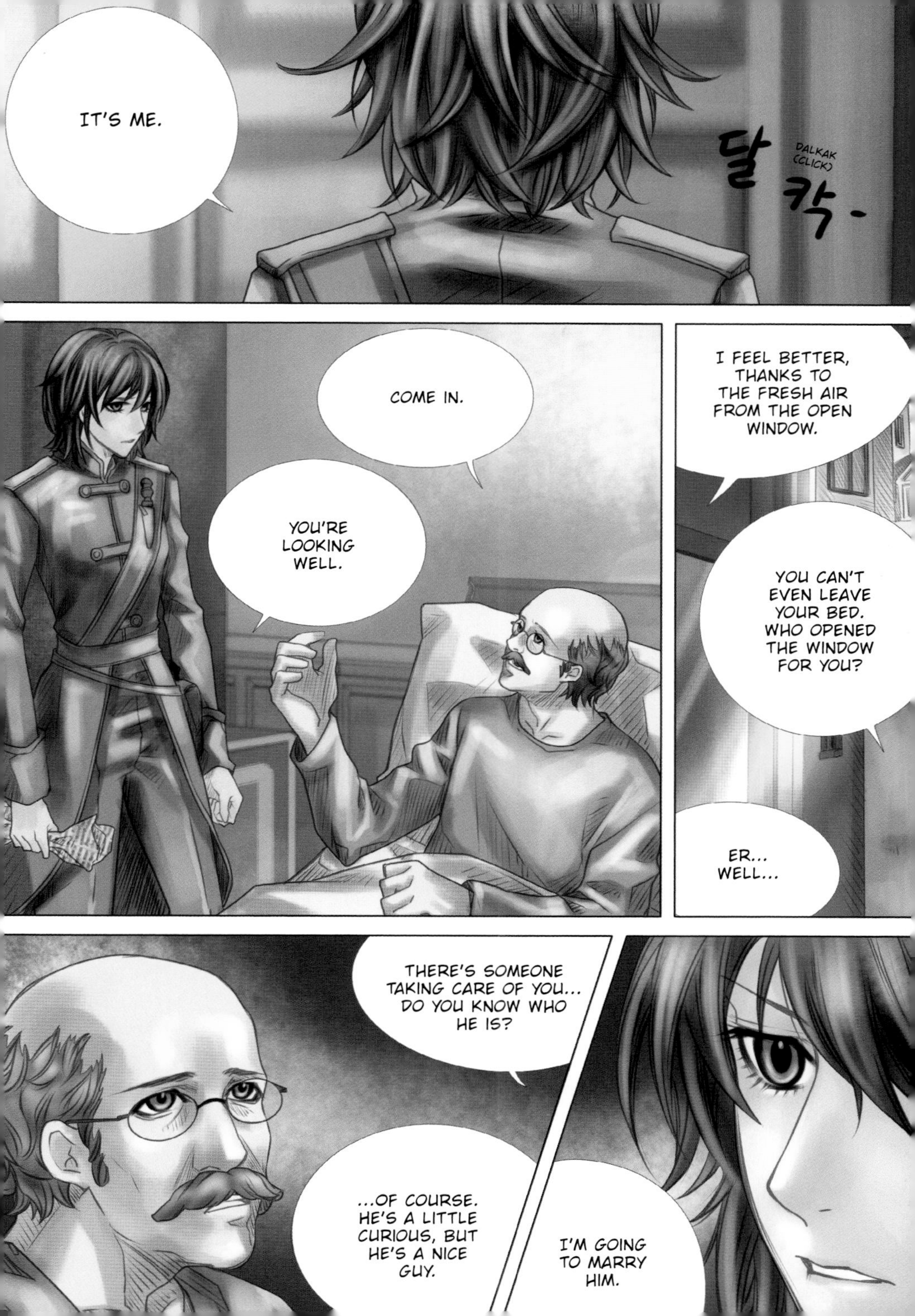
IT'S ME.
달 칵-
DALKAK (CLICK)
COME IN.
YOU'RE LOOKING WELL.
I FEEL BETTER, THANKS TO THE FRESH AIR FROM THE OPEN WINDOW.
YOU CAN'T EVEN LEAVE YOUR BED. WHO OPENED THE WINDOW FOR YOU?
ER... WELL...
THERE'S SOMEONE TAKING CARE OF YOU... DO YOU KNOW WHO HE IS?
...OF COURSE. HE'S A LITTLE CURIOUS, BUT HE'S A NICE GUY.
I'M GOING TO MARRY HIM.

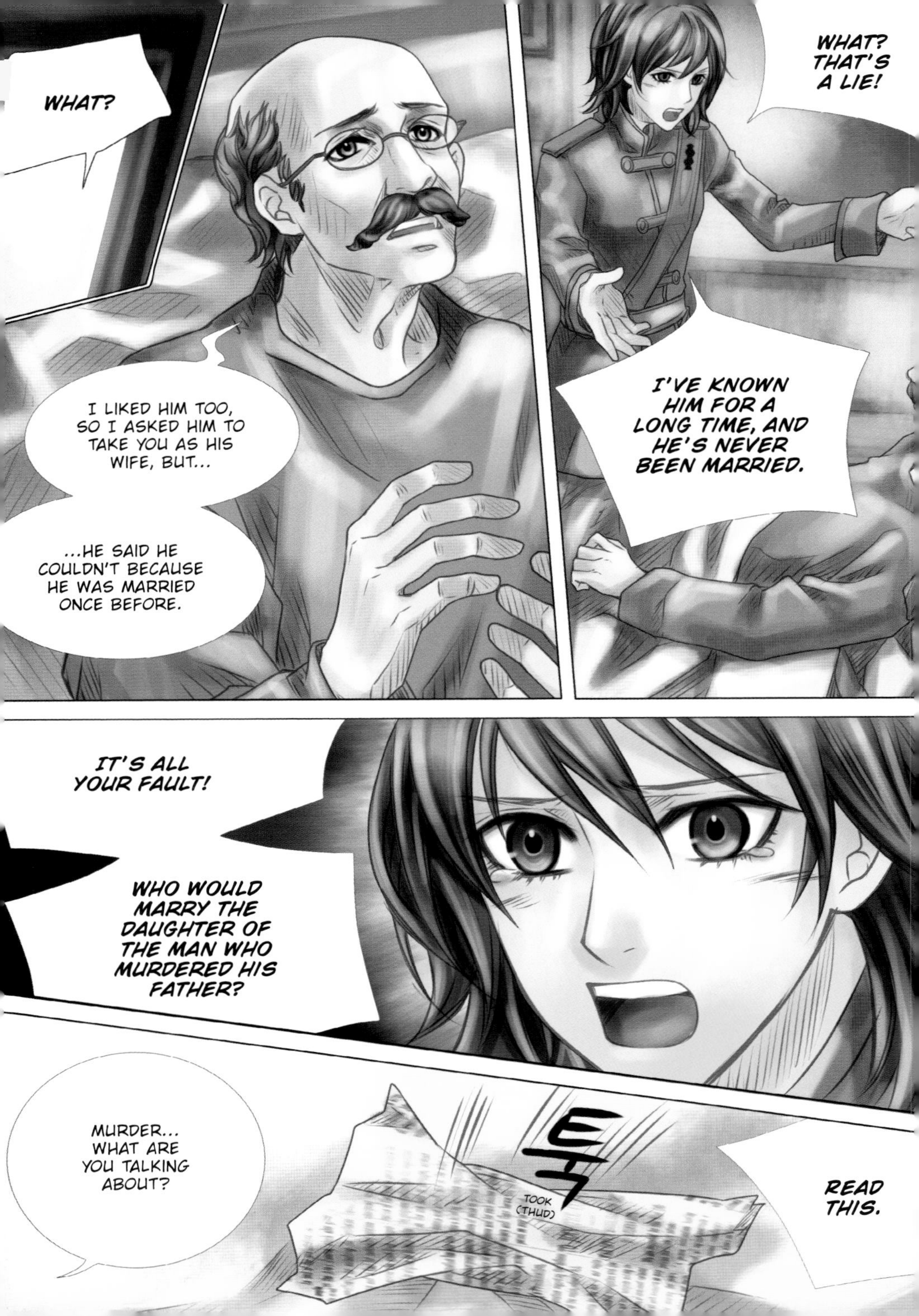
WHAT?
I LIKED HIM TOO, SO I ASKED HIM TO TAKE YOU AS HIS WIFE, BUT...
...HE SAID HE COULDN'T BECAUSE HE WAS MARRIED ONCE BEFORE.
WHAT? THAT'S A LIE!
I'VE KNOWN HIM FOR A LONG TIME, AND HE'S NEVER BEEN MARRIED.
IT'S ALL YOUR FAULT!
WHO WOULD MARRY THE DAUGHTER OF THE MAN WHO MURDERED HIS FATHER?
MURDER... WHAT ARE YOU TALKING ABOUT?
툭
TOOK (THUD)
READ THIS.

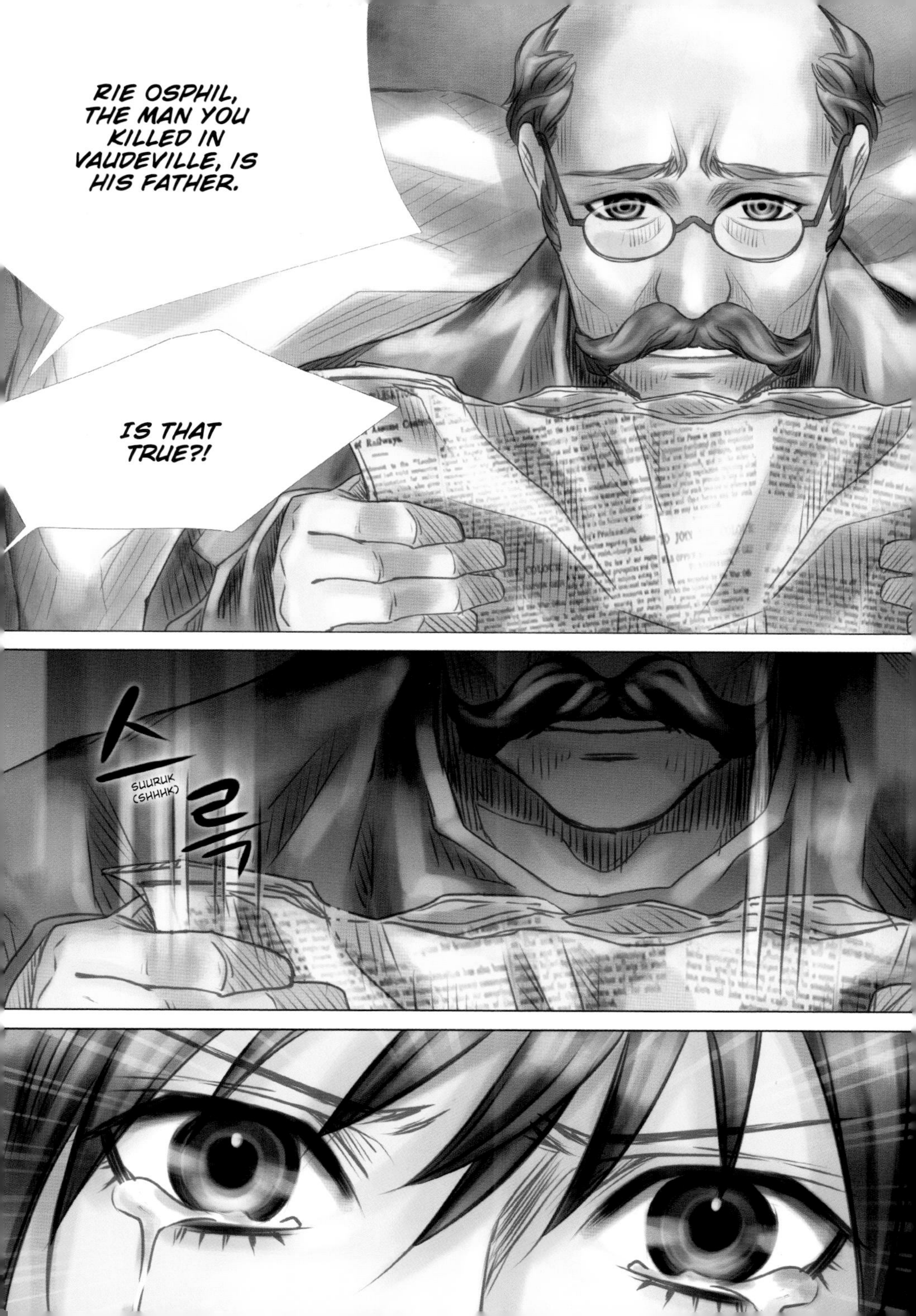
RIE OSPHIL, THE MAN YOU KILLED IN VAUDEVILLE, IS HIS FATHER.
IS THAT TRUE?!
SUURUK (SHHHK)

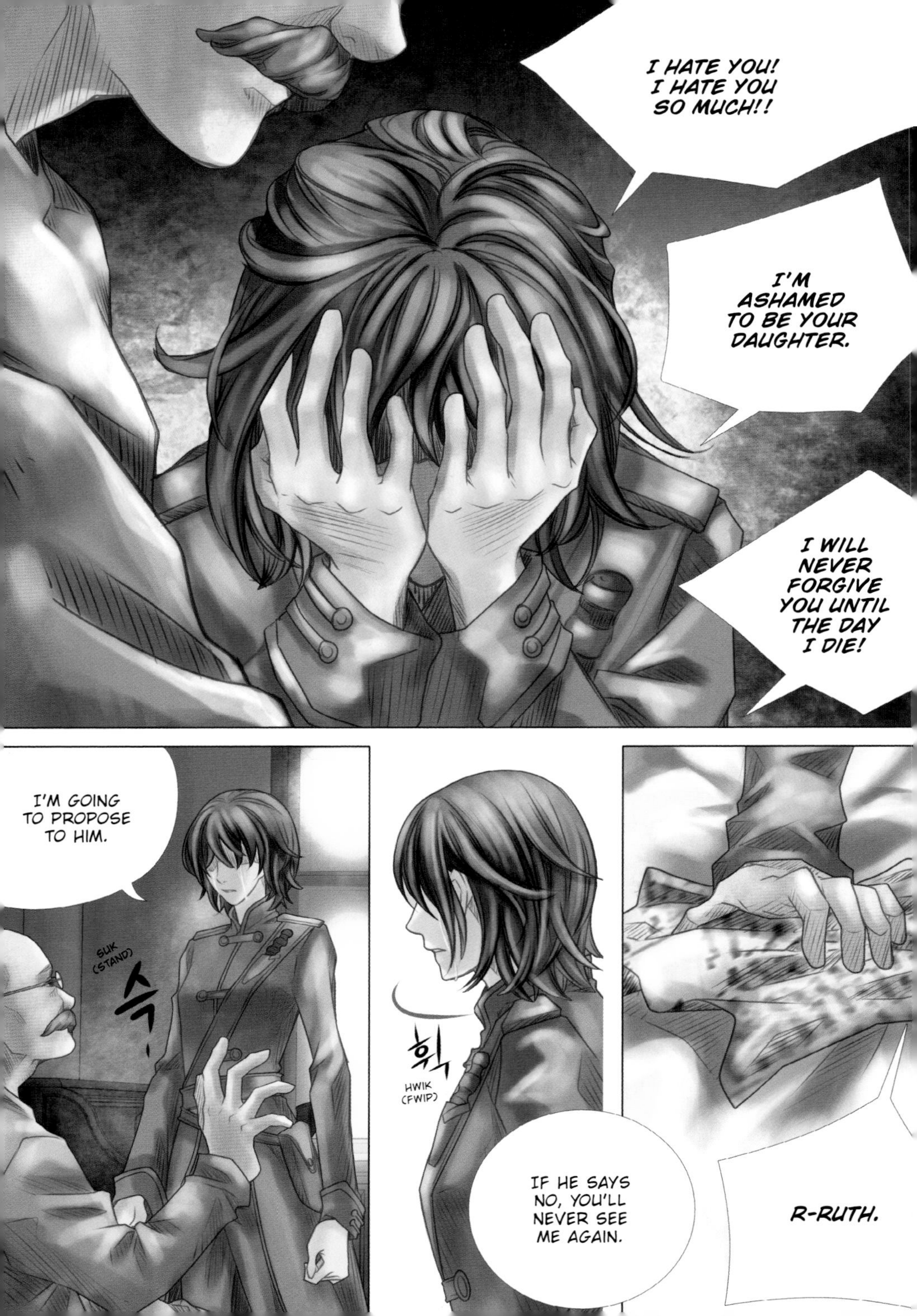
I HATE YOU! I HATE YOU SO MUCH!!
I'M ASHAMED TO BE YOUR DAUGHTER.
I WILL NEVER FORGIVE YOU UNTIL THE DAY I DIE!
I'M GOING TO PROPOSE TO HIM.
SUK (STAND)
스
HWIK (FWIP)
휙
IF HE SAYS NO, YOU'LL NEVER SEE ME AGAIN.
R-RUTH.

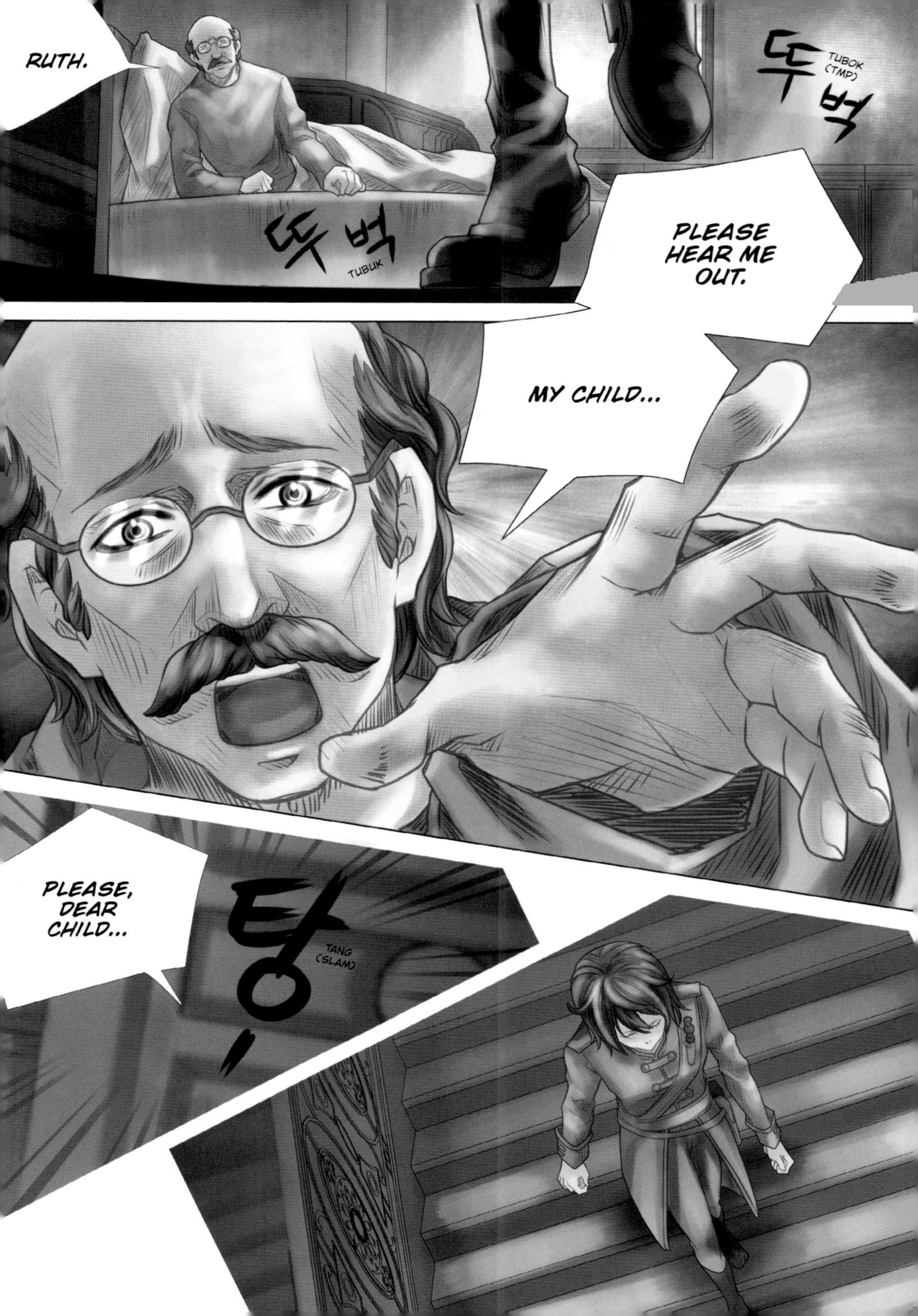
RUTH.
뚜벅
TUBOK (TMP)
뚜벅
TUBUK
PLEASE HEAR ME OUT.
MY CHILD...
PLEASE, DEAR CHILD...
탕!
TANG (SLAM)

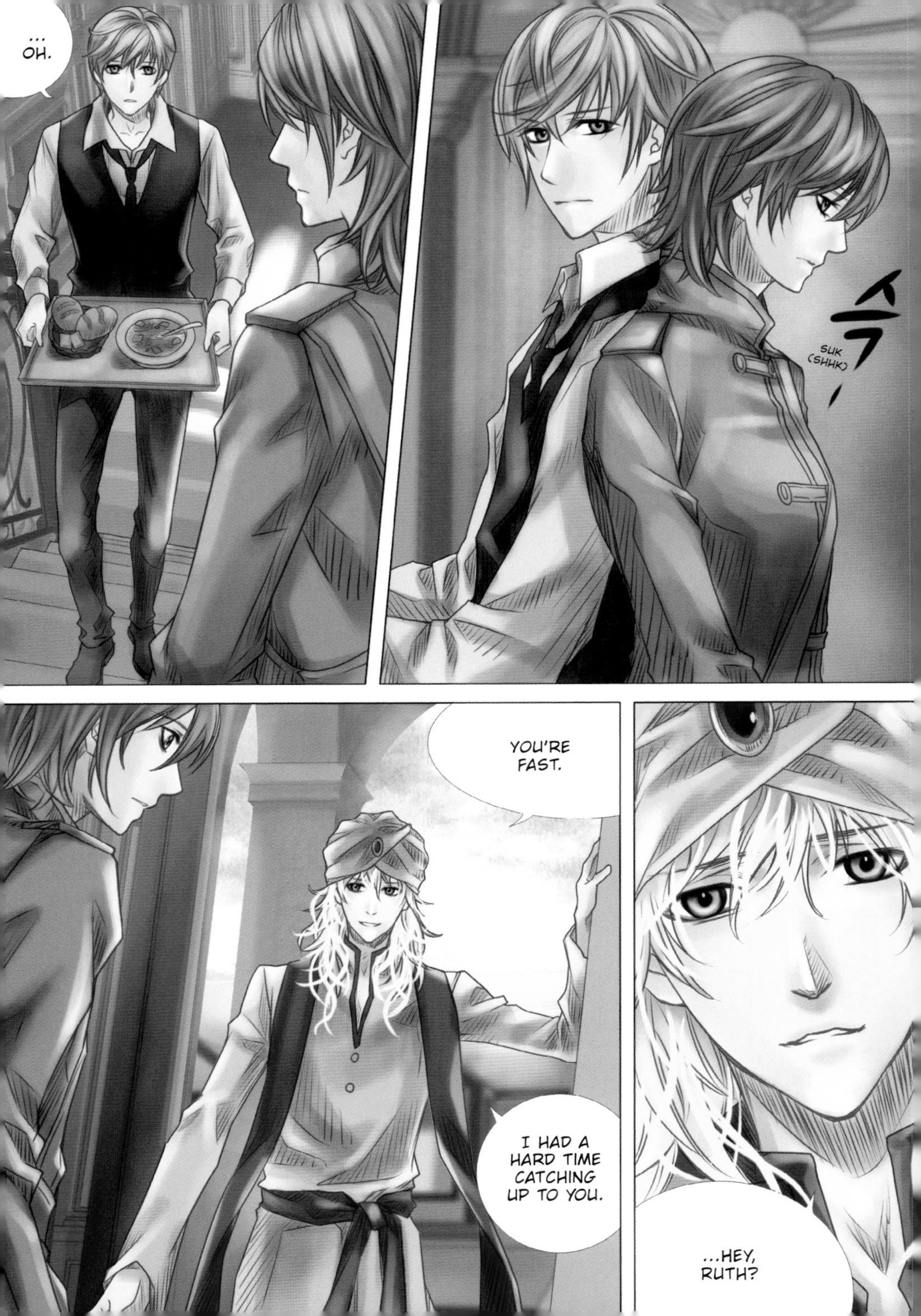
...OH.
SUK (SHHK)
YOU'RE FAST.
I HAD A HARD TIME CATCHING UP TO YOU.
...HEY, RUTH?

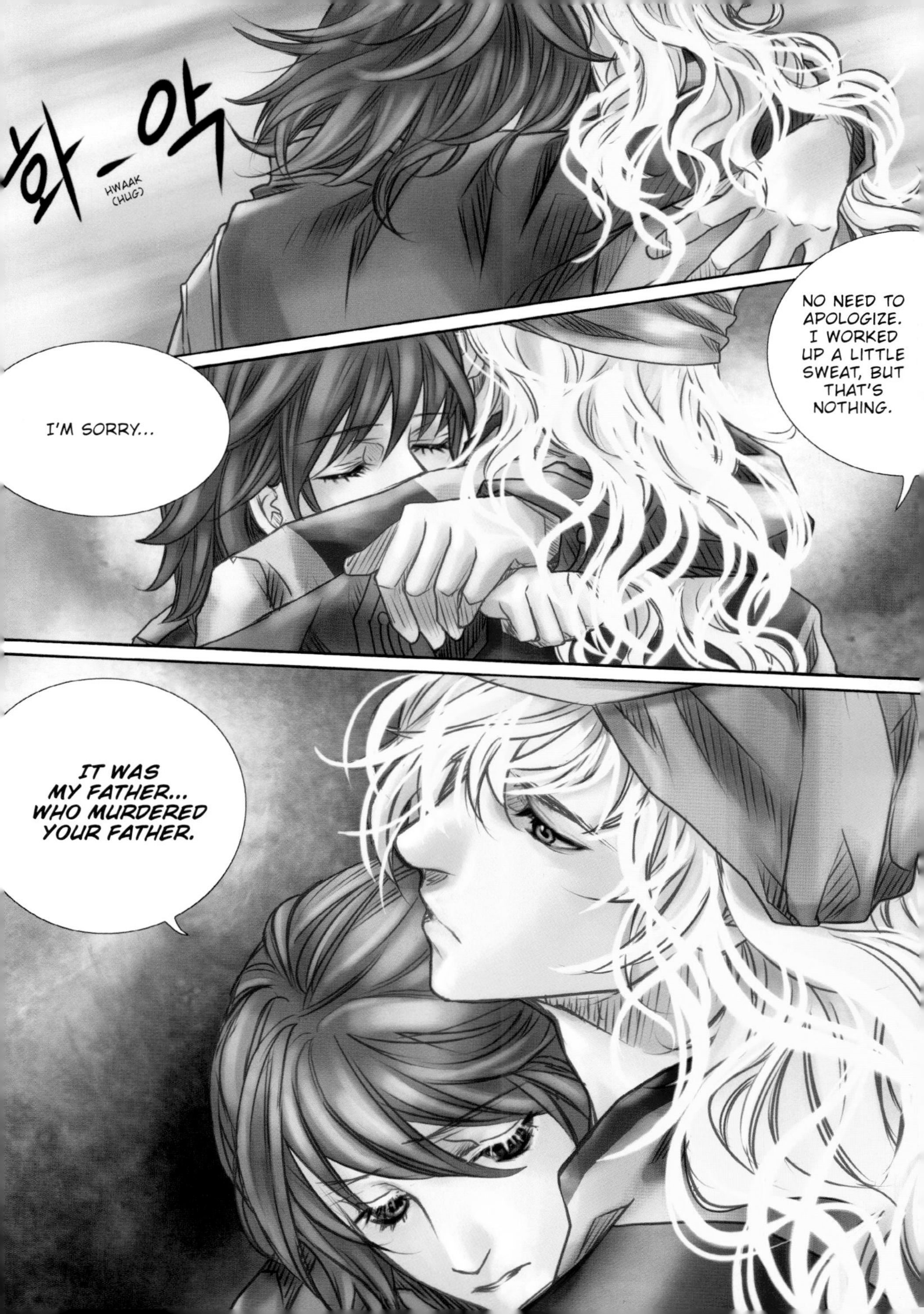
화-악
HWAAK (HUG)
I'M SORRY...
NO NEED TO APOLOGIZE. I WORKED UP A LITTLE SWEAT, BUT THAT'S NOTHING.
IT WAS MY FATHER... WHO MURDERED YOUR FATHER.

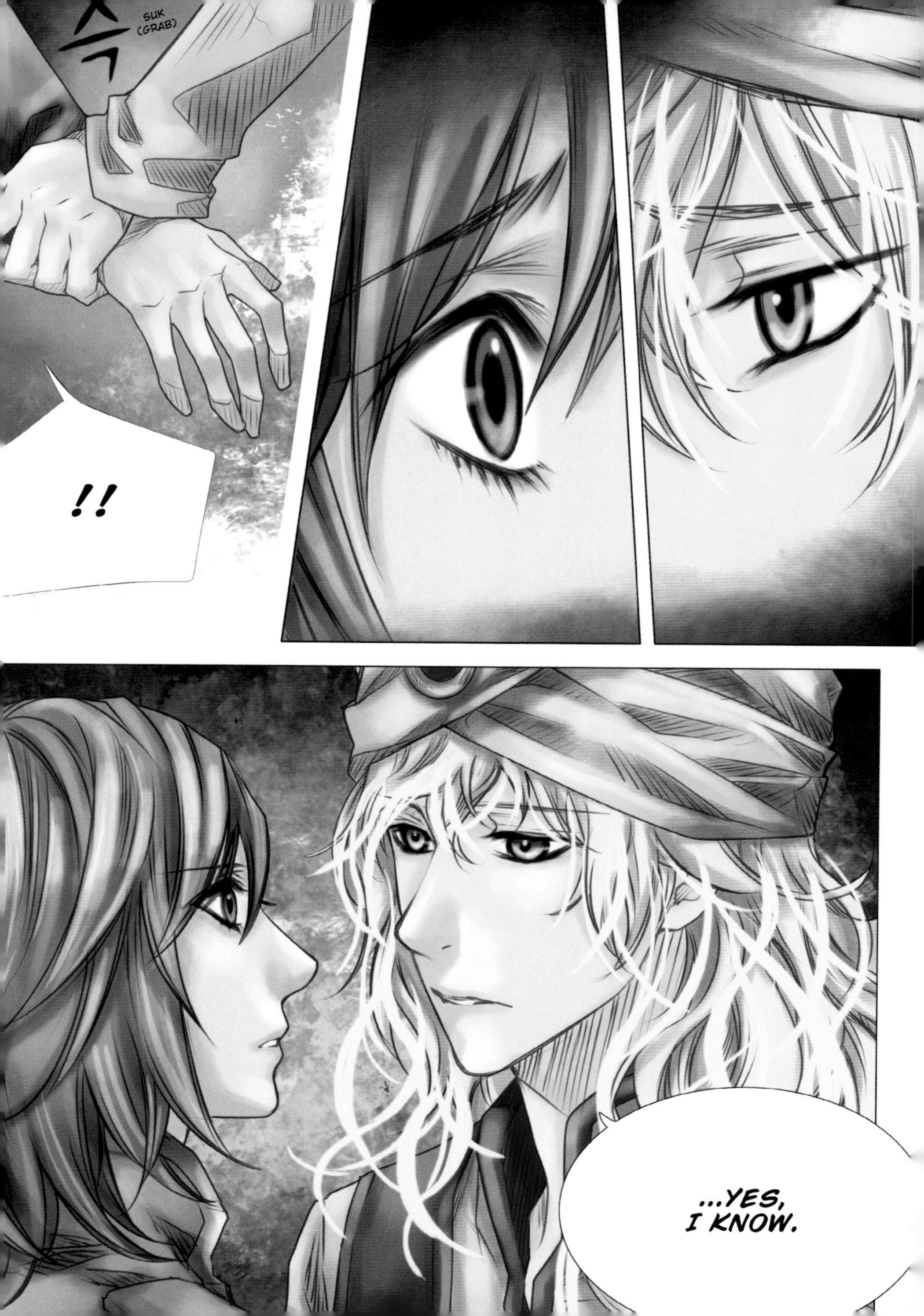
SUK (GRAB)
!!
...YES, I KNOW.

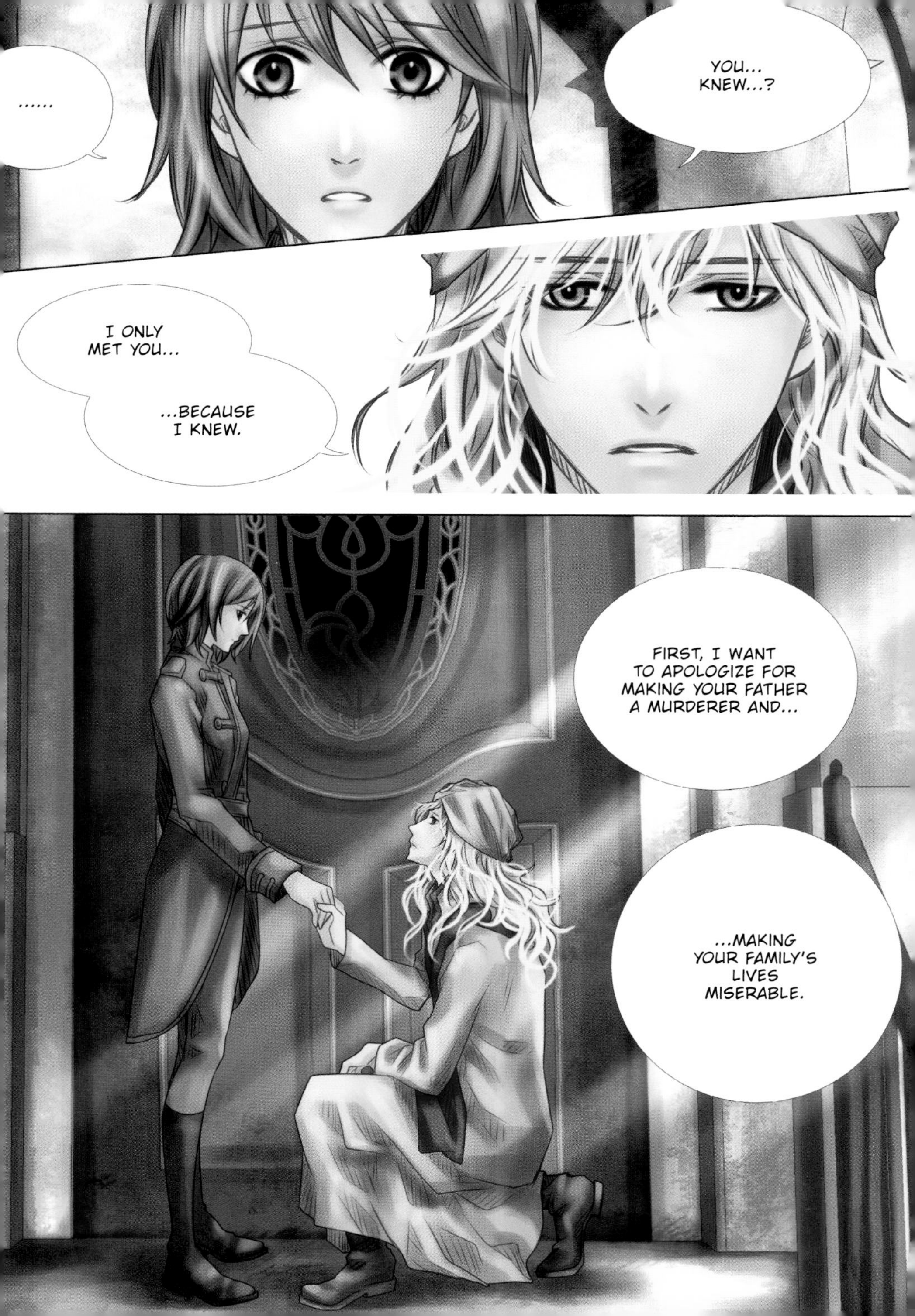
......
YOU... KNEW...?
I ONLY MET YOU...
...BECAUSE I KNEW.
FIRST, I WANT TO APOLOGIZE FOR MAKING YOUR FATHER A MURDERER AND...
...MAKING YOUR FAMILY'S LIVES MISERABLE.

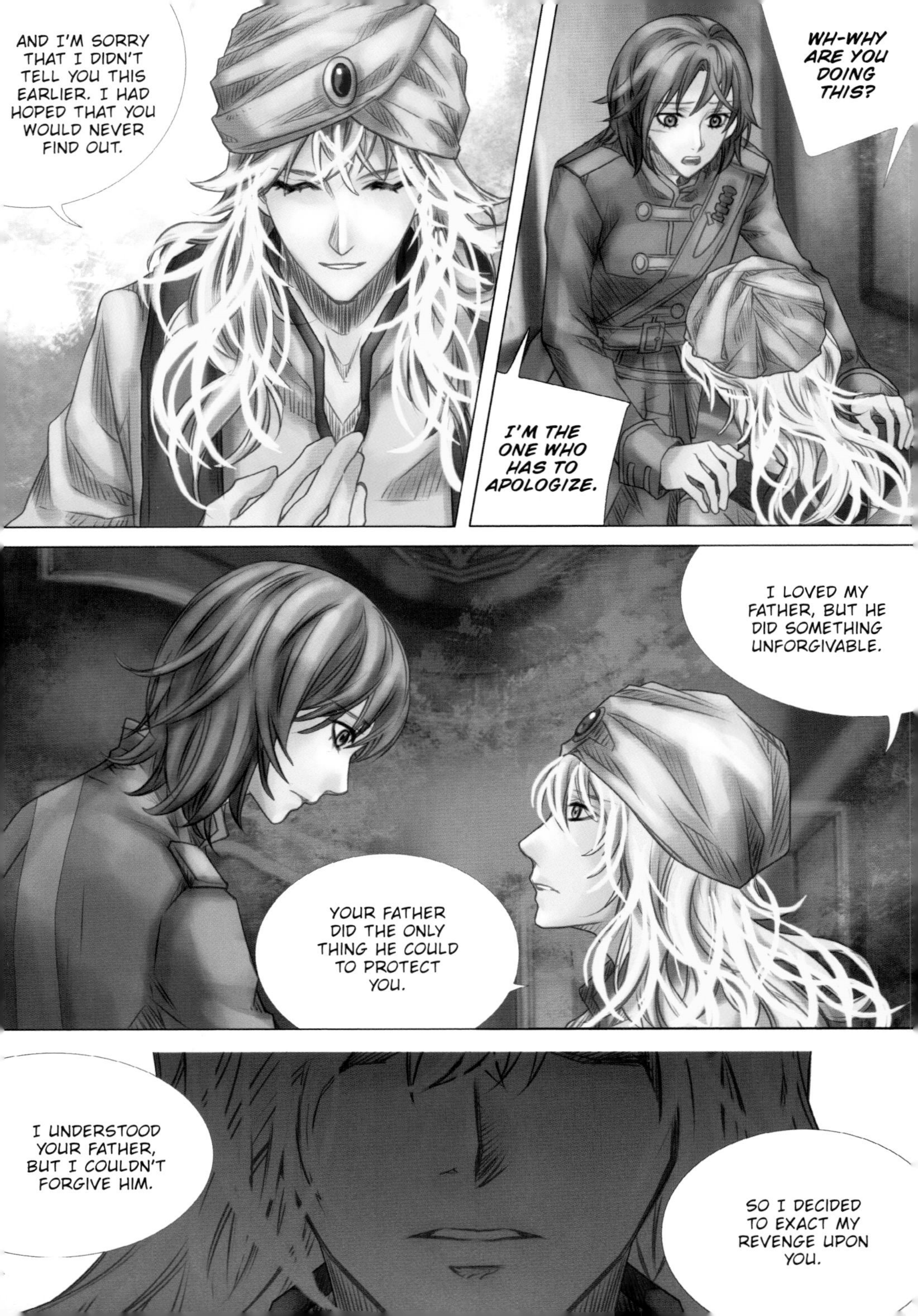
AND I'M SORRY THAT I DIDN'T TELL YOU THIS EARLIER. I HAD HOPED THAT YOU WOULD NEVER FIND OUT.
WH-WHY ARE YOU DOING THIS?
I'M THE ONE WHO HAS TO APOLOGIZE.
I LOVED MY FATHER, BUT HE DID SOMETHING UNFORGIVABLE.
YOUR FATHER DID THE ONLY THING HE COULD TO PROTECT YOU.
I UNDERSTOOD YOUR FATHER, BUT I COULDN'T FORGIVE HIM.
SO I DECIDED TO EXACT MY REVENGE UPON YOU.

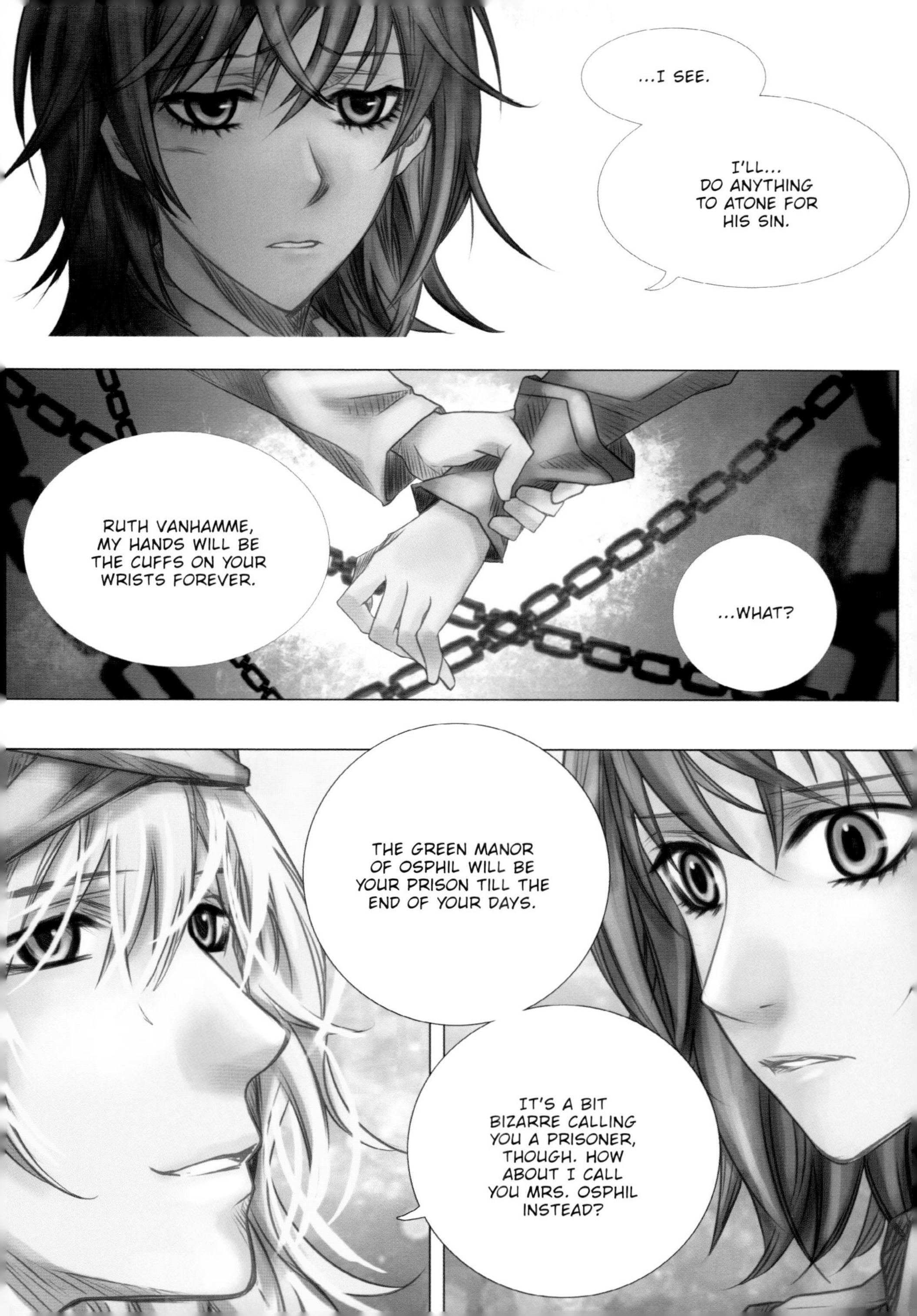
...I SEE.
I'LL... DO ANYTHING TO ATONE FOR HIS SIN.
RUTH VANHAMME, MY HANDS WILL BE THE CUFFS ON YOUR WRISTS FOREVER.
...WHAT?
THE GREEN MANOR OF OSPHIL WILL BE YOUR PRISON TILL THE END OF YOUR DAYS.
IT'S A BIT BIZARRE CALLING YOU A PRISONER, THOUGH. HOW ABOUT I CALL YOU MRS. OSPHIL INSTEAD?

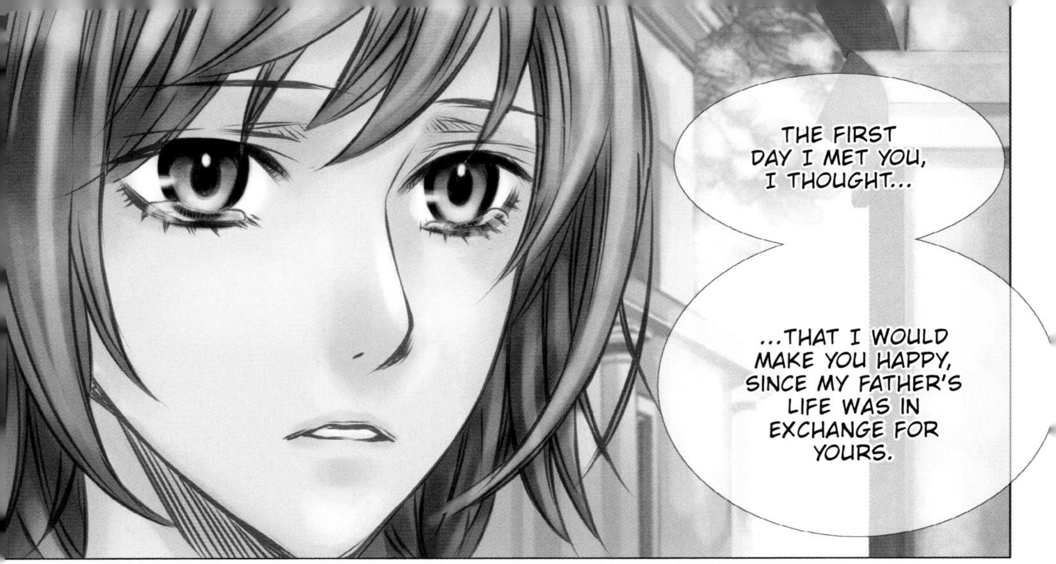
THE FIRST DAY I MET YOU, I THOUGHT...
...THAT I WOULD MAKE YOU HAPPY, SINCE MY FATHER'S LIFE WAS IN EXCHANGE FOR YOURS.
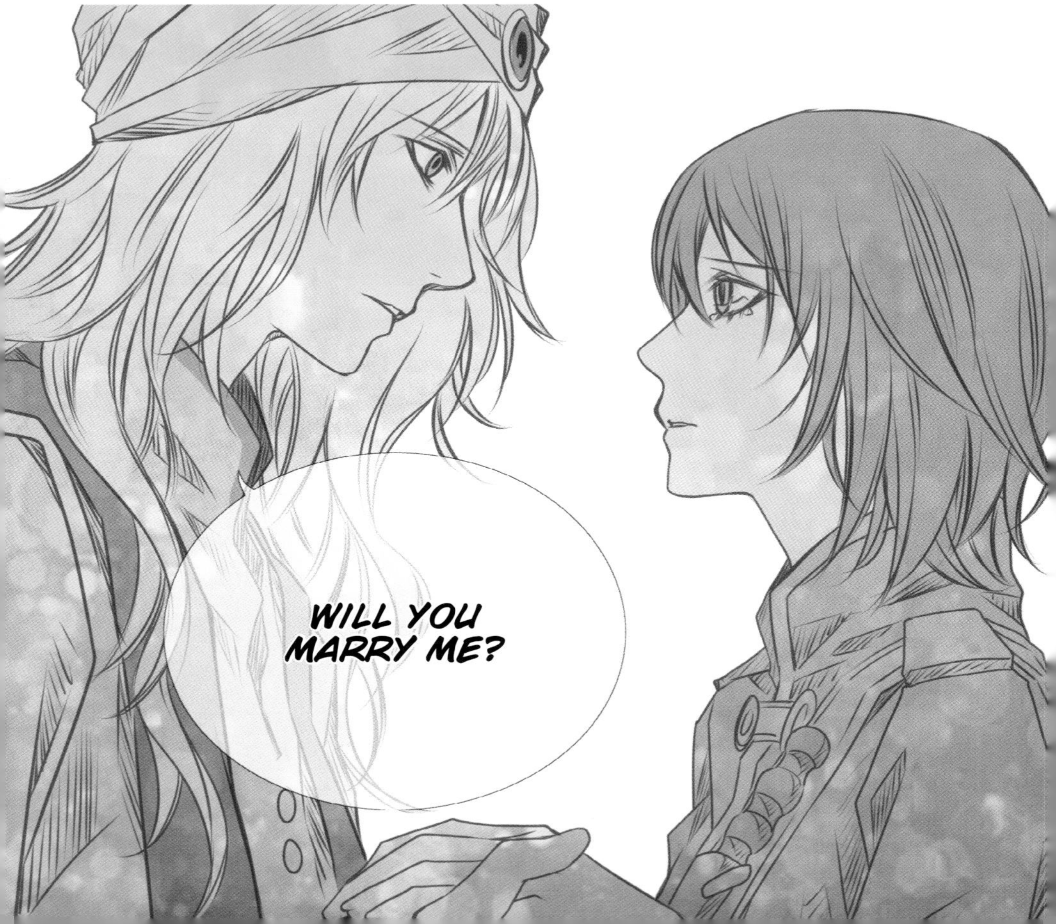
WILL YOU MARRY ME?

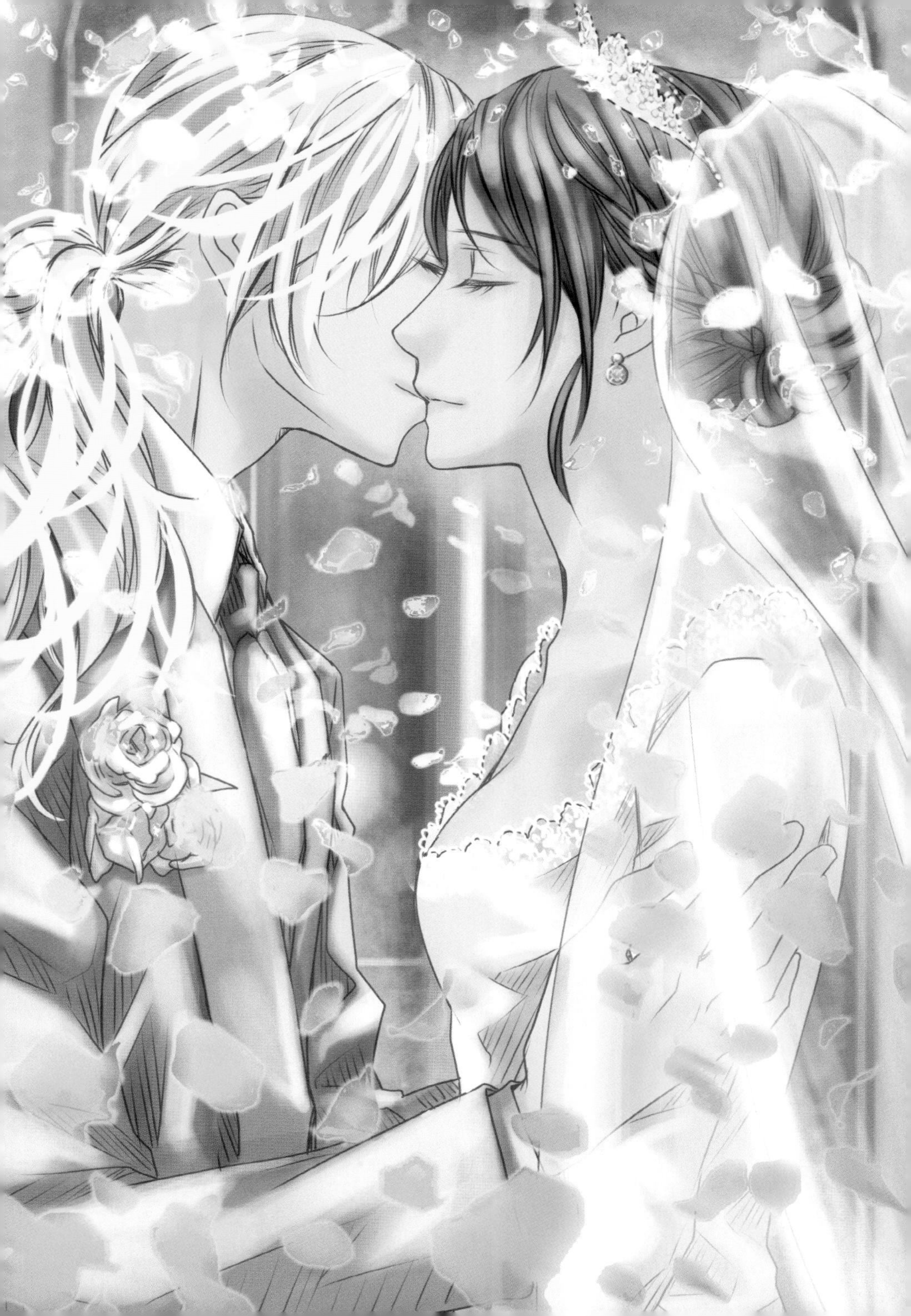

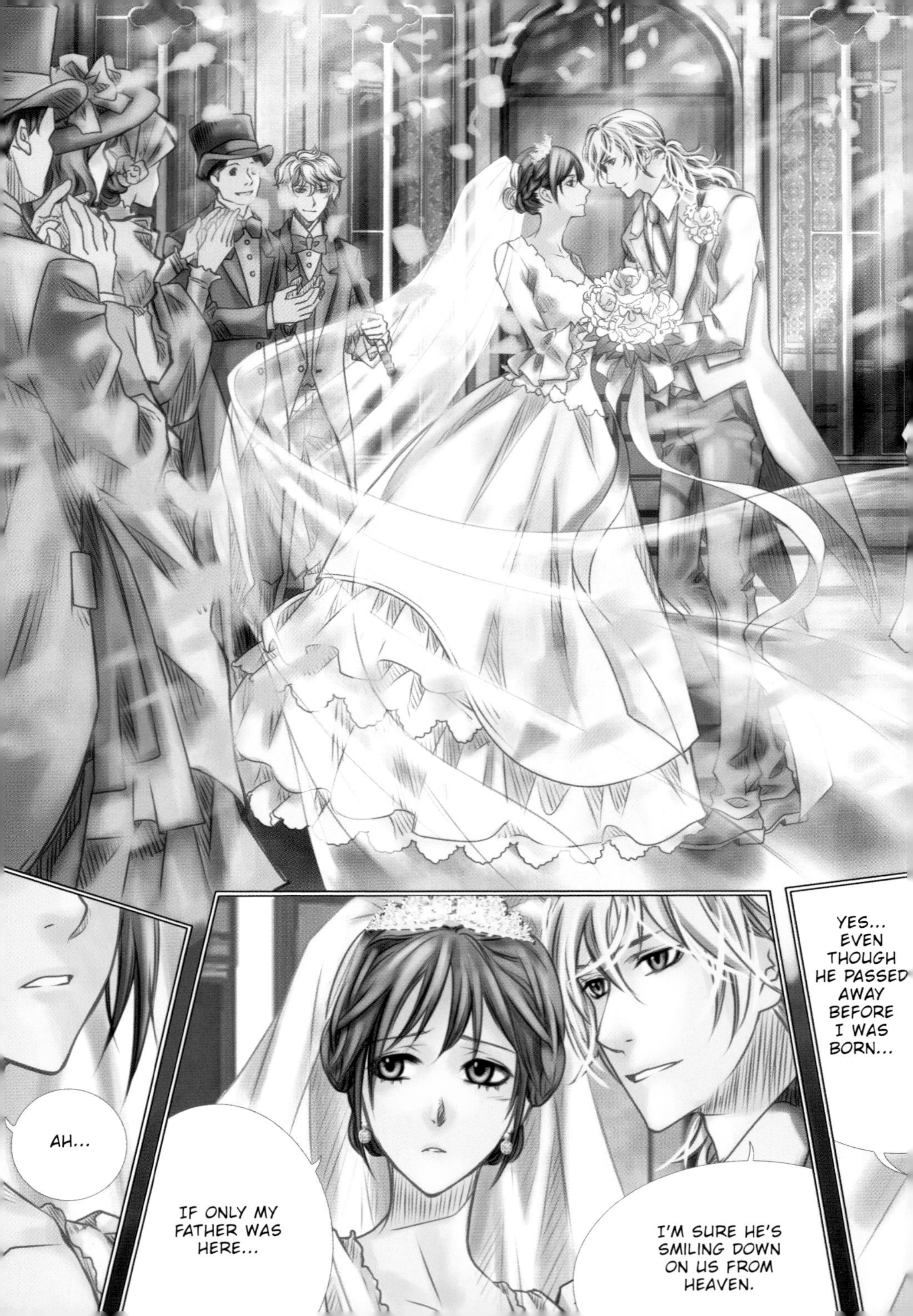
AH...
IF ONLY MY FATHER WAS HERE...
I'M SURE HE'S SMILING DOWN ON US FROM HEAVEN.
YES... EVEN THOUGH HE PASSED AWAY BEFORE I WAS BORN...

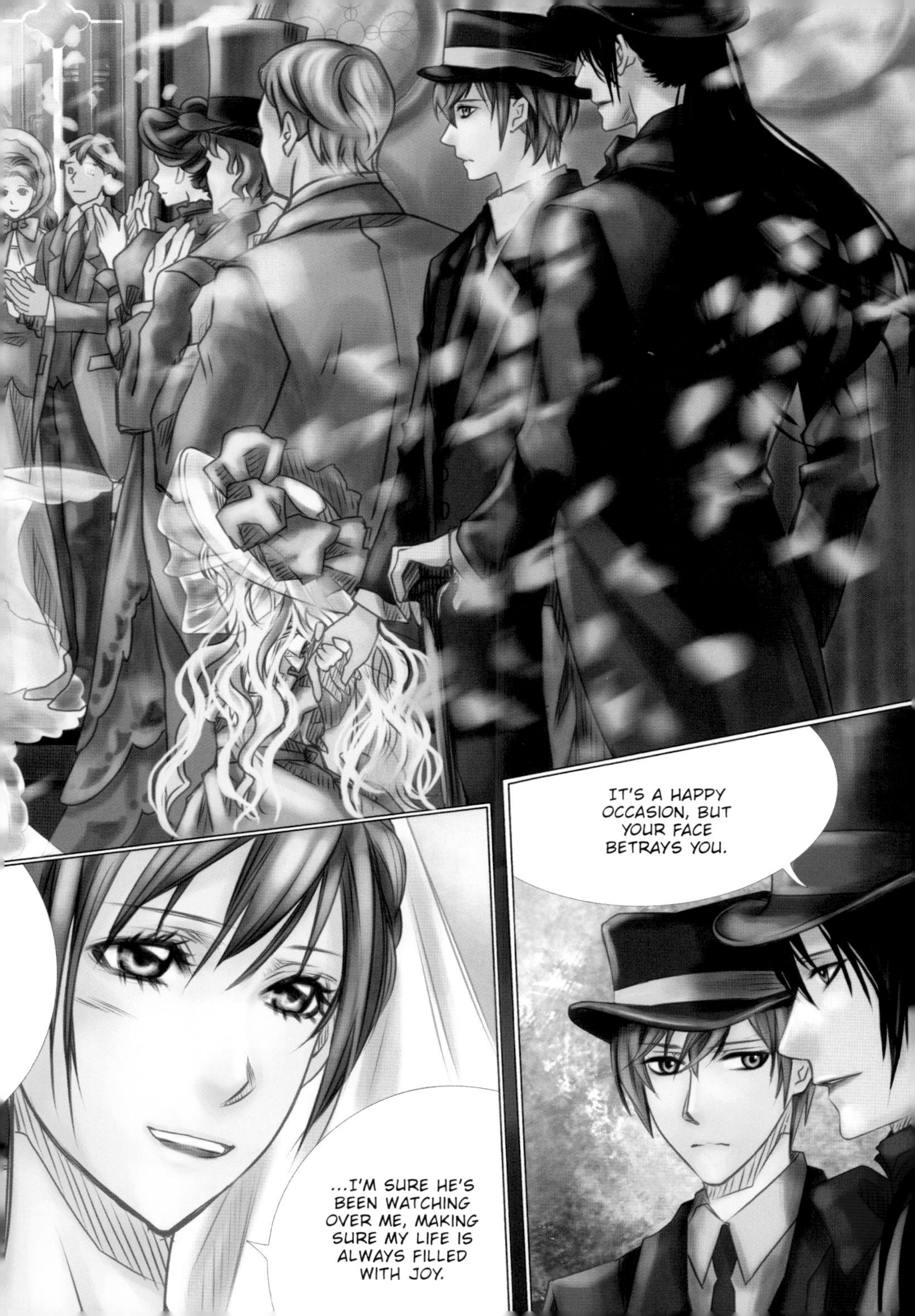
...I'M SURE HE'S BEEN WATCHING OVER ME, MAKING SURE MY LIFE IS ALWAYS FILLED WITH JOY.
IT'S A HAPPY OCCASION, BUT YOUR FACE BETRAYS YOU.

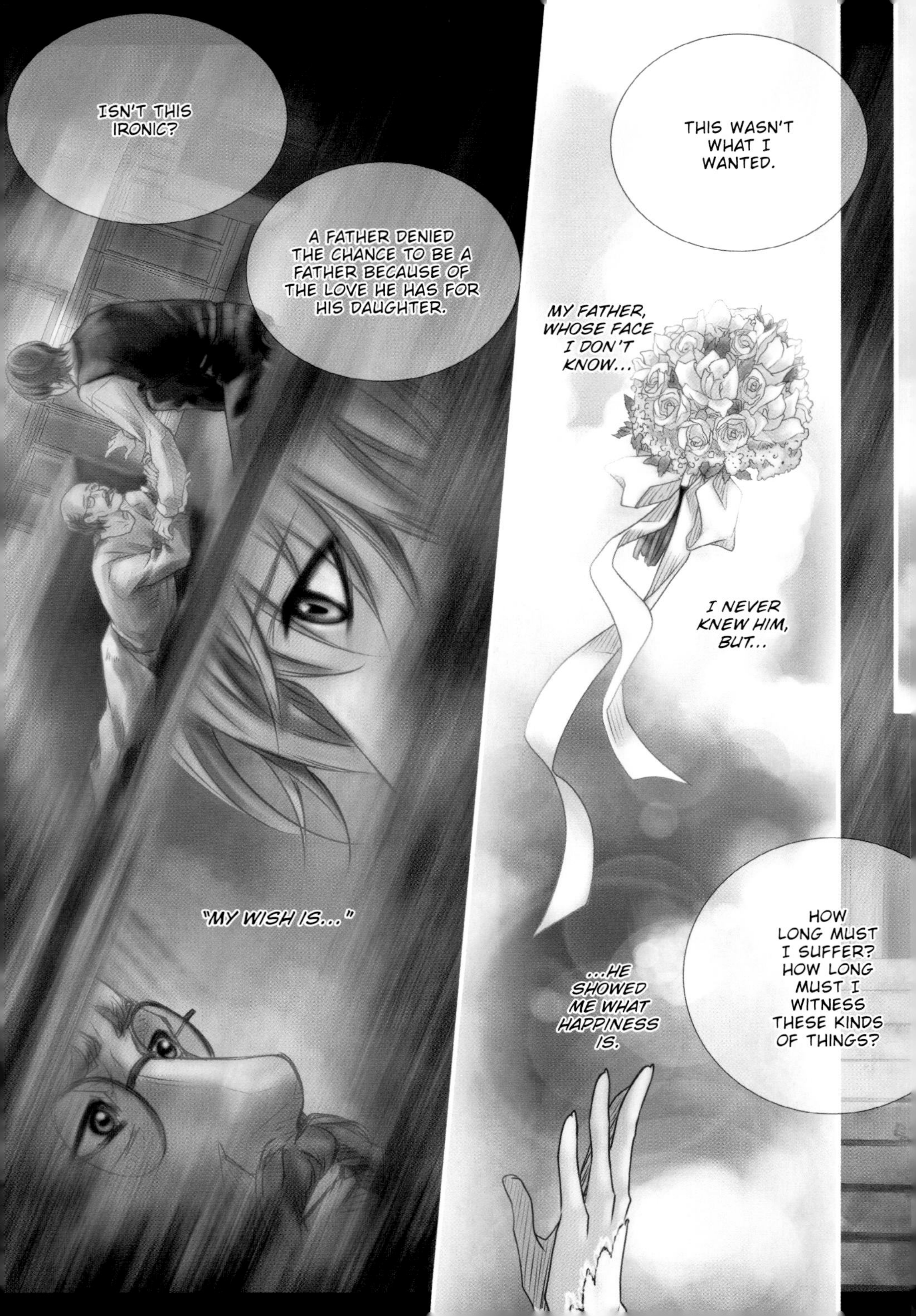
ISN'T THIS IRONIC?
A FATHER DENIED THE CHANCE TO BE A FATHER BECAUSE OF THE LOVE HE HAS FOR HIS DAUGHTER.
"MY WISH IS..."
THIS WASN'T WHAT I WANTED.
MY FATHER, WHOSE FACE I DON'T KNOW...
I NEVER KNEW HIM, BUT...
...HE SHOWED ME WHAT HAPPINESS IS.
HOW LONG MUST I SUFFER? HOW LONG MUST I WITNESS THESE KINDS OF THINGS?

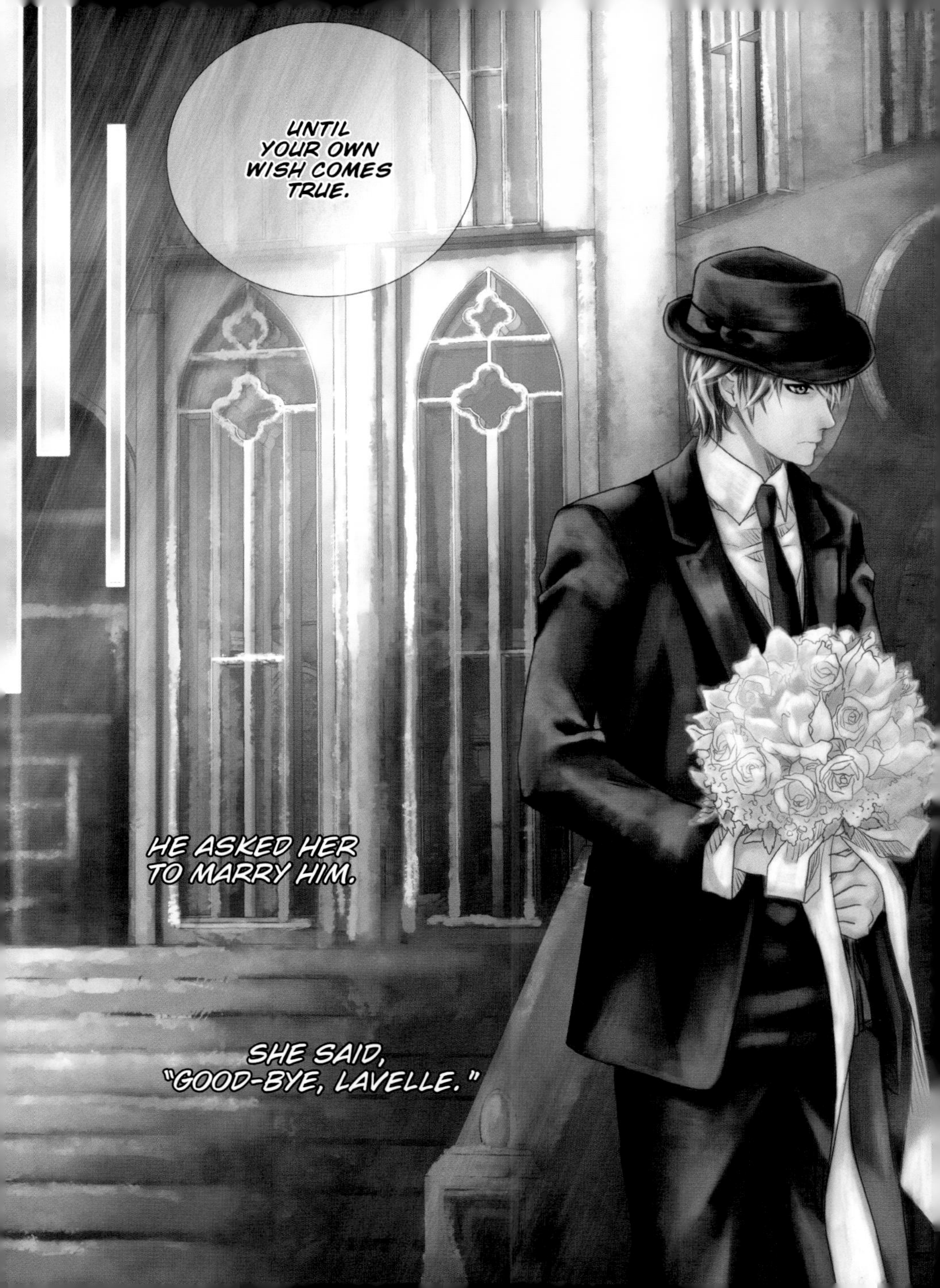
UNTIL YOUR OWN WISH COMES TRUE.
HE ASKED HER TO MARRY HIM.
SHE SAID, "GOOD-BYE, LAVELLE."

Void's Enigmatic Mansion

"

But who would use
their only wish for
someone else?

"

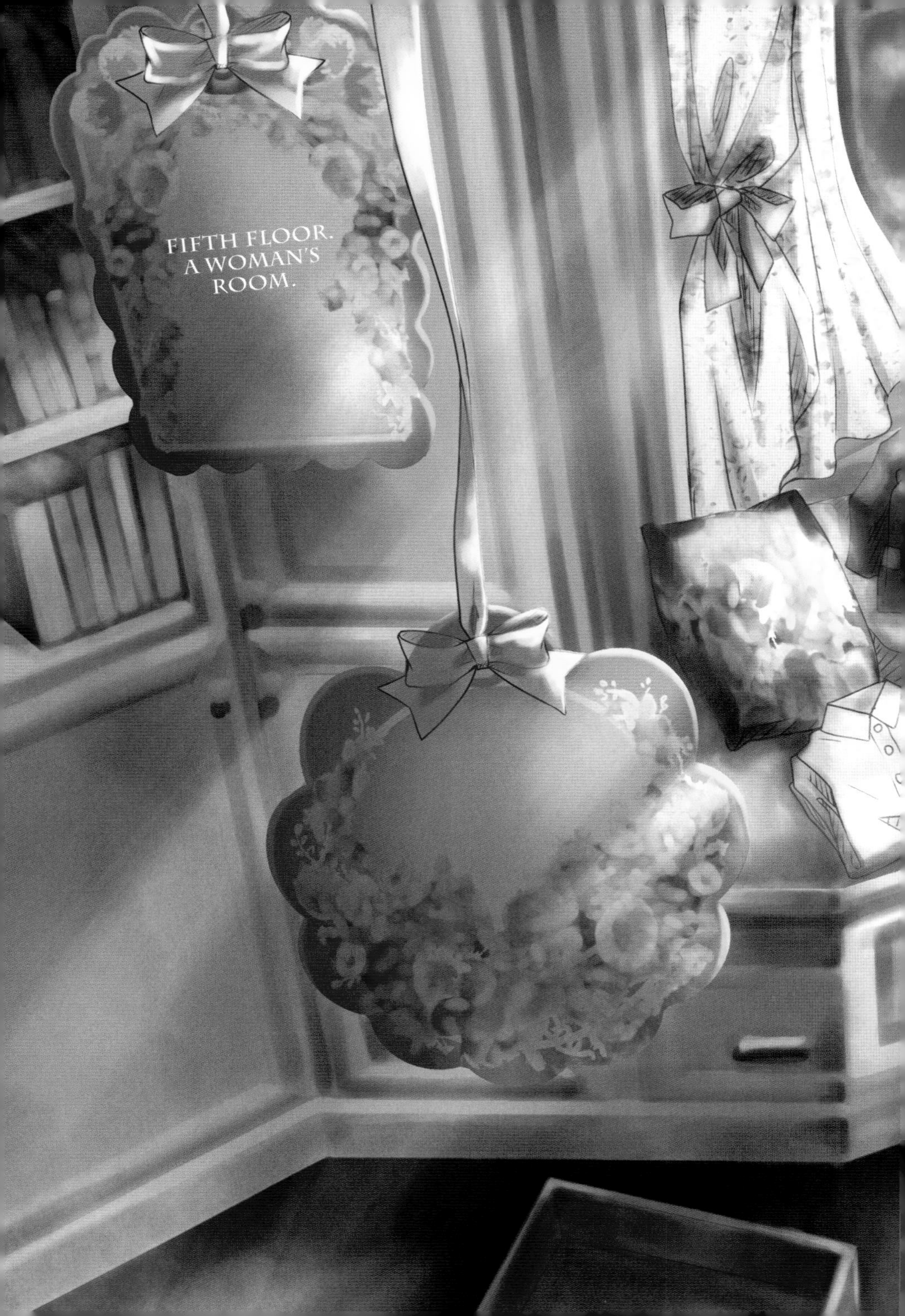
FIFTH FLOOR.
A WOMAN'S
ROOM.

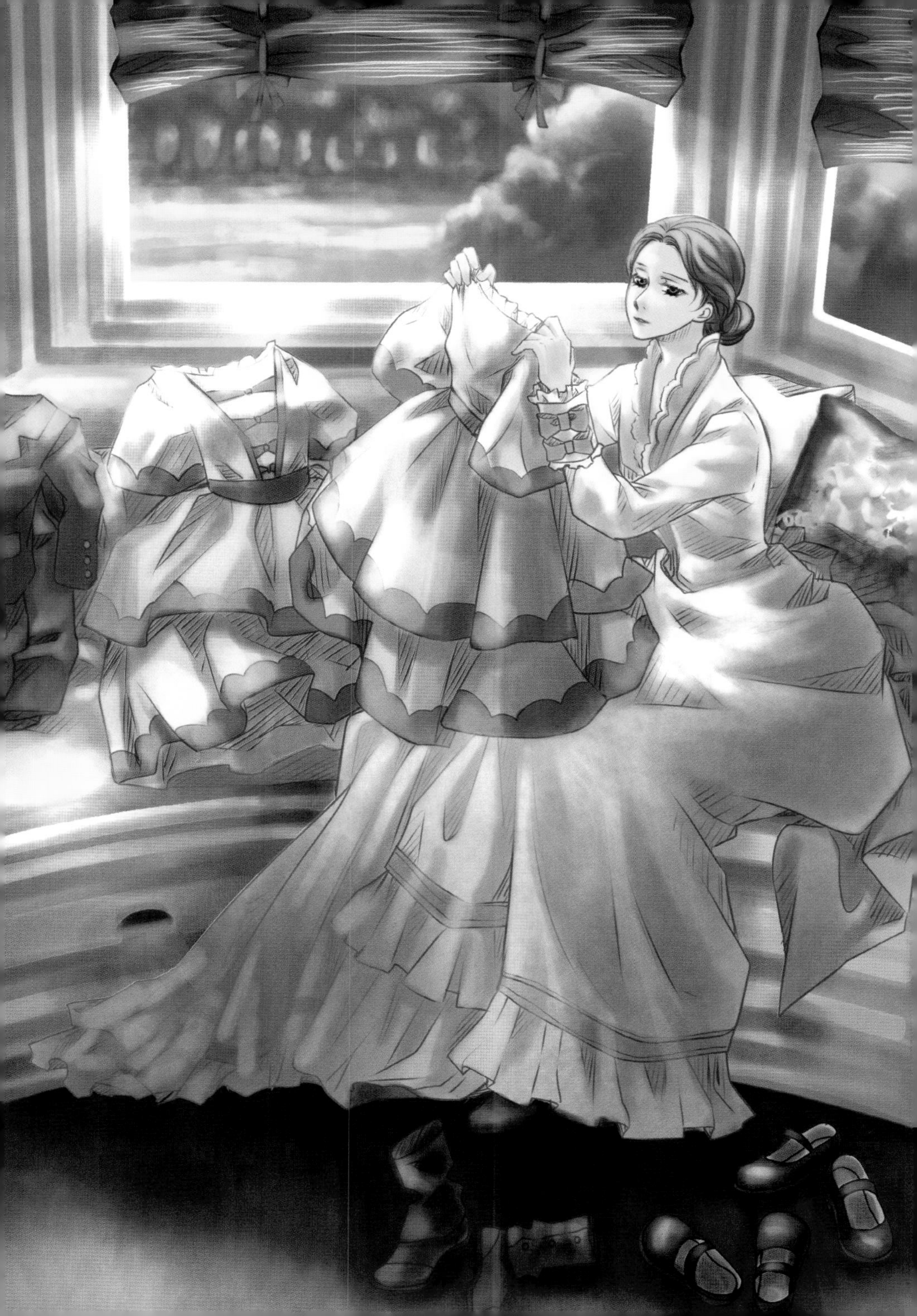

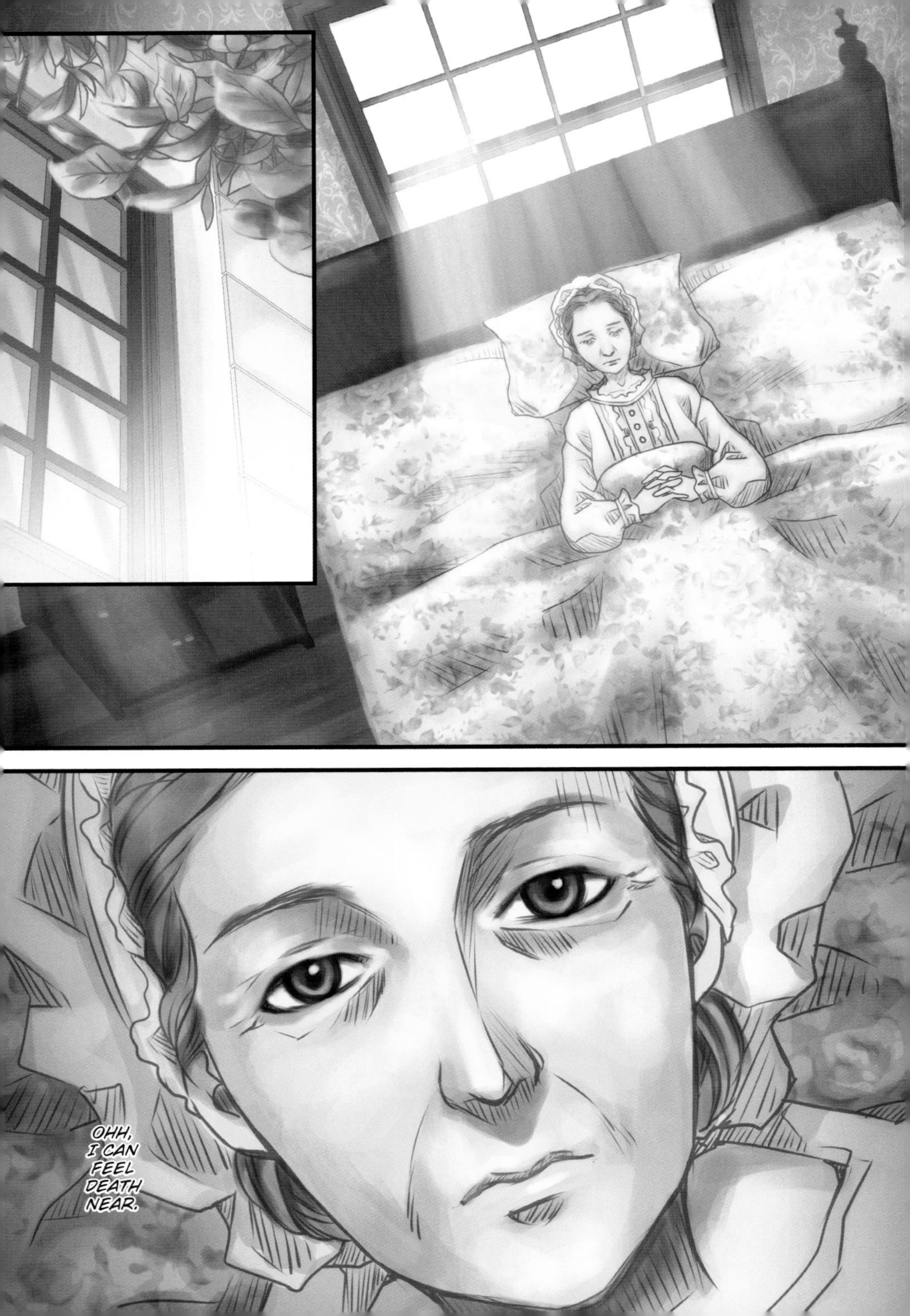
OHH, I CAN FEEL DEATH NEAR.

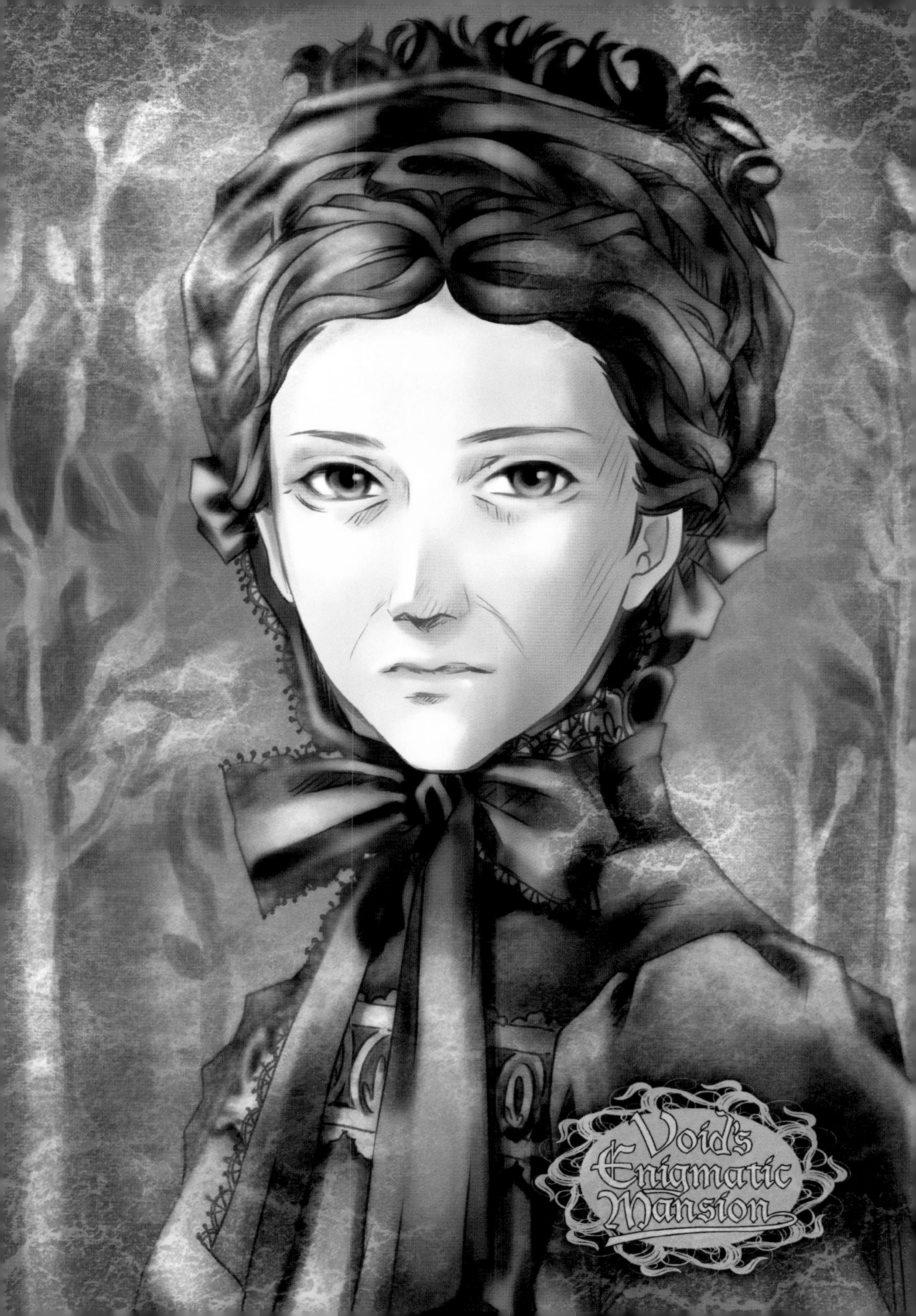
Void's
Enigmatic
Mansion

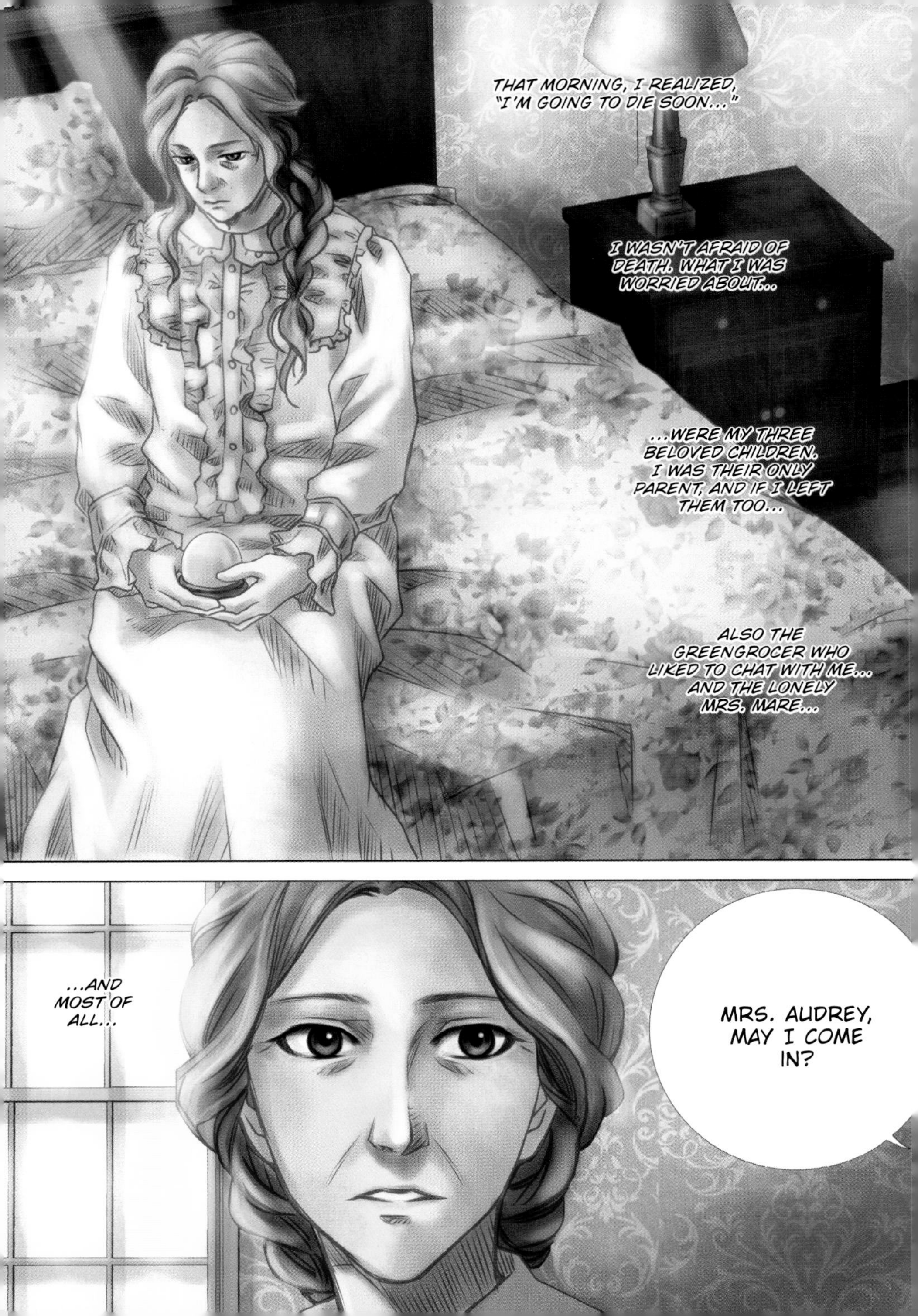
THAT MORNING, I REALIZED, "I'M GOING TO DIE SOON..."
I WASN'T AFRAID OF DEATH. WHAT I WAS WORRIED ABOUT...
...WERE MY THREE BELOVED CHILDREN. I WAS THEIR ONLY PARENT, AND IF I LEFT THEM TOO...
ALSO THE GREENGROCER WHO LIKED TO CHAT WITH ME... AND THE LONELY MRS. MARE...
...AND MOST OF ALL...
MRS. AUDREY, MAY I COME IN?

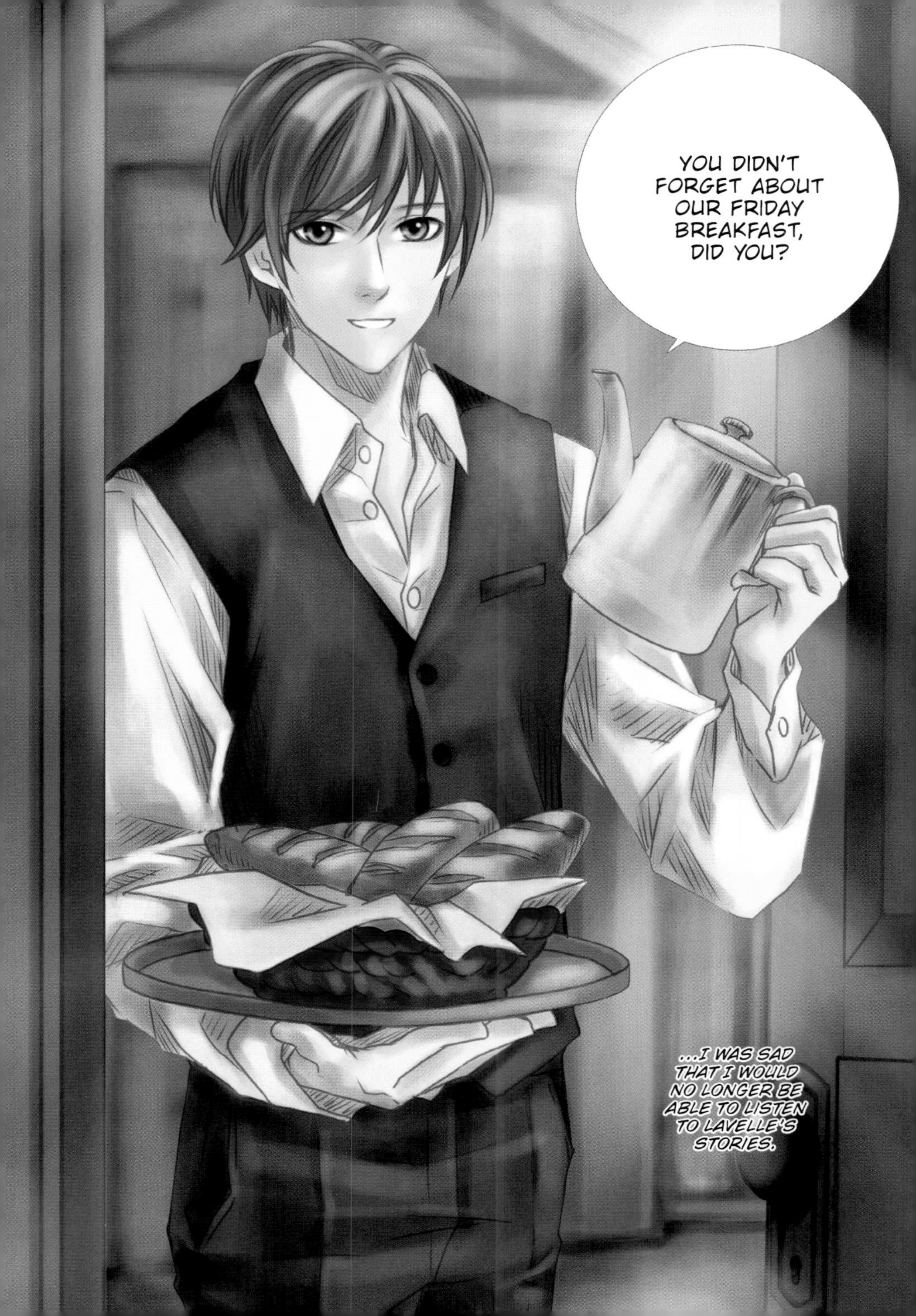
YOU DIDN'T FORGET ABOUT OUR FRIDAY BREAKFAST, DID YOU?
...I WAS SAD THAT I WOULD NO LONGER BE ABLE TO LISTEN TO LAVELLE'S STORIES.

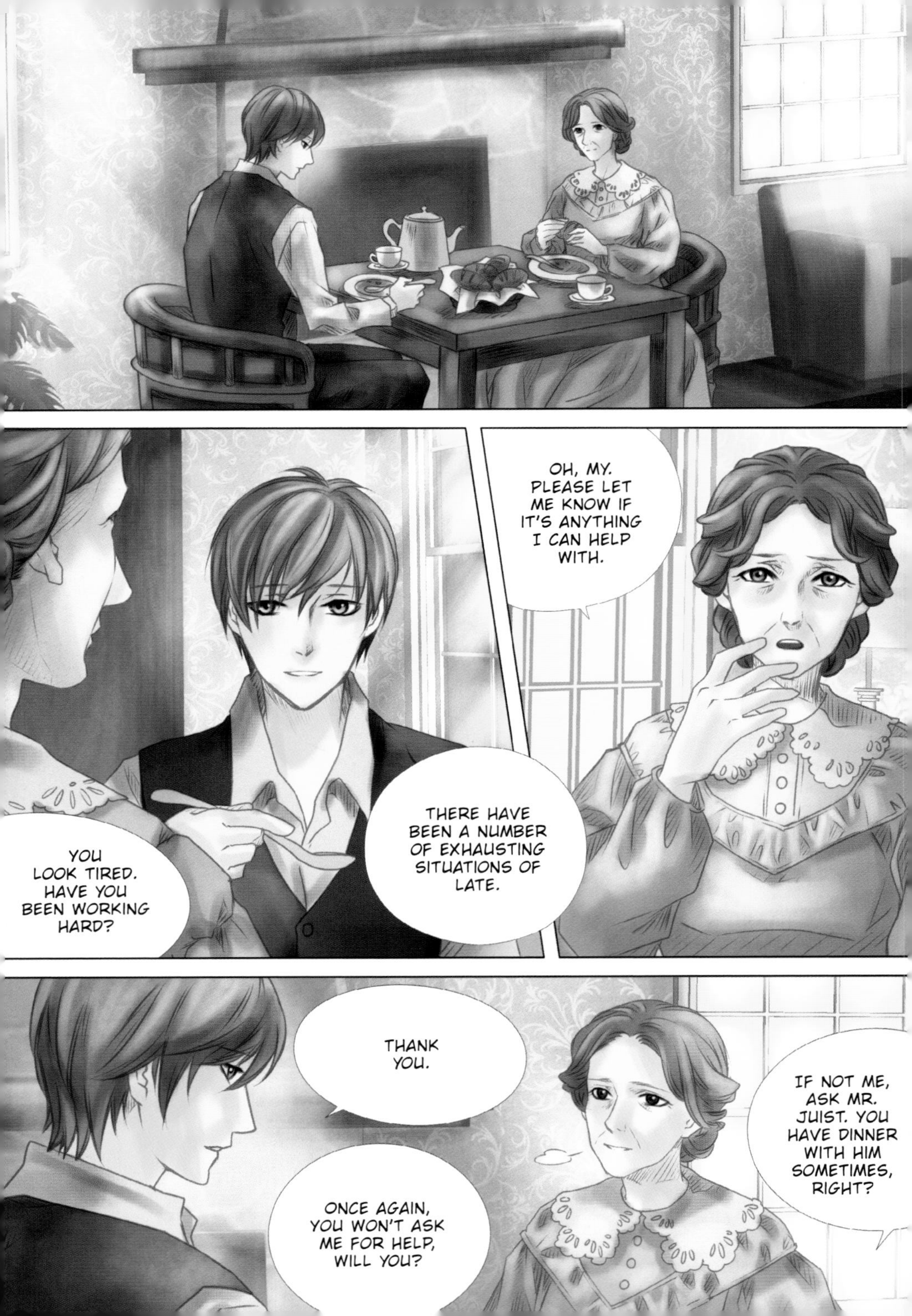
YOU LOOK TIRED. HAVE YOU BEEN WORKING HARD?
THERE HAVE BEEN A NUMBER OF EXHAUSTING SITUATIONS OF LATE.
OH, MY. PLEASE LET ME KNOW IF IT'S ANYTHING I CAN HELP WITH.
THANK YOU.
ONCE AGAIN, YOU WON'T ASK ME FOR HELP, WILL YOU?
IF NOT ME, ASK MR. JUIST. YOU HAVE DINNER WITH HIM SOMETIMES, RIGHT?

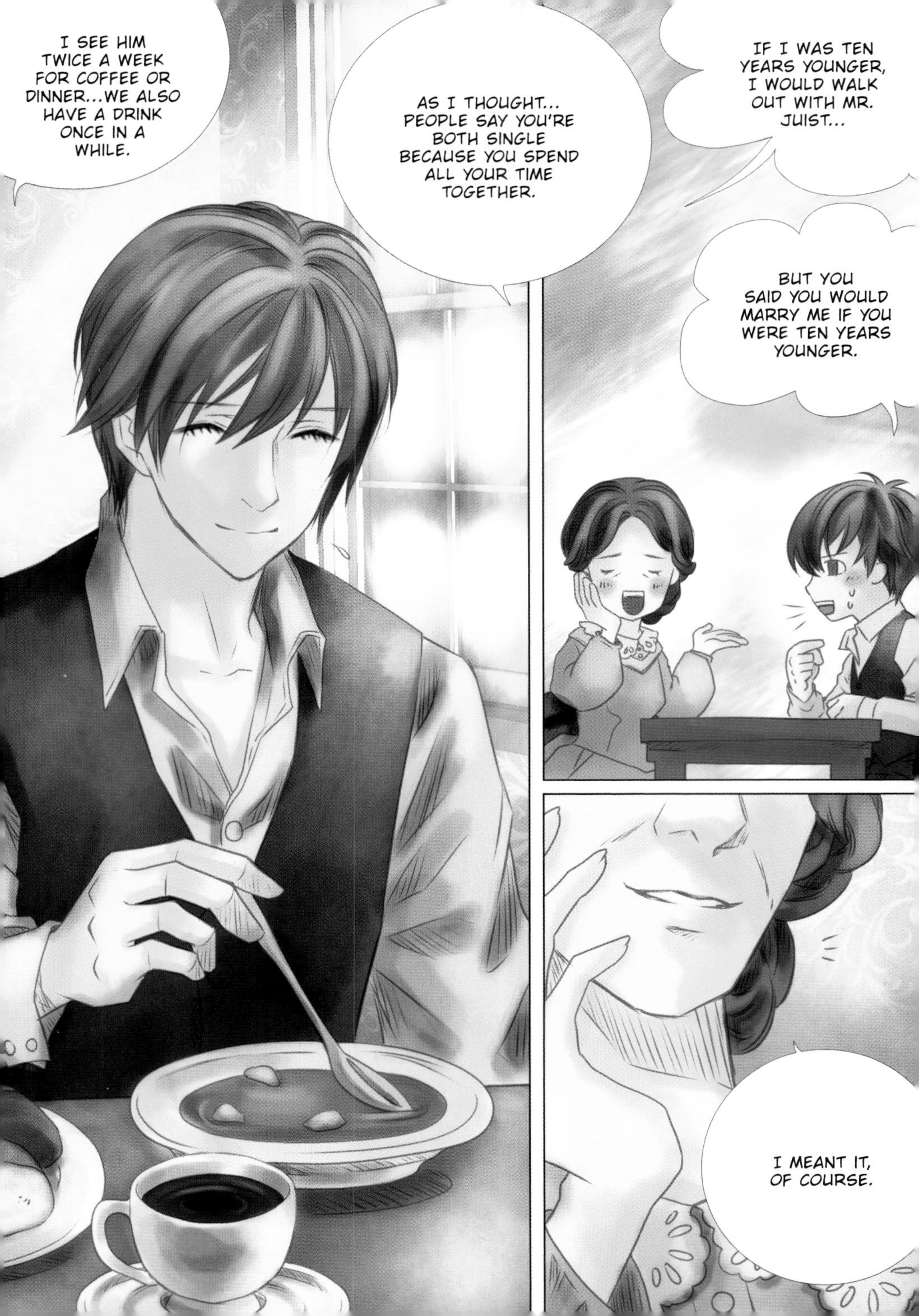
I SEE HIM TWICE A WEEK FOR COFFEE OR DINNER...WE ALSO HAVE A DRINK ONCE IN A WHILE.
AS I THOUGHT... PEOPLE SAY YOU'RE BOTH SINGLE BECAUSE YOU SPEND ALL YOUR TIME TOGETHER.
IF I WAS TEN YEARS YOUNGER, I WOULD WALK OUT WITH MR. JUIST...
BUT YOU SAID YOU WOULD MARRY ME IF YOU WERE TEN YEARS YOUNGER.
I MEANT IT, OF COURSE.

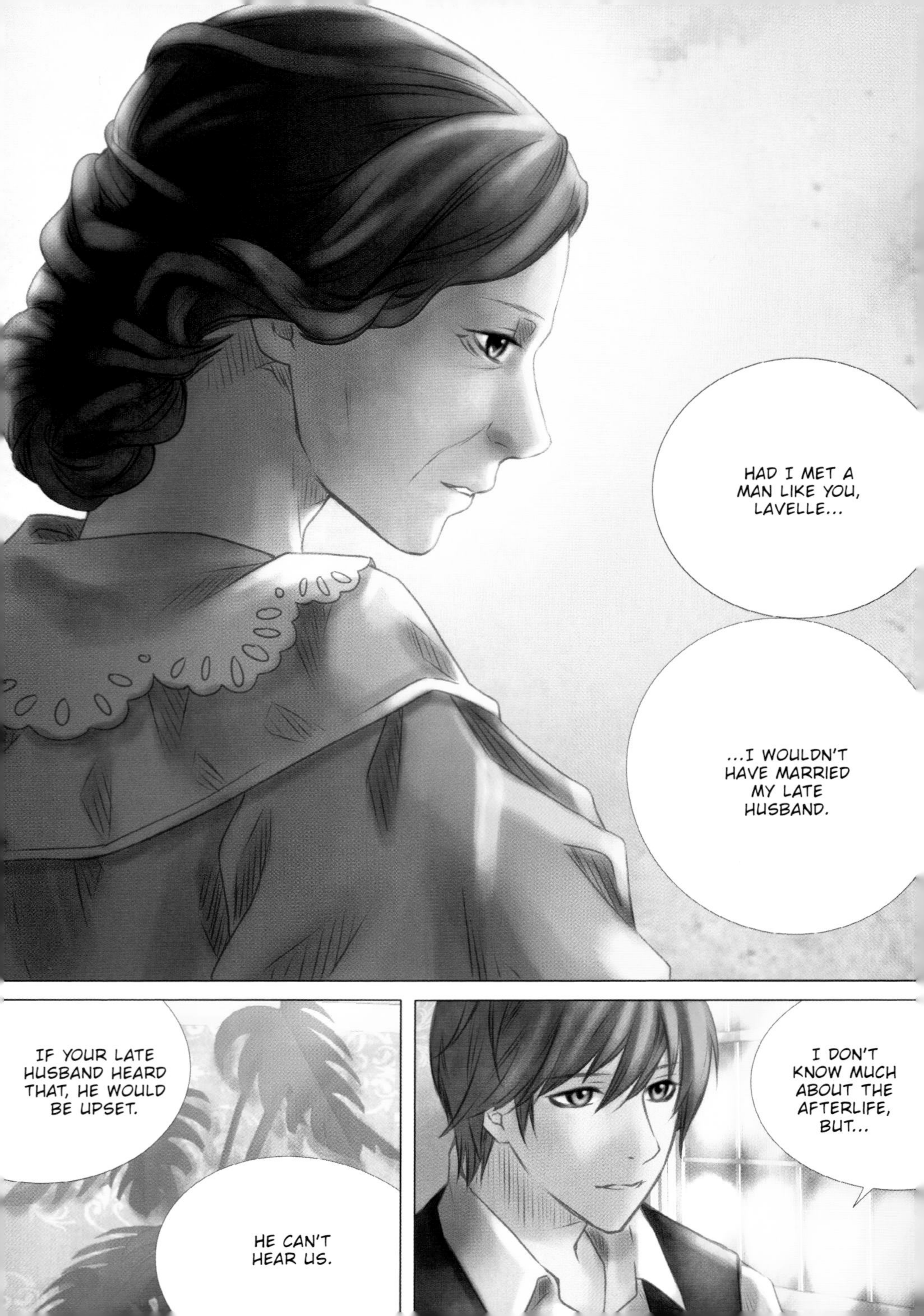
HAD I MET A MAN LIKE YOU, LAVELLE...
...I WOULDN'T HAVE MARRIED MY LATE HUSBAND.
IF YOUR LATE HUSBAND HEARD THAT, HE WOULD BE UPSET.
HE CAN'T HEAR US.
I DON'T KNOW MUCH ABOUT THE AFTERLIFE, BUT...

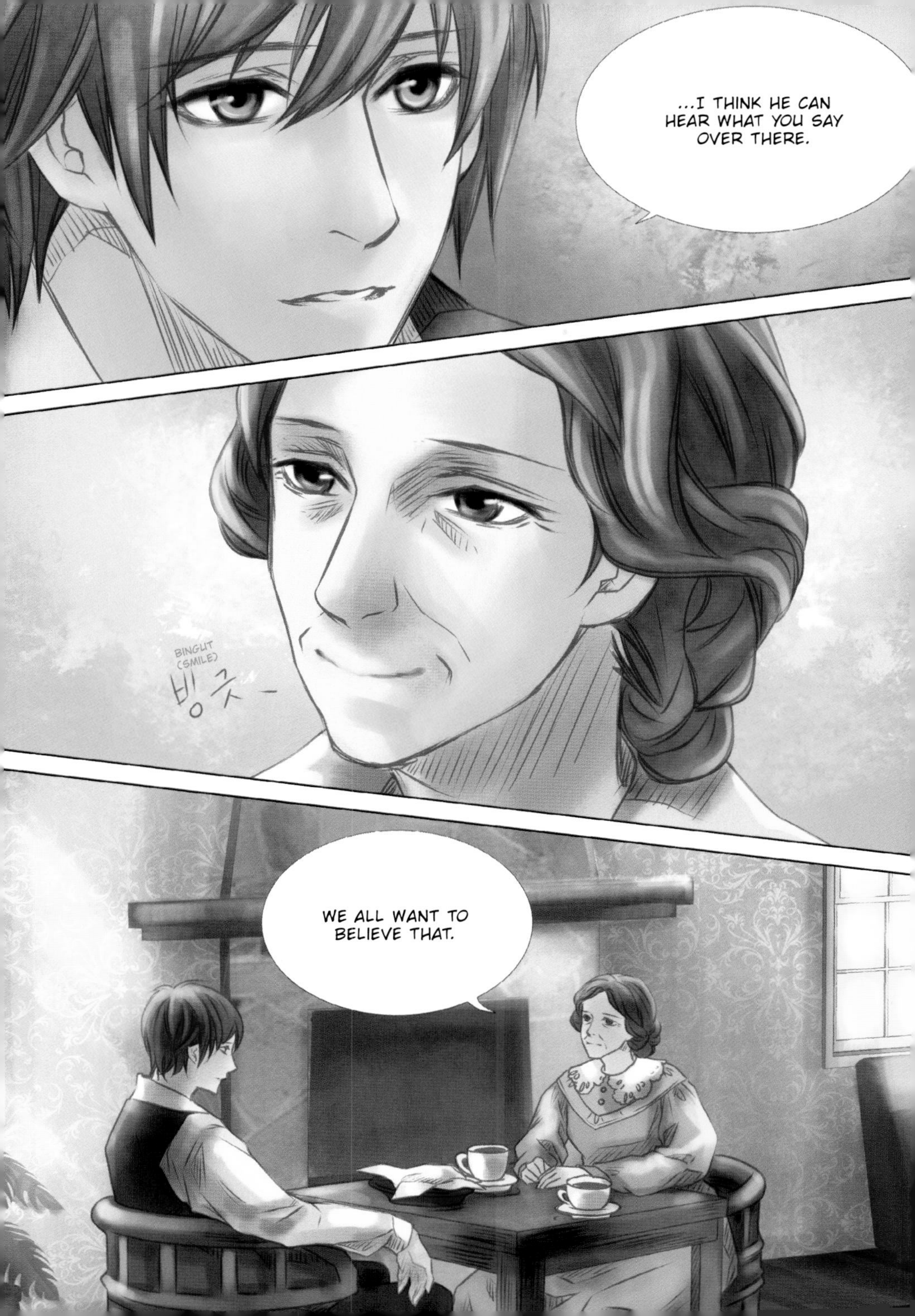
...I THINK HE CAN HEAR WHAT YOU SAY OVER THERE.
BINGUT (SMILE)
빙긋
WE ALL WANT TO BELIEVE THAT.

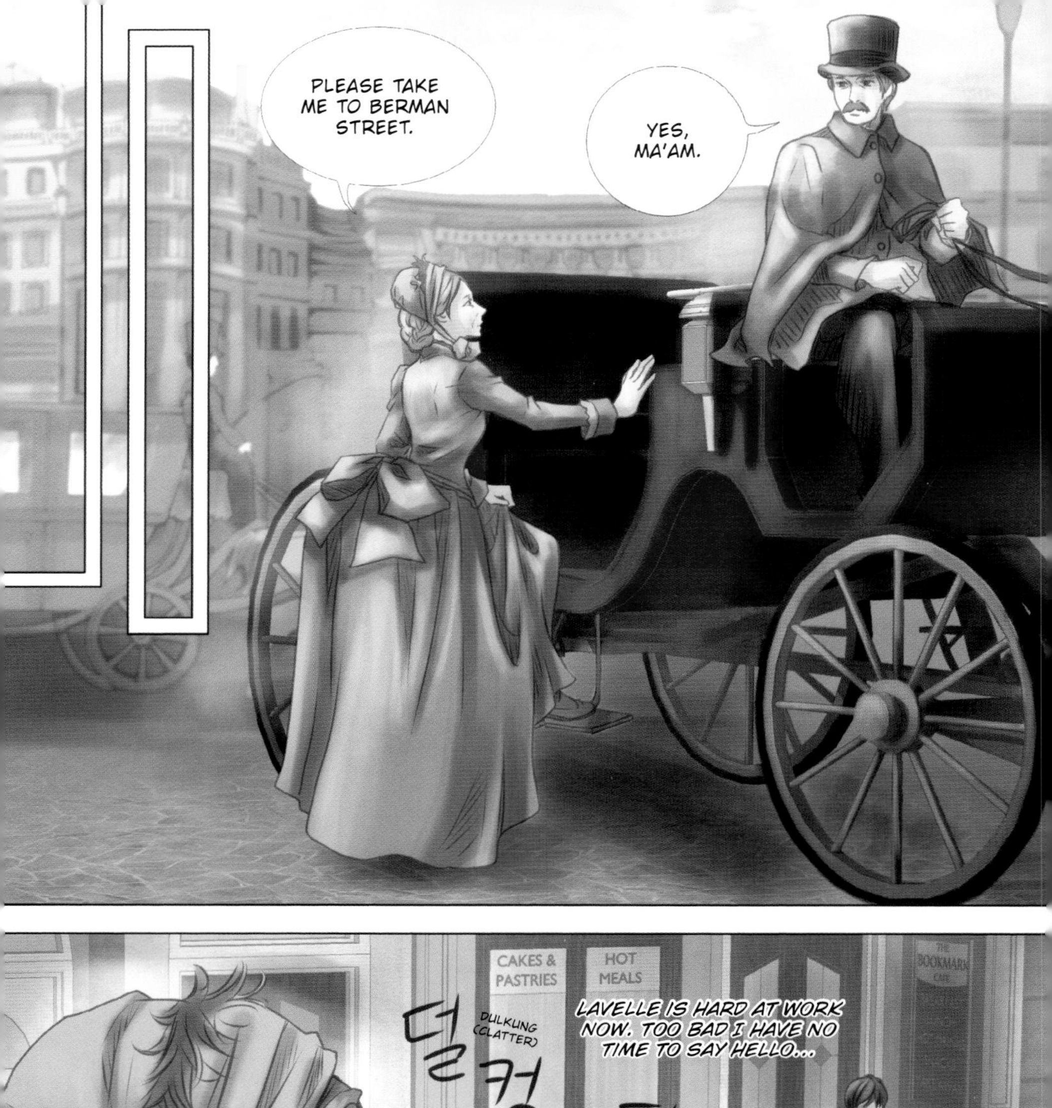
PLEASE TAKE ME TO BERMAN STREET.
YES, MA'AM.

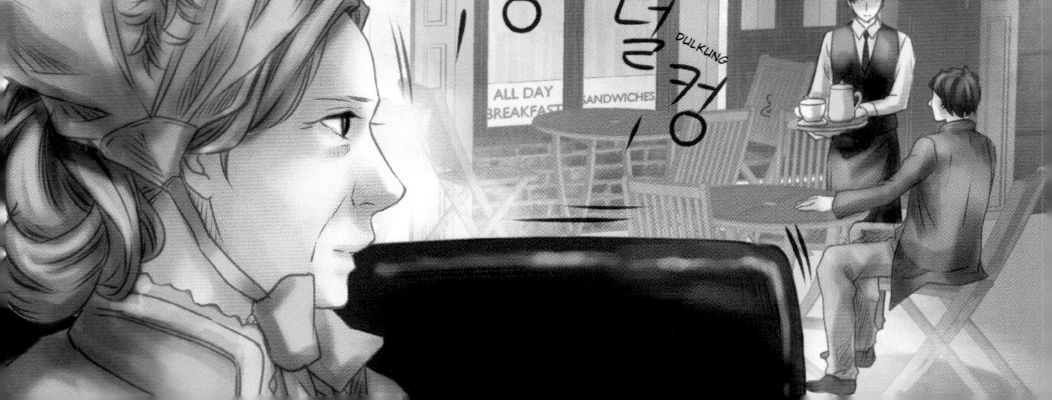
CAKES & PASTRIES
HOT MEALS
THE BOOKMARK CAFE
덜컹
DULKUNG (CLATTER)
LAVELLE IS HARD AT WORK NOW. TOO BAD I HAVE NO TIME TO SAY HELLO...
덜컹
DULKUNG
ALL DAY BREAKFAST
SANDWICHES

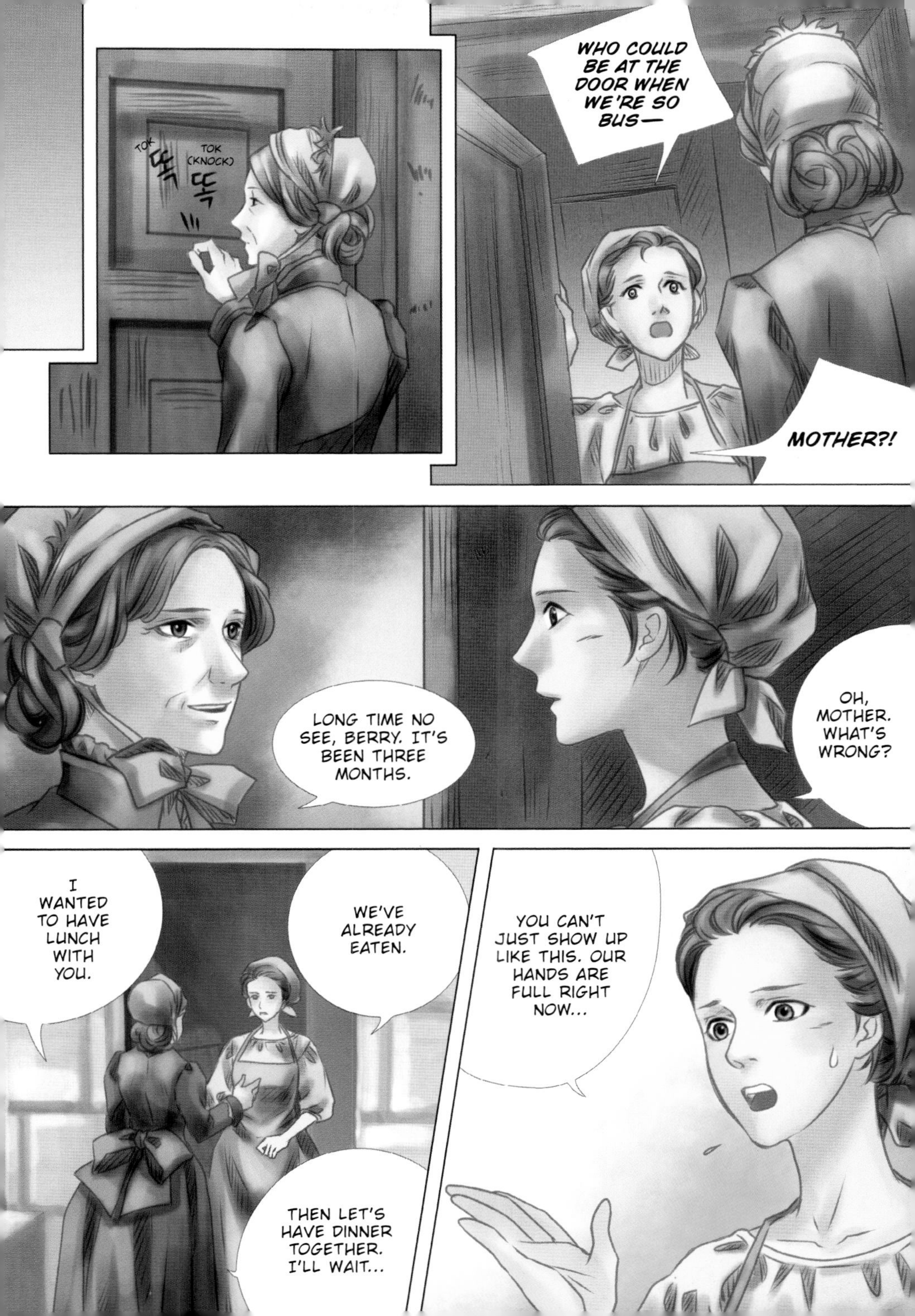
TOK
똑
TOK (KNOCK)
똑
WHO COULD BE AT THE DOOR WHEN WE'RE SO BUS—
MOTHER?!
LONG TIME NO SEE, BERRY. IT'S BEEN THREE MONTHS.
OH, MOTHER. WHAT'S WRONG?
I WANTED TO HAVE LUNCH WITH YOU.
WE'VE ALREADY EATEN.
THEN LET'S HAVE DINNER TOGETHER. I'LL WAIT...
YOU CAN'T JUST SHOW UP LIKE THIS. OUR HANDS ARE FULL RIGHT NOW...

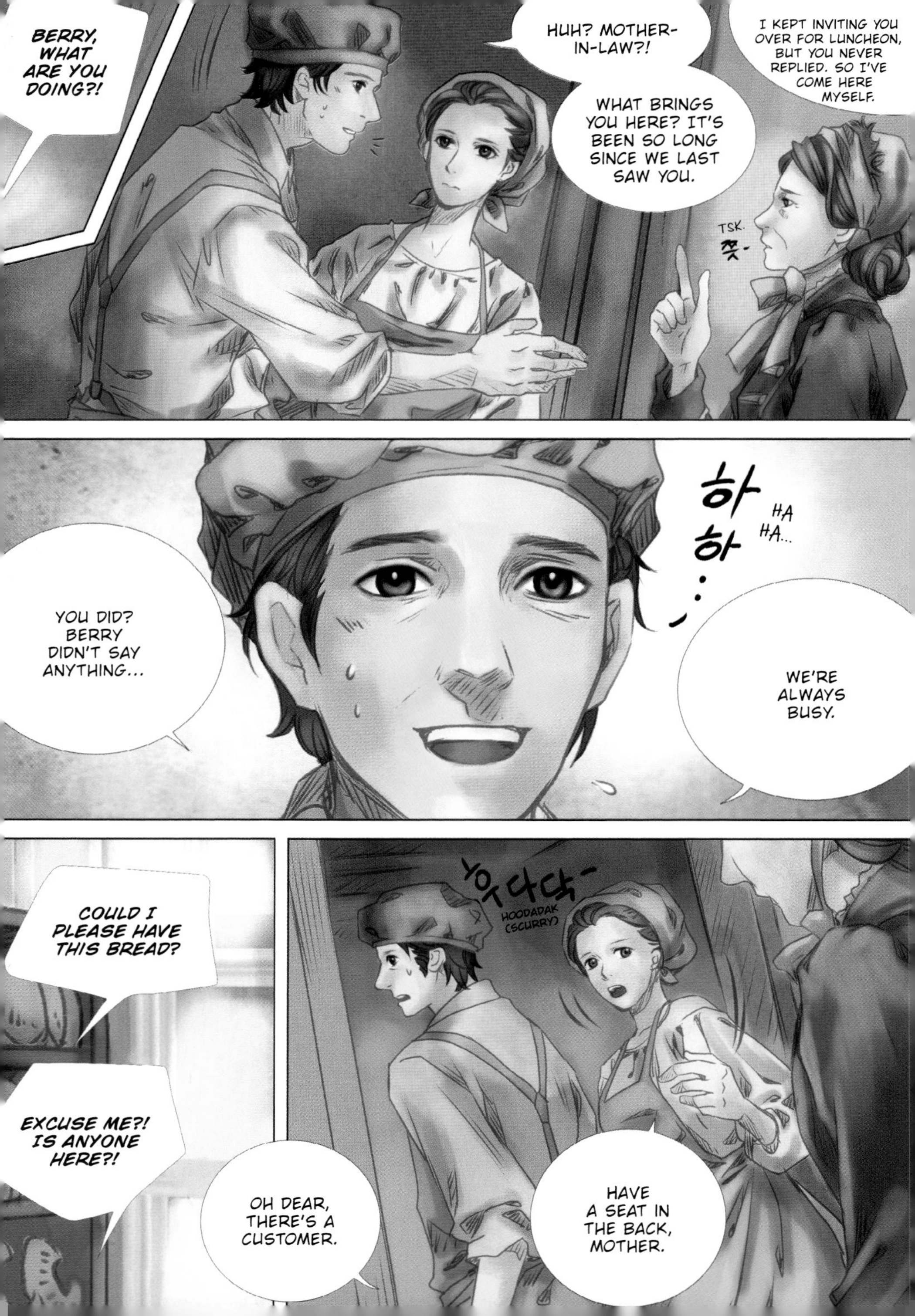
BERRY, WHAT ARE YOU DOING?!
HUH? MOTHER-IN-LAW?!
WHAT BRINGS YOU HERE? IT'S BEEN SO LONG SINCE WE LAST SAW YOU.
I KEPT INVITING YOU OVER FOR LUNCHEON, BUT YOU NEVER REPLIED. SO I'VE COME HERE MYSELF.
쯧
TSK.
하하…
HA HA...
YOU DID? BERRY DIDN'T SAY ANYTHING...
WE'RE ALWAYS BUSY.
COULD I PLEASE HAVE THIS BREAD?
EXCUSE ME?! IS ANYONE HERE?!
후다닥-
HOODADAK (SCURRY)
OH DEAR, THERE'S A CUSTOMER.
HAVE A SEAT IN THE BACK, MOTHER.

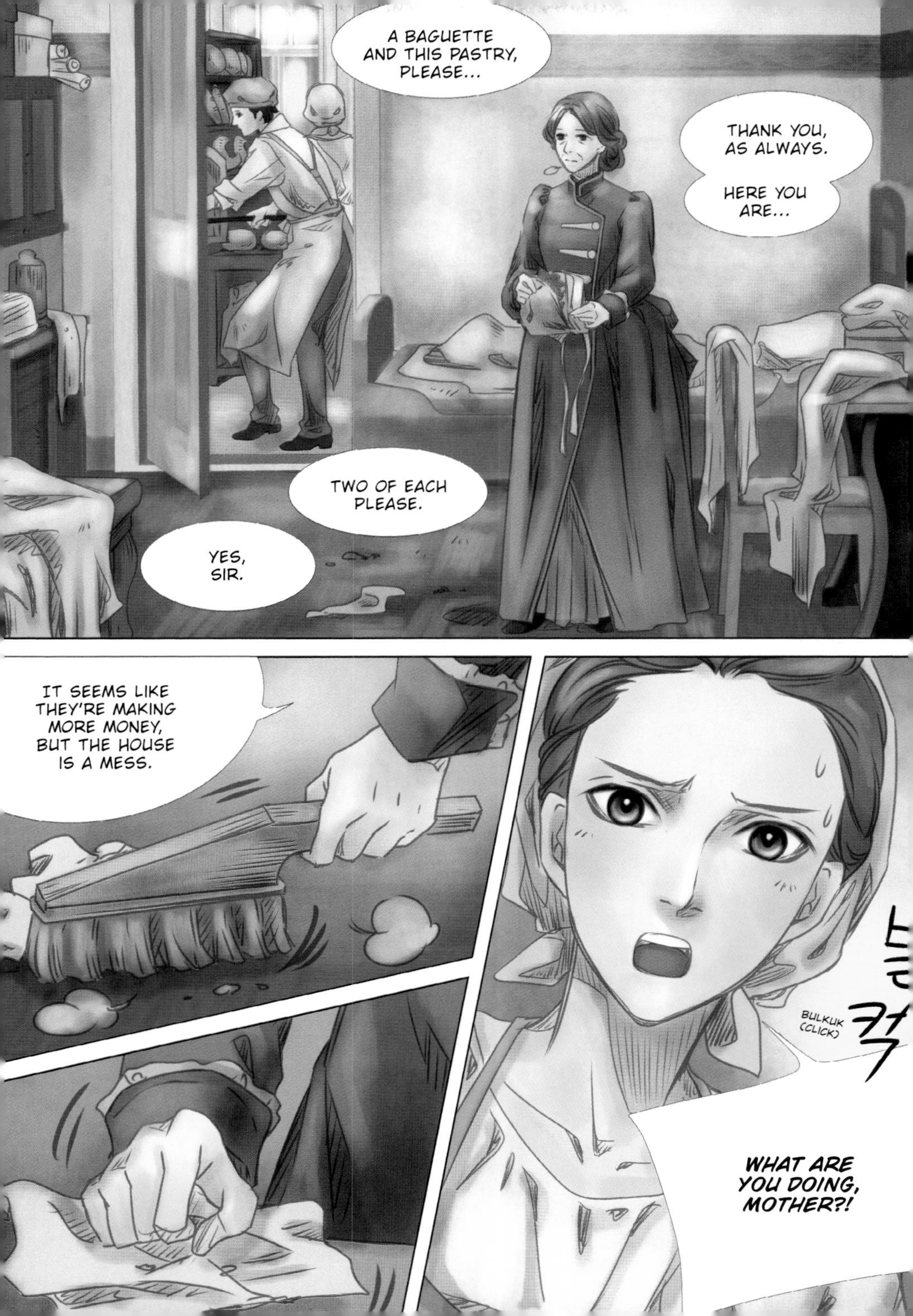
A BAGUETTE AND THIS PASTRY, PLEASE...
THANK YOU, AS ALWAYS.
HERE YOU ARE...
TWO OF EACH PLEASE.
YES, SIR.
IT SEEMS LIKE THEY'RE MAKING MORE MONEY, BUT THE HOUSE IS A MESS.
BULKUK (CLICK)
WHAT ARE YOU DOING, MOTHER?!

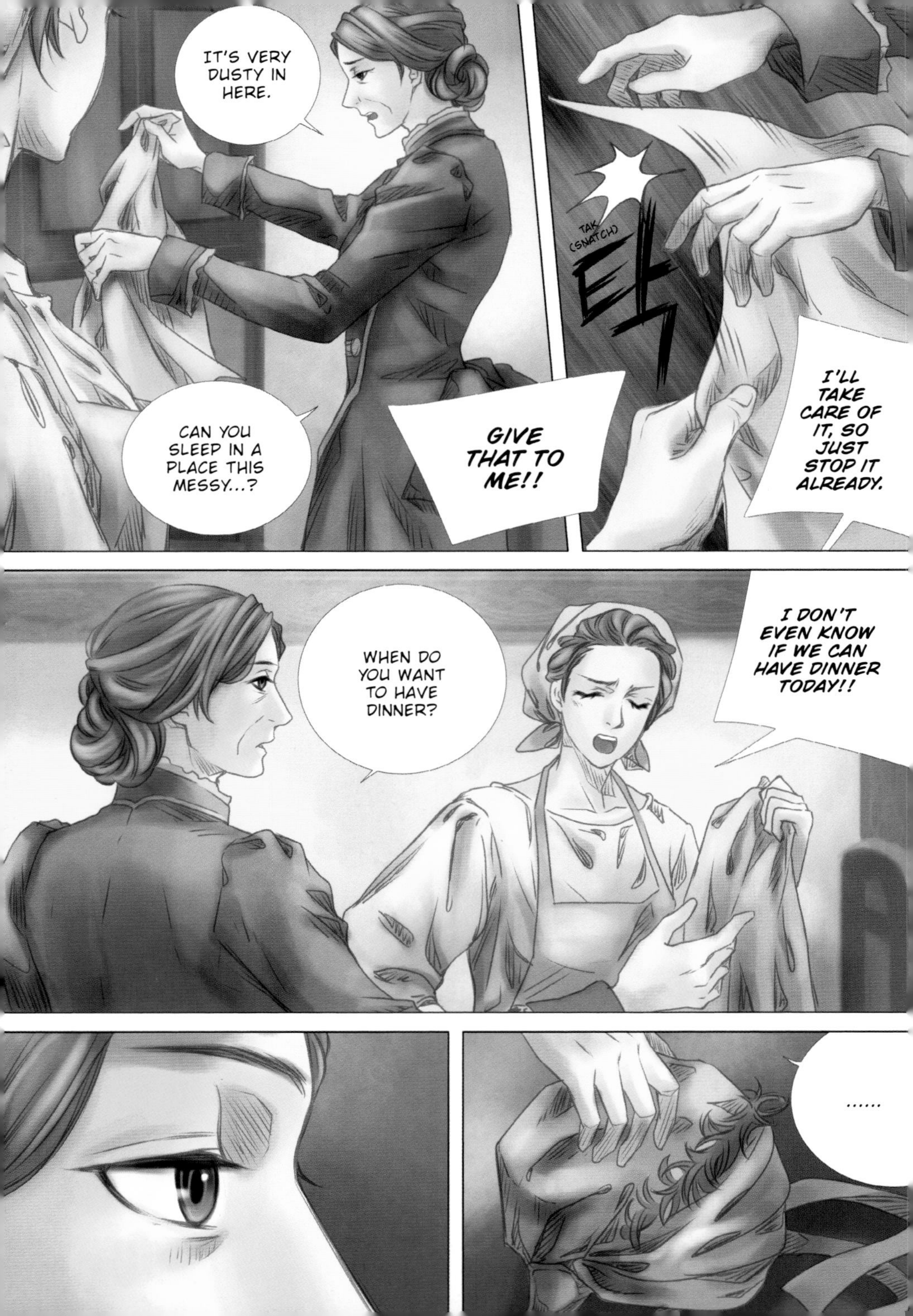
IT'S VERY DUSTY IN HERE.
CAN YOU SLEEP IN A PLACE THIS MESSY...?
GIVE THAT TO ME!!
TAK (SNATCH)
I'LL TAKE CARE OF IT, SO JUST STOP IT ALREADY.
WHEN DO YOU WANT TO HAVE DINNER?
I DON'T EVEN KNOW IF WE CAN HAVE DINNER TODAY!!
......

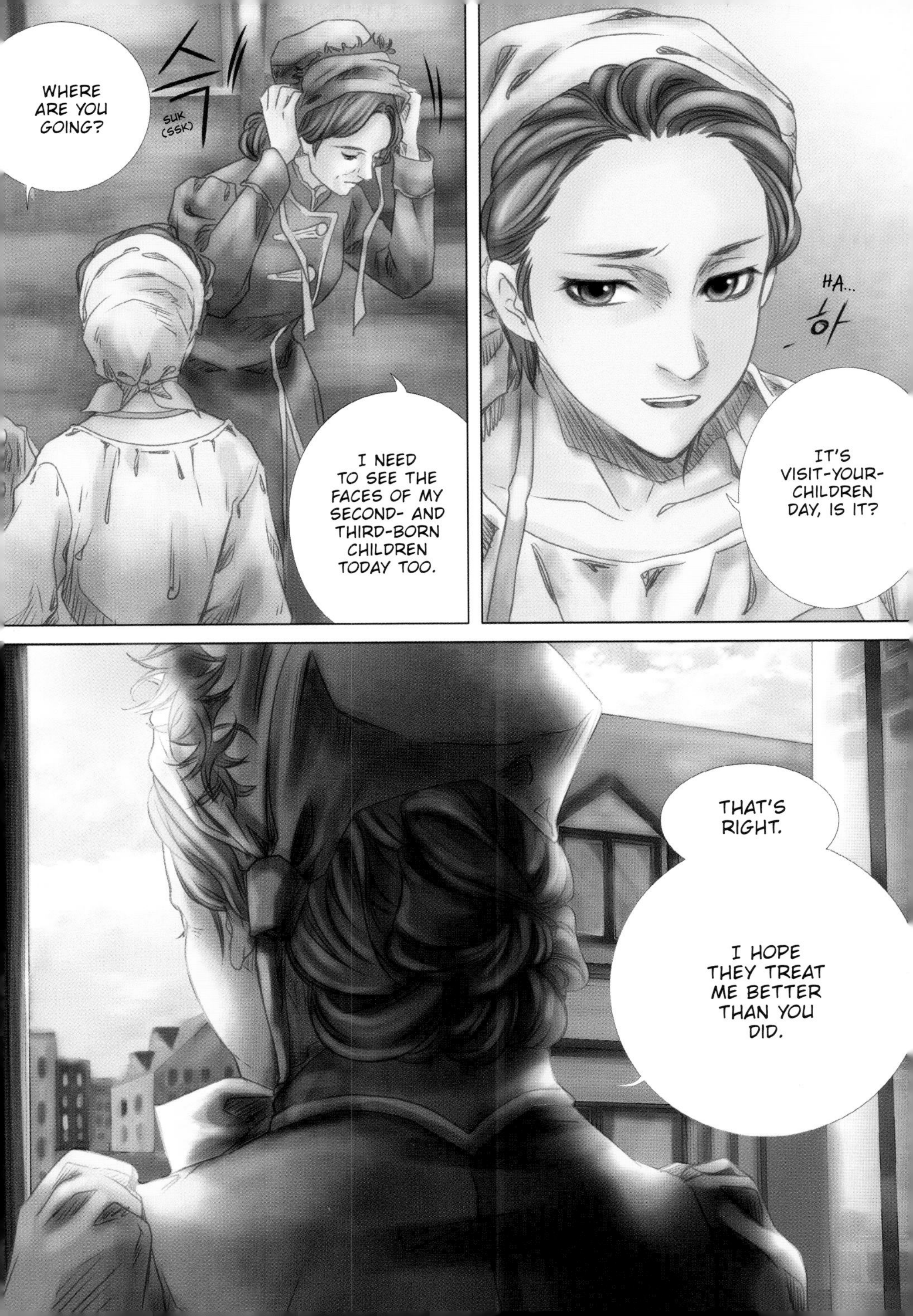
WHERE ARE YOU GOING?
SUK (SSK)
I NEED TO SEE THE FACES OF MY SECOND- AND THIRD-BORN CHILDREN TODAY TOO.
HA...
IT'S VISIT-YOUR-CHILDREN DAY, IS IT?
THAT'S RIGHT.
I HOPE THEY TREAT ME BETTER THAN YOU DID.

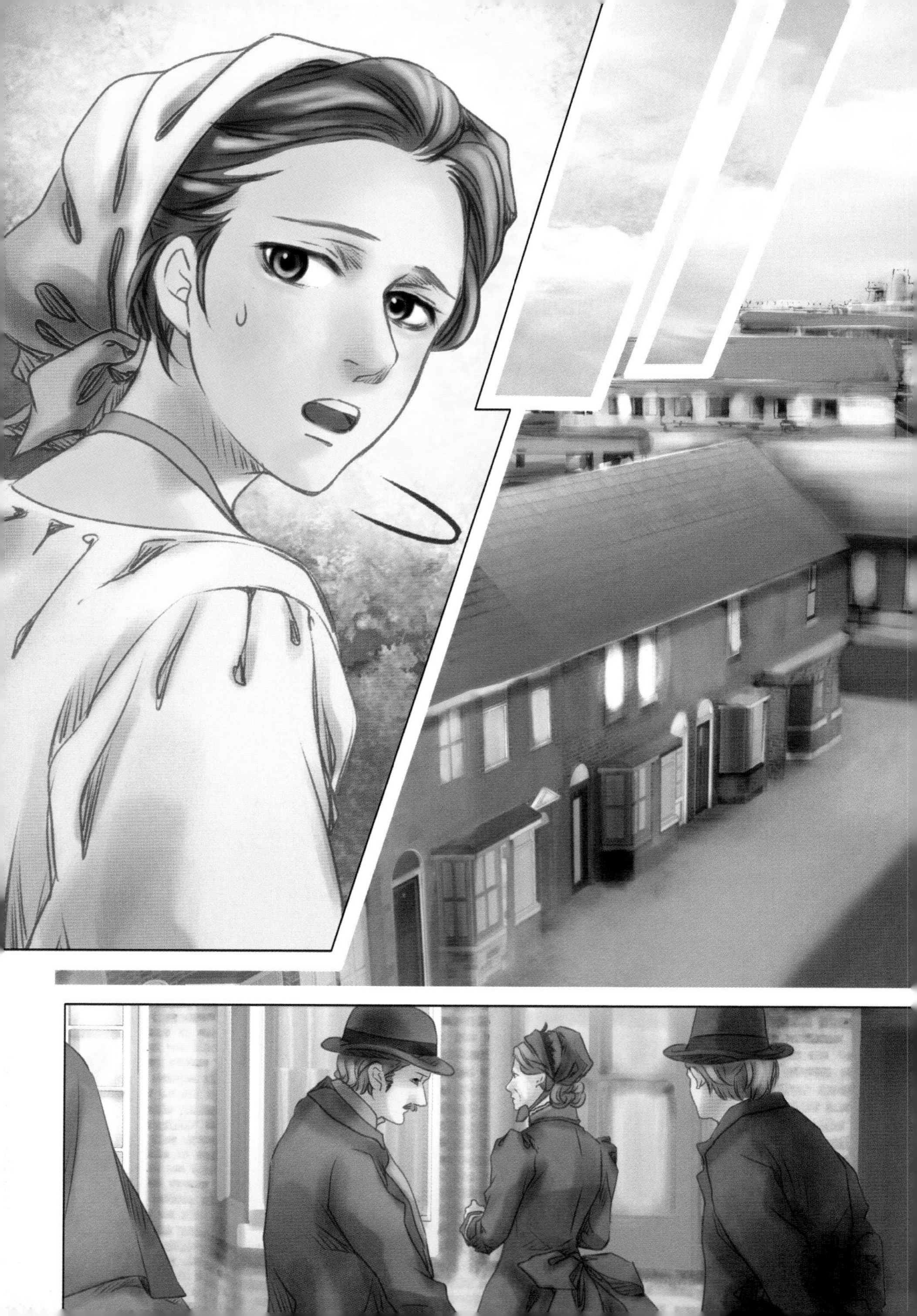

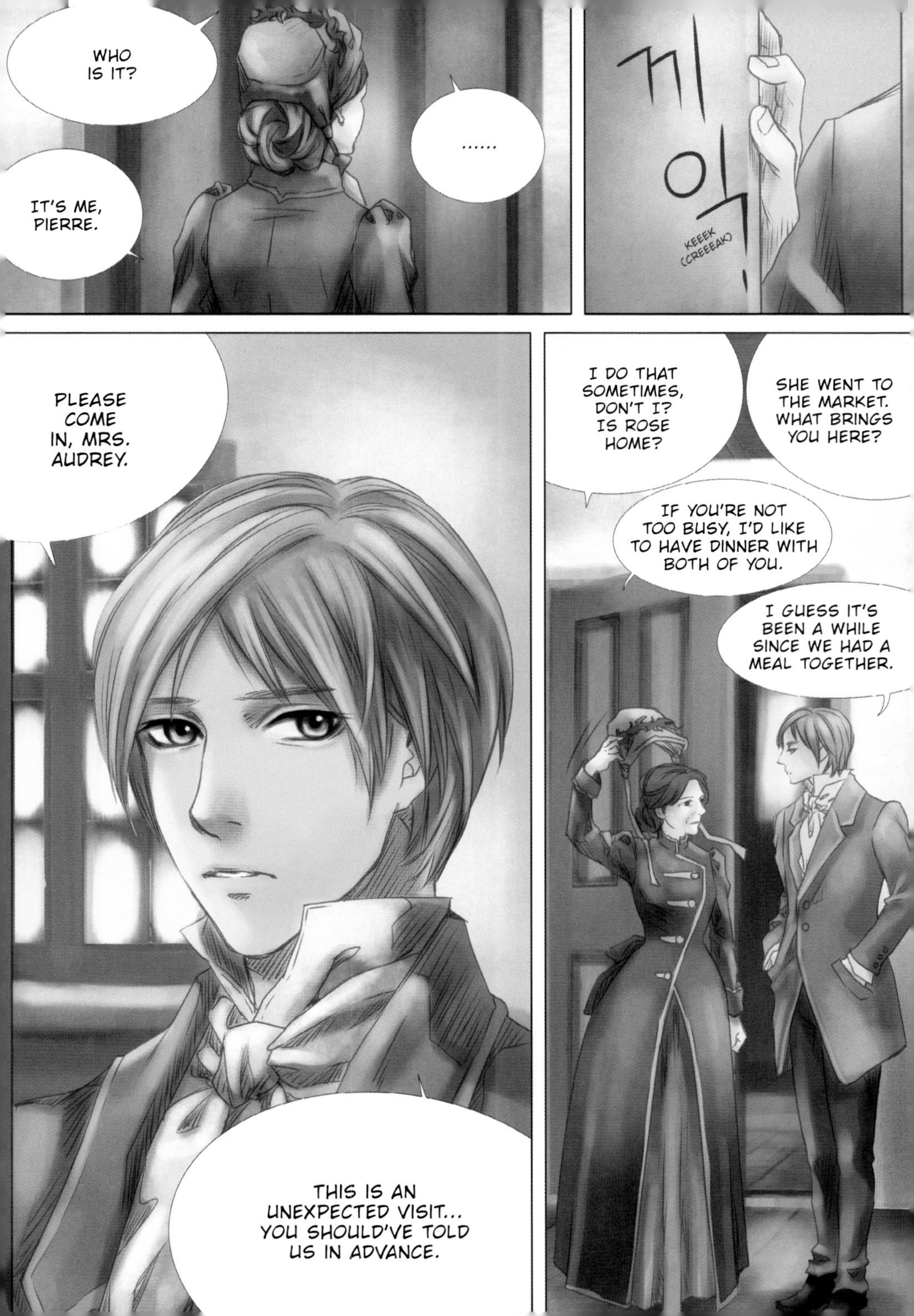
WHO IS IT?
IT'S ME, PIERRE.
......
끼익
KEEEK (CREEEAK)
PLEASE COME IN, MRS. AUDREY.
THIS IS AN UNEXPECTED VISIT... YOU SHOULD'VE TOLD US IN ADVANCE.
I DO THAT SOMETIMES, DON'T I? IS ROSE HOME?
SHE WENT TO THE MARKET. WHAT BRINGS YOU HERE?
IF YOU'RE NOT TOO BUSY, I'D LIKE TO HAVE DINNER WITH BOTH OF YOU.
I GUESS IT'S BEEN A WHILE SINCE WE HAD A MEAL TOGETHER.

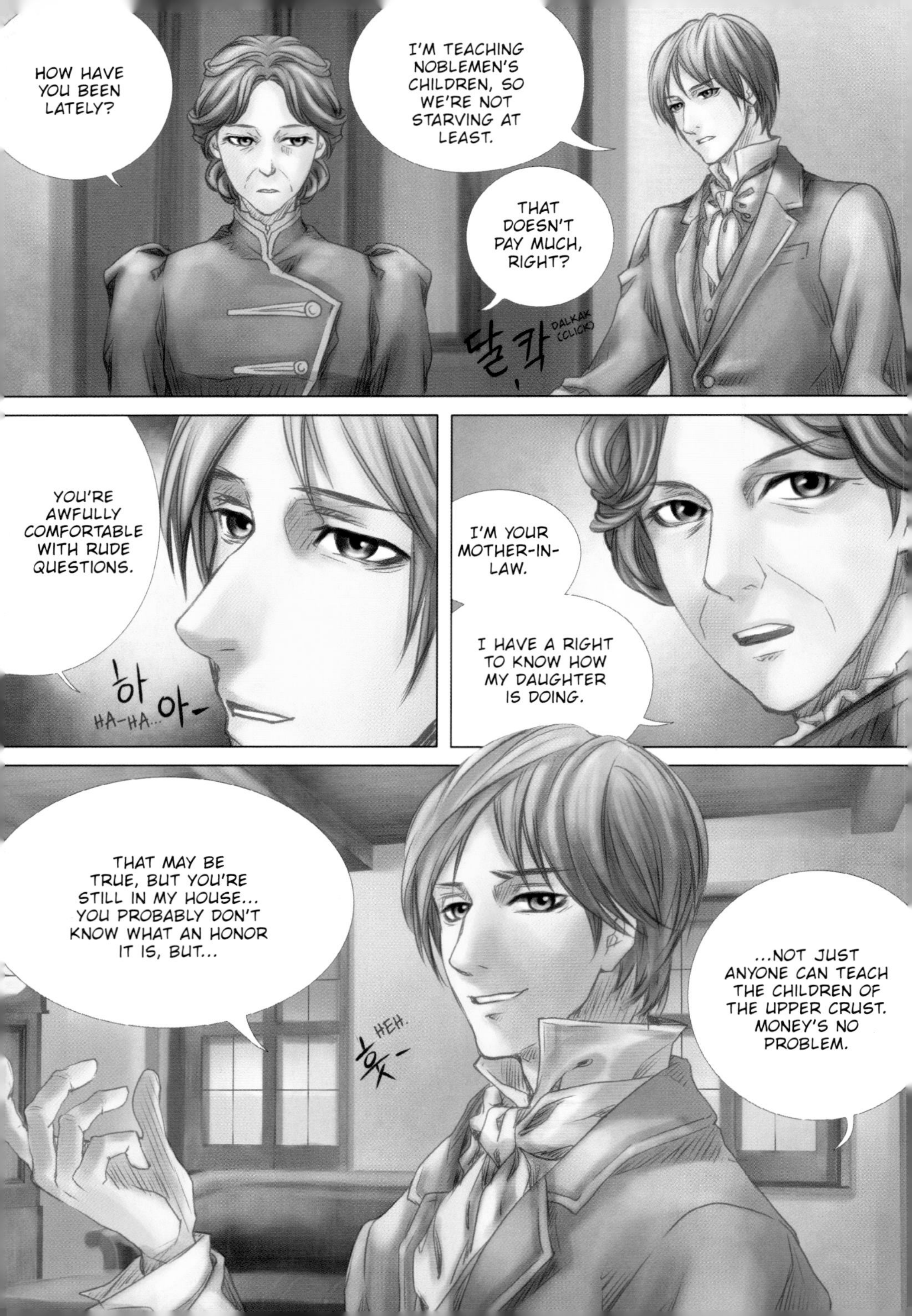
HOW HAVE YOU BEEN LATELY?
I'M TEACHING NOBLEMEN'S CHILDREN, SO WE'RE NOT STARVING AT LEAST.
THAT DOESN'T PAY MUCH, RIGHT?
달칵 DALKAK (CLICK)
YOU'RE AWFULLY COMFORTABLE WITH RUDE QUESTIONS.
하아- HA-HA...
I'M YOUR MOTHER-IN-LAW.
I HAVE A RIGHT TO KNOW HOW MY DAUGHTER IS DOING.
THAT MAY BE TRUE, BUT YOU'RE STILL IN MY HOUSE... YOU PROBABLY DON'T KNOW WHAT AN HONOR IT IS, BUT...
훗- HEH.
...NOT JUST ANYONE CAN TEACH THE CHILDREN OF THE UPPER CRUST. MONEY'S NO PROBLEM.

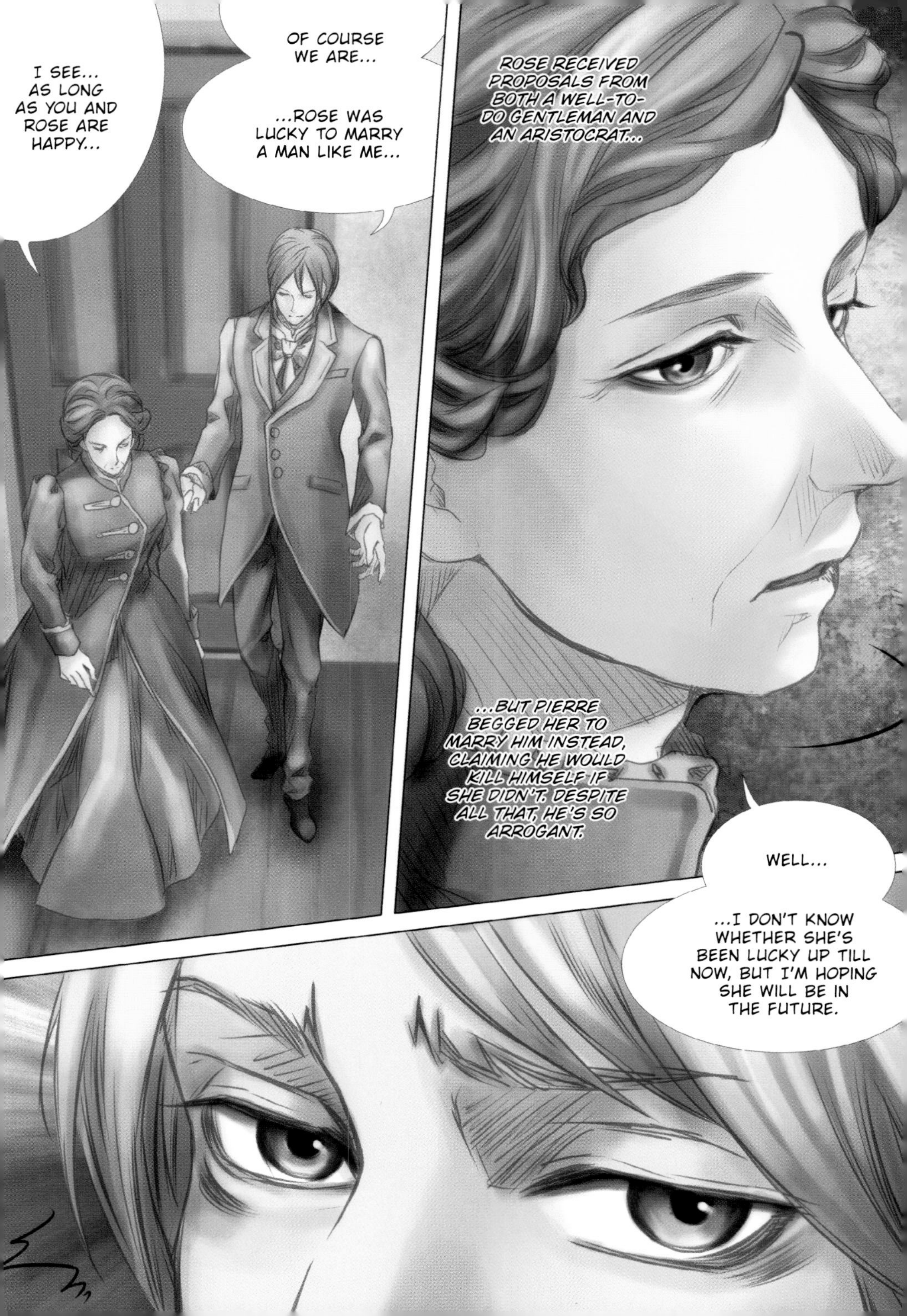
I SEE... AS LONG AS YOU AND ROSE ARE HAPPY...
OF COURSE WE ARE...
...ROSE WAS LUCKY TO MARRY A MAN LIKE ME...
ROSE RECEIVED PROPOSALS FROM BOTH A WELL-TO-DO GENTLEMAN AND AN ARISTOCRAT...
...BUT PIERRE BEGGED HER TO MARRY HIM INSTEAD, CLAIMING HE WOULD KILL HIMSELF IF SHE DIDN'T. DESPITE ALL THAT, HE'S SO ARROGANT.
WELL...
...I DON'T KNOW WHETHER SHE'S BEEN LUCKY UP TILL NOW, BUT I'M HOPING SHE WILL BE IN THE FUTURE.

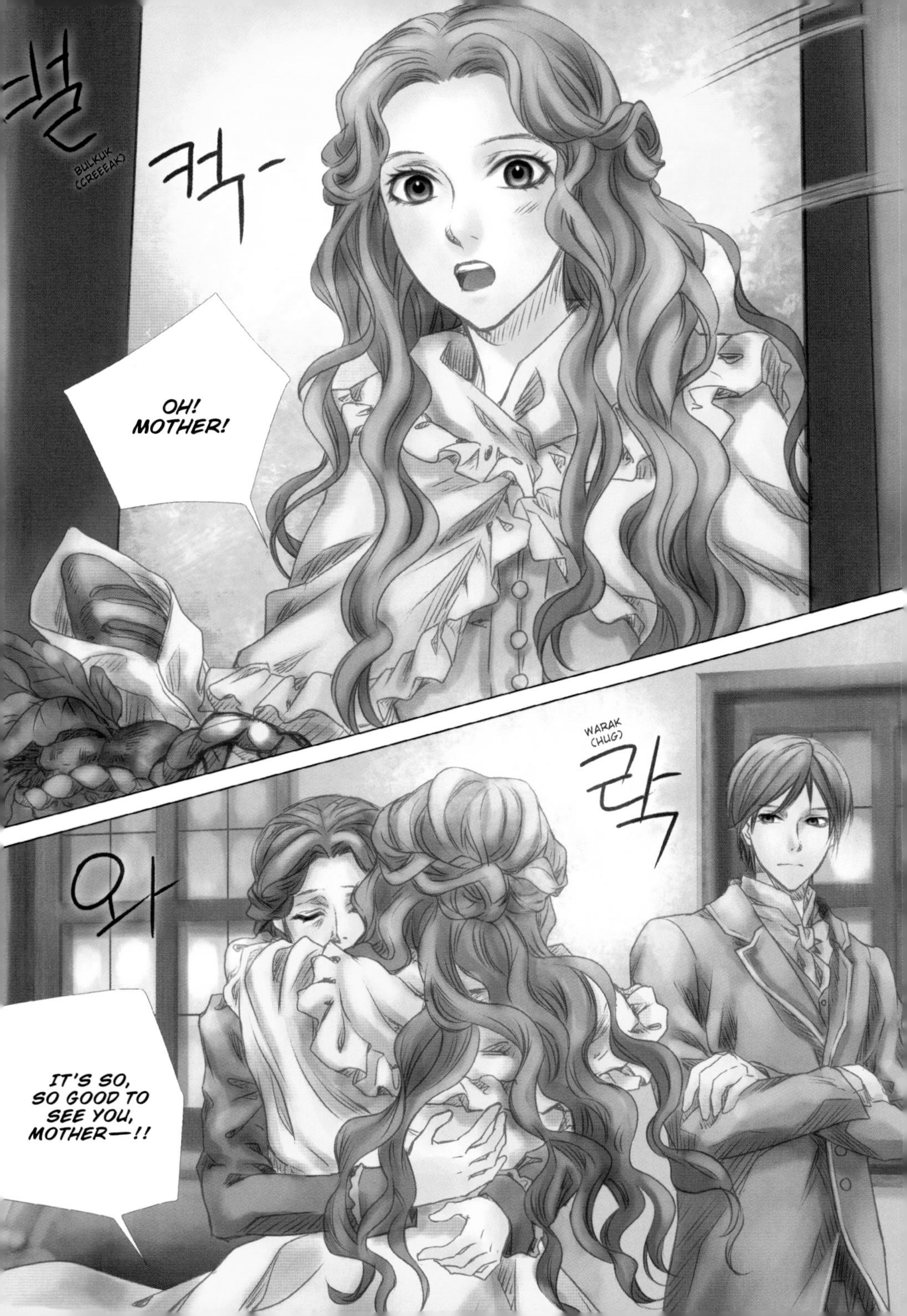
벌
BULKUK (CREEEAK)
컥-
OH! MOTHER!
WARAK (HUG)
와
락
IT'S SO, SO GOOD TO SEE YOU, MOTHER—!!

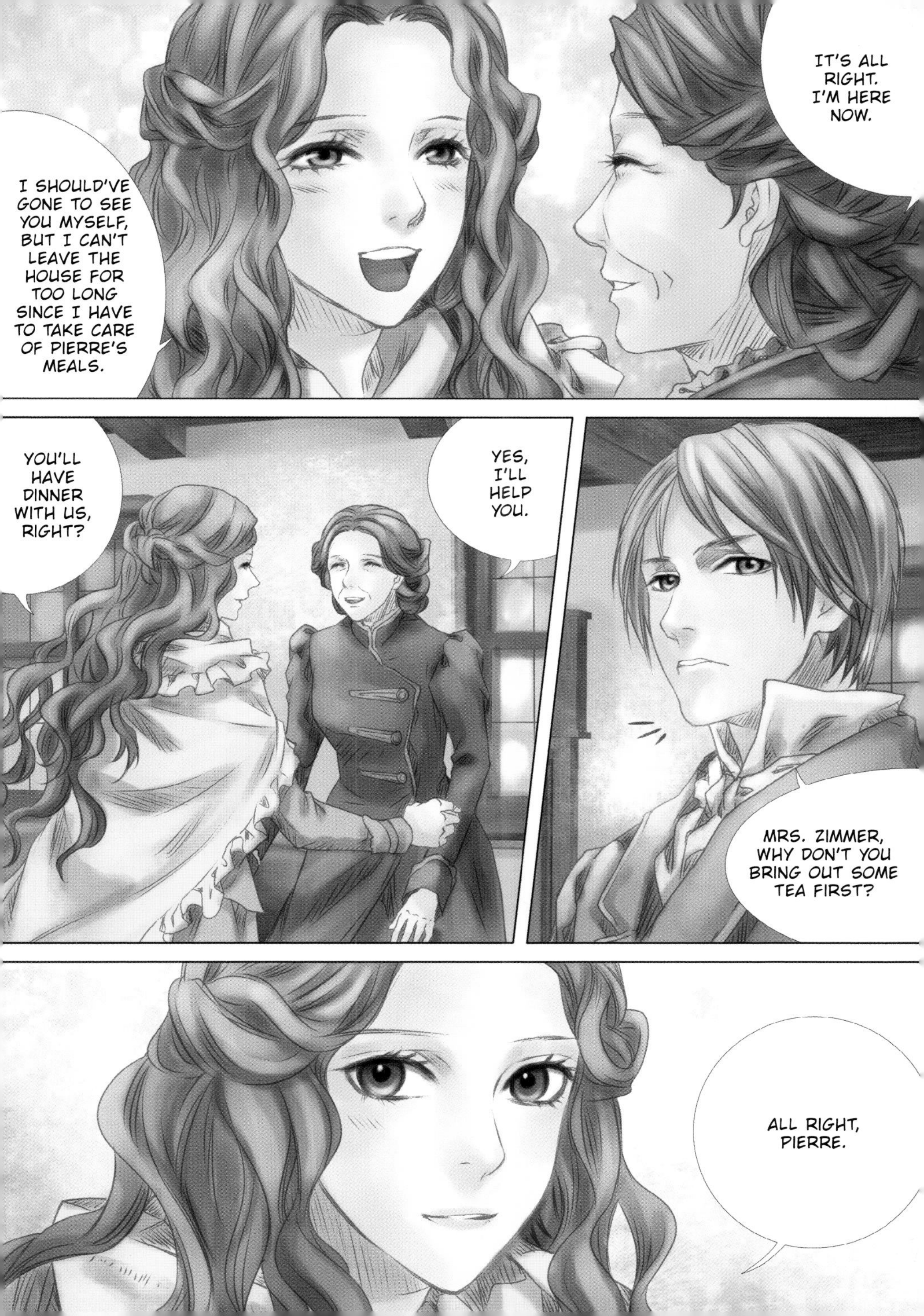
I SHOULD'VE GONE TO SEE YOU MYSELF, BUT I CAN'T LEAVE THE HOUSE FOR TOO LONG SINCE I HAVE TO TAKE CARE OF PIERRE'S MEALS.
IT'S ALL RIGHT. I'M HERE NOW.
YOU'LL HAVE DINNER WITH US, RIGHT?
YES, I'LL HELP YOU.
MRS. ZIMMER, WHY DON'T YOU BRING OUT SOME TEA FIRST?
ALL RIGHT, PIERRE.

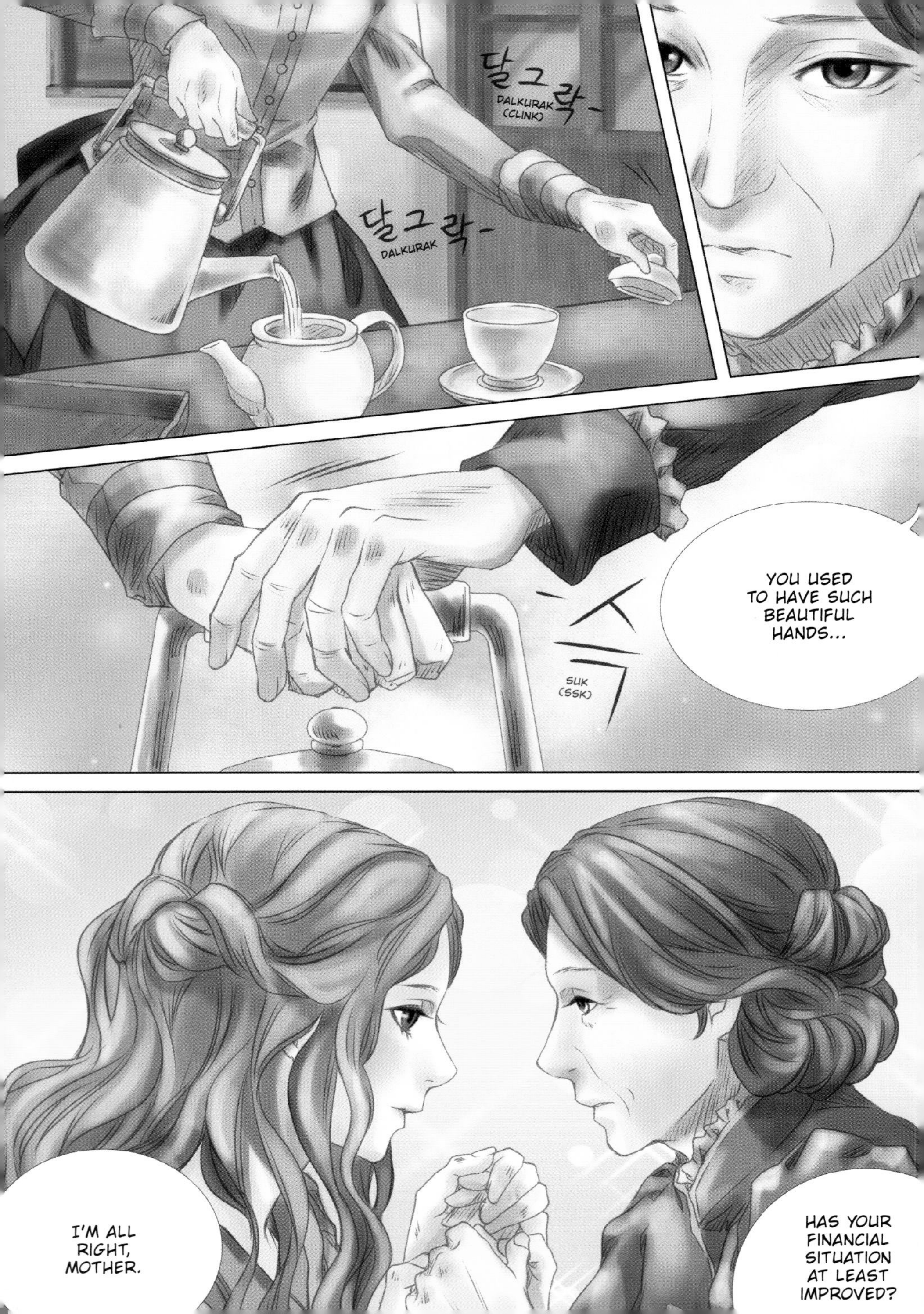

달그락-
DALKURAK
달그락-
DALKURAK
(CLINK)
SUK
(SSK)
YOU USED TO HAVE SUCH BEAUTIFUL HANDS...
I'M ALL RIGHT, MOTHER.
HAS YOUR FINANCIAL SITUATION AT LEAST IMPROVED?

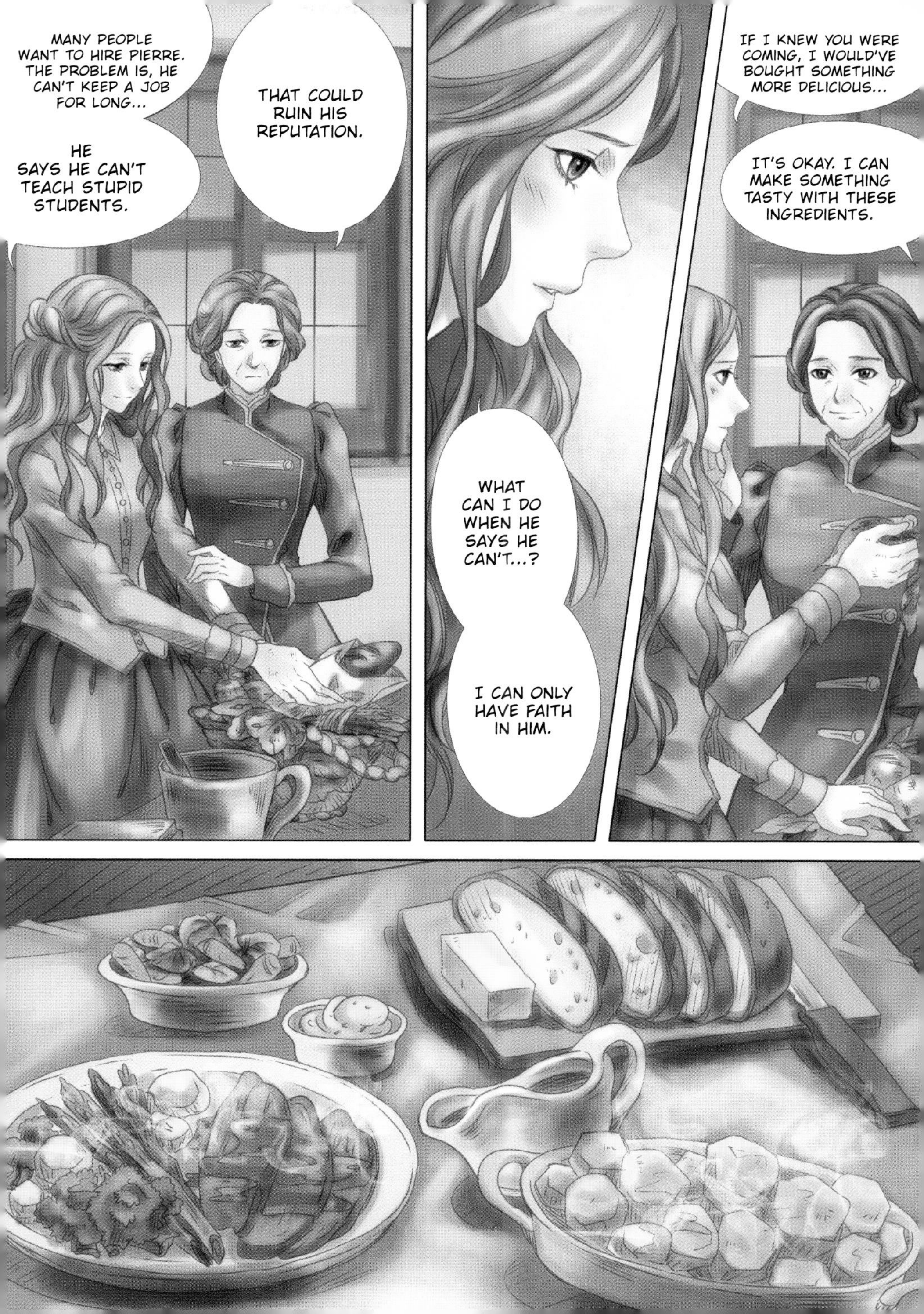
MANY PEOPLE WANT TO HIRE PIERRE. THE PROBLEM IS, HE CAN'T KEEP A JOB FOR LONG...
HE SAYS HE CAN'T TEACH STUPID STUDENTS.
THAT COULD RUIN HIS REPUTATION.
WHAT CAN I DO WHEN HE SAYS HE CAN'T...?
I CAN ONLY HAVE FAITH IN HIM.
IF I KNEW YOU WERE COMING, I WOULD'VE BOUGHT SOMETHING MORE DELICIOUS...
IT'S OKAY. I CAN MAKE SOMETHING TASTY WITH THESE INGREDIENTS.

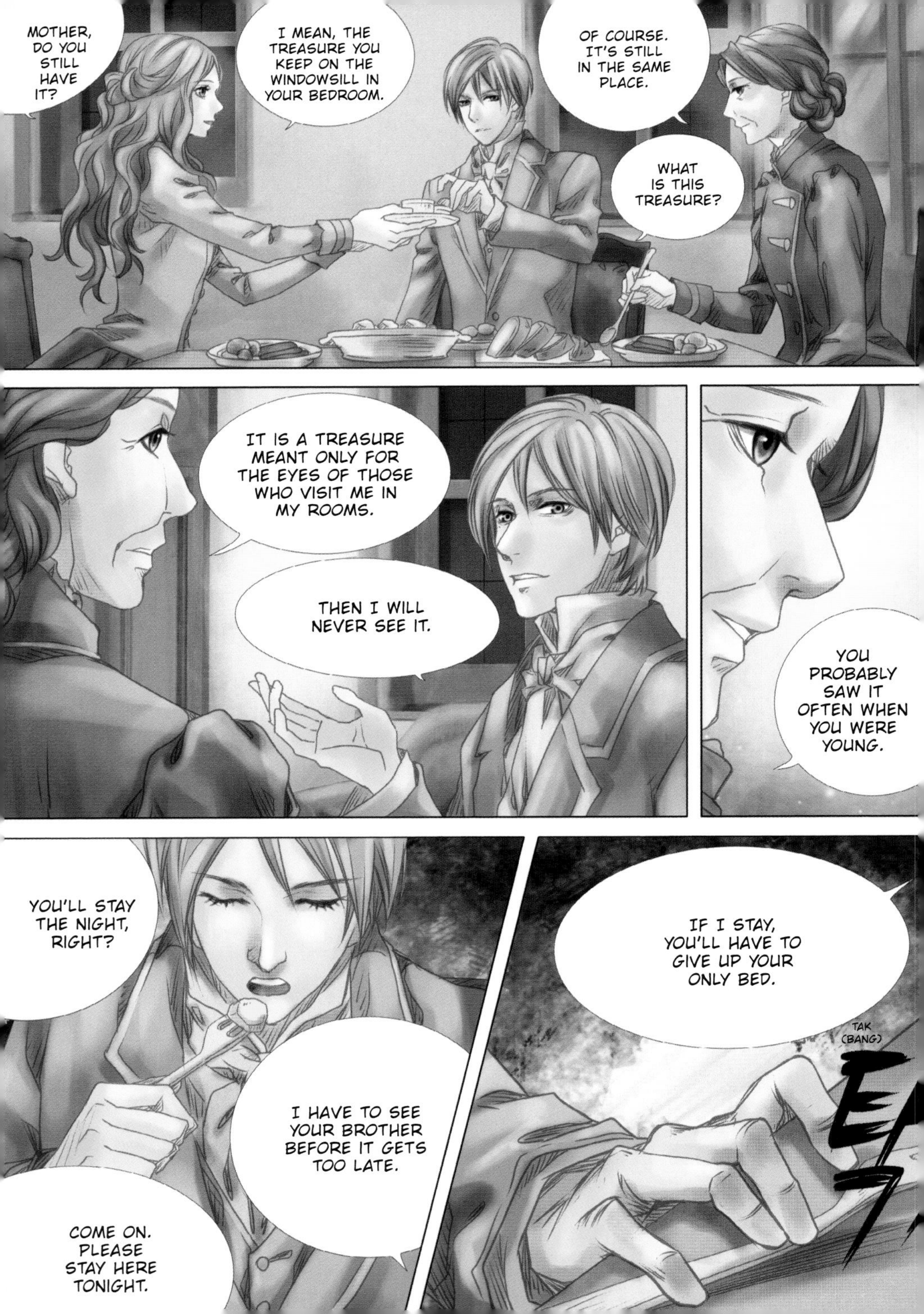
MOTHER, DO YOU STILL HAVE IT?
I MEAN, THE TREASURE YOU KEEP ON THE WINDOWSILL IN YOUR BEDROOM.
OF COURSE. IT'S STILL IN THE SAME PLACE.
WHAT IS THIS TREASURE?
IT IS A TREASURE MEANT ONLY FOR THE EYES OF THOSE WHO VISIT ME IN MY ROOMS.
THEN I WILL NEVER SEE IT.
YOU PROBABLY SAW IT OFTEN WHEN YOU WERE YOUNG.
YOU'LL STAY THE NIGHT, RIGHT?
I HAVE TO SEE YOUR BROTHER BEFORE IT GETS TOO LATE.
COME ON. PLEASE STAY HERE TONIGHT.
IF I STAY, YOU'LL HAVE TO GIVE UP YOUR ONLY BED.
TAK (BANG)

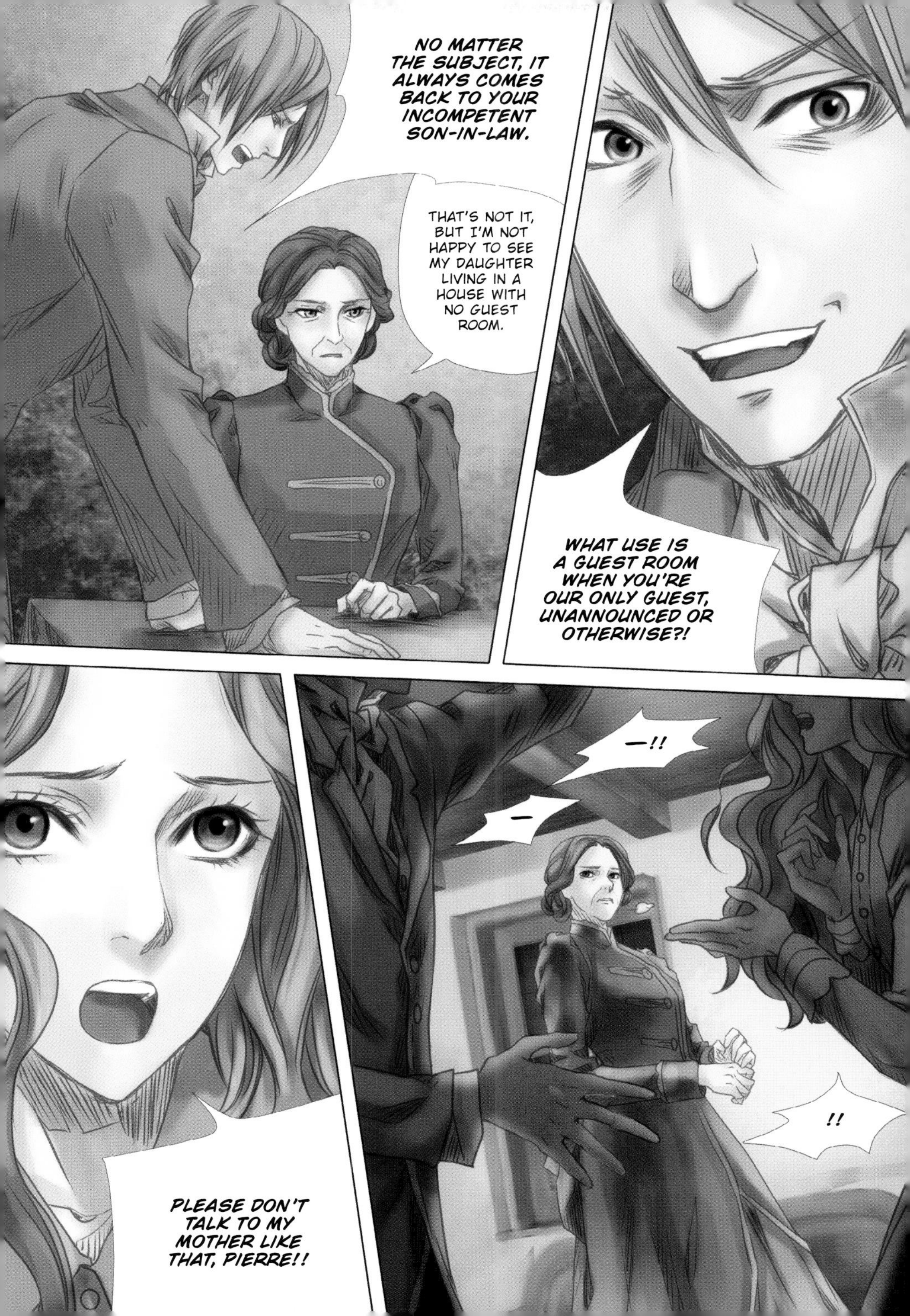
NO MATTER THE SUBJECT, IT ALWAYS COMES BACK TO YOUR INCOMPETENT SON-IN-LAW.
THAT'S NOT IT, BUT I'M NOT HAPPY TO SEE MY DAUGHTER LIVING IN A HOUSE WITH NO GUEST ROOM.
WHAT USE IS A GUEST ROOM WHEN YOU'RE OUR ONLY GUEST, UNANNOUNCED OR OTHERWISE?!
PLEASE DON'T TALK TO MY MOTHER LIKE THAT, PIERRE!!
—!!
—
!!

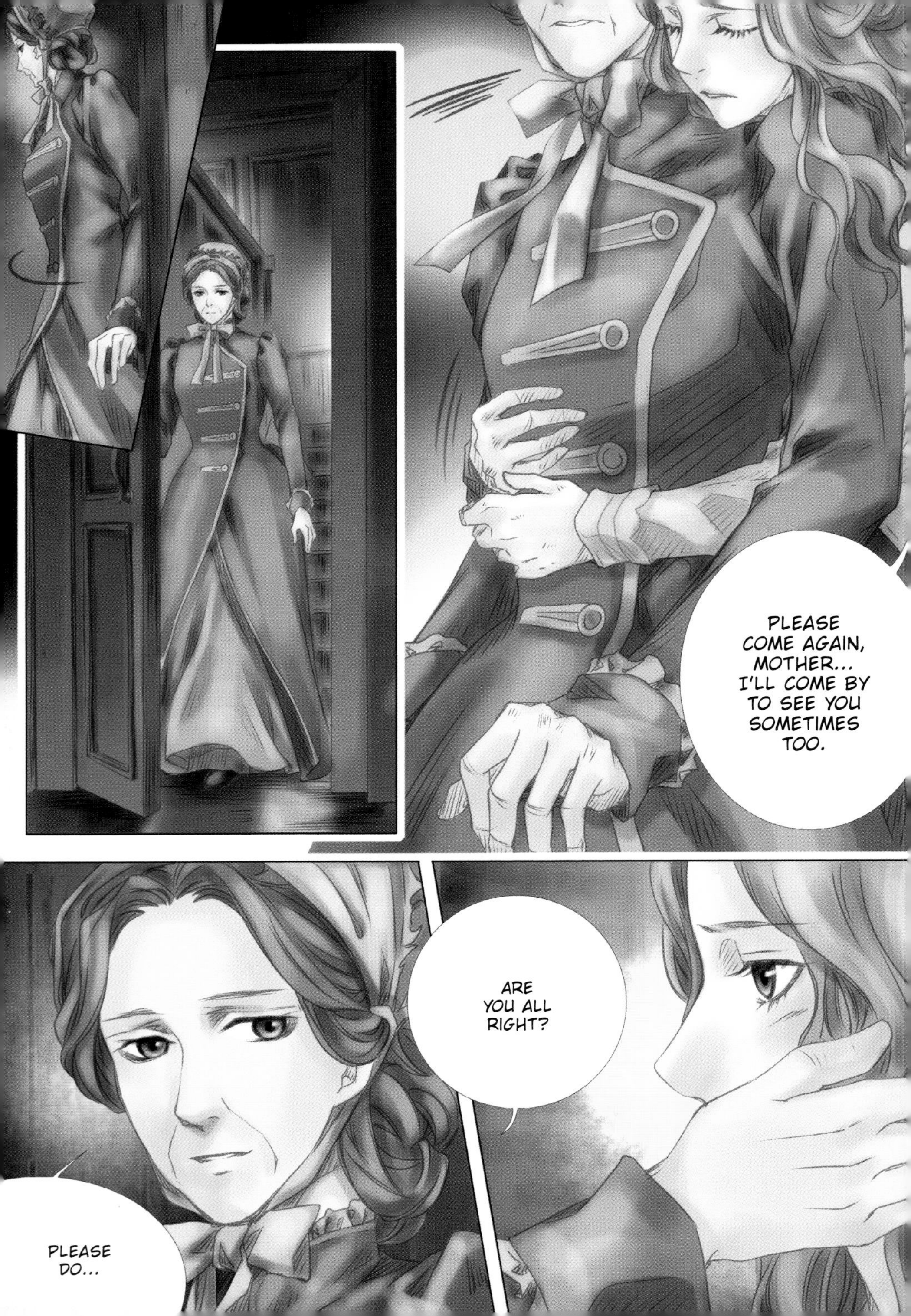
PLEASE COME AGAIN, MOTHER... I'LL COME BY TO SEE YOU SOMETIMES TOO.
PLEASE DO...
ARE YOU ALL RIGHT?

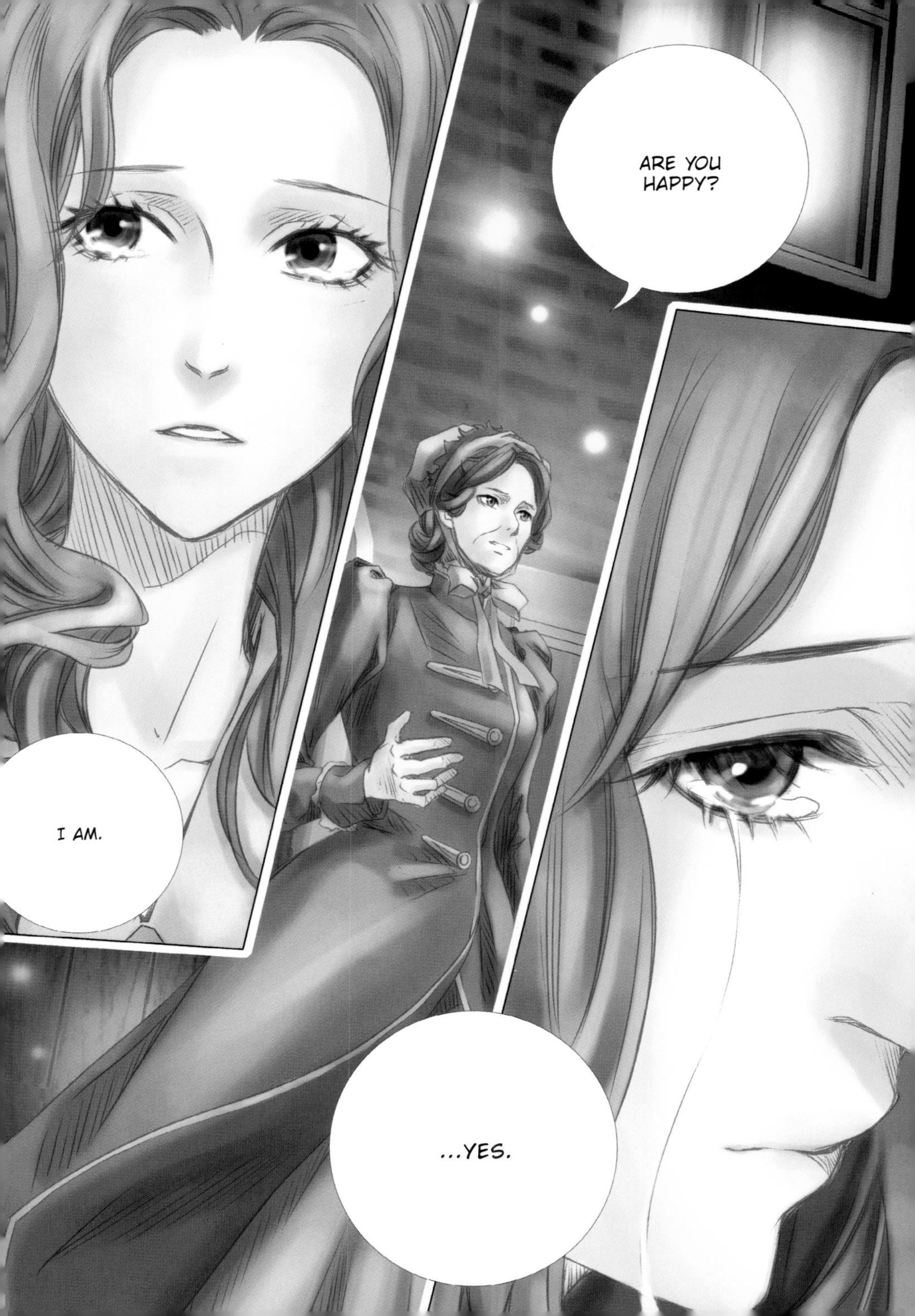
ARE YOU HAPPY?
I AM.
...YES.

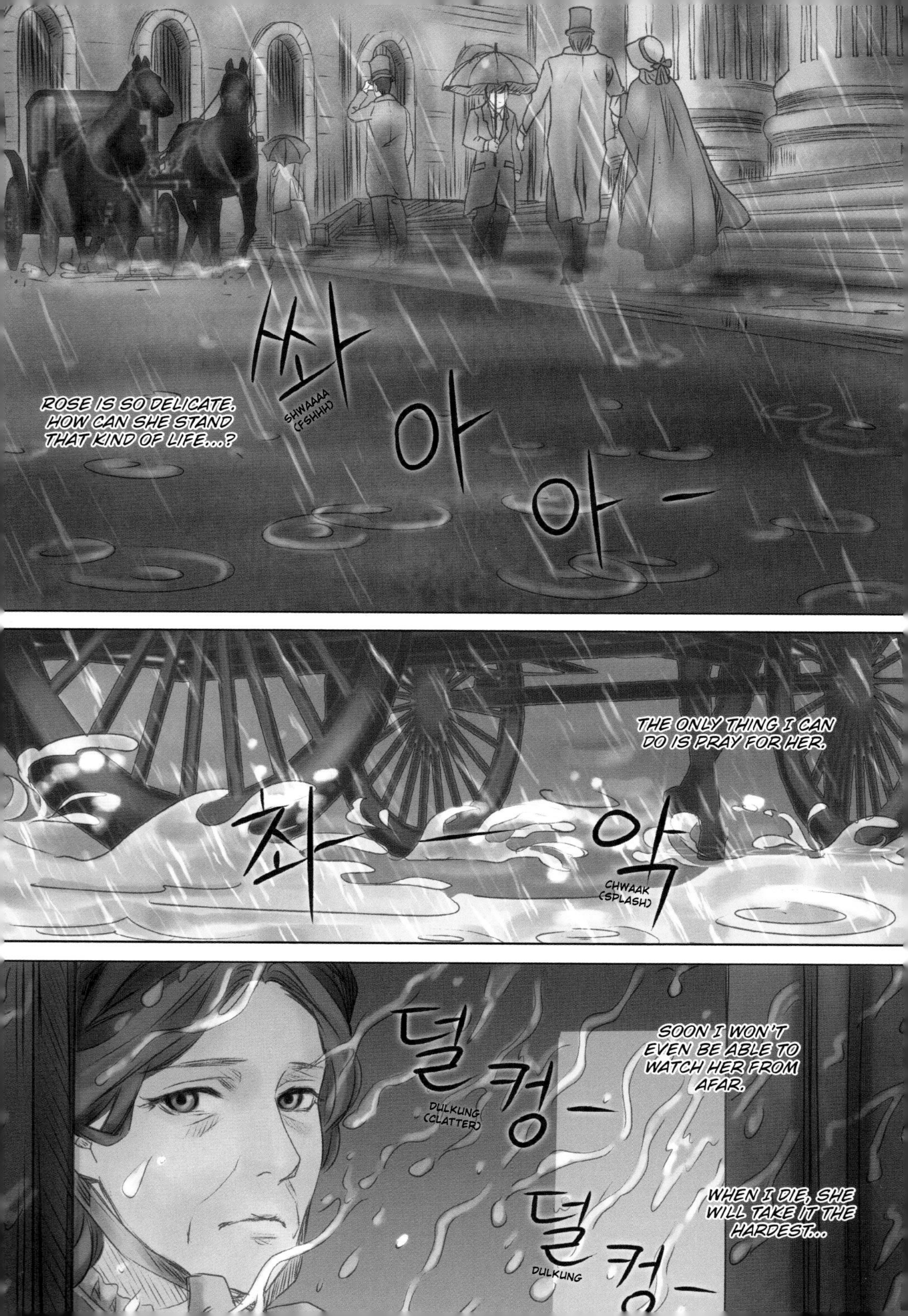
ROSE IS SO DELICATE. HOW CAN SHE STAND THAT KIND OF LIFE...?
쏴아아-
SHWAAAA (FSHHH)
THE ONLY THING I CAN DO IS PRAY FOR HER.
촤-악
CHWAAK (SPLASH)
덜컹-
DULKUNG (CLATTER)
SOON I WON'T EVEN BE ABLE TO WATCH HER FROM AFAR.
WHEN I DIE, SHE WILL TAKE IT THE HARDEST...
덜컹-
DULKUNG

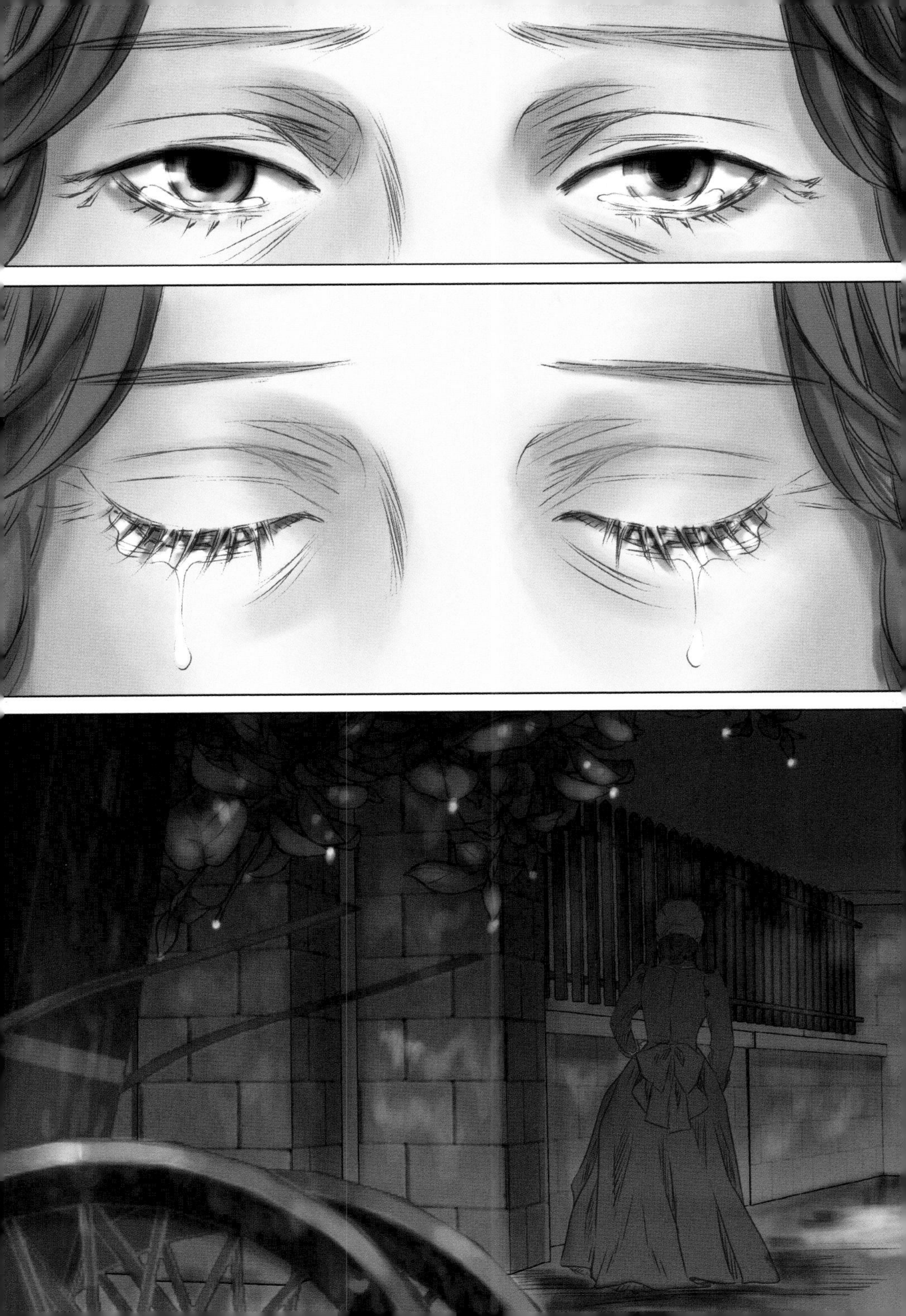

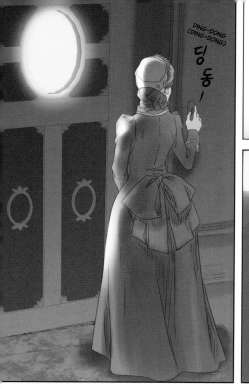

DING-DONG
(DING-DONG)
딩 동!

우당탕
WOODANGTANG
(WHAM)

KYAH-HA-HA!
까 하하
까
KYAH!

NO WONDER THEY CAN'T HEAR THE DOOR-BELL.

AND THE DOOR IS UNLOCKED ...

IT'S BEEN TOO LONG, THEO.

MOTHER?

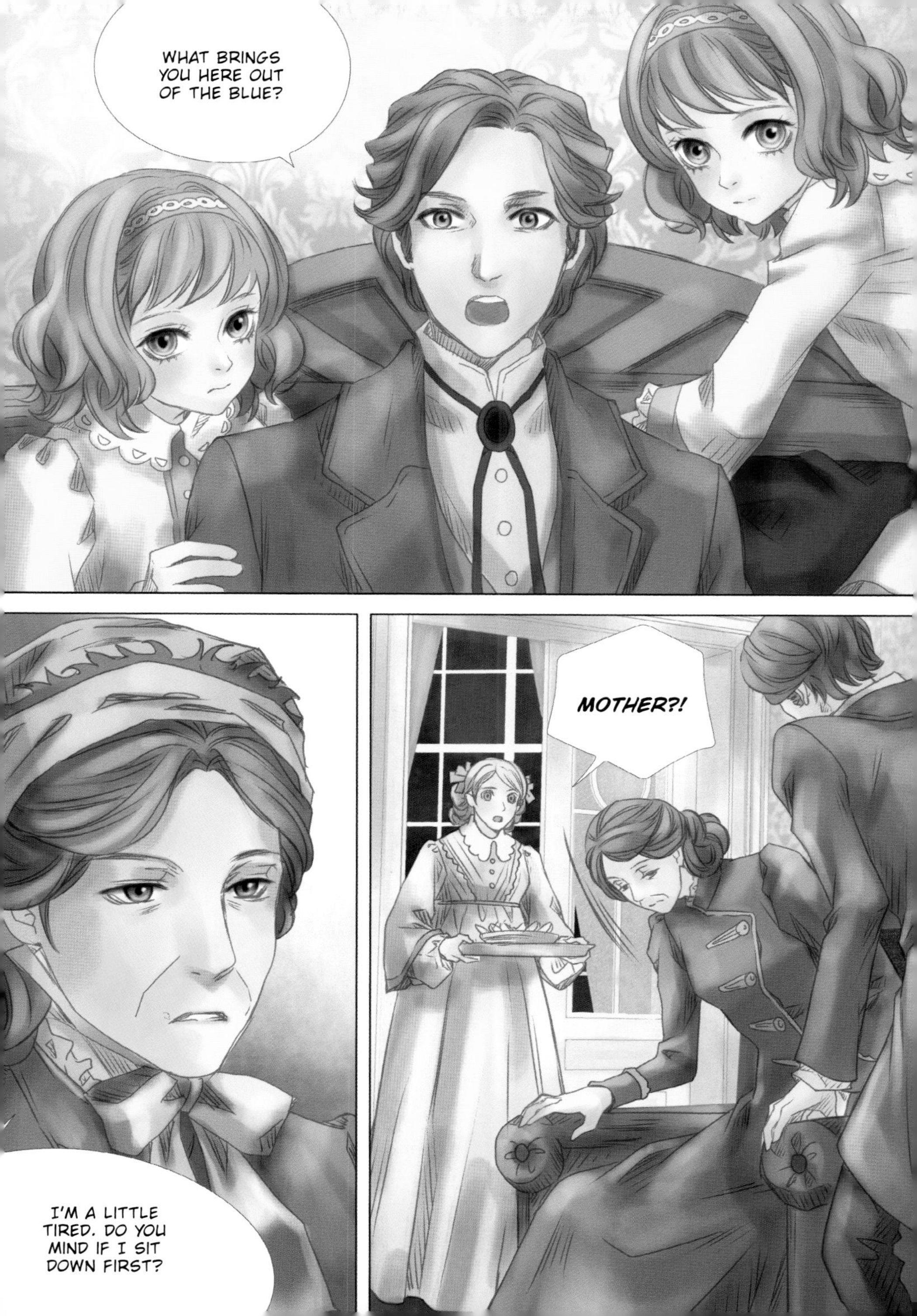
WHAT BRINGS YOU HERE OUT OF THE BLUE?
I'M A LITTLE TIRED. DO YOU MIND IF I SIT DOWN FIRST?
MOTHER?!

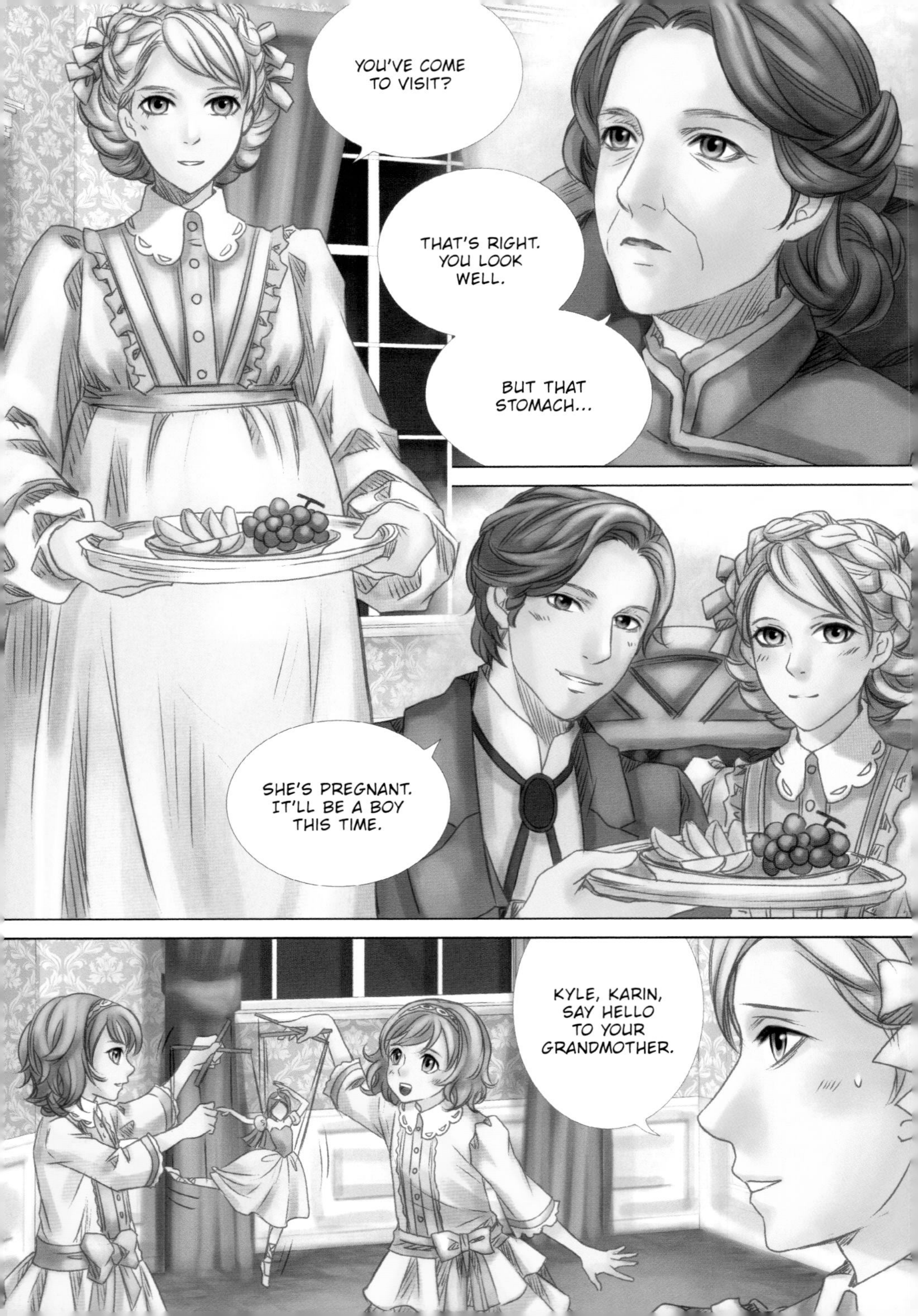
YOU'VE COME TO VISIT?
THAT'S RIGHT. YOU LOOK WELL.
BUT THAT STOMACH...
SHE'S PREGNANT. IT'LL BE A BOY THIS TIME.
KYLE, KARIN, SAY HELLO TO YOUR GRANDMOTHER.

OH. HELLO, GRANDMOTHER.

CHUPYUT
(SHY)

CHUPYUT

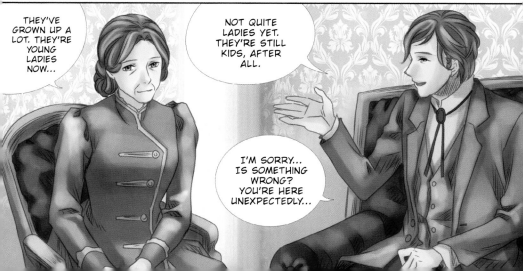

THEY'VE GROWN UP A LOT. THEY'RE YOUNG LADIES NOW...

NOT QUITE LADIES YET. THEY'RE STILL KIDS, AFTER ALL.

I'M SORRY... IS SOMETHING WRONG? YOU'RE HERE UNEXPECTEDLY...

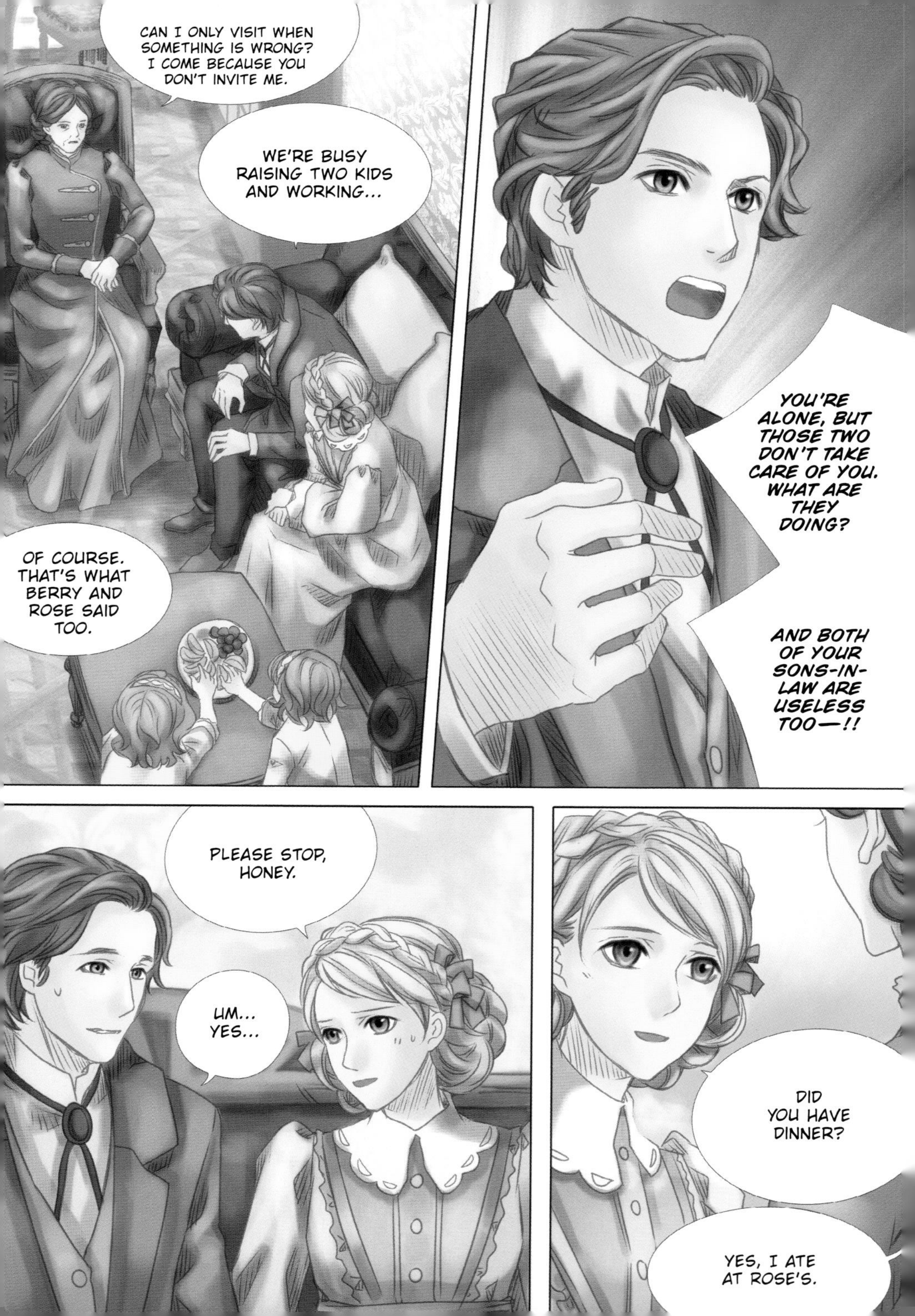
CAN I ONLY VISIT WHEN SOMETHING IS WRONG? I COME BECAUSE YOU DON'T INVITE ME.
WE'RE BUSY RAISING TWO KIDS AND WORKING...
OF COURSE. THAT'S WHAT BERRY AND ROSE SAID TOO.
YOU'RE ALONE, BUT THOSE TWO DON'T TAKE CARE OF YOU. WHAT ARE THEY DOING?
AND BOTH OF YOUR SONS-IN-LAW ARE USELESS TOO—!!
PLEASE STOP, HONEY.
UM... YES...
DID YOU HAVE DINNER?
YES, I ATE AT ROSE'S.

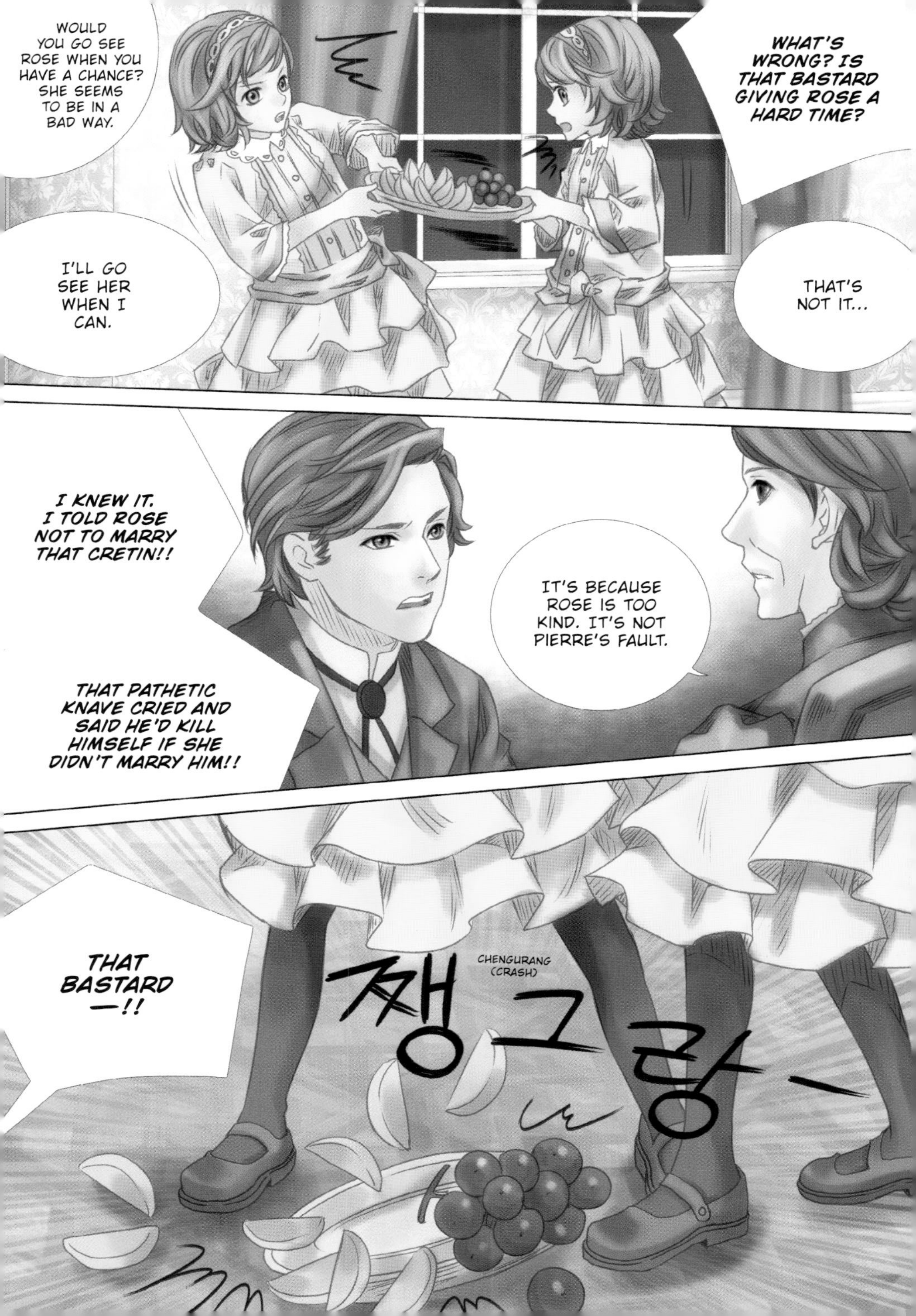
WOULD YOU GO SEE ROSE WHEN YOU HAVE A CHANCE? SHE SEEMS TO BE IN A BAD WAY.
WHAT'S WRONG? IS THAT BASTARD GIVING ROSE A HARD TIME?
I'LL GO SEE HER WHEN I CAN.
THAT'S NOT IT...
I KNEW IT. I TOLD ROSE NOT TO MARRY THAT CRETIN!!
THAT PATHETIC KNAVE CRIED AND SAID HE'D KILL HIMSELF IF SHE DIDN'T MARRY HIM!!
IT'S BECAUSE ROSE IS TOO KIND. IT'S NOT PIERRE'S FAULT.
THAT BASTARD—!!
CHENGURANG (CRASH)
쨍그랑ー

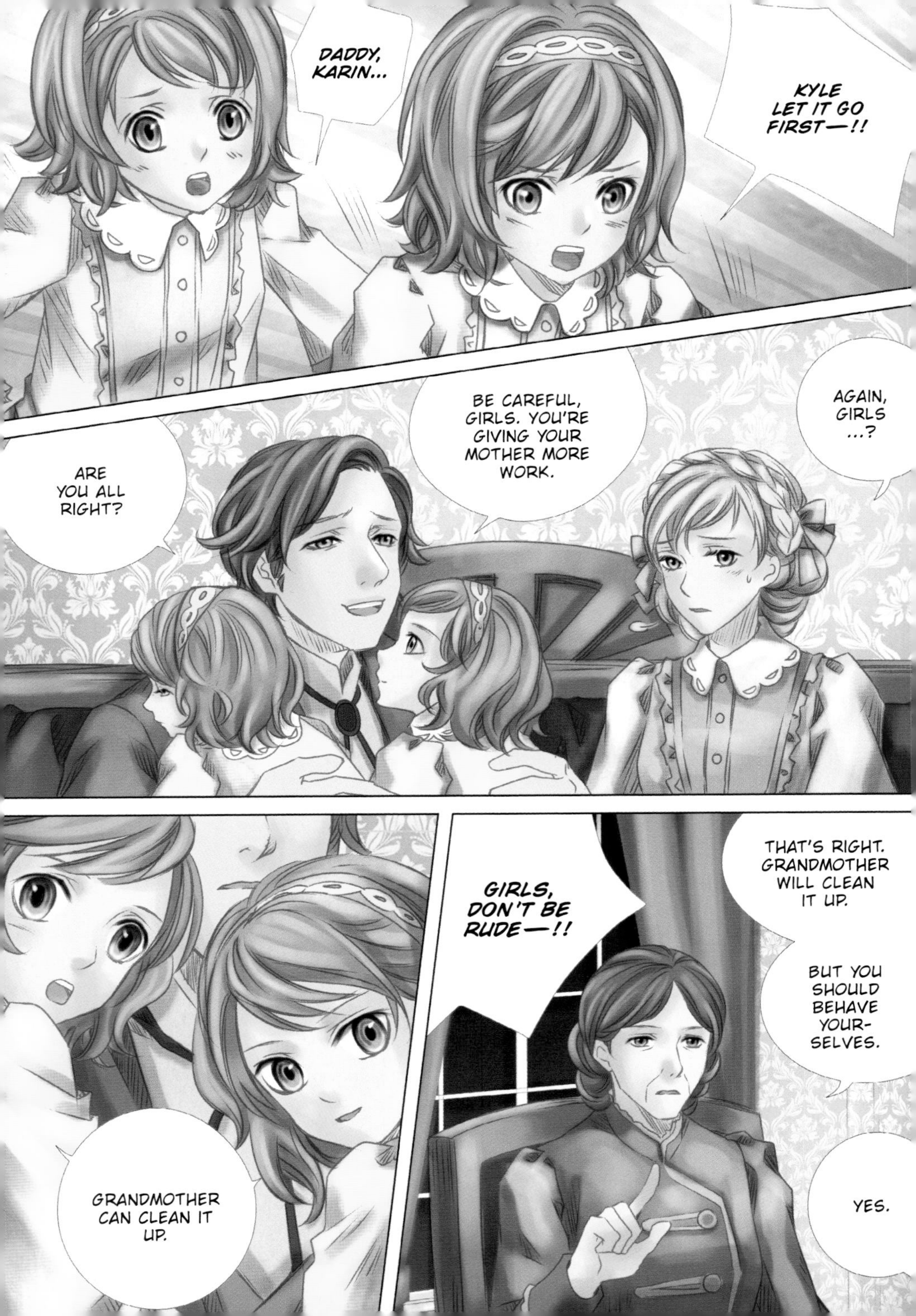
DADDY, KARIN...
KYLE LET IT GO FIRST—!!
ARE YOU ALL RIGHT?
BE CAREFUL, GIRLS. YOU'RE GIVING YOUR MOTHER MORE WORK.
AGAIN, GIRLS ...?
GRANDMOTHER CAN CLEAN IT UP.
GIRLS, DON'T BE RUDE—!!
THAT'S RIGHT. GRANDMOTHER WILL CLEAN IT UP.
BUT YOU SHOULD BEHAVE YOUR-SELVES.
YES.

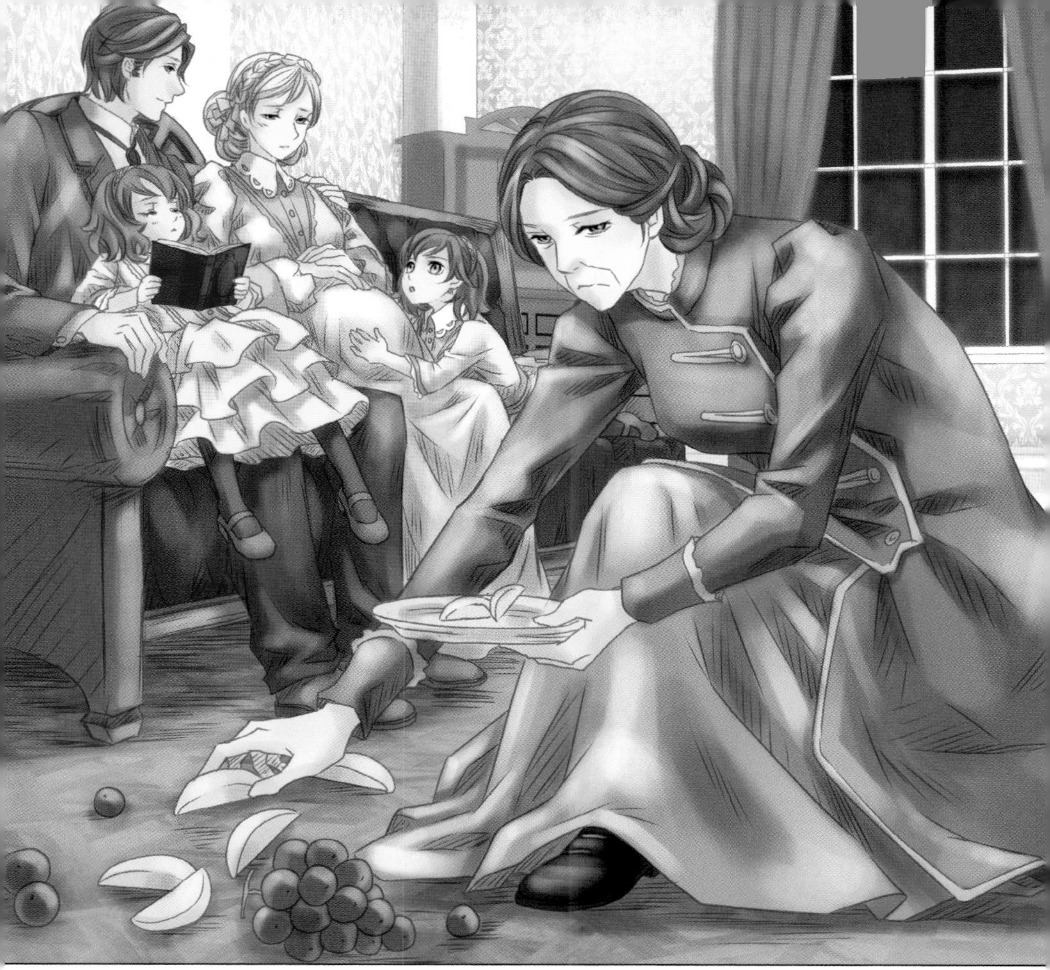

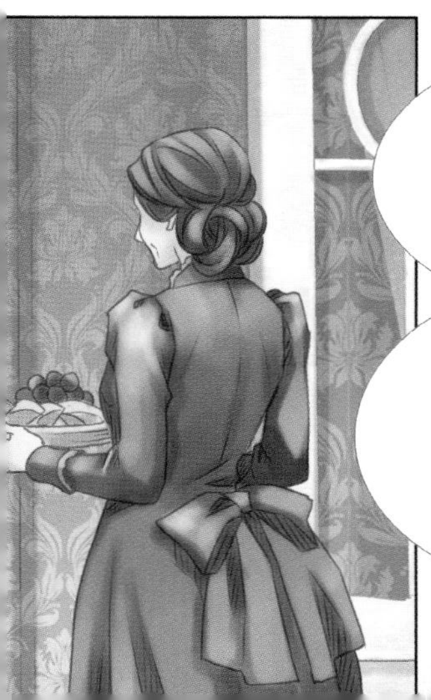

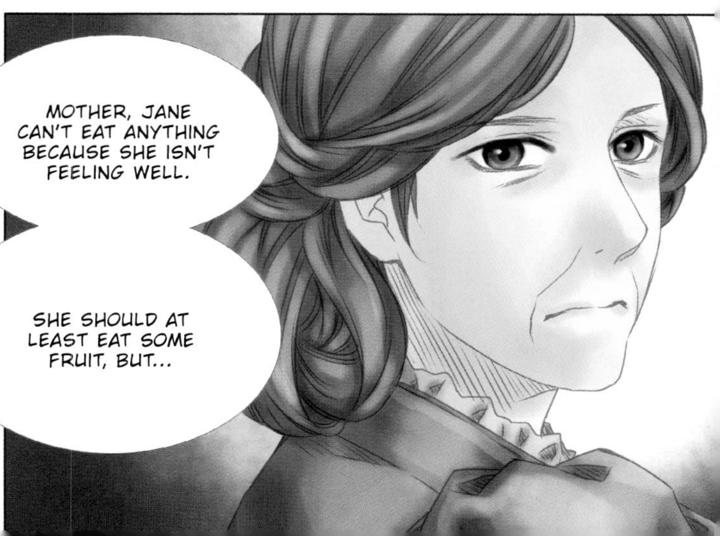
MOTHER, JANE CAN'T EAT ANYTHING BECAUSE SHE ISN'T FEELING WELL.
SHE SHOULD AT LEAST EAT SOME FRUIT, BUT...

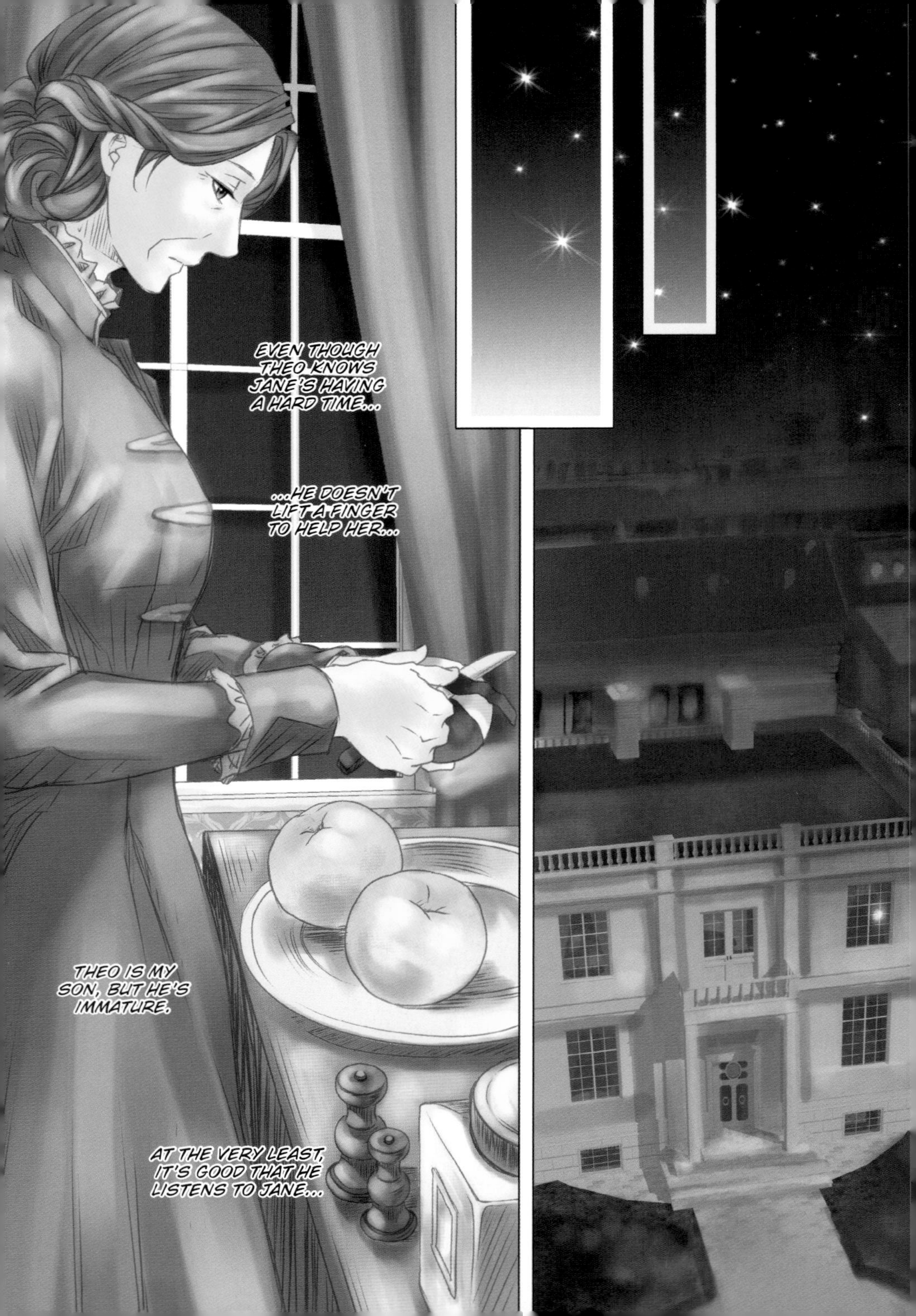
EVEN THOUGH THEO KNOWS JANE'S HAVING A HARD TIME...
...HE DOESN'T LIFT A FINGER TO HELP HER...
THEO IS MY SON, BUT HE'S IMMATURE.
AT THE VERY LEAST, IT'S GOOD THAT HE LISTENS TO JANE...

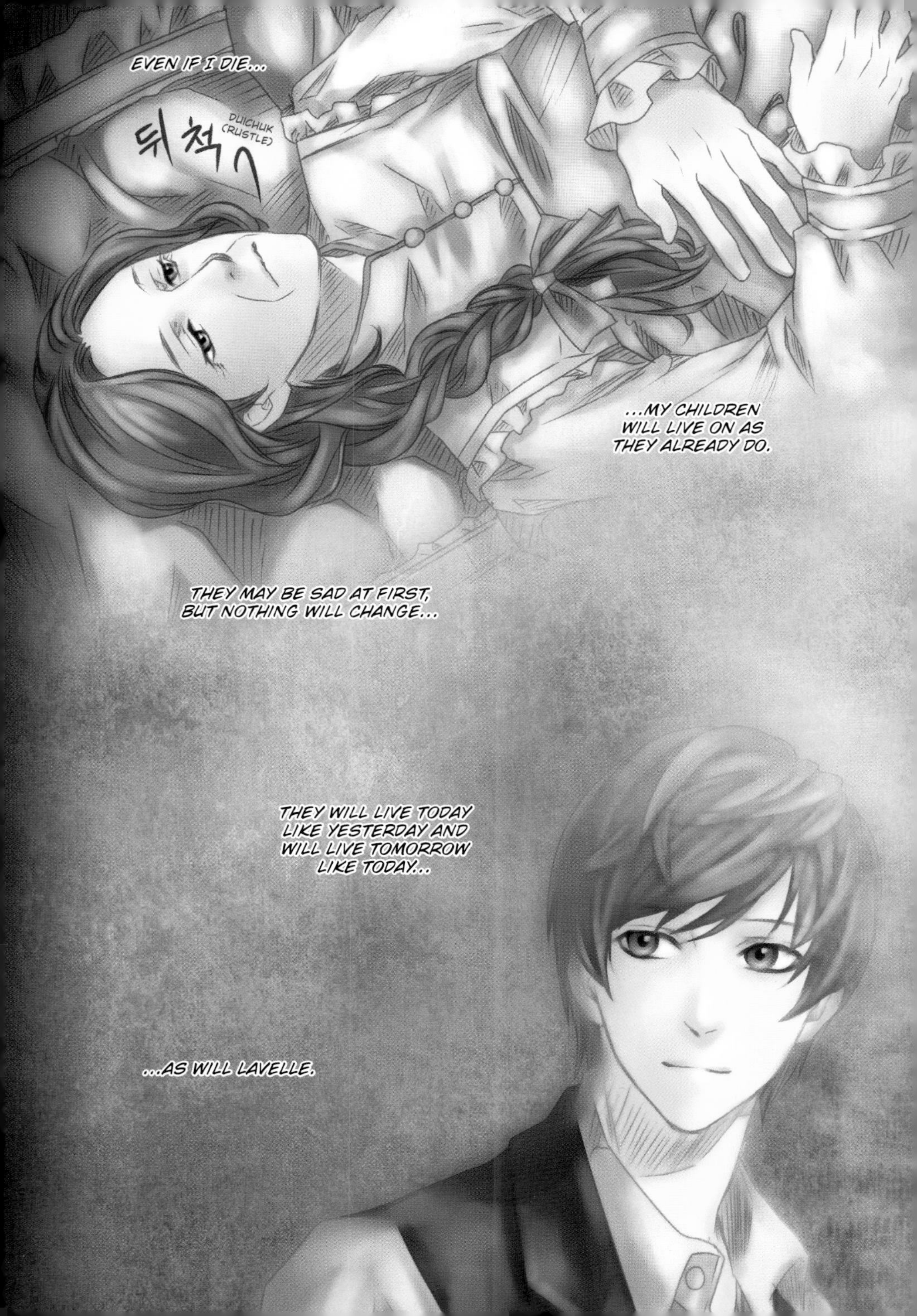
EVEN IF I DIE...
뒤척
DUICHUK (RUSTLE)
...MY CHILDREN WILL LIVE ON AS THEY ALREADY DO.
THEY MAY BE SAD AT FIRST, BUT NOTHING WILL CHANGE...
THEY WILL LIVE TODAY LIKE YESTERDAY AND WILL LIVE TOMORROW LIKE TODAY...
...AS WILL LAVELLE.

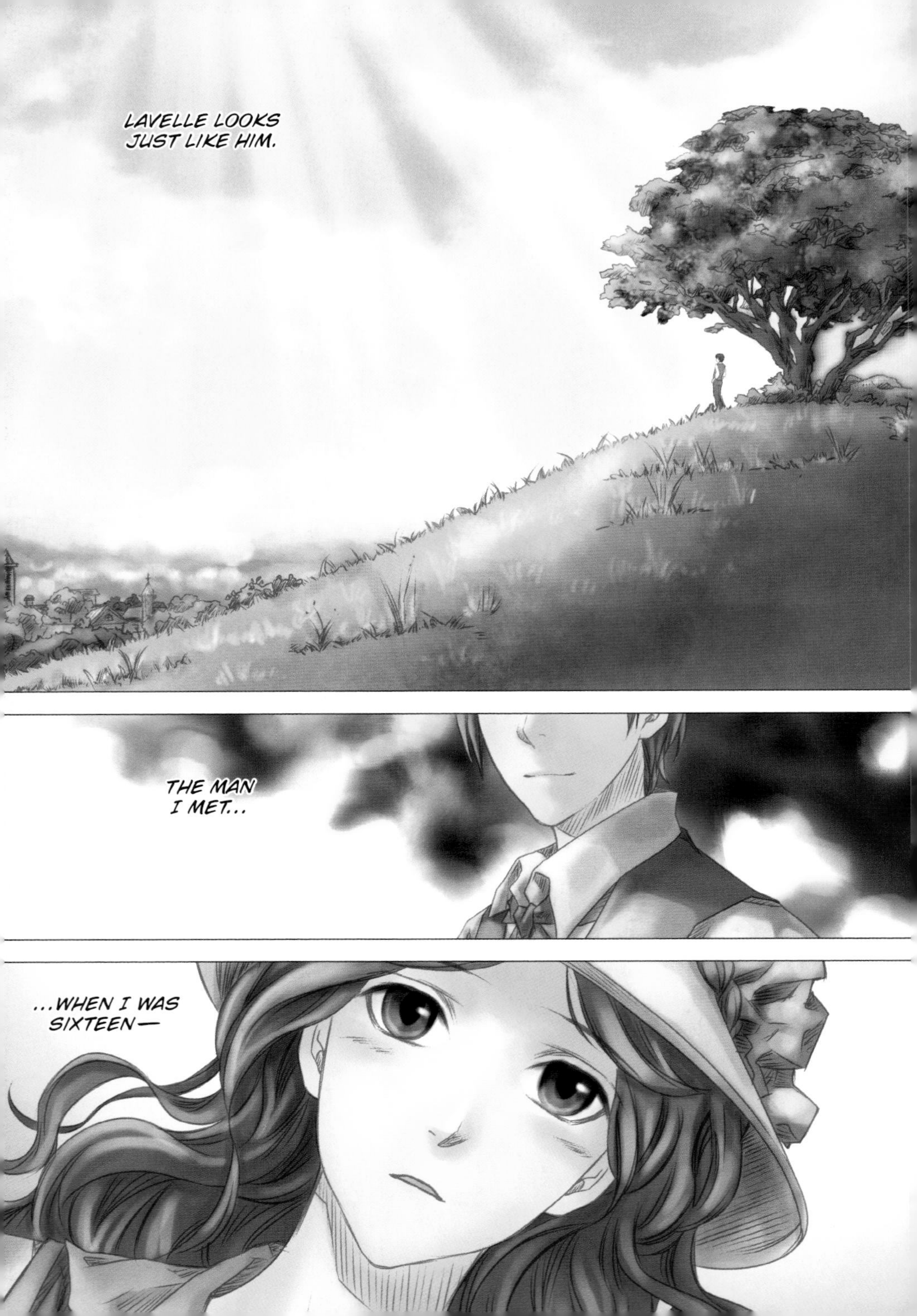
LAVELLE LOOKS JUST LIKE HIM.
THE MAN I MET...
...WHEN I WAS SIXTEEN—

Void's
Enigmatic
Mansion

To be continued in Volume 4...

Void's Enigmatic Mansion

Visit artist HeeEun Kim's blog at http://blog.naver.com/kimnoran!

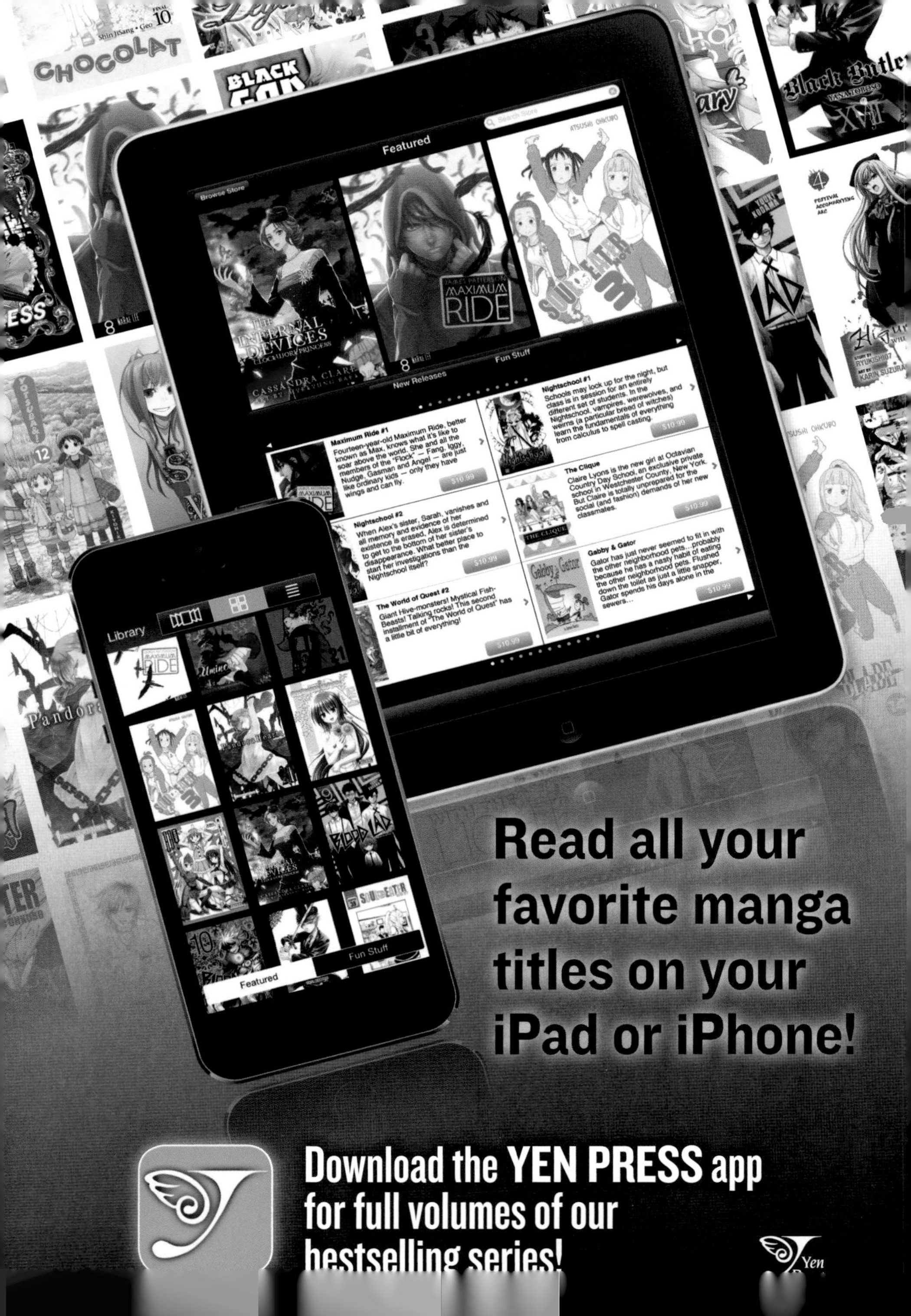
Read all your favorite manga titles on your iPad or iPhone!
Download the YEN PRESS app for full volumes of our bestselling series!
Yen

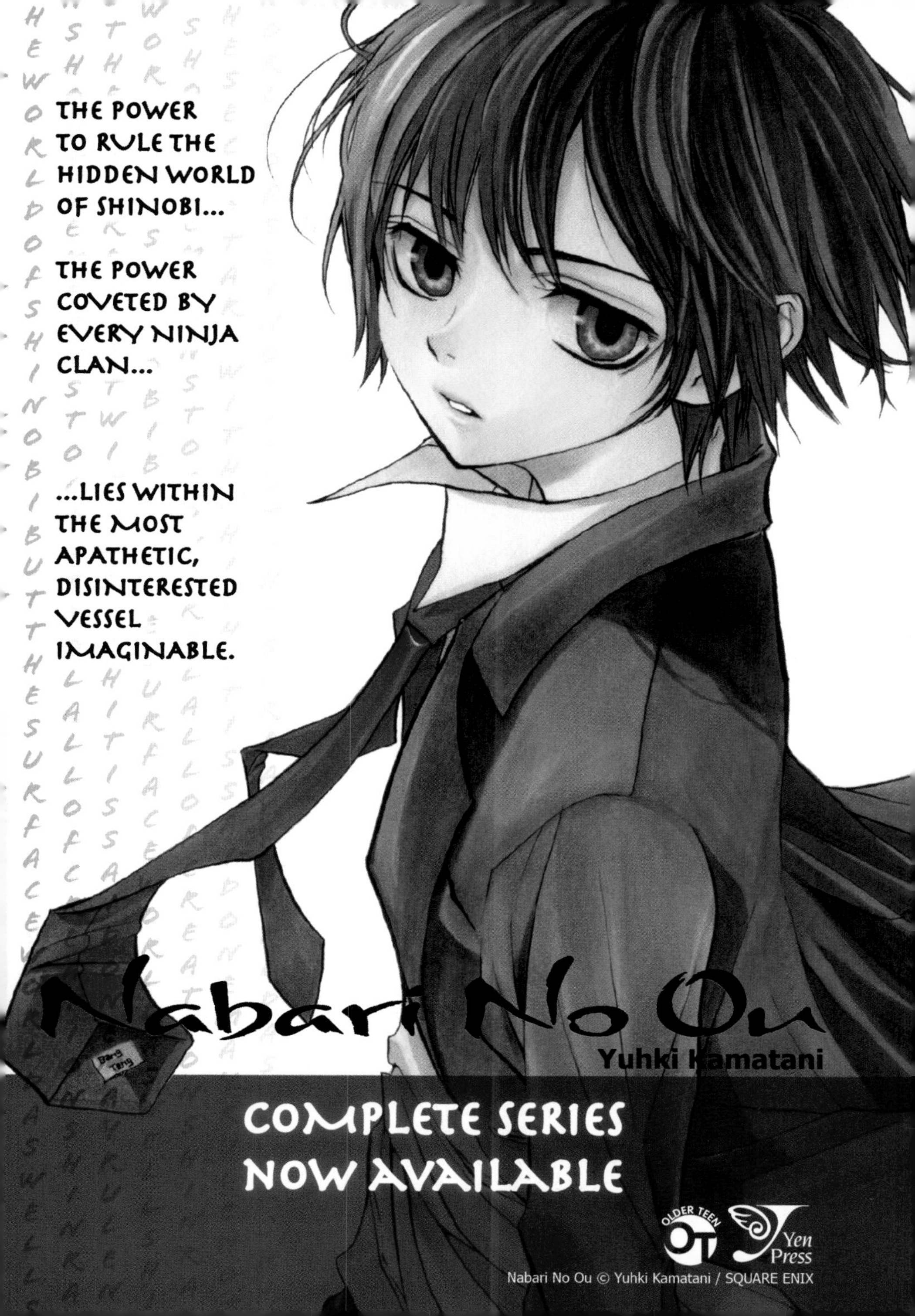
THE POWER TO RULE THE HIDDEN WORLD OF SHINOBI...
THE POWER COVETED BY EVERY NINJA CLAN...
...LIES WITHIN THE MOST APATHETIC, DISINTERESTED VESSEL IMAGINABLE.
Nabari No Ou
Yuhki Kamatani
COMPLETE SERIES NOW AVAILABLE
OLDER TEEN OT
Yen Press
Nabari No Ou © Yuhki Kamatani / SQUARE ENIX

DURARARA!!

DRRR!! 1

CREATOR
RYOHGO
NARITA

CHARACTER
DESIGN
SUZUHITO
YASUDA

ART
AKIYO
SATORIGI

The Phantomhive family has a butler who's almost too good to be true...

...or maybe he's just too good to be human.

Black Butler

YANA TOBOSO

VOLUME 21 AVAILABLE NOW!